The Sword Saint

Empire of Salt: Book Three

C. F. IGGULDEN

PENGUIN BOOKS

PENGUIN BOOKS

UK | USA | Canada | Ireland | Australia
India | New Zealand | South Africa

Penguin Books is part of the Penguin Random House group of companies
whose addresses can be found at global.penguinrandomhouse.com.

Penguin
Random House
UK

First published by Michael Joseph 2019
Published in Penguin Books 2020
001

Copyright © Conn Iggulden, 2019

The moral right of the author has been asserted

Printed and bound in Great Britain by Clays Ltd, Elcograf S.p.A.

A CIP catalogue record for this book is available from the British Library

ISBN: 978–0–718–18681–4

www.greenpenguin.co.uk

MIX
Paper from
responsible sources
FSC® C018179

Penguin Random House is committed to a
sustainable future for our business, our readers
and our planet. This book is made from Forest
Stewardship Council® certified paper.

To all those who work in bookshops and libraries.
Thank you for your patience – and for keeping me safe
and warm, when I should have been in school.

Acknowledgements

I have always loved stories. I used to write them in a sort of wild state, flinging words into the air from an old PC and golfball printer. Those around me were patient, though I spent years tapping away on my own, lost in chaotic imaginings.

I acknowledged some of the authors I've revered in the first book. To those, I should add the people who turned all that phantom-of-the-opera madness into actual printed books. Victoria Hobbs was the first to say yes. Nick Sayers was the first editor to accept. Katie Espiner and Susan Watt and Amanda Ridout and Victoria Barnsley all played vital roles. Tim Waller copy-edited my first book and just about every one since, including *The Dangerous Book for Boys*. He is a shadow of his former self as a result. In Penguin Random House, Alex Clarke, Louise Moore, Jillian Taylor and Tom Weldon nurtured, allowed, championed – just made things happen. I could keep going with names. It takes a village to put a book in your hand – and you, of course, to pick it up. Thank you.

Conn Iggulden

Prologue

The boy crouched on a ledge, resting his chin on his knees, eyes bright as he watched the old priest pass below. His mother had told him not to visit the little temple on the hill. She'd made him swear he would never set foot in the place. He'd nodded and mumbled his oath, but all the time he'd known he would. Rules were wonderful things, Jean had discovered. Boys, girls, adult men and women, even priests seemed bound by them. They called them laws or traditions and then they raised them up to holy writ. For fear of being caught, Jean supposed. So if he wasn't caught, he could do anything. He *loved* rules, as many as possible. He could argue in his persuasive way that people needed them – to fend off the ache of having to make their own decisions, for example. Or because when they really needed to rebel, to roar and shake their fists at the stars, they could break some petty little law about not defacing coins, rather than running amok with an axe.

Jean smiled as the priest muttered something to himself, utterly unaware of the fourteen-year-old perched high above him. He'd watched the cleric go through his late service over a dozen evenings, peering in from the door. Jean knew his mother would hardly have been able to believe his patience, but he didn't want to rush in, not for this. She still thought of him as a child, but he had a man's growth on him and he could see the way other men looked away as he passed, for all his youth. There was something in his eyes, in the challenge they saw there, that made them drop their gaze. Each time it happened was a little triumph. He hoped it hurt when older men felt their nerve fail. It would never happen to him. He would die first.

His mind filled again with dreams of gold. The old priest may have served some dark god to frighten Jean's mother – and all mothers like her – but the smell of blood was rich and not unpleasant, not noticeably worse than a butcher's shop. And what did it matter really, if some sheep was thrown alive onto a fire rather than being slaughtered and cut into chops first? No, Jean Brieland was not afraid of a skinny priest, half-deaf and milky-eyed. If there was a treasure in that little temple, he would have it. Perhaps he would buy his mother a house. She'd look at him then without the pity and fear he always saw in her. Her disappointment was like acid in that way. It burned him and made him jut his jaw. It made him determined to prove her wrong. He was not his father.

Ahead of him, the priest fiddled with the mechanism of the door to the inner sanctuary – or whatever it was that lay behind it. Jean had only caught a glimpse of the room on one previous occasion, when Father Cormac had been caught in a rainstorm, stumbling in with an armful of firewood, leaving the door open until he'd brought in all he needed.

The room beyond went back into gloom – that was all Jean had been able to see. Each evening, old Cormac completed some ritual in the outer cave, with or without a blood sacrifice. A few of the older hill shepherds still made offerings to the little temple, so Jean supposed it depended on what they had left. He'd only seen a live lamb once and that had been a scrawny little thing, all eyes and legs. Another time, it had just been a packet of kidneys wrapped in cloth. The priest was thin enough for the offerings to be a rare thing. Too lazy to work for a living probably, the old bastard.

When he'd finished his chanting and whispering, Father Cormac tossed a handful of incense on the metal brazier, gleaming beads of tree sap that spat as they melted. He sang then for a time, in a voice that was more like the hissing of geese. Jean had struggled not to laugh out loud when he'd heard the old boy sing for the first time. He'd had to press his hand across his own mouth as he'd peered in, hidden in the long grasses by the entrance.

Little by little, Jean had learned the patterns the priest followed. It wasn't hard when they were always the same. The service and the incense came first, then Cormac would bow so low it always looked like he might not make it back up, first in one direction, then another. After that, he would nod to himself and turn to the back of the temple – and the only true door in the place, leading to who knew what.

Today was the day for firewood, once again. With a sense of excitement, Jean had watched the old man opening up the turf-covered wood store before the service, giving the spiders a chance to escape. The priest had collected half a dozen armfuls and brought them through the temple, past the little altar, to the very rear, by the door.

The old man sighed to himself as he came out for another load. Jean smiled above, hugging his knees in anticipation. It had taken the priest a count of forty to carry the first logs inside, to stack around some stove. That gap had given Jean the chance to get up onto the ledge, hidden from view in the gloom. He'd almost pressed in behind the open door, but it wasn't always pushed right back and there was something glorious about sitting above the heads of others. He'd spent enough evenings on the roof of his mother's building to know that. Up there, out of reach, he could be a king.

Father Cormac filled his arms once more, moving slowly and steadily, stacking the pieces of wood on the crook of his right arm with his left. He passed through the door and Jean dropped down, light as a bird, following him in.

The air was sour somehow, away from the scents of turf and charcoal. It smelled of a single man living on his own, his clothes too rarely washed. Jean knew the smell well enough from his own room and his mother's complaints. It was dark too and as he padded forward, he almost ran into the shuffling priest. Only the man's deafness saved him then as Jean leaned back against a rock wall and held his breath.

His eyes grew accustomed to the dimness, in time to watch Father Cormac enter a side room further down a short tunnel cut into the rock. Jean heard the sound of logs being dropped into a basket and he realised even old Cormac couldn't fail to see him on the way back. He had to get out, but he'd learned nothing. Fear made him angry. He darted forward instead, pattering down the corridor after the priest.

Another door stood open, opposite and a little beyond the first. There was a sense of air and cold from it, with the faintest of lights far away. Jean glanced back at the room Father Cormac had gone into and firmed his jaw. He had spent too long planning this to turn back. He might as well be hung for a sheep as a lamb. That was what his mother said. Jean darted into the opening and felt his mouth drop open.

There was a walkway of sorts, though it had no rail or anything to stop him falling. It was impossible to say how deep the pit went, perhaps all the way to the bottom of the mountain, like a shaft through the heart. Jean could feel depth as he peered over the edge. He fought a mad urge to shout, just to hear the echo.

The tiny light across the pit helped him crush the impulse. He had not come for childish things, but to see why a temple would have been built in such a place and tended, so his mother said, all her life. And who knew how long before that? Temples meant gold cups, or gold coins. Everyone knew that.

Fearing the edge, Jean made his way around the pit. The path was wide and flat, almost as if it had been paved. Even so, he went slowly, in case the floor was not as solid as it seemed. There were no surprises. When he reached the other side and looked back, he was awed at how far he had come. He could see the dim shape of the doorway he'd passed through, the one that led to the outside. He smiled in the darkness, feeling the life coursing in his limbs. He stood tall and wide-shouldered, confident in his own strength and speed. He was not afraid. There was nothing in the world he could not fight or outrun. Still, the silence was unnerving. He wondered if there had ever been more light falling in there than this eternal gloom.

The gleam he'd seen from the far side of the pit was produced by a single lamp. He was obscurely disappointed at the ordinary sight of matches, spare wicks and a canister of oil on a rock shelf. It was easy to imagine the old man shuffling along there every evening to refill the reservoir, or to spark a new flame. If the pit turned out to be nothing more than his toilet, Jean had already wasted too long on it. He fought not to giggle at the idea, though it was more a release of tension than real humour.

Disappointment touched him as he searched, running his hands along the edges of a dozen shelves cut into the rock – and right to the back of each one, though he feared the nip of some scaled thing. Nothing. No crowns, no bags of gold coins, no hoard to make him rich. A dusty leather belt hung on a nail and he reached for that as something moved in the gloom, rushing closer.

He had not heard the priest creep up. Jean shrieked a high note as Cormac lunged at him. His hand scrabbled with the belt, yanking it free as he tried to lash out with it and drive him back. Jean could see something flash silver in the old man's hands as he came at him, jabbing and slicing the air.

He retreated and the priest howled when he saw Jean whipping the belt back and forth. In a frenzy, the old man lunged again. Jean felt the horror of an iron blade across his throat, but there was no pain, no hot blood coursing. He gaped at the priest and felt his neck. Father Cormac seemed to have lost his mind and continued to slash at him. Jean raised one arm to protect his face and saw a wicked little blade slide across his skin without leaving a mark. He held the belt in one hand and as he looked at it, something gleamed beneath the dust. Jean grabbed the priest's arm.

He was fourteen and strong. With the belt in one hand, he gripped the old man's robe, shaking him back and forth in soundless rage. Father Cormac was gasping fit to burst his heart as Jean took his stick-like wrist and turned it, shoving the little blade into the old man's chest.

It was over in an instant. All the struggle died away and the priest looked at him.

'You're just . . . no. You don't . . .'

Father Cormac fought for breath, but the pit was huge and deep behind him and Jean could not resist the pull of it. He pushed the old man hard, watching him stumble against the edge and then fall, vanishing into blackness with a cry like a gull.

Jean found himself on his knees by the edge, gasping hard. Without thinking, he took up the little lamp and tossed it down. It fell a long way and, at the bottom, he saw the splayed body of Father Cormac and around him a glimpse of black shapes, like statues standing guard.

True darkness flooded in as the lamp winked out. It filled his mouth and eyes and ears like liquid and the silence was profound and eternal. Until something moved, a scrape of rock that filled Jean with horror. He still had the belt wrapped around his hand and he was up and shuffling, with the wall at his back, trying to guess how far away the door was. He thought he sensed something watching him, something that would cry out his guilt. His own breath was the loudest thing in the world. When he felt the door frame under his hands, he almost wept and clung to it in relief. He never saw the shadow detach from that much deeper darkness and follow him. It was no bigger than a cat, though it crept on more than four limbs.

I

Canis

Lord Canis stepped down from his coach. Pale and thin, in a black suit with his hair oiled close to his head, he was as elegant as any undertaker. The new road shone blue and grey, like fish scales. It was good-quality work. Canis knew the roadmen's costs to the last penny, but it looked both neat and hard-wearing, well worth the expense. In most parts of Darien, people still trudged through slop older than they were, a foul mixture of mud, hog blood and other things too noisome to consider. Here, the council building sat in a shining sea of flint. Lord Canis nodded to himself. A city needed good roads.

His servant, Albert George, came round, holding a small brush in each hand. Albert George may have had a surname, but it was never used. The man was in his sixties, short, spry and neat in manner. Though his own hair had long ago retreated to a silver shore, he looked healthy, the dome of his head suntanned and slightly freckled. On that day, the bristles in his nose and ears had been trimmed right back to a mat of stubble. Nothing was out of place. Though Lord Canis was a head taller, the scene had an air of a father inspecting his son before sending him to be married, or to accept his degree.

Canis stood coolly while Albert George used the brushes

in quick sweeps. If there was a glimmer of affection in the older man, it was not returned by the lord and council member. Nor did Albert George expect thanks. When he was finished, he stood back and bowed his head. Only one other coachman waited to be dismissed, ready for Albert George to swing up so he could take the carriage round to the stables.

The flow of bustling people and carts had slowed as a crowd gathered, but no one called out, in greeting or insult. A sight of the Canis coach brought dread in that city. For most of them, it meant tragedy. If Lord Canis had looked up, he might have been interested to observe how many of the watchers turned their heads so as not to see him, as if they could banish his dark cloth and black coach from the reality of their lives. He did not look up, however. His mind was on the vote of that morning and the business still ahead in the afternoon.

The huge door to the new council building stood before him, constructed with a tithe taken from every working citizen and subject in Darien. Canis had been involved in that vast undertaking, the fortification of the city two years before. A small piece of that funding had created an impressive building of six storeys, in brick and sandstone. Stone lions guarded the entrance. One was asleep, but the other had raised its head to observe the city, a symbol of eternal vigilance. Inside, the walls were panelled and floored in waxed oak, lighter and less oppressive than some of the older public buildings in Darien. Not cheap, however. Canis had seen the receipts and checked the accounts himself.

'All done, my lord,' Albert George said. 'I hope the afternoon session goes well.'

Canis nodded. As he'd risen before dawn, it had already been a long day, though he showed no sign of weariness. Albert George had known him for forty years, ever since the family stone had been used on a child so full of grins and pranks it had seemed he might burst. That laughing boy had died where he'd lain in the Canis gardens, robbed away by the wall that had crushed him – and the stone that saved his life.

Canis held out his hand and Albert George passed him a slender leather case, holding it steady while his master's grip closed on the handle.

'Listen for the bell at Frith Street chapel,' Canis said. 'The one by the west gate is running five minutes slow. Four o'clock, Albert George. I will be ready then.'

Something changed in the crowd. It was a subtle thing, but it broke the rhythm of the city around them and Albert George looked past his master to see what it was. He might have done the same if the drone of a wasp nest under a window had suddenly ceased, unnoticed until it was gone.

The house of Canis had never been much beloved. The family was known to be cold and there were enough dark stories about their stone. The pavement had been left clear between the coach and the entrance to the council building. Canis needed no guards to keep people away, not when even his touch was said to bring ill fortune. There was barely a grain of truth in any of it, but who would risk those they loved? While Albert George had brushed his master's coat, not half a dozen citizens had scurried across, heads down and backs bent, trying to escape notice. Hundreds more had interrupted their own busy afternoon to simply stand and stare at the head of one of the twelve noble families of Darien. They made their own wall to those behind.

In an instant, three men broke through. They wore brown cloaks that swirled around them. Two rested arms on each other's shoulders and laughed together, while the third seemed to dance. They were all tall and slender and Albert George turned, the instinct of years in the legion making him move to face a threat. He was not fast enough.

The laughing men enveloped the manservant for a few moments, never pausing as they swept past. Knives flickered under the cloaks and Albert George gave a grunt at the bite of iron.

'Murder!' he roared, startling the three even as they capered and shoved one another. Blood spattered on his breath and Albert George clung to the one who had stabbed him, holding on as his legs folded. The attacker struggled to pull his fingers from the thick cloak, dipping to a crouch.

All the fake laughter had vanished as the violence began. While one of their number still wrestled with the dying servant, the other two drew long knives and darted at the man they had come to kill.

Lord Canis tossed his satchel at them, so that one had to bat it from the air. It was just a heartbeat's respite, but it allowed him to draw a dagger from a black scabbard on his hip. It was no longer than his forearm, more symbol than weapon of war. Yet it was like a razor. If they had expected the lord to cower from them, or stand stunned as his servant died, they were mistaken.

Canis whipped his blade across the arm of one as the man lunged for him. He was rewarded with a slash of red and a yelp of surprise. The lord was slim and quick in his movements, his eyes utterly cold as he assessed the threat. The second one charged him, keeping him off-balance and under attack. For a time, Canis could do nothing but fend off both men. His expression never changed, though he took cuts on the forearm and across the ribs. The attackers were fast and careful with their blades. They knew how to fight, but still Canis remained on his feet.

The third attacker wrenched his cloak free at last, plunging his knife again and again until Albert George's grip suddenly weakened. As the fellow rose in ugly triumph, Lord Canis saw the dark shape of his coachman leap from above, driving a short sword through the killer's shoulders. They crashed together onto the hard flints. It had been a mortal blow, which left just two. Yet Canis could feel his strength beginning to fade. He was no longer young. Worse, his cuts bled profusely, stealing his will and concentration.

His sole advantage lay in each beat of time that passed. Canis did not smile when he heard shouts raised in the council building, nor at the running steps he could hear over the yells and screams of the crowd around them. He adjusted his stance as the two attackers flew at him again. Perhaps they sensed time running out. For frenzied moments they snarled and panted and struck at him. Killing a man was hard work.

Canis took a second wound on his forearm, but the attacker rolled his wrist as he struck. The blade tore through a sleeve to pass under his elbow and between the ribs. Canis felt it as a great thump in the chest, as if he had been punched. His riposte was across the man's throat. The assassin's body continued to pant, though his lips were suddenly still.

Instead, the throat pulsed obscenely as air rushed in and out of the wound. Fear showed in the man's eyes at last.

'Why, there is *always* a price,' Canis said softly to him. 'Did you not know?'

Three guards in white uniforms had come pounding out of the council building. One of them began to shout, but the other two engaged without any warning. They could not know friend from foe, but they were experienced men. The coachman staggered upright only to be knocked flat and knelt on. The one still attacking Lord Canis was a more obvious threat. The guards cut him down from behind as he struggled past his dying companion, still trying to finish the job.

Those who lived remained on high alert, panting and looking for threats that did not come. The crowd had pulled back and there had been some shrieking while the fight was going on. In that moment, there was a vast silence. It would not last – it never did – but for a time, the men involved stood apart somehow from their fellows. They looked at each other and gave private thanks for having survived. Then the moment of brotherhood faded and the noise of the city swelled in around them.

Canis slumped against the side of his coach. His coat hid the worst wounds, but he could feel his hands and feet getting numb. At the same time, a warm line ran from his belly down one leg. It reminded him of having wet himself and he hoped they had not pierced his bladder, looking for the dark stain against the blacker wool.

His coachman cried out for the guards to get off, scrambling up in stunned horror at what had erupted in the street. He reached Lord Canis as his master began to slip down against the polished carriage door. The coachman had not touched Lord Canis in a dozen years. The lord invited no intimacy of any kind. Yet he would certainly have fallen if his man had not held him upright.

'My lord, where are you hurt?' he said. The coachman gaped at the red stain that covered his palm like a child's paint. 'Help! Bring help here! His lordship needs a healer.'

'Let's get him inside,' one of the guards said.

He and his colleagues were still struggling to understand what had happened, but the street was too open and the crowds were pressing closer in horror and fascination. Who knew if there were more attackers, just watching for another chance? The council guards felt their backs exposed, so they took hold of Lord Canis and his dead manservant, forcing the coachman into service to carry the feet of Albert George. The black coach and the other bodies were left behind as the group vanished through the doors of the council building. By the time more guards came out to take control of the scene, the killers had been stripped of weapons, rings and pouches of coin. The satchel remained on the road and the coach itself lay untouched, though the door creaked back and forth in the air. Embroidered cushions were clearly visible inside, but no one wanted anything of the Canis house.

Inside the council building, the clatter of heels on polished marble echoed. Clerks stood rooted to the spot as whispered questions began. No one knew what was going on.

In a meeting room off the main entrance, the guards swept a table clear and laid Lord Canis down. His manservant was clearly dead and they rested the body of Albert George on the carpet, folding bloodied hands across his chest. Word of the attack travelled through the building like smoke. Slowly, every doorway and stair filled with staring faces.

Tellius came out of the new dining room, wiping his mouth while one of the clerks informed him of the tragedy. He tossed the cloth aside as he saw Lord Canis stretched out on the meeting-room table. The man's chest still rose and fell, but barely. Tellius went to him, ignoring the Aeris guards, who stood back respectfully in his presence. In Darien, Tellius was consort to Lady Sallet and speaker to the council. Some of the families knew too that he was part of the royal line in Shiang, though not many. Either way, they made no protest as he entered the room and took charge, glaring at those leaning in to stare.

'What is this, a show?' Tellius demanded. 'Get back to your labours, all of you.' Many of those watching turned away, though others hesitated and remained. Tellius swore under his breath as he glanced at the Aeris guards. 'One of you fetch the king's surgeon. Run, now! Master Burroughs has rooms on Whiteharte – out of the door and left, not a quarter mile from here.'

Tellius took Canis' hand then and looked down upon him, wincing at the cool stiffness already in the flesh. Canis was very pale and each breath seemed to catch, as if something blocked the draw of air. It was not a good sign.

Tellius leaned right over then to murmur into the ear, where small curved wrinkles joined it to the man's scalp.

'Shall I have your stone brought?'

'*No* . . . not again.' The man's words came with little movement. His eyes had been weary, resigned to death. Tellius' question brought back a gleam of life and . . . fear. The stone restored, but it also took warmth. It took too much.

'*Never . . .*' Canis whispered.

To Tellius' horror, the lord began to choke. His lungs had filled with blood and he could pull no more air into them. Yet his eyes still moved back and forth, as if looking for a way out. One leg twitched violently, clattering against the polished oak. It was an agonising wait and no one moved until blood began to dry on his lips and the heel no longer drummed. The silence seemed to fill the building. Tellius reached out and arranged the dead man's hands once more across his chest.

'Fetch me linen, would you?' he said. 'A cloth long enough to cover him.'

One was brought and Tellius watched as two servants drew it over the staring eyes. As it settled, a dark spot appeared where it touched the man's lips. Tellius found himself unable to look away as his mind whirred and plotted. Canis had voted against the proposal from the north. His murder meant the council was deadlocked no longer. More, it meant Tellius knew who had to be responsible. The one man in the city he could not touch.

Tellius closed his fists slowly, watching the spot increase to the size of a coin. In his own way, Canis had been a decent and honourable man. His death could not go unpunished. Tellius would just have to find a way.

'Master Tellius?'

Tellius glanced coldly at the young servant sent to fetch him, making him stammer as he went on.

'Y-your p-presence is requested in the chamber. Lady Sallet . . .'

'Yes, I understand,' Tellius said. He rubbed his jaw for a moment. Rage would ruin them. He needed to be cold.

2

Council

The council chamber still smelled of new leather and candle wax. The room was high-ceilinged enough to allow an observer gallery along one edge, a light and pleasant place, with huge windows on the east and west walls. The afternoon sun glittered in thick bands of gold as the representatives of the Twelve Families took their seats, visibly disturbed as the news spread.

Tellius was the last to enter. He nodded to Lady Sallet as he came into the room, exchanging a glance of worry and intimacy they would not be able to share again until they met that evening. He had a role to play first – and a threat to disperse, if he could find a way. Tellius glanced too at the man he was almost certain had given the order to murder Lord Canis. The prince of Féal was not quite able to hide a glitter of triumph in his eyes. Lords of Darien were not assaulted and murdered in the city. Not by three trained men, in broad daylight. Tellius had been out onto the street to examine the bodies of the killers and hear the first, rushed reports. In cells beneath the council building, the Canis coachman had been joined by three witnesses foolish enough to volunteer a description of events. They'd been given paper to write down all they knew and Tellius himself would question them, teasing out every detail. Yet the truth lay in the consequence. That morning, the council had agreed to hold a binding vote. It should have been a formality, but with Canis gone, everything had changed.

As Tellius settled himself, he could not help glaring at the prince of Féal. Youth could be annoying at the best of times. Yet the Fool of Féal, as Tellius had already privately named him, had all the special arrogance of a young swordsman – one who knew he had secured the advantage. The murder of Canis was surely written in that slight smile.

The prince did not sit at the great oval table of the Twelve Families, of course. He had taken a place with his two advisers on padded green benches that ran the length of the room. Petitioners and officials could rest on those while they waited for the council to finish deliberating. Tellius could see the casual, studied pose was a fiction. The young man sat with one leg crossed over the other. He wore a coat of dark blue velvet, with a spill of lace at the wrists and some sort of sapphire and diamond brooch on his lapel. It was gaudy even for a prince – if he was truly who he said he was. Tellius still wondered about that as he read over the notes from the morning and prepared to address the others. As speaker of the council, Tellius being present allowed the afternoon session to begin and he sensed the interest in the room as the whispers ceased. He conferred briefly with two of his clerks before peering over the assembled lords and ladies of Darien.

The knowledge of tragedy was clear in their faces, drawn and stern and still in shock. The body of Lord Canis lay under its sheet in an antechamber not forty paces from where they sat, yet they were forced to continue as if one of their number had not just been cut down like a dog in the street.

Tellius shook his head. There was a time for formality, but this was not it.

'It is my duty to announce the death of a friend and colleague in Lord Canis. Given the sudden and violent events of this morning, I move this meeting be suspended out of respect for his family. We can reconvene when the investigators have finished their report. I assure you, those responsible will end their days in regret. All those in favour . . . ?'

Before he finished speaking, the voice he had come to know only too well drawled over him.

'Master Speaker,' the prince began. He seemed utterly unaware of the protocols he ignored, speaking as if he had just been invited to respond. 'I wish my grief and personal sorrow to be included in the record, as the representative to Darien of the kingdom of Féal. I did not know Lord Canis beyond the discussions in this very room, of course, but he was clearly a man of integ . . .'

Tellius tried to speak over him. 'All those in favour, please raise your right hands.'

A few of them went up, but the prince continued as if no one else had spoken. From the first moment he had addressed them in session, Tellius had noticed the young man did not seem to mind talking over anyone else. He would rattle on without pause or obvious breath, trampling all reasonable discourse under his silver-buckled boots. Perhaps the council members bore it from a foreign prince, who might be excused lapses in good manners. It made Tellius want to strike him, but in his role as Speaker and Father of the Council, he had to endure the constant interruptions with a patience he had never learned.

'. . . integrity,' the prince went on, as he had never stopped speaking. 'Yet I am forced to indelicacy by the seriousness of my duties here. King Jean of Féal sent me to gain a response to his proposition. You have completed the preliminary voting and . . .'

'And we were deadlocked, with six on each side,' Tellius snapped, loud enough to be heard through the smooth torrent of words. 'Would you take advantage of a murder, Prince Louis? The body of Canis is not yet cold! To ask us to vote on this matter at such a time would be an insult to the city and this council. Is that your intention?'

The prince of Féal rose to his feet to address them. Tellius hid clenched fists under the rim of the table. He had not meant to ask a question, but his anger had given the prince an opening.

'My lords and ladies,' the prince said, shaking his head in reproof or regret. 'I must ask your patience once more – and risk your disapproval. I must risk even insult. My father is not a patient man and I have already spent days in constant talk in this very chamber. I understood this morning that you would move to a formal vote in this session, a final tally. My time here is at an end and I tell you, however this turns out, I must leave tomorrow, to take the news home. What that will be I do not yet know. His Majesty, Jean Brieland of the kingdom of Féal, asked me to secure the southern border of his territories. "Bring me a treaty for peace," he said! If I cannot secure that alliance, the insult will not be yours, but *ours*, my lords. My father fights every day against a cruel and dying empire to the far north. All he asks – all I must ask – is for an alliance with you, so that we do not have to guard two borders. Is that so terrible? I have asked you to agree a treaty of peace and trade with a neighbour hard-pressed by his enemies. If you refuse . . . if you force me to return with news that you will not give my father those reassurances . . .' The prince shook his head and ran a hand through the locks of his hair. 'What do you expect will follow? When my father subdues his enemies in the north, when that war is won, what do you think he will say then about the city on our southern border? The city that said to us "Do not call us allies", that forced us to keep legions nearby in time of war – legions we desperately need in the north.'

His voice had grown in passion, but it was still a performance, Tellius could see. He wondered if the young man was truly any relation to a king no one there had ever known. Over just a few years, Tellius had heard the first reports of a new territory being formed from a dozen smaller fiefdoms and cities to the north. Barely eighteen months before, the trickle of rumours had become a torrent, with tales of battles won and gold flowing like a river. Tellius spent a fortune in Darien coin each year to be told of new things. For hundreds of miles, his traders and spymasters paid silver for anything of interest, collecting all they were told in monthly reports and sending it back for him to pore over.

Reading those reports, Tellius felt he had come to know the man who called himself King Jean Brieland. The man's struggle to bring Féal into the world had been like watching a canvas filling slowly with colour, or a child born still – until its heart beat and there it was, suddenly alive. As that beat had sounded, the prince had arrived in Darien. The kingdom of Féal called itself a nation, that was true.

The man who ruled there wore a crown and took the name of king. Of course, anyone could, with soldiers and a few villages behind him. The rest was hard to gauge. From the beginning, the prince of Féal had argued for speed, pushing and needling them to make a decision. It was the hallmark of a con and Tellius had never lost that first hint of doubt.

For a week, the council had argued and discussed the offer. Tellius still wondered at the pressures the prince had been able to marshal in his defence. Blackmail? Certainly. More than one of the lords had changed his vote with a face so bright red and humiliated it could only have been forced. Bribery seemed less likely, though Tellius thought Lord Aeris had probably been bought, perhaps Woodville as well. One by one, he had watched the votes turn with each session and each preliminary vote. Until they had deadlocked that morning, at six on both sides. There had been no give in any of them and Tellius knew he had won. A draw meant nothing changed – which meant they would not be signing any treaty with an unknown power. As they'd broken for lunch, Tellius had signalled he would hold a formal vote that afternoon, then send the prince of Féal away from Darien with their regrets. That formal vote would have been written into the records of the city, no more than a footnote. Now, Canis was gone and the deadlock of the morning was in pieces.

'You call yourself a friend to this city,' Tellius said slowly, 'though you threaten us in the same breath. I wonder, if I stand against you, will there be knives waiting for me as I leave?'

His words caused an intake of breath, though Lord

Regis growled 'Good man' across the table. He had voted consistently against the proposal from the beginning.

'I am appalled to hear such cynicism from the speaker of this council,' Prince Louis responded, though he seemed utterly unruffled by the implication. As he began to go on, Tellius too rose to his feet, his voice growing stronger.

'You come here with bribes and threats, to the free city of Darien. Telling us you want to secure a border and nothing more, that the alliance will be a trading agreement, with resources shared. Yet it will be your courts administering those trade agreements, your officials setting tariffs and licences to trade. Your king allowing all – and our free city will be just a vassal.'

'You do not speak *for* the council,' the prince of Féal said. 'You are merely "the" speaker – and the oldest in this chamber. I offer trade, yes, and peace, yes – and how else would you negotiate between our great trading houses? Goodwill between competitors? I do not deny the role our courts will play. If you send us salt fish, must we take any standard? Or will you allow us to demand, assess – and then pay for – the best?'

'Markets decide prices, not you. Yet the judgement remains with you,' Tellius replied, shaking his head. 'If there is a complaint, your courts will assess our goods, and then what? Fines? You expect us to believe you won't beggar our merchants to promote your own?'

The prince spread his hands in appeal.

'Nations cooperate, even when a great one is facing a lesser competitor. I have asked for nothing you cannot afford to give. Don't you see . . .'

'So you do understand perfectly well! Do you think we

are fools? If your courts interpret the law, they *make* the law!' Tellius shouted over him. 'At a stroke, you will have us place your courts over ours! You come here with lies spilling from your mouth. You ask for an alliance and promise nothing! You say your king desires a safe southern border. What is that to us? What do we gain?'

'You gain our gratitude, and trade – and wealth beyond the dreams of this small table,' the prince retorted. He looked angrier than he had to that point, with bright colour darkening his cheeks. His hand trembled as he jabbed a finger at Tellius. 'And you gain safety. You gain the knowledge that you will not be considered our enemy.'

Even as the prince spoke the threat, he understood he had gone too far. His expression changed subtly. With an effort of will, he smothered some of his own fire.

'Yet we are not enemies. All I ask . . .'

'Yes, you have said,' Tellius replied. 'All you ask is that your courts decide our right to trade – our laws. That your government will consider fining us if we do not follow those laws. I tell you, when another man makes the laws under which you must live, if *you cannot amend those laws*, you are a slave! That is what you ask. That is why we must refuse.'

'I see the speaker is more obstinate than the noble families of the council,' the prince said. 'Well, call the binding vote, Master Speaker. See if you have the votes you need.'

'Take your seat, Prince Louis of Féal,' Tellius said. 'We will not vote on this today. If you must truly leave tomorrow, it will be without a treaty.'

There was a moment of stillness, then Lord Aeris cleared his throat. Tellius pressed his hands hard onto the oak table as he turned to face the lord whose traitorous brother had almost brought the city to ruin four years before. For most of the families at the table, their right to rule sprang from ancient ownership of a stone. Over the centuries, some had been destroyed, or taken as a spoil of war. Two or three stoneless families retained their seat on the council from a combination of vast wealth and stubbornness. Yet the Aeris family had been poor. When their stone had been lost, they'd made themselves soldiers, in hereditary command of five thousand men. It gave them status still.

Four years before, an Aeris son had gambled his family honour and lost. He'd brought the legion against the city during the Reaper Festival. It had been a night of savagery and that particular general had not survived it. The Aeris legion had endured decimation as a punishment, one man in ten murdered by his friends. It was a stain on all those who sat at that table, but it was not forgotten and there were scowls when the young lord spoke. The current Lord Aeris seemed a lesser man than his brother, at least as far as Tellius could judge.

'I think, Master Speaker, that we might test the waters here,' Aeris went on. He would not meet Tellius' eyes as he spoke. 'I would like to move for a vote on this issue.'

The man was not quite shameless in his refusal to look up, but Tellius let the contempt ring out in his voice.

'You'd vote, with Canis dead in the anterooms? Are you the creature of this foreign prince, then, Lord Aeris? What did he offer you for your honour?'

There was a grumble of anger from some of the other lords at that, along with a cry for Tellius to sit down. None of them were used to being spectators. They wanted to be heard.

Tellius paused long enough to allow one of his clerks to whisper in his ear. He shook his head and murmured a few words, sending the man away at an unseemly pace.

'I have been informed that Henry Canis has arrived in the building. He has the right to vote in his father's place.'

'How old is he, ten?' Aeris demanded.

Tellius shrugged.

'If he was about to speak his first word, that word could be his vote, my lord Aeris. His father is dead. The boy *is* Lord Canis, from that moment.'

'Has the royal physician pronounced the death, then?' Lord Woodville said suddenly, forcing Tellius to turn his head from the seething Aeris. 'I cannot accept some boy's vote without even a certificate of death, acknowledged and accepted by this council. No, we are all here. I move we vote at once.'

Tellius summoned another of his clerks for instruction, bending to his ear and sending him off at greater speed even than the last.

'Seconded!' Lord Aeris snapped. 'The vote before this council is whether to accept a peace treaty with the kingdom of Féal. Terms as discussed this morning and yesterday and right back to the crack of recorded time, as far as I can tell. Will you have us grow old and grey in this place, Master Speaker? Call the vote now. I cast mine for the treaty.'

Tellius could feel the meeting slipping away from him in the smile that creased the prince of Féal, watching his every move. Almost as one, the gathered nobles looked for some sign of the new Lord Canis or the doctor's death certificate on their way. The doors remained closed and every face

years. The truth would always be there to see. It was a small comfort.

'Those in favour of suspending proceedings, raise their right hands.'

Tellius counted slowly and consulted with the tellers making their marks on a wax slate before transferring the tally of five votes to the permanent record – all while Aeris tutted and huffed in impatience, hurrying them on.

'Those against.'

As Canis could not vote, the result was five to six. There would be no further delays allowed.

Tellius glanced once more at the door to the hall, still firmly shut. He breathed out, closing his eyes briefly in resignation.

'Very well. The vote is passed. We return to the original motion before the council – whether to accept alliance with the kingdom of Féal.' He pronounced it to rhyme with 'fail', though the prince had always given the name a sound closer to 'heal'. Whatever they called it, the treaty was a form of vassalage. Yet the struggle was lost.

'Those who wish to accept the terms of the treaty as laid out by Prince Louis of Féal, raise their right hands.'

Aeris was first, with Woodville. They had surely been bought with gold. Tellius hardly knew the Herne family, or the new Lord Bracken. He thought the old master of the Bracken house would never have given up freedom for mere trade, but they'd had a stone then. Perhaps that loss made a difference.

The hand of Forza rose a beat behind them. Tellius had known the young man's mother. She would have been disgusted with her offspring, he thought. Or perhaps the reason these families had thrived for so long was because they bent with the wind. Reeds survived the keel that cut the channel. Tellius shook his head in disgust.

The last of the six in favour was the house of Saracen, said once to be the keepers of an extraordinary weapon, though they had not brought it out when the city was threatened. Tellius wondered if it wasn't just another myth. He'd heard a rumour the thing had been stolen, though no one was saying anything. The prince of Féal must have spent fortunes to buy those families – or promised them attractive terms. That was more likely. They would refill their family coffers and expect the city to remain around them, quiet and subservient. Tellius had lived above those streets for many years. He wondered if they understood the strength of resentment that could build. Men will bend the knee to those they respect, for a long, long time. Then, one morning, they will not – and the streets run red.

'Against,' Tellius ordered. He jerked as the doors banged open and the royal physician himself came through, holding a white paper in his hand.

'My lords!' he began.

Guards stepped in front of Master Burroughs and he was forced to come to a halt. Tellius saw nervousness on the face of the prince of Féal for the first time. Yet it was too late. Aeris looked round in triumph and actually laughed, though the son of a murdered man stood just a few paces away, shaking in grief.

'Let him through,' Tellius ordered.

The guards stood back and the physician approached.

'My lords, I bear the death certificate of Lord Canis, murdered close by these rooms.'

'Well done, sir,' Lord Aeris replied in waspish triumph. 'His son will be sworn in the very instant we have finished this current vote. Carry on, Master Speaker.'

'Against,' Tellius called grimly. When they had written the council charter, it had been all too easy to imagine false alarms interrupting key votes. Once they had begun, only the rarest of emergencies could halt them. Tellius had pushed his luck and his authority as far as he could.

Lady Sallet raised her hand, as did Lord Regis and the new Lord De Guise, a cousin from a distant holding. Lord Hart added his vote and Lord Garland was a beat behind him. Five.

Tellius waited while the tellers wrote it into the official record.

'The motion is passed, six to five. The treaty is accepted.'

'Thank you,' the prince of Féal said. Once more he rose from the benches, hardly able to hide his relief. 'I am only sorry to have had this moment marred by such terrible tragedy. There will be a toast to Canis tonight in my house on Vine Street. You are all invited to share in the better part of the news – our alliance. His Majesty King Jean of Féal will be delighted.'

The prince dipped his head and left in a swirl of cloaks, his two advisers falling in behind. Tellius watched him go every step, until the door closed. He turned then to the new Lord Canis.

'Henry, Lord Canis, will you swear loyalty to this council, as the Goddess watches you and knows your heart?'

The boy shrugged off the hand of his father's servant on his shoulder and stood as tall as he could, showing for an instant the man he would become.

'I will,' he replied, his voice firm and cool.

There was more life in his eyes than Tellius had ever seen in the father, but there was also anger there. Tellius met the eyes of Lady Sallet in silent communication. The boy would have to be watched for a time, at least until the prince of Féal was out of the city.

3

Tellius

'I wanted to *strangle* him, Win,' Tellius said, pacing. He had returned to the Sallet estate, within the city. He had rarely appreciated the privacy of gates and walls quite as much as he did at that moment. 'I wanted to have the guards smash that smug expression off his face and throw him in a ditch. Or tie him backwards on a horse and return him to his father. You saw them! That damned prince of "Fail". Some two-horse king, that's all his father is. And then Aeris and his cronies! How long is it since his traitor brother brought the legion into the city? Four years, five? I'd have thought it takes longer than that to wipe away such a stain! I'd have thought it would be a generation or two before that blasted family put their heads up again. And for money? I have known men who would cut your heart out for a ring or a brooch, Win. And they were more honest than those who would sell their city to a foreign king. I swear, I should have cut Aeris' throat, just to even the votes.'

He mimed a slashing blow in the empty air, showing his teeth. Lady Win Sallet waited for his temper to run down, as it always did in the end. The man she loved blew up like summer storms. Over time, she'd quietly removed the sort of thing Tellius might stumble across and kick in her private rooms. Just a week after accepting his position as speaker for the council, he had broken a toe launching an umbrella stand after it became tangled between his feet. It had taken six months of limping and walking with a stick before he could clench his toes again. Even there in the day room, Lady Sallet eyed an orchid on a mahogany pedestal. If Tellius clipped that in his temper, the plant would surely go flying.

'Will you go to the event this evening?' she asked suddenly. 'There will be danger there, Tellius. On his own ground.'

'I don't think so. What is the point? Darien and Féal are allies now, apparently. Though if our traders wish to sell their goods into the "Nation of Féal" – can you believe it, Win? If our traders want to export, they will need to purchase a licence at a cost that would wipe out any profit for the first few years. Yet I see Aeris and Woodville are already gathering trading caravans. It's so blatant, Win! They have had their mouths filled with gold, their honour bought.'

'Trade is a good thing, Tellius,' she reminded him. 'How many times have you said that? It creates wealth where there was none before. Perhaps Aeris and Woodville and Herne and Bracken . . . perhaps they simply see it in those terms. Forza has always been a trading house, before everything. In a way, I am least surprised by them.'

'Yes? Perhaps we differ, then. I would rather be poor and free than a rich slave. This treaty binds us in trade, yes, but with trade come courts to adjudicate between merchants. With courts come binding laws, like threads of silk, Win. And where is the mechanism to undo this treaty? Where are *we* represented in the courts and palaces of this new nation? No, I think we have been bought and parcelled up – and I could not stop it. Perhaps I should have gone back to Shiang.'

'Where half the population are the slaves of the other half,' she reminded him softly.

He sighed and held the bridge of his nose with his eyes closed, breathing slowly and deeply.

'I could have done something about that.'

'Now you are just being contrary, my dear,' Lady Sallet said firmly. 'You were certain before. "Shiang is months of travel away – and my home is here." That's what you told me. Even if you left Darien – and me – you couldn't know the welcome you'd get, or if they would kill you on sight. The uncle who betrayed his own brother? You said yourself there would be poison in every meal, in every flower. Months to cross thousands of miles – and a single day for an assassin to be purchased and to reach you in your bed. That is what you said. And tell me how much you could achieve in that place, so far from me?'

'More than I managed today,' Tellius said, bitterness overwhelming him. He saw how she watched the damned orchid on its stand as he passed it. In response, he put his hands behind his back and clenched them into a mass of knuckles and old scars. Tellius was fit and strong, but in his sixties. As he paced, he resembled an elderly schoolmaster.

Both of them looked up at the sound of a bell tolling a single note nearby. Tellius frowned. Setting up communications between the courts of Shiang and Darien had been a monumental undertaking. Merely building a dovecote for sixty birds had been the least of it. Each of them had to be carried to Darien over mountains and forests, all the way from their home in Shiang. If they had been allowed to fly, they would of course have returned to their original roost, the very quality that made them so valuable. Yet it meant the birds had to remain caged for months. Half of them had died and the remaining thirty had arrived so unfit they could never have managed the return journey. Tellius had overseen the construction of the great pigeon house on the royal estate, where there was space for it. It turned out the smell and noise was less pleasant than he remembered from his childhood.

Inside that enclosure, the birds could at least flap back and forth to recover some of their strength. Yet with such a distance to cross, each message had to be sent with three birds, to have any chance of getting through. When the last of them had been used, the whole process would begin again, on both sides. There was no way to breed birds with that sense of another home. Merely to send a few words from one city to another took fortunes and labours beyond the reach of anyone but a noble house.

For the bell to ring, a messenger had to have run from the royal estate, close by the western gate of the city. Tellius shook his head. By their nature, the messages could not be urgent, but they were always serious. Still, he wanted to wave the sound away and concentrate on the problem of the new alliance.

'Go,' Win said. 'Go and see, before it drives you mad.'

He nodded and bowed to her. To the mistress of the house, and in the presence of servants, Tellius observed proper courtesy. Had they been properly private, he might have squeezed her a little as well.

Out in the courtyard, the sound of the bell seemed to

hang in the air, like a slight pressure. The royal messenger bowed low and held out a tiny tube on his outstretched palm. The first ones had been made from resin, but tortoiseshell was lighter – and weight was everything when it had to be carried so far. Tellius noted the colour of the cap as he unscrewed it. He tapped out a roll of paper, unspooling it slowly as he held it to the light. After a time, he nodded and flipped a coin to the younger man.

'Thank you,' he said.

'Was it good news, sir?' the messenger asked.

Tellius shook his head.

'No, but I am grateful all the same.'

He turned away with a steady step, though what he had read caused his heart to thump and a wave of dizziness to wash through him. They were coming, then, as he had known they would. How could he care for a title he had never truly owned? He had not set foot in Shiang for over forty years. Yet when he closed his eyes, he could imagine the royal precinct and the hub of the city, with scurrying clerks rushing past in robes of white or green or gold. The thought that it was all still going on was oddly comforting. He felt emotions swell in him. What a strange thing it was to grow old! When he had been young, old men seemed to be made of discipline and honour. Now that he had more years than he cared to admit under his belt, it seemed age blurred a man. It took his certainties as well as his strength. Tellius sighed as he went back in. The love of his life had seated herself to wait, her back so straight it would have made a guardsman blush. Win Sallet looked up as he came in through the garden windows. He showed her the tiny tube he still held.

'A nobleman of Shiang is on his way here,' Tellius said. 'It can only be to accept my abdication.'

'I see,' she said. 'How long before he arrives?'

As he began to calculate, she rose from her seat and embraced him, holding him tight. Tellius had been brother to one king and uncle to another. He had not wanted to be the last of the line, but for a time he had been the only survivor of a great house – and king of a city she had never seen.

'The new road reaches two hundred and sixty miles east – more by now, though they'll be writing for new funds any day. My little tavern and the birds I keep there lie at a point exactly a hundred miles from Darien's gate. It is, at most, two hours' flight for an experienced bird, which puts them two, perhaps three days out. Enough time to prepare for them – which is why I went to so much trouble to lay that road and set up the taverns along it.'

He grinned, delighted with one small success on a dark day. It was not hard to imagine a time in the future when carrier pigeons would cross the sky by the thousand, bringing vital information for trade or even war. It was a heady thought, but it did not distract him for long. Lady Sallet kept his hand in hers as she sat by him, looking up as his eyes grew grave once more.

'If I give it up, Win, as I must, they will take down my father's crest from the hall of memory,' he said. 'It will be the end of a line – and everything my father hoped for his sons. That is . . . that hurts, I will admit.' He waved away an objection, though she only watched him. 'I know. I chose this – and it is still the right decision. I will not return – and a king cannot rule from half a world away.'

'But it still hurts,' she said, kissing his cheek. 'I am grateful, you know. In case you thought I was not. If you were torn between Darien and Shiang, I am grateful you chose us – and me.'

He smiled, a little sadly.

'The truth is I was never torn, not really. My past is there, my childhood. What of that? My life now is here, with you. I would not waste a week of it, not to see a dozen Shiangs. You know, when I say it aloud, I feel a weight lift. If they have come to witness me abdicating the throne, I will do it with a glad heart.'

'Good,' she said brusquely. 'The right choice, then. Have you considered what you will tell Masters Hondo and Bosin?'

Tellius thought of the two Shiang swordsmen and how they would react.

'That . . . will be a more delicate conversation. Perhaps I should have them at the meeting, in case this Shiang nobleman attempts to bundle me away, or cuts my throat.'

'Is that a real possibility?' Lady Sallet said.

Her eyes had narrowed and he saw bristling anger that pleased him. He shrugged.

'I have been gone a long time, Win, but yes. If the man has been ordered to kill me, even at the expense of his life, he will obey – or try to.'

'The royal hall can be barred and secured. I will have his retinue overlooked and marked by guns, Tellius. If they raise a hand to you, they will not leave the city.'

He smiled and reached to touch her cheek with the back of his hand. On an impulse, he bent to kiss her, though his back twinged. He hid his tension from her, or thought he had. 'Perhaps I should also ask Master Taeshin to attend,' Tellius said as he broke away. 'If he will even speak to me.'

Lady Sallet concealed her irritation that the man she loved could kiss her and continue to think through the tasks and days ahead. She knew Tellius was burdened, as if his own past had descended on him like a shadow. He would not be free again until the delegation from Shiang had departed.

'You still have time to bathe and change before the event this evening,' she said.

He focused on her then, squinting in surprise.

'You think I should go to the house on Vine Street? There *is* danger there, Win. This Prince Louis of Féal is no friend to me, not after all that was said.'

'Oh, I agree. But we do not turn our backs on an enemy, Tellius. See who else is there, who bows to him, who hangs on his words. In just an hour, you will learn a great deal.'

'And of course if I go, you don't have to,' he said, raising his eyes.

She made a wheezing sound as she laughed, caught by surprise.

'Well, yes.'

'You are the least social woman I have ever met, Win,' he said. There was amusement in his eyes, but also great affection. She had seemed cold and aloof when they'd first met. The loneliness had been well hidden, but it had been there.

Matching the gleam in his eyes, she thought for a moment, taking her bottom lip between finger and thumb in a way that made him want to kiss her. 'Still – take Hondo and Bosin with you. And remind them that your honour is sacrosanct.'

Tellius took her into an embrace with a rustle of material, this time with more than simple affection in it.

The sword saint of Shiang was sweating hard as he increased the pace. Hondo was pleased at his form even so. He ran efficiently, without wasted breath or unnecessary movement. It was true he would need to spend part of the evening with an ice pack on each knee, but it still felt right to run, even in the shadow of Darien's walls.

'This is the last lap, Bosin. Then I am done for the day.'

The man at his side made no reply, as he had asked no question. Hondo reached out and clapped him on the shoulder. He made a point of touching the giant swordsman whenever there was an opportunity. Bosin had been healed by the Canis Stone two years before, saved from death when wounds and fevers had filled his lungs. Hondo could never be certain he would not have recovered on his own, given more time. The truth was that they had needed Bosin's sword arm when the city had come under attack. The big Shiang master had been vital to the defence and Hondo could not regret what they had done to him to secure it. Yet he regretted it anyway. Guilt stabbed him when he looked at the calmness in that face. The old Bosin had been a roaring drunkard, more given to telling lewd stories and eating prodigious amounts of food than the much leaner warrior that ran now at his side.

As with the brashness and temper, Bosin's weight had fallen away. Neither food nor drink seemed to interest him since he had been healed and sent out to fight for a foreign city. Hondo had taken it upon himself to keep Bosin fit and strong. It had begun as a sort of penance, when he saw

43

the big man sitting idly in a corner, staring at nothing and waiting for orders. Those who were healed by the Canis Stone were not incapable of thought or action. They merely lost warmth. Yet in Bosin's case, that warmth had been the very heart of him, the wellspring of his life.

The man who ran alongside Hondo breathed long and slow and showed no sign of discomfort. Bosin may have lost bulk, but his strength had surely increased and he still towered over the sword saint. He had accepted Tellius had the right to give orders – and to appoint Hondo as his trainer. There was a mind there still. It just didn't care.

If Hondo told him to lift an iron weight, Bosin would do it until his muscles could not support the thing any longer, so that they trembled and quivered like a horse beset with flies. If they trained with swords, Hondo had to be at his sharpest. Bosin attacked like the wind and he was so strong, a single blow could send the smaller man staggering and off-balance. There were even moments when Hondo was convinced the old Bosin was there once more, but then he would focus on the man's face and see that blankness – and his heart would sink. On a quiet evening, Hondo had made Tellius swear an oath he would never use the Canis Stone on him, even if the whole world needed the sword saint. Some things were worse than death. The idea that the old Bosin might somehow still be aware, might know and rage at all he had lost – that was an abomination.

The western gate loomed up before them, with a line of carts leading back to the main road. Hondo raised a hand to halt his companion, though of course that had no effect and Bosin ran on, as if he might continue to the end of the world.

'Enough!' Hondo said. 'My knees are aching.'

He reached to his hip to pat the sword hilt before remembering he had left it in his lodgings at the Red Inn. It was a strange realisation. Not only was he unarmed where once he would have scorned the idea. No, he was unarmed in a strange city, thousands of miles from home. Yet he had not left, because the man he had been sent to bring back had ordered him to remain. Hondo and Bosin and the twins had come to bring Tellius to Shiang for justice. The twins had not survived and the man Bosin had been was gone. Yet when the royal nephew had been killed in Shiang, murdered without heirs, Tellius had become king by default – and that had changed everything.

With that authority established, Tellius had used the swordsmen of Shiang as a weapon. For one night, Hondo and Bosin had stood against savage creatures or returned souls, things stronger than men and faster than anything had a right to be. Two years later, Hondo was still not sure what they had been. He had expected to die. Yet he had sworn on his honour to obey the king of Shiang, whoever it was.

None of them were the same after all they had seen and done. As physical injuries healed and scarred, it had taken an entire year before Hondo stopped sitting upright in the middle of sleep, clawing for some weapon or enemy he saw only in dreams. He had begun running around the city to help him sleep, then brought Bosin for company and for the debt he still owed. It was a little like adopting a son, Hondo thought. Bosin was his responsibility, however it had come about. He would not allow another to take the burden. It was an interesting thought.

'Have you eaten?' Hondo asked.

Bosin looked back and shook his head. Hondo noticed the big man was barely breathing hard, though they had run twelve miles at a good pace. He could feel himself still heating up, with new lines of sweat making his clothes stick to him. Still, he was much fitter than a year before. As his first master had said, the body could be trained, at any age, from any standard, to something like fitness. Hondo realised he was probably older than Master An had been then, which was disturbing.

'I will buy you breakfast at the stall inside the west gate,' Hondo said. 'A paper wrap with lamb and vegetables. Will that suit you? Or would you prefer fruit?'

He tried to ask questions that could not be answered with a nod or a shrug. The big man thought about it with a complete lack of interest.

'A wrap,' he said.

Hondo nodded and clapped him on the shoulder once again. He tried not to remember that the old Bosin would have eaten half a dozen of the things and probably ended up betting on his own abilities with the stallholder. Those days were gone.

They walked in through the western gate, both men too well known to the guards to be challenged, though they were stained with sweat and dust. Inside the wall, the stallholder ignored a queue of customers to serve them. One or two grumbled, but only until Bosin appeared to be looking in their direction. Still, Hondo saw three of them were wearing guns. It was becoming a more common sight with each season. He had not yet lowered himself to use the weapons, though he acknowledged their power.

Hondo remembered a friend he had known in his youth, a boy in his class at their first school. They had learned to read and write letters together, but there had been some sort of fever spreading through the other boy's village. When the child returned to school, he had been made dull – and deaf in one ear. There hadn't been any point mourning the loss, nor any way back. Hondo had been almost too young to understand, but he thought he did then, with Bosin. It was a sort of death, if death meant the loss of a particular personality.

He watched Bosin munch his way through the roll of meat and vegetables until it was all gone.

'Come, Master Bosin,' he said. 'I would like to make an offering at the temple, then look in on the king's birds. Will you accompany me? I have a meeting this afternoon with those young fellows I told you about. The riders willing to open up the mountain route to Shiang. We might have a proper postal service in a few years. Can you imagine that?'

Bosin shook his head and Hondo cursed under his breath, passing over a coin to the stallholder.

'Come on, then. You should bathe and be rubbed down or you will be stiff tonight.'

They left the crowd staring after them, as at any novelty. Hondo felt their eyes on his back and, worse, their pity. He remembered the bright voice of the boy's mother when she came to pick him up each day – 'And how was it? Did you work hard? Did you learn your letters?' – while her son just stared at her. Sometimes, a line of spittle had dripped from his open mouth. Hondo recalled her eyes would fill with tears then as she took his hand and walked him home.

4

Deeds

Vic Deeds smiled to himself. If his mother could only see him now. He'd grown a dark-blond moustache over the previous year that had become his pride and joy. He wore a black tunic and shirt over cream leggings and black boots that had seen better days, despite the vigorous polish he'd given them that afternoon. There was always a chance he'd be recognised, of course, despite the changes he'd made. With his work as a fixer for the old Aeris legion, he'd met a lot of people. Deeds had thrown away his yellow waistcoats and white shirts when he'd let his hair grow long. Darien was a fine, busy place, anyway. A man could lose himself there, regardless of what he'd done in the past, at least if he was reasonably cautious. It was also where the jobs were, if you happened to have been blackballed by a logging union and suffered a losing streak in cards. About the only thing left had been farming, and Deeds preferred clean nails and easy work.

The house on Vine Street was a grand place, refurbished over the previous month so that everything gleamed new and clean and smelled of money. The main hall could hold two hundred and that evening it looked as if it was going to. Everyone the prince of Féal had invited seemed to have decided to come. At first, Deeds had worried he might meet someone who knew him, but no one looked sharply in his direction. They were all too busy watching each other. He'd counted nine of the twelve families of Darien, there in some form or other. Not every family head had come, but Deeds could see they'd made sure they were represented. A Canis cousin could be seen, pale and stern in the corner; an oldest Herne daughter had arrived in place of her mother. Beyond those and men like Forza and Regis were a whole sprinkling of cousins, stepchildren and presumably mistresses and single-use lovers. As was the way of golden tickets, hangers-on had swelled the numbers. If they continued to arrive, Deeds thought there would hardly be room to raise one of the crystal glasses when it came to toasting the foreign prince who spent gold like chilled wine.

Deeds took a sip as he watched the crowd thicken and swirl. He caught the annoyed glance Lord Woodville cast his way, so decided to put the glass down. Truth be told, Deeds had lost more fortunes than he had made, certainly in the last few years. By thirty, he'd expected to be rich, with a wife and a mistress. He'd hoped to own a minor tavern or perhaps a whorehouse. Somewhere he could put his boots on the table and not care a damn for what anyone else thought. Instead, he'd taken a few wrong turns. One or two of them would have him dragged to a rope and executed, if they ever came out. Vic Deeds was not a man who dwelled on the past, however. He was not even sure it existed and had amused himself more than once making the point to men who discovered they couldn't prove it did.

As Lord Woodville turned to greet a young woman

with a sapphire necklace that drew the eye to an extraordinarily deep bosom, Deeds snatched up his glass once more and drained it. He still watched the young woman, but her weapons were not the sort that might interest Lord Woodville's personal guard.

Musicians sawed away in the corner, though the music they made was in danger of being smothered by voices and laughter. The crush meant there was certainly no prospect of dancing, for which Deeds was grateful. The favourite nobles and merchants of Darien stood in small groups, elbow to touching elbow, filling even that great room with a noise like clattering pigeon wings, or a wooden ratchet spinning free.

There were more dangerous men present than on the average battlefield, Deeds could see. Some of them noticed his attention and returned it in grim appraisal. It was an odd sort of professional courtesy between those who were there to protect a particular noble or wealthy trader. They nodded to one another, but it was also an exchange of awareness. 'I see you, mate,' Deeds murmured to himself more than once as he dipped his head and smiled to one of the others. They stood out for their balance and physical health, as if they wore tabards with the word 'killer' on them. He chuckled at the thought, though the sound drew Lord Woodville's cold stare once again. Deeds sighed to himself. There would be no bonus that night, he was reasonably sure. The tight old bastard had arrived in a coach he'd hired for the evening, with a jacket of pale grey velvet that smelled of cedar from years of moth protection. Money was not exactly flowing in the Woodville household, Deeds surmised. Still, he imagined they had the sense not to refuse to pay a man who wore a long pistol on each hip. 'Louder than words,' he'd said at the hiring, as he'd shot playing cards to pieces in a ripple of thunder. Of course, the Woodville steward had looked blankly at him until Deeds remembered they had him down as 'Israel Jenkins'. It did not please him to hide his name, but the truth was he had creditors who had just about given up on him being alive. A few of them could be in that very room.

Deeds wondered if it would somehow break the rules for him to fill a plate at the food table. It groaned under dozens of dishes, while servants rushed to and from the kitchens to heap more on. Deeds thought he could hear his stomach making a sound like wet leather, a fair mournful creaking. Somehow he knew Lord Woodville would be appalled, as if a personal guard should be above the need to eat, or to empty his bladder. On that subject, Deeds tried to gauge how long it would be before he had to leave the old sod alone and find a pot or a lavatory. Perhaps if he waited for Prince Louis to give a speech, he could slip away while his employer listened. Deeds managed to snatch another glass of white wine as a tray went past him. He still had fast hands, he told himself smugly.

He almost choked on the drink when he saw who entered then. His first casual glance was at the swords the two men carried, then with dawning horror Deeds realised he had seen them both before, in a logging camp far from the city. He edged back from instinct at the memory of how they had moved, like insects almost, skittering across open ground towards him. He'd fired on four of them and killed one, he was certain. In all honesty, he thought he'd hit the big one as well, as least twice. Yet there he was, a head taller than anyone else in the room. He'd lost some of that bear-like bulk, though, Deeds thought, maybe while recovering from wounds. Deeds looked around him, marking the position of the closest door. There were limits to bought loyalty. Lord Woodville would just have to fend for himself against those two, if it came to it.

It took an effort of will to strangle the voice whispering in his ear for him to leave. It had been two years since he'd fired those shots in the logging camp. What would they possibly remember of a half-glimpse in near darkness? No, it was not the time to panic. Behind the two men of Shiang came a third. Deeds knew him by sight well enough. He'd even sat in a cell at the Sallet estate for a brief time. Yet Deeds had been amongst many then, swept up together in the civil unrest. The one they called Speaker 'Androvanus Yuan-Tellius' wouldn't know him from any other bright-faced lad, he was reasonably sure. No, it was the man's Shiang guards Deeds feared.

He reminded himself he still wore his guns, the very same weapons that had chopped one of them down and stopped another. He patted the hilt of the right one and was reassured by it. If they came for him, he'd answer in fire and thunder, just as he had before. There was no need to be afraid. He raised his head and summoned his courage.

On the other side of the room, the roving eye of the big one seemed to have fixed on Deeds. Something like a frown crossed the face of the Shiang swordsman, until Hondo nudged Bosin in the ribs, making him blink and turn away.

*

Tellius remembered how much he disliked crowded parties of exactly this sort. As he moved through the room with Hondo and Bosin, his status produced some interesting results, unimaginable just half a dozen years before. Within moments of his arrival, every man or woman there knew he had entered the room. Those who faced him reported his movements to those still turned away, so that he never had to approach a closed group; they opened like flowers as he made his way over to allies and greeted them. Hondo and Bosin caused a ripple of unease, of course, but of the two hundred or so in that room, perhaps half were there to protect the other half.

Tellius bowed his head to Lord Forza, though he still felt disappointed at the way the man had voted in council. The younger man's mother had been a force in the city, but the wheel turned and the best always seemed to be taken. Tellius rubbed his jaw as Forza bowed and asked after Lady Sallet. Perhaps it was just part of getting old. Optimism was for the young.

Around that room, Tellius could sense clusters where he would not be welcome. It was in the way they stood and whispered, their awareness of his presence leading to stiffness and resentment rather than any pleasure. The vote had split the council in half, it seemed, a wound that would not soon heal. Tellius wondered if everyone there would live long enough to regret the new partner of Darien.

The representative of that kingdom appeared as if summoned from a door at the back of the hall, surrounded by a phalanx of servants. Tellius already knew the pair introduced as the prince's 'advisers', though he assumed they would be handy men. He wondered if there might be a way to prod Prince Louis into a challenge against Hondo or Bosin. That would be small recompense for the death of Canis, but it might knock the man's smile awry. Tellius began to consider it while the prince's men tapped glasses with fingernails or eating knives, making a ringing sound that brought a greater hush.

'My friends, lords and ladies of Darien, thank you all for coming,' the prince said. 'Your presence here gives me hope for the future – and our joint enterprise.' Some of the weaker men in the room began to raise glasses and respond, but the prince held up his hands and they quieted. 'I only wish the shadow of tragedy did not hang over us all this evening. In what might have been a celebration, I am instead minded of your loss. Such violence in the open street is too common wherever men gather. It shames us all. Perhaps, with the new wealth of our trade, we can put a guard on every corner, to keep the peace.'

Tellius felt one or two sideways glances land on him, watching to see how he would react. The prince himself never looked in Tellius' direction, playing the room like a harp. He was young and handsome enough to be an arresting figure, with a good speaking voice. Yet Tellius saw only cold calculation. He judged a man by what he offered – and there was not much honour in buying the poorest noble houses of Darien. Yet even there, at the prince's moment of triumph, Tellius could see strain, even hatred, in some of the faces watching him, ready to echo the toast. Whatever the prince had done to secure those votes had not made them allies. Oh, Lords Woodville and Aeris seemed happy enough, but Tellius saw how Lord Forza grinned like a skull. There was bright sweat running down

Lord Herne's neck. It was something to think about, Tellius considered. For that insight alone, he realised Win had been right to send him. She always was, at least when it came to the Twelve Families. He truly didn't deserve her, but she didn't seem to mind.

The prince was handed a glass of wine by a servant. He raised it immediately.

'To absent friends,' he said.

Tellius grimaced, but he could not refuse that particular toast. Not when Lord Canis was being prepared for death by his servants that very evening, across the city. As one, those in the room echoed the words and drank. A moment of stillness followed. The prince of Féal stood with his head bowed and Tellius could practically see him counting the beats before he looked up once more and smiled. Duty done, then. Murder committed.

Tellius had no doubt who had been behind the three killers. He still wondered if they'd expected to escape with their lives. In a way, he hoped so. Fanatics made unpleasant enemies. Tellius would always rather deal with men who expected to go home and kiss their wives, or enjoy a cup of tea by the fire that evening. Perhaps the three assassins hadn't expected so robust a response from Lord Canis and just a couple of servants. Tellius clenched his fist on the stem of his glass as he drank. When he'd gone out to the street, he had seen a smear of blue on the lips of the one the coachman had felled. The witnesses he'd questioned had confirmed someone in the crowd had come forward and pressed a hand over the mouth of that man, as he'd moaned and thrashed and spat blood. They'd all assumed it was a doctor, or some official from the council.

It seemed the writhing man had grown still after that touch – and the stranger had vanished back into the crowd.

The scene in the street had been chaotic and roughly planned, as far as Tellius could tell. The infuriating thing was how well it had worked. Canis was dead and the vote for an alliance had been won. The sheer brazen arrogance of it still shocked him. Tellius had known a fair share of malign men in his life, but very few would have pushed through something like that so openly, with a body cooling in the next room. The truth was, every man and woman in that hall knew who had killed Lord Canis. Yet they drank the murderer's wine and raised his glasses in the air and pretended it was all a tragic mystery. Tellius despised them, in that moment, even as he did the same. He loved Darien. He loved Lady Win Sallet. In his most private thoughts, he might have admitted to paternal feelings for the boy-king and some of the lads who'd fought for the city. Yet he hated the Twelve Families. Oh, there were a few he admired, like Lord Canis or the late Lady Forza. The rest, though, seemed made from a different clay.

Tellius was a loyal man. He knew it in his innermost heart. He had roots – roots he'd torn from the ground in Shiang and planted deep and still and dark in Darien. Perhaps that was why he was so loyal. He was a part of the city, wound into the veins and noise and gangs and stinks and trade. He was home and he would fight to protect it.

He had never forgotten the strange absence of so many of the Twelve Families on the night the city had been attacked by the Aeris legion years before. He'd assumed they had been caught by surprise, but it was just as likely they had been out in their gardens, burying gold and artefacts. With only a few honoured exceptions, the families were the sort to survive, or so they believed. As the prince of Féal caught his eye and dipped his head in a public show of respect, Tellius wondered if they had welcomed a ravening wolf amongst all the little lambs of Darien.

He decided to leave. He'd shown his face and that was probably enough to avoid any accusation of a snub. Politics seemed to involve a constant process of moving on from bad decisions, like a man refusing to go back to the beginning of a maze and instead just pushing on, fork after fork, regardless of where he ended up. Tellius knew he should at least acknowledge the five families he had led to a defeat. Lord Regis was off to one side, red-faced with laughter at some story his wife was telling. The new Lord De Guise stood at the older man's shoulder, visibly unsure of himself. His wife was a pretty little thing, looking entranced at all the grand families in attendance. Tellius shook his head, suddenly tired of them all. He gave the merest nod to Hondo and began to turn away.

The prince of Féal had approached him in his moment of indecision. Tellius might have knocked into him as he turned if Hondo hadn't nudged Bosin into the man's path. The move was perfectly judged so that Tellius barely caught a glimpse of Prince Louis before Bosin took a half-step between them, moved off-balance by a touch. Prince Louis was left facing a broad Shiang back. Tellius flashed a tight smile at his senior bodyguard. If the prince had been intent on another attack, it would have been interrupted.

'Excuse me,' the prince said, his mouth twisting sourly. The enormous Shiang swordsman turned on the spot and looked down on him. Tellius saw the prince meet Bosin's gaze with perfect confidence.

'Thank you, Master Bosin,' Tellius said, touching the big man lightly on the arm. 'You may stand down. I'm afraid Prince Louis is not used to swordsmen.'

Bosin stepped aside with a blank expression, utterly unruffled at being used like a wall. His only response was to dip his head in acknowledgement, but Prince Louis blinked, closing his mouth on whatever he had intended to say.

'Not used . . . Not used to swordsmen? I believe you are mistaken, Master Speaker! I grew up with them.'

Tellius found his smile widening. It seemed there were weaknesses in the man after all. He had found one in that easily stung pride – too late, but still.

'You may believe what you wish, of course, Your Majesty. Forgive me, I didn't mean the ordinary sort in Féal.' Tellius pronounced the name to rhyme with 'fail', as he always did. He was rewarded with a slight tightening of the man's eyes. 'I meant the masters of the blade in Shiang. We have a royal school in Darien now.'

'Perhaps I can find time to visit, before I leave.'

Tellius suspected the man's supporters in the Twelve Families would be only too happy to arrange such a thing, but he pushed a needle in even so. The king owed him a favour or three, if it came to it.

'Ah. I'm afraid that will not be possible, Your Majesty. The lessons are private – not for foreign eyes. Secrets of state.'

'Not even for new allies, Master Tellius? Are we not all friends here?'

The prince chuckled and reached out to clap the older man on the shoulder. At the same time, Hondo turned and accidentally bumped the prince with his hip, so that the hand flailed in the air.

'Your pardon, Majesty. It is very crowded here,' Hondo murmured, bowing.

The prince seemed to understand he was being blocked, and what that meant. His colour deepened and Tellius wondered what the consequences might be if the young man returned home in a wooden box to his father. War, perhaps, if he was much loved. A delay to any trade treaty, at the very least. He swallowed, forcing such thoughts back down into the acids of his stomach, where they could not cause trouble.

'These . . . gentlemen are swordsmen from Shiang, are they not?' the prince said. 'I wonder how they would fare against my father's elite guards.'

'Very well indeed, Your Majesty,' Tellius replied smoothly. 'But do not take it to heart. Shiang is a city built on mastery of the sword. They have no equal – though perhaps we will have a sword saint of Darien in a few years.' He ignored the slight grunt from Hondo as he spoke. The idea of teaching Mazer steps to foreigners still had the sting of heresy.

'I would love to see these extraordinary skills,' the prince said. There was a note of anger in his voice still and Tellius continued to prick him, casting away caution.

'There is a story told in Shiang of two masters, Your Majesty. One challenged the other to cut flies from the air with his blade. The older master stood perfectly still and when a fly came close, he drew and cut. The fly continued on its way. "You missed!" cried the younger man. "I did not miss," the older swordsman replied. "He will not be fathering any new flies, not now."'

Hondo snorted as he understood. The prince blinked, his irritation growing in opposition to Tellius' enjoyment of it. On a sudden whim and spike of temper, the prince tossed his empty wine glass into the air. He had intended to interrupt the smug condescension he felt from the speaker to the council. The glass would shatter on the floor and perhaps they would remember to treat him with respect. Had he not brought Darien to the table and wrenched a treaty from them that very day? All that flashed through his mind in a childish spasm. He jerked the glass up and watched as Bosin took it from the air, as smoothly as if they had practised the move a thousand times. The man had moved with no perceptible lag, just reached out and caught the glass as it rose.

'Ah, would you like a refill, Your Majesty?' Tellius said lightly. He could hardly believe the petty temper in the young man. There had been no sign of it in the council meetings. In that, Tellius felt the sting of failure. He should have found the weakness and used it when it would have done some good.

'That is kind of you, but no. I would like to see your man spar. A little action to take the taste of sweetness from my mouth. Do you understand? I will wager my man against yours, if you are willing.'

Tellius saw the prince's gaze flicker over Bosin. The man's size was intimidating. Yet Hondo was watching calmly, waiting to be asked. Tellius knew the sword saint would never forgive him if he gave the task to Bosin.

60

'It would be our honour, of course. Should it be to the death?'

There was no sound in that room as the crowd waited for the prince to reply. He felt the pressure of so many listeners and barely hesitated.

'Why, of course. A man's life as the stake, then.'

'And . . . what, four thousand in gold?' Tellius added. It was a sum as great as the prince must have promised the house of Aeris or Woodville for their vote. It would make Tellius a rich man in a single night. Unless Hondo lost, of course. Then he would have to go on bended knee to Lady Sallet and explain why she had to sell her town house to keep him out of slavery.

'Why not?' the prince said more coldly. 'Four thousand in gold.'

'You have that much here, Your Majesty? Or would it be an order to be drawn on a later date?'

The prince had paled as Tellius poked him, over and over. He felt able to push back a little at that.

'You don't think my written word would be good?'

Tellius chuckled, the sound oddly muffled in a room with two hundred silent people thinking he had lost his mind to be infuriating the prince in this way.

'I prefer gold, Your Majesty. Coins I can hold in my hand. Would you like a lower stake?'

The prince hesitated. He probably didn't have so vast a sum in Darien, but his honour and desire to strike back were overruling good sense. To Tellius' delight, the prince turned to Lord Aeris.

'Will you stake me, Aeris? I cannot match so great a sum tonight.'

Lord Aeris raised a hand to his face, scratching a cheek in a nervous gesture. The fingers trembled, Tellius saw in delight. He had been wandering through a maze, but found, if not the centre, at least a spot to stop and laugh. Lord Aeris had no real wealth. Tellius was forcing the prince to ask for the return of the very bribe Aeris had accepted from his hand. The crowd would guess why Aeris was trembling so – seeing his new confidence drain away. The man nodded like a twitch, already aware he had hesitated too long.

'Of course, Your Majesty.'

'Excellent,' Tellius said. 'Then we have a bet. And a little entertainment. Better than your musicians, anyway.' He saw the anger in the prince's eyes, though the man smiled.

5

To Lose

The house in Vine Street had clearly been refurbished with
no expense spared. Tellius could smell fresh paint as the
entire party trooped out to an inner yard. There, too, was
evidence of an army of workers, though the space was
stark and still mostly bare. Trimmed bushes spilled from
raised stone beds, like clumps of moss or tumours. Paths
wound between them, with a central space left for a table
and chairs in wrought iron. Even the lines of moss between
the path stones had been scrubbed out and lifted up,
removing the grime of decades. Servants of Féal came out
with the chattering guests, whisking away tables and
chairs. Still more moved swiftly to replenish any empty
glass. It was an impressive performance in its way, Tellius
thought. Within moments, the centre of the courtyard was
clear. Lamps hung overhead on metal wires from the floors
above. Tellius glanced up to see black spars jutting from
the brickwork, while Féal servants raised long poles to
light each wick. One by one, pools of light made the courtyard a place of serenity and austere beauty. Tellius rather
liked it, with his Shiang sensibilities. Yet he would end the
evening in blood, even so.

Hondo and Bosin waited at his side, with more space
around them than before. The crowd seemed to understand

that at least one of them would enter a mortal ring. They pressed back, so that the three Shiang men found themselves apart, almost in the centre of the courtyard. The house rose around them on all sides, making Tellius wonder if the sun ever reached the ground. It would explain the empty flower-beds if it did not. There seemed to be an unnatural chill there and he shivered.

The prince was performing for the crowd, there was no other way to describe it. The young man moved from group to group, explaining the event they would witness and leaving them beaming. Whatever else the man was, Tellius could admit, he had charm. Even those who had voted against the alliance were rewarded with a few brief words and a flashing grin. It made Tellius' stomach grind to watch a politician flatter and amuse men and women who should have been immune.

Hondo showed no sign of tension as Tellius glanced at him. Even so, Tellius took a slow breath before he leaned in to whisper to his man. Shiang honour was a piece of glass in that place. Tellius stood as his patron and master that evening. As his king. He had forced Hondo to accept that royal authority by right two years before, when Tellius had needed the sword saint to defend Darien. With ene-mies all around, Tellius would not shame the man with a single note of doubt in his abilities.

'You will have to kill whoever he puts up,' Tellius said under his breath.

Hondo inclined his head a fraction in answer.

'I want to win; I want him also to lose,' Tellius murmured.

There was a slight tightening around Hondo's eyes at that. The words were well known in the history of Shiang.

Once again, Hondo dipped his head and Tellius moved away with Bosin at his shoulder.

Unlike the man who would actually fight that evening, Tellius felt his heart beating hard and fast, fresh sweat breaking out on his brow. In all ways, he was a subject and citizen of Darien. In all ways but one, perhaps. Tellius loved the grace and mastery of the sword in a way that few from his adopted city could appreciate. He could not have had better seats that evening in any theatre. This was the play.

Lord Regis had fought alongside Hondo and Bosin two years before, when part of the city had been consumed in fire. Tellius was gratified to see the red-haired lord scaring up bets from the crowd – and having trouble getting any takers. They knew not to bet against a man who had won the title of sword saint from a city that revered masters of the blade.

The prince of Féal had conferred with one or two of his servants while the crowd assembled. He and his senior officers stared openly at Hondo, trying to gauge the man's strengths and weaknesses. Perhaps they had a choice of champions. Tellius leaned back against one of the raised stone beds, pressing into dense shrubbery. It cradled him as he settled, so that green leaves and stems quivered on the edge of his vision.

The crowd fell silent as Hondo's opponent arrived. Even if Prince Louis had not gestured, calling him to the centre, it could hardly have been anyone else. The man was not especially large, though he stood a head in height over Hondo. At that point, the sword saint was watching his opponent with intense concentration, judging gait and posture for any sign of old injuries. The man seemed to sense that scrutiny, so that he looked over and glared in challenge. He wore his hair short, revealing a fine scar that ran from his scalp and down into one cheek, as if pressed by a claw. He had survived a terrible wound at some point.

'My lords and ladies,' the prince said, making his voice echo from all sides. 'I would like to introduce Master Emil Cartagne. Champion to the king of Féal.'

The prince flashed a glance of triumph at Tellius as he spoke. In the same moment, his man went into a pattern of strikes, a combination of knees and elbows. The Féal man carried no sword and Tellius wondered if the prince had somehow misunderstood. Before he could voice the thought, a servant brought up a short sword resting on his outstretched arms. It was little more than a machete, weighted at the tip. The short length lent itself to being swung and the king's champion obliged, making silver blurs in the air. The crowd gasped and murmured.

The air was heating up with so many of them crammed in. One or two fanned themselves without looking away for an instant. They were close enough to be flecked with blood and they knew it. Tellius could see excitement rising in them like sap.

He saw the prince had extended a hand to him. Tellius came off the flowerbed to stand straight. His voice was strong enough to silence the whispering nobles.

'On our side stands Master Hondo, the saint of swords.' A thought struck him and he went on. 'Bodyguard to the king of Shiang.'

Prince Louis blinked at that, though Tellius was sure he would have been told. Well, if the ambassador of Shiang was coming to accept his abdication, he hadn't arrived yet. Tellius had not been crowned, but if it had ever been true, it was still true that evening.

'One bout, then, between royal champions. To the death,' the prince said.

Confidence came off him like heat and Tellius found himself staring intently at the fighter named as Emil Cartagne. The man looked fit and strong, with the sort of bone-hard body that can only be made in constant battle. It was too easy to imagine the flat, wide face twisting in anger and implacable strength.

Tellius scratched a line of sweat as it ran down his cheek. He could not help wondering if the prince had set him up. There had been no sign of the king's champion in any of the council meetings. Prince Louis had kept him back, perhaps for just such a trap as this.

The prince seemed intent on his role as master of ceremonies. He gestured to Hondo and his own fighter, summoning them to face one another. In response, Hondo held up a hand, interrupting proceedings. With the slowness of ritual, Hondo untied the wide belt at his waist, then unbuttoned the jacket underneath, handing both to Bosin to drape over an arm. Emil Cartagne stood bare-chested in the lamplight and Hondo chose to match him, rather than wear armour of any kind.

Beneath the coat, the sword saint wore a strap-pouch with his money and a variety of slender blades. He removed that and added it to the bundle Bosin held. A thin linen shirt followed, then a skin of silk that fitted closely. Tellius knew that final layer would trap an arrow in its wound, so that it could more easily be drawn out. Silk was a wonderful weave for warriors. As Hondo added that to the rest, Tellius wondered how it would fare against bullets. He also wondered if it might be a wonderful weave for old men who felt the chill in winter.

When Hondo stood wearing only high-waisted leggings, he took back his sword from Bosin's hand, the scabbard of orange and black he had been given at the moment of his triumph in Shiang, years before. He bowed over it to Tellius and drew the blade with a note like a bell struck. The sound hung in the air, making eyes round and nervous. Hondo would have given the scabbard to Bosin then, but Tellius held out his hand for it. It was an honour, from patron to master swordsman. Hondo showed no expression, but Tellius thought he was pleased as he passed the scabbard over. It was warm in Tellius' hand, or perhaps he was just cold.

Servants of the prince marked two lines on the centre of the courtyard, roughly the height of a man apart. The space was more cramped than Tellius would have preferred, but no more so than a sparring hall, where a hundred men struck for a minute of frenzied activity, then paused on order, moving on to the next in line. Tellius had never known exhaustion like those days and the memories were thick as they rose in him.

Hondo bowed to Tellius as his patron and strode to where the prince waited with Emil Cartagne. He bowed again, to his opponent and then to the prince, for his role as master of ceremonies. The simple courtesies were from a sparring culture. Tellius felt his mouth tighten in irritation at the prince's smile and exchange of glance with his fighter. Men of Féal had no right to be amused by the customs of Shiang. They knew nothing of honour.

'When the bell sounds, begin,' the prince said. He showed his teeth then, a wolfish expression that had Tellius checking all around and above for some attack. Was this just a diversion? He would not have been surprised. He was on the verge of calling Hondo back when a dozen of the prince's servants stepped forward from every entrance to the courtyard. As one, they took hold of the lamps that hung on their wires and swung them away.

The only sources of light spun crazily, making the courtyard flicker in gold and shadow. Tellius saw the Féal champion ready himself as the prince stepped back. A real bell sounded, the note much deeper than Hondo's blade leaving the scabbard.

The crowd roared as the two men came together, though the sound died away as quickly as it had risen. Tellius had watched ten thousand bouts in his youth. He knew how to look for a blow. Yet he had barely had time to register the speed of the champion of Féal before Hondo flicked the tip of his sword through the right side of the man's throat.

When the Shiang patron of a swordsman demanded not only a victory, but that the other man lose, he asked for the humiliation of an enemy. Hondo had chosen to attack in the first instant, without respect or gaining a sense of the other man's skill. In that way, it was a contemptuous cut, an insult.

It was also a killing blow, though Emil Cartagne immediately held a hand against the gash. Blood poured through his fingers and his expression was one of complete surprise. He went down to one knee, choking. As Tellius began to exult and prepare what he would say to the prince, Hondo suddenly curled over and slumped to the ground. Tellius went forward with the rest and the space in the middle vanished.

Tellius felt the crush of people around him in something like panic. Bosin was there at his shoulder, trying to watch every quarter for an attack, but he was still vulnerable. There were surely enemies in that courtyard, more than before. Still, he could not abandon Hondo.

Tellius knelt at the side of the sword saint, examining him. Hondo had been gashed across the ribs, exactly the sort of blow an experienced fighter might make to feel out his opponent. The champion of Féal had shown too much respect. That was what had killed him. Yet Hondo's wound was not a serious one, barely a six-inch cut, with the white bone showing. Blood dribbled from it, but Tellius was surprised it had felled Hondo, even for a moment. He leaned close and sniffed at the wound. There was a faint tang there, a memory.

'Fetch me the other man's sword,' Tellius said.

It was Lord Regis who stood closest to the fighter from Féal. Emil Cartagne still lived, with servants already trying to wrap his throat, binding his hand against the wound while they summoned a surgeon. Tellius glanced once at him and saw huge, dark pupils as the man's life and strength ebbed. He had no sympathy. Regis collected the man's short blade and Tellius touched the tip of one finger to it, then to his tongue. He felt numbness spread immediately and cursed, letting the blade fall.

'Succinylcholine. Pass me his belt, Master Bosin.'

He knew he had to act quickly. A small dose of the substance acted as a paralytic drug. No one would ever have known, not if Hondo had been quickly decapitated, or struck through the heart. No, that first slight gash would have been the end of him if Hondo hadn't ended the bout in the same split second.

The prince pushed his way through the crowd and heard Tellius speak. The young man blushed scarlet, in shock or fury. When the prince reached for the Féal sword, Bosin put his foot on the blade rather than allow him a weapon at that moment. The prince tried to grab the hilt and Tellius could see Bosin was about to bring a club-fist down on his neck.

'Prince Louis, please,' Tellius snapped. 'Master Hondo has been poisoned. I need an antidote in his belt. My man will be forced to defend us both if you persist.'

The prince looked up, aware of the sheer size of the Shiang master looming over him. He gave up scrabbling for the hilt and stood, brushing nonexistent dust from his coat.

'Very well. I had no part in any treachery, I assure you.'

'Of course, Your Majesty,' Tellius said, giving him the honour of his title as his response.

Bosin untangled the belly-strap Hondo had worn under his coat and Tellius pulled everything out of it, spilling an array of slender blades and pieces of parchment to the ground. Three small resin tubes were held flat in the thing. They resembled the ones carried by pigeons and contained only a scrap of dust. Each was a different colour, but of course Tellius could not know which was which.

Hondo stopped breathing and began to make a clicking sound deep in his throat. The muscle relaxant had been used to kill enemies for a thousand years, rendering them completely helpless. It was cruel, but brutally effective, as it stole strength, then breath and, at the end, the beating of the heart. After that, there was no way back. The antidote was not exactly a chemical opposite, but a stimulant of such ferocity it could burst veins in a healthy man. Tellius had carried tubes like the ones he held then forty years before. He had memorised their use, but it was all a lifetime ago. In his panic, with Hondo dying, he struggled to remember the other two. One was surely for snake venom, the other . . . He gave up and emptied all three into Hondo's gaping mouth, rubbing the powders onto the man's gums and tongue with his finger.

'Hand me that wine glass,' Tellius ordered, reaching for whoever held it. He poured the liquid into Hondo's mouth and prayed he was not drowning him.

They all waited. The sword saint of Shiang looked too much like a corpse in his stillness, made pale by the lack of blood moving in his muscles. When he breathed again, it was answered by a gasp across the faces of the crowd. Many of them had been holding their breaths unconsciously, staring.

The swinging lights were made still, so that the blurring shadows settled and normality returned. Tellius wondered if the prince had thought it might be an advantage to his man, or if it had just been a gesture to add to the drama of the moment. It did not matter then. The body of Emil Cartagne, champion of Féal, had been carried away from the courtyard, leaving a great stain of blood on the flagstones. Everything he had been had been taken from him.

Once he was sure Hondo would not stop breathing again, Tellius rose to his feet and faced the prince. The young man had recovered his dignity, but there was a glitter in his eyes: uncertainty, or a trace of fear.

'I must apologise for the actions of my man,' the prince said. 'I assure you it does not reflect the honour of Féal. If he had survived, I would have had him executed.'

Tellius felt old and tired. He was not in the mood for small barbs, not when the main battle of the evening was his victory.

'I believe you, Your Majesty. Now, I'll need to take my man to the royal physician. Can I prevail on you for a couple of servants to help carry him? My coach will be outside.'

'Of course.'

The prince snapped his fingers and two of his men stepped forward. One of them reached for Hondo's sword, where it had fallen. Tellius moved sharply at that.

'Not the sword. Allow me.' He stooped and picked it up.

'Should I examine that blade as well?' Prince Louis asked.

It was a mistake, said in bitter jest, but Tellius was not in the mood to let it pass. He grew very still and it was the prince's turn to wonder if he had gone too far, with a man who held a sword within striking range.

Tellius reached out with the blade, making the gesture slow enough not to be seen as a threat. He had no idea how many assassins mingled in that crowd. He did not want to startle one of them into rash action.

'Reassure yourself, if you wish. Be careful though, Your Majesty. It is sharper than you know.'

As if mesmerised, the prince wet his finger and touched it to the cold metal, rubbing a strip that made Tellius cringe internally. The prince tasted his own skin and seemed disappointed there was nothing more than a trace of oil. Tellius wrapped the sword in Hondo's jacket then, without sheathing it. That single touch would leave a permanent mark if it wasn't polished clean.

Some of the prince's confidence returned, perhaps with the unconscious awareness that both men had fallen. Hondo lay limp and the victory was less clear than it might have been. As Tellius readied himself to leave, some of the other nobles came to make their goodbyes, as if they were leaving a party like any other. Tellius could see it did not seem like the humiliation and failure it actually was. He felt a whisper of anger uncoil.

'So, Your Majesty. Will you send the four thousand in gold tomorrow morning? If Aeris staked you, perhaps you could have him drop it in to me.'

Tellius spoke casually and the prince's sick expression was its own reward. Prince Louis had indeed forgotten the bet in the presence of death.

'Y-yes . . . yes, of course,' the prince replied, biting one half of his lower lip.

'It will help with the doctor's bill, I imagine,' Tellius said, enjoying the discomfort. 'I hope you will tell your king that his champion died with dishonour. Such things are important. I'm sure he can find another as . . . skilled.'

The prince waved away the suggestion, his anger flaring in bright colour. For an instant, it was as if he and Tellius stood alone.

'Oh, we have ten thousand swordsmen, Master Speaker. In the royal guard alone. Do not concern yourself on that score.'

It was a threat, delivered by a foreign prince in the heart of Darien. Tellius knew he should just leave. He should incline his head and take Hondo out to his coach. Instead, he looked at the crowd around them, searching for a man he'd noticed in the first moment of arrival, who had edged away rather than crane to see, like all the others – and so made himself obvious.

'You, sir,' Tellius called across them. The man in question tried to disappear behind a row of guests and Tellius sighed. 'Vic Deeds, I believe. Come here.'

Not for nothing had Tellius trained and deployed spies across the city, in every noble and trading house. He knew the names, habits and vices of all those watching in Vine Street that night. He knew Deeds had called himself Israel Jenkins, as well. The idea that Lord Woodville could hire a new personal guard without a few questions being asked was laughable.

Deeds came forward with some real bravado and at least the same amount feigned.

'Stand there, son,' Tellius said. He pointed to the long pistols of black iron that hung in holsters on both hips. At his side, he felt Bosin lean forward, frowning and present in a way he had not quite been before. Deeds glanced only once at the big man, then kept his gaze firmly lowered.

The prince still stared in confusion. Tellius turned to him to answer.

'Your Majesty, swords were my life once, in Shiang. But I am a man of Darien now. And we have guns.'

The threat was clear, though he smiled. Tellius bowed then, judging the depth to a nicety wasted on the young prince, then spun on his heel and departed.

Outside, Tellius oversaw Hondo being put into his coach. The evening had been satisfying, in its way. He'd learned a great deal more about the prince. Yet he thought the cost had been too high. Bosin climbed up on the outside with the coachman, making the springs creak and lean. The whip snapped and they rode away into the darkness, to wake the king's physician before dawn.

6

Ambassador

Hondo came awake in his own room in the Sallet estate, under clean white sheets. Bosin sat in a chair at the foot of his bed, staring at nothing. Hondo watched him for a time, content just to lie there and recover his thoughts. He remembered killing the champion of Féal. That was beyond dispute. The blow had been mortal and he'd registered the satisfaction of a victory as he'd struck.

Hondo felt heat and swelling in his side, but none of the sense of wrongness that accompanied more serious wounds. He knew instinctively that he'd had worse and survived. He put that pain aside. His memories of the party ended at the moment of striking. He did recall Tellius' order – 'I want to win; I want him also to lose.' It was a line from the legends of Shiang, a demand from a master to his guards not only to bring victory, but to humiliate his enemy to such a degree that suicide was his only possible response.

Hondo felt heat begin to rise in his cheeks as he considered the choices he had made. He could not say he had fulfilled the spirit of the order. He might have taken the Féal champion apart a strip at a time, for example, until he was a bloody mess, begging Hondo to end his torment. That would have been a spectacle worthy of the ancient command.

Instead, Hondo had sought an ending so fast it would be in itself a humiliation. He had skirted his duty, trying to obey, but retaining subtlety and nuance. He shook his head slightly, as if refusing to answer a question. Two years in Darien had changed him, he realised. Not like Bosin, but still, something. The people of the city knew nothing of Mazer swordsmen, or unthinking fealty. They preferred to bargain and trade favours, to insult and take revenge. Life in Darien was crude and clumsy and occasionally obscene, but Hondo saw the value in it. There were times when he missed Shiang with the power of a homesick child – and other times when he understood completely what Tellius saw in all the noise and dirt and sheer chaos. Order was agreeably restful, but disorder could be stimulating.

Bosin sensed the gaze on him. The big man turned his head slowly, as if returning from far away. When he saw Hondo was awake, Bosin nodded once.

'Muscle-weakener,' he said.

Hondo nodded, though he felt his cheeks grow hotter in response. He was the sword saint of Shiang! Twenty years before, it would not have mattered if an opponent had coated his sword with some poison. Hondo would not have been cut. There had been a time . . . Hondo sighed and closed his eyes. He felt rested. If he had learned anything over two years in Darien, it was not to dwell too long on the past. That was a major difference between the cultures. In Shiang, there were a thousand tales of men or women whose lives had been ruined by a single error, often in their youth. In Darien, they seemed to accept their younger versions were mostly idiots. It was not so much forgiveness, as a mature response to something that could not be changed. The past was dead.

'I polished your blade,' Bosin said. 'The prince touched it.'

Hondo cursed under his breath as he threw back the cover and put his legs down to the floor. His ribs were bound, but there was little pain. He patted the square of bandage.

'Good work,' he said. It was unusual to have any kind of conversation with Bosin and he searched for something else to add.

'Are you all right?' he heard himself say.

Bosin turned a blank expression on him.

'Yes,' he said with a shrug. Bosin rose from the chair. 'The ambassador from Shiang is coming.'

'Thank you,' Hondo said faintly. He watched as the cold mask settled on Bosin once again. The big man did not look round as he crossed to the door and went out, closing it behind him. Bosin would not have hesitated to carry out Tellius' humiliation order, whether it was justified or not. Nor would he have wasted time thinking about it afterwards. Hondo imagined it was a peaceful existence, though it was still a kind of death. He shuddered as he reached under the bed for a porcelain pot to empty his bladder.

Tellius found he was sweating again. The early-evening sun had turned a harder gold, lighting the highest walls and towers in bands of brass. The prince of Féal had left Darien that morning, though the house on Vine Street remained open. Tellius had expected reports of it being shuttered, but instead, more worrying news had come of offices and clerks being installed. It felt just a little like an infection, allowed into the city and then given free rein. Worse was the arrival of another message from the eastern road. There was hardly time to congratulate himself on the success of the warning system he had created. The ambassador from Shiang was moving faster than Tellius had expected. Perhaps the sight of a good road had spurred him on, but the last birds had come from a tavern just forty miles from the city. It meant they could be at the gates of the city the following morning, if they chose to push on. Tellius had no one closer on the road, though he had twice thought of sending gallopers a few miles out to give him a final warning. They would be seen, however. If the ambassador was the competitive type, it could turn into a race for the walls.

Tellius had informed the court, of course, passing the tiny thread of paper on to the king's advisers. There were matters of etiquette involved that were appallingly complex. If Tellius was king of Shiang by right of inheritance, he could not go himself to greet the ambassador. The man and his retinue had to be escorted to the royal palace of Darien as a diplomatic party, there to be given rooms to rest and recuperate after the long journey.

Tellius wiped beads from his forehead as he bustled down a corridor of the Sallet estate, the captain of the guard at his side. Captain Galen was a good man, proven in loyalty. He seemed amused by Tellius' state of nerves, for reasons Tellius could not understand or stop to ask.

'This is no good,' Tellius said. 'I must know where he is on the road. I need a warning. Can we have someone sent up a high tower? That would win me a few minutes, wouldn't it?'

Galen nodded to one of the young serving lads trailing in their wake.

'You can run, Peter, I've seen you, when there's work to be done. So – east wall guard tower. When you see any sort of group on the road, come back here to me. Understood?'

'Not to you, captain,' Tellius interrupted. 'To the palace. I'll be there, I think. Lady Sallet thought that would be best . . .'

'Very well, sir. Peter, did you hear that? Don't nod at me, boy. Say, "Yes, captain." Very good. The palace, then. When you see them, come like the wind, all right? Well? Are you waiting for a little push to get you started? Go!'

The boy peeled off from the group and Tellius nodded sharply, over and over.

'Who do we have on the greeting group – at the gate?'

'Royal stewards in full livery, three of those,' Galen counted off on his fingers. 'Lord Hart will join them. He has agreed to guide the ambassador to the palace. Lord Hart has promised six of his guards in their best ceremonial blues. There'll be more men along the route – and the ones you wanted in the crowd in case there's trouble.'

'You have sawhorses out ready to block the junctions? The detour signs?' Tellius asked. He had asked the same questions twice before and Galen raised his eyes briefly to the ceiling of the cloister as they reached the end of it.

'All ready. Whenever he arrives, the ambassador will be

guided straight through the city gate with Lord Hart, then escorted to the palace. The royal estate will open before him and he'll be taken to the Bee rooms to rest and refresh himself. You and the king will meet him in the early evening. The meal will be duck.'

Tellius stopped and glanced at Galen.

'Really?'

Galen chuckled, a little embarrassed.

'Actually, yes. I heard the cook discussing the menu when you sent me out there this afternoon. He has a number of soups ready as well, though I forget the names. Leek was involved in one of them.'

Tellius waved a hand, feeling the tightness in his chest ease.

'Thank you, Galen. I can see it's all in hand. I just . . .' He trailed off, unable to explain.

Galen smiled.

'I understand, sir. I have a mother-in-law.' Tellius blinked at him and Galen went on. 'It's a little bit like that – someone you need to impress, coming into your house. You've been in Darien a long time, sir. You just want to make a good impression on someone from the old country. We'll do our bit, don't worry. This city owes you a good show.'

'Galen has that right,' Lady Sallet said, appearing in the doorway. She reached out and let Tellius kiss her cheek. 'Now. There is a bath filled and I have laid out your clothes for the morning. Simple, dark colours as you said.'

'My blue jacket?'

'With the white shirt. It's too warm for a coat, so I've kept it simple. Just the sword, on a black leather belt.'

Tellius kissed her again and swept past, shrugging out of his tunic as he went.

Ambassador Anson Xi-Hue maintained the cold face as he started up the royal hall, his retinue like rustling geese behind him. He prided himself on his ability to hide all emotion, an asset in foreign courts – and sometimes his own. So he gave no sign of the astonishment he felt, though he reeled from it. He had not expected huge walls and fortifications. Just a glance back as he passed through the gate confirmed intricate mechanisms, walkways, guardhouses and steps down to the street. He had certainly not expected crowds staring in hostile fashion from behind enormous sawhorses stretched across the road. The fact that his presence prevented them going about their lives had somehow been abundantly clear in their expressions and the way their eyes had followed him. In friendly company, with a little wine, Xi-Hue might have claimed a kinship with such common men. His mother had been high-born, it was true, but his father had been a simple mathematics tutor. Xi-Hue had avoided the airs and sneering of some of his generation. It was true he disliked crudity in all forms, but perhaps he saw a nobility in the honest carpenter or the layer of bricks that others in the diplomatic corps never could. He prided himself on that common touch.

It had been disconcerting to have the crowds in Darien call out insults as he passed. He still did not know if it was the fact that he rode a beautiful grey gelding, or his tunic of blue silk, or that his retinue wore matching coats. He had been called a 'peacock' as he'd arrived that morning and although he had halted his horse and pointed out the offender, the guard he addressed had only looked blankly at him. Xi-Hue shuddered at the memory of the wet clot from the road that had arced overhead, missing by inches. It made him wonder if his hosts even understood their own honour was bound up in his protection. The slightest attack on his dignity would be tenfold upon theirs.

For the first time in many years, Xi-Hue felt discomfited by conflicting information. The palace was clearly new and impressive, in a crude style. It suggested a good base of wealth and a vigorous class of nobles. Yet the manners of the people were those of savages. He tried not to think of the strange contraption they had provided as his toilet, but to his horror, the memory made his cheeks burn. It sat above the floor! With an urgent need upon him, he'd stared nonplussed at a mushroom of white porcelain. Driven by need, he'd climbed on to crouch with his feet on either side of the hole. Even then, he might have finished all he needed to do if he hadn't leaned on a metal handle, placed at convenient height. When that had suddenly moved, he'd fallen off the seat to the accompaniment of rushing waters. It had been at what could only be described as the worst possible time. The mess had been appalling, putting him in mind of prisoners who defiled their own cells. He had even somehow marked the wall as he slipped sideways.

For a diplomat to be kept waiting was one thing. Keeping a king waiting was an extraordinary discourtesy. Yet Xi-Hue's memory of the afternoon was mostly clatter and frenzy as his servants tried to restore the bathing room without revealing to their hosts what had happened. Xi-Hue himself had insisted on two separate baths. The first had been alone, without even his personal staff attending.

By the time he and his retinue were finally ready to leave the rooms, it was almost dark and torches had been lit all over the palace grounds. Xi-Hue wondered if the toilet had been intended to humiliate him, but it was hard to see how he could possibly ask, without revealing his difficulties. He had to resist the urge to smell his hands again, though he had scrubbed them so hard they were cracked and raw. On his first night in a city for months, he had not expected to miss the forests, where a civilised man simply found a sapling to hold and dug a little hole.

The king of Darien was a boy, as Xi-Hue had been warned in the exchange of pigeons that had preceded his entry to the city. Shiang kept no network of spies in Darien and that was just about the extent of Xi-Hue's information. He had a reputation for adaptability, he knew – the quality any diplomat must have when presented with some food or drink of dubious provenance. Or indeed a boy-king who had sat on the throne for almost five years. Xi-Hue had expected to meet a lad of seventeen or so, but the throne dwarfed its inhabitant. The king might have been ten, perhaps twelve at the most. Xi-Hue swept on, easing a smile onto his face.

The long hall was lined with subjects and guards. Xi-Hue was not sure what to make of the fact that neither he nor his retinue had been searched for weapons. It was either innocence or arrogance, he could not yet decide which. The court of Shiang had the same practice, which was the first thing he'd noticed in common since his arrival. Either way, he had on his person two thorn-rings to kill a man with a touch, while his retinue included Master Wai, the most accomplished quick-poisoner in Shiang. No doubt there were men with similar skills watching him make his way towards the boy-king of Darien.

Xi-Hue halted as one of the king's men raised a hand, stepping forward.

'Ambassador Anson Xi-Hue,' the man announced. 'Lord of the white, plenipotentiary to the court of Shiang.'

The details had been passed on while Xi-Hue had been taking his second bath. The moment was upon them all.

Xi-Hue had discussed with the council at home how much respect he should show to a foreign king. Shiang recognised no other authority as an equal, though there were a number of degrees of respect for trading partners and foreign chieftains. Back in Shiang, it had seemed reasonable to offer the bow of master-to-favoured-servant. Yet Xi-Hue had been promoted to high office for exactly this sort of fine judgement. Darien was a hub of power. He had sensed that from the first moment inside the gates and seen the length of the shadow they cast.

On instinct, he dropped to one knee and bowed his head. In the silence, Xi-Hue heard the slight intake of breath from his retinue as he did so, though the hiss of clothing assured him they had copied his action. He had dressed them in dark gold for the first meeting. Having them all kneel at the same moment would have looked like the beat of a wing, especially on that dark, polished floor.

Xi-Hue held the position long enough to count 'one emperor' in his head, then rose.

Years of training prevented any sharp movement as he saw the king had come to stand before him. The boy moved like a wraith! There had been no sound, Xi-Hue was certain. Yet the child-king had left his throne and walked two steps down. Was this more of the magic of Darien? They seemed so assured, these people, hardly deferent at all. Perhaps he had wandered into a nest of foreign wizards and would be lucky to get out with his skin.

Xi-Hue settled his initial shock as the boy looked up at him with a faint smile, clear-eyed and straight in his posture. He was clearly waiting for Xi-Hue to speak.

'Your Majesty, I am delighted to see your city for the first time,' Xi-Hue began. 'It is a wonder. I have been made most welcome.'

'You *are* welcome, ambassador. May I call you Xi-Hue?' To Xi-Hue's surprise, the young king pronounced it perfectly as 'Tsee-hway'.

'Your Majesty is welcome to use any name he might wish. I am your most humble guest and visitor. I only hope you will forgive any breach in custom that arises from my ignorance of your ways.'

'Then you may continue to call me "Your Majesty",' the king said. Xi-Hue bowed once more in response. 'Were you satisfied with your rooms? Some of your servants were found trying to burn garments in a walled garden on the palace grounds. They seemed distressed. I have had wine sent to them. I hope that is all right?'

'Of course, Your Majesty,' Xi-Hue replied, though he was mortified to have his dishonour on the cusp of being public knowledge. 'They are not . . . familiar with the customs here.'

'No, I suppose not,' said the king. 'Though perhaps they can learn. I am interested myself in learning, ambassador.

Master Tellius says so little about his home. It is like squeezing a stone. You would do me a great honour if you'd sit at my side as we dine, to tell me about Shiang. Perhaps I will have the pleasure of visiting one day.'

'When you are older,' Xi-Hue said, beginning to relax.

The king looked sideways at him.

'Yes . . . when I am older, as you say. Until that happy day, though, I will just have to remember everything you told me. I hope you like duck well done, ambassador. My cook has been threatening to leave my service if we didn't come to the table. And I would not like to lose him.'

Xi-Hue found himself unclenching as he walked alongside the boy-king, Arthur. He did not signal his retinue to follow and so they remained where they were. He was on his own, a task for which he had been well trained.

As they reached the end of the hall, he and the king approached two huge doors that hinted at lamplight and the smell of good food beyond. Another man stepped out of the shadows then, to stand on Xi-Hue's right shoulder as the young king stood on his left. Xi-Hue glanced at the fellow, seeing a tall and slender man of around his own age, with good bearing and features . . . The ambassador stumbled, suddenly clumsy. He might have fallen if Tellius hadn't taken him firmly by the arm.

'Ah yes, I suppose you've never met,' Arthur said. 'Ambassador Xi-Hue, let me introduce Master Speaker Androvanus Yuan-Tellius, king of Shiang. Now please, we really must attend to this duck, or my cook will pack his bags and be gone by the morning. And gentlemen, that would be a tragedy to overshadow anything else.'

Xi-Hue steadied himself, though he felt faint. It had

been a long day. To top it all, as a veteran of a thousand diplomatic meals, he knew with near-certainty that the duck would be overdone. It always was. He took a deep breath and forced the cold face once more as the three of them swept into the dining room. Some forty men and women rose in greeting, with bare plates and untouched napkins arrayed before them. Candles lit the table almost intimately, though it stretched the length of the room. Xi-Hue felt his confidence return. Regardless of the state of the duck, despite all the surprises he had endured, he was in his element.

7

Kingdom

Prince Louis found his confidence grew as he crossed the border – and not just because he and his companions rode Féal land. The formal border itself had been just a tiny outpost in the middle of nowhere, barely a wooden beam to block the road. It had pleased Louis to halt and present his travel papers to the guard there, signed and sealed by the king's clerk. The prince had saluted the lonely officer and received a salute in return before riding on. It didn't matter that he and his men could just as easily have gone round. Louis was back in the kingdom. With every mile that passed under their hooves, there were more signs of order, from the solid roadbed and clipped hedges, to fields marked by stone walls, like a net thrown over the land.

Ambling along a sunny road, with hills on either side, Prince Louis felt calm descend. The southern marches had been lawless when he had been born twenty years before. By all accounts, a policy of massed hangings had put an end to the worst of it, so his father said. These days, the villages to the south were quiet, respectful places. More than one householder came out to see who was riding through and then stood with their heads bowed when they recognised the prince's livery, rolling their caps to rope in their hands. They were decent, hard-working sorts, he thought. Men of the soil, who asked nothing more than sun and rain for their crops. They built their own low-roofed homes with sweat and strength and skill, like badgers rooting in the black earth. He rather envied them the simple beauty of their lives.

Louis' father still told the story of meeting one of their headmen or village elders. A skinny old fellow, chosen to speak for his people, yet who still claimed not to lead. In gentle reproof, the king of Féal had explained how things would be. All men were ruled, he had said, though some could never see it. The natural estate of man was to bind himself in laws – and to appoint strangers to enforce them. In short, man feared his own nature. To emphasise the point, the king himself had returned the man's head to his family. He had walked into their village alone and spent an entire morning sinking a hole for a sharp stake, hammering it deep, packing stones around it, then placing the head on top, in the very centre of their main crossroads. The man's wife and two sons had come out to watch him, but there had been something in the king that day that prevented them from speaking a single word. He left them staring at the slack-featured thing as he walked back the way he had come.

That had been a very different world, when King Jean Brieland had been young and unforgiving. He told the story as a cautionary tale in later years, saying he should have sent in his men to burn the village first, not risked his life just to make a point. Yet the village had not risen up against the stranger who'd strolled in amongst them. If the wolf walks slow, his father said, the geese are sometimes too afraid to run.

When the officials and taxmen of Féal had come in the weeks and months after that first visit, they had not been refused a building in the high street. Or when the first villagers died in their beds of old age and there were the taxmen of Féal with their pouches for the new 'death duty', no one had dared complain. They remembered the king who had walked so cheerfully in with his tools, with his spade and long hammer.

The secret, so his father said, was to strike hard, then squeeze gently. The taxes he imposed were never too harsh, though he increased them just a touch each yearly review. Even in that, his father's sly humour could be seen. Each 'review' was announced with talk of the burden of costs, as if one day it might actually lower taxes. Somehow they always went up even so.

The prince dismounted at his father's breaking grounds. King Jean Brieland was out in the summer air, of course, tending the warhorses that carried his most feared knights into battle. Prince Louis watched his father mount a huge young stallion, leaping onto a rug across its back without saddle or stirrups. The king wore dark yellow gloves and a wide tunic that left powerful arms bare and brown. The leggings were shiny with age and horse sweat, cinched at the waist by the old belt he always wore. For a while, Louis watched, unable to look away. The horse fought the man gripping him, leaping and plunging its head. It was a contest between two leaders of the herd and Louis thought he could hear his father laughing over the whinnies and snorts. There were times when Prince Louis wondered if his father cared at all for the kingdom, or if he was simply a man who preferred to dominate – to ride rather than to be ridden. It was an energy and determination King Jean brought to all parts of his life, whether it was bargaining with suppliers, or convincing some pitiful village that they had a new master and were part of a glorious future.

If King Jean Brieland had simply taken all they had, life would have been much simpler. All men understood robbery. Yet instead, the king employed them by the thousands, as clerks and judges and prison guards and chancellors – men whose living depended on maintaining his regime, whose families depended on supporting him for their bread. More, he paid men and women to spend the royal treasury – on roads, on doctors, on schools for the poor children. It was perhaps the ultimate demonstration of his will, that those he had crushed went on to cheer him as he paraded past. In their own towns.

Louis looked on his father with awe and more than a little dread. The prince was still dusty and stained from the road. He knew he had made good time and the news from Darien could hardly have gone ahead of him. He should have been coming home in triumph, but his father would decide whether he had earned praise or censure. Yet Louis was confident, his spirits borne up by the extraordinary trade deal he had made.

His father slid down, landing lightly. He slapped the horse on the rump, almost in insult, making it snort and toss its head. The king grinned, standing far too close to a still unbroken animal that could have crushed him, but showing no fear.

'That will do for today,' the king said to the trainers.

They formed a ring to try and get ropes on. Confused, the big horse bucked, the hooves coming close to his father, before it was off once again, galloping around the enclosure. Prince Louis watched and waited, ready for his father's attention to fall on him. King Jean knew he was there, of course. Like the horse, Louis could run around and around, but never break free.

Your son is here. Won't you greet him? Has he displeased you? No, he is loyal — more loyal than you deserve. Yet you ignore him while he stands and waits. You give him no honour, in front of your men.

'Honour must be won,' Jean Brieland snapped. 'It cannot be given.'

He had spoken aloud and shot a warning glance to his shadow, sitting in the dust of the corral like a stain on the ground. His son took his words as an opening and immediately stepped forward. The king of Féal felt the shadow's silent triumph. His hand drifted to his belt, hooking one thumb inside and letting the fingers fall like a wing. He took comfort in that touch.

'I believe I have won honour,' Prince Louis said. He patted a leather satchel on a long strap. 'As perhaps you hoped, Father. I have here an alliance with Darien, a trade agreement that will benefit us both.'

He paused in hope of some reaction but his father's gaze was on the horse he had broken. The animal knew that he watched. It kicked and bucked in a show of rebellion that had not been evident while it bore his weight.

'I bought a property there . . .' Prince Louis went on. 'And had it refurbished as our official residence.' He trailed away as his father glanced at him, one eye squinting almost closed in an expression of irritation.

'You had your men mark the positions of the city gates, the heights of the walls?'

The prince reached into the satchel, pleased to be able to report success.

'Yes, Father. They worked without sleep. I have plans of every district, in as much detail as we could manage in a short time. Darien is . . . a wondrous place.'

'I see. A city that employs a legion in its defence. Five thousand men.'

Prince Louis hesitated for just an instant, trying to choose his answer. In response, he sensed his father's interest turn on him like a flame.

'A few years ago, perhaps. They have armed the people of the city since. I could not say how many carry guns now, though I saw them on the streets, worn openly. I didn't get the chance to see any other defences – the Sallet Greens, the Regis shield. The De Guise sword . . .'

'They do exist,' his father said, though his attention seemed to have drifted away. It was as if he spoke to a patch of dry earth nearby. When Prince Louis stammered on, the king looked at him in surprise.

'I-I am sure. But the defences of the city were not shown to me, Father. Still, they have agreed to trade and to good-will between us. The council of the Twelve Families voted and I must say, it was . . .'

'I thought they would refuse,' the king said over him. 'I sent you, because I thought you of all my sons would surely fail. Oh, don't look so downcast! I didn't think anyone could win an alliance with Darien. They are so proud – and too wealthy to bribe. No, I thought they might give me the pretext to invade. By killing you, or imprisoning you, or humiliating my representative. Something like that. Instead, you return waving papers in triumph! What am I going to do with you now, eh? With all my plans in disarray?'

'I thought you wanted . . .' the prince began, breaking off. 'If you had told me your plans, perhaps I could have made a worse job of the approach!'

It was a rare flash of anger in him and the king heard it. Jean Brieland turned his back on the warhorse, glancing just once at the patch of ground that had fascinated him before. Prince Louis had learned not to follow that distracted gaze. There was never anything there.

'I gave you an impossible task and you succeeded anyway. Perhaps you are my son after all, as your mother always claimed. Eh?'

'I hope so,' Prince Louis murmured.

His father snorted.

'I hope so too, after all the time I have put into training you. Darien was not meant to be an ally, Louis! If I attack them now, I will be betraying a sovereign state bound to me in trade and by oath. It would be like raping a friend, do you understand? No one would ever trust me again.'

'Then trade, Father,' Prince Louis said. 'Instead of war, let me make peace with them. You have not seen the new walls around the city, nor the merchant ships like fat wasps on the river, flitting in and out at all hours of the day and night. Let them be an engine for wealth, perhaps to fund the campaigns you still plan. Doesn't that make sense?'

The king came closer and Prince Louis tried not to recoil as he felt the man's breath on his face. It was always slightly sweet.

'I could have whatever falls from their table, yes. Or I could take it all.'

'But why? You have already conquered lands and cities and . . . mountains. What do you need with more? Will you spend your whole life in the saddle, riding to battle?'

To Louis' surprise, his father suddenly laughed.

'I think I might, if I could remain young as well. Galloping on stone and heath, breaking a fighting line. Those are for men whose joints don't ache on cold mornings, whose lungs don't wheeze in the winter months. No, son, I need a little more than that to be content. It is summer now – and I am strong in summer. It is my season. Come on, I reek of horse sweat and I am hungry. Come and eat something with me.'

The king gave a low whistle and three of his rangers stepped in to secure the warhorse and lead it back to its stable. Louis noticed the animal was still watching his father. As they walked, the horse's ears suddenly dropped flat and it pulled away from one of the rangers. It looked as if a rat had scurried beneath its hooves, though Louis saw nothing.

'That is a fine destrier,' he said in genuine appreciation.

'Ox-head? He will be, when I have gentled him. My beloved Benedictus is twenty years old. If his son is only half the horse his father was, it will still be good enough. He just needs to learn to trust me.'

Prince Louis knew his father was capable of layering his meaning – speaking of one thing while teasing out something else. He wondered if he was meant to blindly trust the king, or if he would have to be broken first. It was a troubling thought.

King Jean Brieland took off his dark yellow gloves and tossed them to one of his servants trotting alongside. They anticipated his needs well, Prince Louis thought. Perhaps that was the lesson.

'I am forty-four years old, Louis. In some ways I am in my prime – in planning, in all I have learned. I have not wasted my life! Yet in other ways, I am closer to the end than the beginning.'

He glanced at his son, expecting the young man to object. Instead, Louis merely walked on, a frown on his face. The king sighed.

'And so it is not too hard to look ahead, to think . . . how will the world be, once I am gone? I know, I know – your mother always said it was a kind of madness. She said it was a sign of my lack of trust – that I try to order the world because I do not believe anyone else is capable. She was a woman of rare wisdom, Louis. But she is dead – and all that wisdom is gone into the earth. So I plan ahead and ahead, and ahead. Do you understand? No, not yet. But you will. Strong men breed weak sons, all too often. Yet if you are mine, I have not broken you too hard, have I? If you live long enough, you will stand one day before my tomb and you will speak my name and weep.'

'I swear I will,' Prince Louis said.

'And I hope I will hear it! I hope there is something more – *anything*. I have read fanciful tales, of punishments for the sinful dead, of lakes of fire and torment . . . and all I could think was how wonderful it would be! How magnificent to know there is *more*. If one day I burn for my sins, Louis, my balm will be the knowledge that this world is not all there is. That will cool me well enough, I think.'

'You will not burn,' Prince Louis said softly.

'No? Why not? I have burned others. It would be fitting, if there is any justice in the world at all.'

Your mind is wandering. Look at his worry, his confusion! Speak clearly, Jean Brieland. Let him see you need him.

'My point, Louis . . . my point, is this. There were nations once, so long ago that pages crumbled as I read them, sifting into dust. Not just one or two cities, but many. A dozen, a hundred like Darien. Not living as slaves, but as brothers . . .' The king stopped and gripped the bridge of his nose with his eyes closed. 'Nothing lasts for ever, Louis. But those nations came close. They were all born from small kings, bonded in blood and conquest into something much greater. Bordered by sea or mountain, or great river. On one side, a mighty people under a single crown; on the other – strangers, foreigners. Is it not a grand dream? I have half a dozen cities in the north. They call me king, though some still lick the wounds I gave them. Perhaps it is true I'll never know peace, Louis! I don't mind that life you mentioned – always in the saddle, always riding to war – because you or one of your brothers will inherit a nation. When the wounds have all healed at last, when we have one or two capitals and our roads stretch to the mountains in the east and the sea in the west, we'll have made something new. No, something *old* in the world, something reborn. And it will last, because it will be too strong to fail.'

Prince Louis saw the light in his father's eyes and felt it kindle his own, colder heart in turn. The man had always been able to do so, when he talked of creating new lines of horses bred for war, or roads connecting every village and city, so that no one was alone and all men could be reached. King Jean Brieland was inspiring because he believed his own dreams.

'Of course he sees now!' the king growled suddenly. '*Do* you see, Louis? Do you understand why I cannot have a mere alliance with Darien? I cannot swell a nation around them, leaving them to grow untended. Nations end in mountains and the sea, not on friendly borders. Not if I make it to last. When I am gone, I want a golden age, of peace and wealth for a thousand years. I want the lands around Darien to grow crops and boys to be my soldiers. So no city-state, no small king, can *ever* rise up and cast us down again. That will be my balm, while I sit in flames and laugh and laugh.'

The king glanced waspishly aside, though Louis had not said anything.

'Oh, don't worry, Louis. You have not wasted these months. Your skill, your negotiations, will have lulled them to sleep. I can hardly believe they didn't just flog you and send you back for your impertinence. Did you spend all the gold I gave you? Or is there a sum to be returned to the treasury?'

'All you gave – and more. I staked Aeris for his vote, but I had to borrow it back on a bet.'

The king paused and relief washed the tension from his gaze.

'How much?'

The prince steeled himself to reply.

'Four thousand in gold. I bet on Emil to win a bout, but he . . . failed.'

The king waved the loss away.

'There it is. Why did you not say before? I can nail a man up on four thousand, Louis. Whether I owe it to him, or he owes it to me. Debts are the destroyer of friendships, son. They can even be the lever that tips us all into war.' He tapped his fingers on the raised sections of the belt as he thought. 'Don't worry so much, Louis! There is never just one plan.'

8

Memory

Food and wine had passed across the table in a number of courses. The duck had been edible, though overdone, as the king's chef had warned. The man himself had delivered the dishes to the table, then waited for some word of satisfaction in a most irritating manner. Xi-Hue had rebuked him with a slight frown as he'd tasted the first mouthful, though the taste had been delicate enough. The chef had been almost in tears as he'd left.

Conversation had been light for the duration of the meal. Xi-Hue accepted his host's right to command the subject, of course. To please him, the ambassador had regaled the young king with stories of the court and society of Shiang. The ability to spin a tale was one of his talents and some of the other guests spilled wine as they snorted with laughter. No serious business had been discussed, for which the ambassador was grateful. He enjoyed the theatre of a grand meal in fine surroundings. It was such a shame to spoil it with work.

It was hard to judge the lateness of the hour when the king dismissed the other diners and ushered Xi-Hue and Tellius into his private chambers. The windows were dark, with no moon visible to reveal the city beyond. There too, Xi-Hue had been impressed. He liked wood and the chambers were panelled and warm, with thick carpets underfoot. They had the look of formal staterooms still, rather than the lair of a young boy. Xi-Hue had wondered for one horrible moment if he might encounter a wooden horse, or coloured building blocks, so that he'd had to stifle an urge to smile. Yet for all his apparent youth, the king seemed completely at ease in those surroundings. Servants filled glasses with a palatable red wine and the fire warmed them as they sat and gazed at the flames. Xi-Hue doubted they were truly alone. The king would surely fear an assassin. Yet the last of the servants left a decanter on a low side table where Tellius could reach it, then closed the double doors.

Xi-Hue looked up. He felt warm, relaxed, full and a little sleepy. For a few moments, he imagined his two young sons being crushed by a cart, calling for their father. It always helped to sharpen his wits, though he thought they were more likely to be asleep in their beds.

'You have been a very generous host, Your Majesty,' Xi-Hue ventured. 'Darien is so far from my home, I was not sure what to expect.'

'Though it grows closer, every day,' Arthur murmured. He had not touched any wine, Xi-Hue noticed. For one so small, perhaps it was too strong a drink.

'Closer, Your Majesty?' Xi-Hue asked.

'The road, Xi-Hue. It takes, what, three or four months now to make the crossing in summer? Half of that is still over rough land and forests, with a mountain pass hardly worth the name. Our road will widen that pass and halve the journey time, with way stations and taverns all along the route for weary travellers. Darien and Shiang do indeed grow closer every day.'

'Your Majesty is very wise, of course,' Xi-Hue said. He

did not show his concern, so he was surprised when Tellius broke in.

'An army would also be able to use the road, don't you think? When it is finished. I'd say there was an even chance we'll meet in the middle. Neither Shiang nor Darien will want to be surprised, so they'll have marching ranks set off as soon as there's a good route through. We should prepare the spot now, perhaps. Some sort of stone marker for where our forces will meet.'

Xi-Hue looked in concern from one to the other, unsure if they were toying with him or whether it was a real threat. He saw a glimmer of amusement in Tellius, but the boy-king was surprisingly hard to read.

'I believe you are expressing a real concern, Your Majesty . . . er . . . Master Tellius.' He had addressed the man who was king of Shiang, but in all his career, Xi-Hue had never met two kings at the same time. It was a little confusing and Tellius laughed as he understood.

'Please, as a countryman, you may call me Tellius when we are alone.'

'And I am "Your Majesty",' Arthur added solemnly. Both men looked at him and he sighed. 'All right. Arthur. For tonight alone, Tellius – and nowhere else. It is good to be king in Darien. I won't lay it down.'

'The road . . . is a real concern,' Tellius went on. 'Though we will not build all of it. Darien could never complete it without cooperation. It is my hope to persuade the new king of Shiang to meet us halfway on quarry and building costs, which are considerable. I'd like to see that meeting-point stone I mentioned, but in peace. One road, shared, could be a trade route to join us both.'

'Then I would be delighted to take your proposition to the king-in-waiting,' Xi-Hue said.

Tellius reached down to the side of his chair and presented a thick leather wrap to the ambassador.

'It's all there. Costs, plans, everything. I imagine they gave you all the authority you need, ambassador. It is not an unreasonable demand, not in the circumstances.'

'Thank you,' Xi-Hue replied. He did not confirm what Tellius had said, though he noted the choice of words. He could feel the weight of a much slimmer wrap in a hidden pocket of his tunic. Could this possibly be the time? He had expected to spend days in Darien, but these men seemed to move quickly.

As he had the thought, Tellius spoke again, confirming his impression.

'So . . . which family is to lend its sons to the throne of Shiang?'

Xi-Hue settled himself and sipped the wine, barely wetting his lips for courtesy now that he knew he would need to be sharp.

'The Hong clan is ascendant. They have gathered the most support, though the Diamatei were a close second, with the eastern nobles. You know Shiang, however, Your Maj . . . Tellius. Once Lord Hong is confirmed, order will be . . . retained.'

Xi-Hue could have pinched himself for coming so close to admitting the bloodshed that had plagued Shiang in recent months. The armies of four noble houses had fought it out on the streets of the city and the surrounding territories. The Hong father and son had brokered alliances with great skill, winning the crown for themselves.

All they needed was for Tellius to scratch his abdication in ink on vellum and the city could breathe in relief and peace once more. Xi-Hue had indeed been given considerable leeway to negotiate a settlement. He only hoped it would be enough. He feared the road Tellius wanted might be the least of it.

'Is it a condition that I hand over the Yuan sword?' Tellius had unstrapped the weapon that lay alongside his thigh, leaning it on the arm of his chair. The scabbard of dark red looked as if it was made of enamelled blood and it fairly hummed with menace. Xi-Hue could not help glancing at it, though he had ignored its presence studiously before.

'It is a symbol,' Xi-Hue replied. It was answer enough and he saw Tellius was resigned to its loss.

'It won't work for Lord Hong, of course. It won't cut the way it does for one of my line.'

Xi-Hue hesitated only for a moment as he decided whether to reveal the plans of the new royal house. Tellius was being brisk and candid with him and he decided to return the favour.

'I believe Lord Hong's son is to marry a bloodline cousin of yours. They hope to retain the qualities of the sword for a future generation.'

Tellius smiled, though he felt a pang at the news. Of course they were planning ahead. Shiang looked into the centuries to come and then worked to bring them about.

'I see. That makes sense. I hope it works. My father carried this sword, as did my brother and his son. It is beyond value, but I will hand it over to you. So . . . what else? You'll sign a treaty on behalf of Lord Hong to build your half of the road, I give you the sword he needs to wear for the crowds and the other houses . . . I sign your abdication. What else were you told to offer me, ambassador? I won't waste your time. I want Shiang as an ally, especially now we have agreed a trade treaty with the kingdom of Féal. Shiang is almost unknown here, Xi-Hue. Yet it was my home and I would see us brought closer before I die. There, I have told you all.'

Xi-Hue showed his excitement only in three rapid blinks as he considered and forced himself to be cautious. Tellius was offering everything he wanted, at far greater speed than Xi-Hue had dared to hope. And for what? A road? No matter how great an undertaking it was, Lord Hong would pay it to resolve the impasse at home with the Diamatei faction. He decided to lay out another piece of his offer.

'I have been authorised to grant a royal pension of a thousand a year in gold as well as the right to a title, currently in abeyance. You would retain nobility and an estate in Shiang. It might have some use in later years perhaps, or for your descendants.'

'I have none,' Tellius said. 'Yet I will accept. Was there anything else? I am tempted to sign tonight, sir! Let me see an end to this – and the beginning of a new friendship.'

Xi-Hue began to reach into the inner pocket for the slim leather wrap that contained a single sheet of perfectly white vellum.

'Lord Hong only asked me to enquire about the four swordsmen. Masters Hondo, Bosin, Hi and Je. We've had no word of them in our exchange of birds. Do they still live?'

Lines appeared around Tellius' mouth as he considered his reply. He had not answered queries about Hondo and Bosin, nor wanted to consider what might happen if he gave up his right to command their service.

'Masters Hi and Je died two years ago, in defence of this city,' he said after a moment of silence. 'There is a statue raised to them on the outer ring road – that area of the city is already known as "The Twins". I will take you to see it – the only monument to men of Shiang in Darien, ambassador. Masters Hondo and Bosin still live, though . . . Bosin was damaged in battle. It is hard to explain his exact condition. He is not the man he was.'

'I have never met him,' Xi-Hue replied, 'though I heard he was, ah . . . impressive. I am saddened to hear of the death of the twins. That is a great loss. Yet if Masters Bosin and Hondo are able to return home, Shiang will be the richer.'

Tellius found his thoughts racing.

'I would like to make their continuing service a condition of my abdication,' he began, though he felt objections forming as he spoke. He saw concern return to the ambassador. Perhaps having to disappoint him explained why Xi-Hue fell back into formality.

'Your Majesty, they are bound by free oath to the crown of Shiang . . . and I have orders for them to return home. I cannot accommodate this, though I wish I could. I can go as high as two thousand a year as the pension for service, however, as compensation.'

It was a fortune, befitting the dignity of a man who had, even briefly, been king of Shiang. Tellius still felt the sting of losing Hondo and Bosin. It was not just the protection and loyalty they gave him. They were men of his home city, almost the only ones in Darien. He did not know if he could call them friends, exactly. He thought Bosin had gone beyond such a concept, to a colder place. Yet they knew streets he had known as a lad, foods he had eaten, all the strange customs and days of celebration. Hondo in particular was a link to home that Tellius had told himself he'd never needed – when Shiang had been somewhere he had escaped. The thought of losing those men was surprisingly painful and Xi-Hue saw it in him and wondered. As the ambassador looked over in concern, he saw Tellius make a hard decision with a sharp nod.

'Write up the terms, Xi-Hue. I will sign it all in the morning.'

'Are you sure, Tellius?' Arthur said softly.

The old man nodded.

'My life is here. If this gets the road built, perhaps I'll visit Shiang again before I die. I would like to show the places of my youth to Win.'

Tellius felt a sting as his eyes prickled with tears, astonishing him. He had grown softer in Darien, without a doubt. Or with the passing years. Just the thought of standing one last time at his father's tomb, with the scent of cypress trees and jasmine on the air, was enough to hurt him.

Ambassador Xi-Hue rose to his feet and knelt to both men, holding the position for much longer than he had in the royal hall.

'May I withdraw?' he said. Arthur and Tellius both nodded, then smiled at one another. 'I think I had better try for sleep before tomorrow morning,' Xi-Hue went on. He paused for a moment, then decided to continue. 'Thank you, Your Majesties. It has been a great honour. I will not forget what we have discussed here.'

Hondo had been surprised at the size of the pile of trunks and leather bags he had collected. He had been forced to purchase his own cart to take them all. Ambassador Xi-Hue had made no objection, indeed he seemed delighted to be travelling in the company of a sword saint.

Hondo shook his head and sighed at his own melancholy. He had arrived in Darien two years before with little more than the clothes he wore, his sword, and what he now knew was a decent sum in gold. It had never been his intention to remain in the city, but to get quickly in and out with a prisoner. The idea that he would ever have learned to bargain with stallholders and traders in Darien, or developed a love of carved wood, or purchased extraordinary magical items with his salary, would have seemed impossible to the man who had first crossed the shadow of Darien's walls. Hondo also thought of the variety of pistols and assorted parts wrapped in fine oilcloth to keep them dry. There would be makers in Shiang who could reproduce them, of course. It would not be too long before the Hart and Regis workshops had competition.

Bosin had contributed almost nothing to the pile of goods and chattels. As far as Hondo knew, the big man had never spent his salary or even asked about it. Tellius and the Sallet estate provided clothes and food. Beyond a comb, toothbrush and the sword on his hip, Bosin had few other needs. When word had come that they would be going home, Hondo had drawn Bosin's salary in silver and been surprised at the sheer weight of coin. Not that he regretted his own purchases. Half the things in the bags would make Hondo a very wealthy man indeed, once he was back in Shiang. The rest would adorn the house he would build with those riches. He found he was excited to be returning, though there was a thread of loss running underneath that he did not wish to examine. He would miss Darien. If the road ever did open, he knew he would return.

'Are you ready to go?' Hondo asked Bosin again, for the third time that morning. Bosin nodded even so, showing unnatural patience.

'You have everything you want to take with you?' Hondo pressed him. 'You know we won't be coming back any time soon? Perhaps never. So if there is something you need to do, do it now. Understand?'

'I understand,' Bosin said, though he did not move from where he sat, his back perfectly straight, his pelvis tilted forward just a fraction so that he rested on the bones, ready to spring up. A swordsman of Bosin's calibre did not slouch.

Hondo felt the starch stiffness in his coat as he watched servants take out the last bags. He followed them into the sun and Bosin rose like smoke to walk alongside. Hondo looked back at the room that had been his home for the best part of two years. It was bare, as if he had already been forgotten. He shook his head, surprised at the sense of sadness. Tellius had signed an abdication agreement. He was no longer king of Shiang. The man Hondo had been sent to capture and return as a prisoner two years before had no call on him any longer, no formal authority over the sword saint. Yet it had not been too great a burden. Hondo found himself smiling at memories as he passed into the bright afternoon.

He halted then, with Bosin suddenly still at his side. The courtyard of the Sallet estate was full of people. They had left a passage clear to the main gate, but the rest were packed in and smiling. As Hondo looked up, they cheered.

Hondo could only gape for a time. He recognised the staff and servants of the estate, along with some of the pupils from the Mazer school. Captain Galen was there, as well as the guards Hondo had spent time training and getting fit. They too hollered and applauded, smiling when they caught his eye.

It was overwhelming, in its unexpectedness and simple affection. Hondo looked up at Bosin and the man's utter lack of interest helped him to maintain his own dignity. It would hardly do to have the sword saint of Shiang wiping his eyes as he left another city.

The trunks and bags were still being loaded onto a flatbed cart, with a bench seat and two small mares to pull it. Hondo looked past that to the smaller group of Lady Sallet, Tellius and Ambassador Xi-Hue, the latter looking completely astonished at whatever he was witnessing.

Hondo acknowledged the crowd as he crossed the yard, then bowed deeply to the lady of the estate and the man who had been his king for two years.

'Lady Sallet, Master Tellius, ambassador . . . thank you. I will miss this place.'

'Perhaps you will be the ambassador to Darien, when the road is finished,' Tellius said, clapping him on the back. 'Who knows Darien better than you?'

'It is a long way, but I hope so,' Hondo said. He was departing a gracious host and it cost him nothing to say the words. He was surprised how much they made his spirits rise, just at the thought of coming back.

Hondo kissed the hand Lady Sallet held out to him and watched as Bosin bowed in perfect balance. Hondo wondered if the big man had family in Shiang, or those who might have missed him in his absence. There would surely have to be explanations, when they returned. Hondo shook his head, marvelling at all they had seen and done. He was leaving Darien and regrets faded in the face of that promise. The open road, the forests and mountains once more – and at the end of it, his home. He suddenly wanted to be off and it was an effort to shake hands and acknowledge those who had come far to see him.

Hondo waved his hands to them and, to his surprise, the cheering died away. He looked at Tellius in confusion and the old man murmured 'speech' to him.

Hondo bowed to them.

'I have been made most welcome in Darien,' he said. 'More than I could ever have believed. Thank you. You have . . . surprised me.'

It was an awkward moment and Hondo was red with embarrassment, but they cheered him again even so. Tellius touched him lightly on the shoulder, both men aware that Hondo permitted the act as a mark of respect. Tellius had to lean closer and speak into his ear to be heard.

'Ambassador Xi-Hue has agreed to take sixty birds back to Shiang. The carts are out in the street, ready to go. I'm afraid it will be a slow journey, Master Hondo, once you leave the road. I'm sending a couple of bright lads with you to tend the birds, as well as the dozen who came with Ambassador Xi-Hue. I have personal letters as well, though I have gone through all that with the ambassador. Is there anything else?'

'I don't think so,' Hondo said over the noise of the crowd.

He looked down at the hand Tellius held out to him.

'Then thank you, Master Hondo. For how you fought to save us, to save me. For all you have done. If I thought you would stay just because I asked, I would . . .'

Hondo looked down at his feet.

'I have orders to return,' he said.

Tellius nodded. He understood.

'Look after Bosin, please. Use three of the birds to let me know you arrived safely, if Lord Hong will allow you to. I wish you peace and good fortune.'

The gates onto the street were drawn open and saddled horses brought out. Hondo saw a man standing on the street side of the gate, coming hesitantly closer as the opportunity presented itself. The Sallet guards were instantly alert, stepping forward to block a view of Lady Sallet or Tellius. With so many guns in the city, they had learned to react quickly to any threat. Hondo frowned, knowing he had seen the man before. His mind cleared as he remembered him from the party in Vine Street. A guest, or more likely a personal guard to one of the guests.

Tellius turned to see the object of their attention. He looked surprised at the changes in Vic Deeds. Someone had clearly given him a proper beating in the day and a half that had passed since Vine Street. The young man's eyes were black and swollen and there was a crust of blood under his nose. His clothes were torn and Tellius could see no sign of the expensive guns Deeds had worn on his hips. The man's fortunes had obviously taken a turn for the worse, as sometimes happened to cocky young devils in Darien. Yet Tellius wanted no interruptions while he was saying goodbye. He signalled to Galen to make the problem vanish. The Sallet captain was an old hand and he approached Deeds with the weight of experience.

'Come on, son. Whatever it is can wait, I'm sure.'

'No, it can't. It was your master who called me by name in front of all of them. I'm a marked man now. So I think I'm *owed* something.'

'Not today. Go on your way, Deeds,' Tellius said. He wanted the man gone while the ambassador of Shiang stood waiting. 'If your past has caught up with you, perhaps there's some justice in that.'

Hondo had been in the act of stepping up to the bench seat on the cart of his belongings. He paused with one foot in the air and set it back down. The sword saint of Shiang turned slowly to face the gate and everyone near to him felt his sudden focus like a crackle in the air.

'Deeds,' Hondo said. '*Vic* Deeds?'

He touched the hilt of his sword.

9

Parole

When the gates opened, Vic Deeds rubbed the back of his neck, forcing out his bottom lip. He'd been robbed, beaten and left unconscious for an entire day. He was lucky to be alive and he thought the fact that he was would probably surprise the men who had attacked him. Also, his jaw clicked when he spoke, which was driving him to distraction. He was starving, with no money left to buy food. He imagined his teeth were too loose to eat anything anyway. He wouldn't have gone anywhere near the Sallet estate that morning if he hadn't been desperate. Yet Tellius was the one who had called him by name in the house on Vine Street. However the old man had known him, it had been Tellius more than his assailants who'd stripped away his new clothes and the fine blond moustache. That hurt in more than one sense – half of the hair had been torn out during his kicking the night before, leaving a great swollen scab on his upper lip where the skin had gone. Deeds felt lower than he could remember – and if there was one man responsible, it was the speaker to the council.

Deeds ignored the Sallet guard captain strolling out to move him on from that spot. He'd been moved on by better men before. Deeds knew he hadn't stepped over the boundary to the Sallet estate, marked as a white line on the ground. Yet he didn't retreat either, even when Tellius told him to take himself off, as if he was a beggar at a rich man's gate. Deeds had nothing left. No savings and nowhere to sleep that night. He'd never felt quite as alone as he did then. His options were to rob travellers heading to Darien, which would almost certainly get him killed, or to beg for some scrap from the man who had dropped him in his current crop of troubles. Nor had Lord Woodville said a word either, as he'd sniffed and disappeared in his rented coach.

It had been a rough patch and the last thing Deeds wanted was to be there, with his hand out. However, pride rarely survived starvation. Deeds clenched his jaw, wincing as it clicked. He was determined not to let them send him on his way.

Deeds was vaguely, muzzily aware of the crowd in the courtyard, revealed as the gate swung open. If he'd been surprised at the sheer number of people, it had faded in his satisfaction at spotting Tellius and Lady Sallet themselves, standing almost in reach of the road. Yet as the crowd fell silent, Deeds found his attention drawn to one figure amongst them, suddenly very still.

He swallowed when he recognised the swordsman, the one they called the sword saint. Deeds had never felt more unarmed than at that moment, when Hondo rested his hand on a sword hilt of black and orange. On any other day, Deeds might have run, but he was bruised and sore and practically helpless as he stood there, peering from one good eye with the other swollen almost shut. His mother had always said he would hang, he recalled. It looked like she was wrong about that.

Deeds heard Hondo say his name and saw that the man

recognised it. He sighed and waved a hand, fatalism and bad temper warring almost equally in him.

'*Yes*, "Vic Deeds",' he said to Hondo. 'All right? What of it? Your man came at me in the woods and I shot him, yes. Your great bear stepped in the way and I shot him as well. We call it self-defence in Darien, meneer, whatever they call it down your way. Now, if you'll excuse me, I would like to apply for a job here.' The thought struck him as he spoke and Deeds went on. 'I managed to take down two Mazer masters with my guns, Master Tellius. Which I have heard since is no easy thing to do. So although I am at a low point today . . . although you have me at a disadvantage here and now, I am not a man to overlook.'

'What guns?' Tellius said. He glanced aside at Hondo, but the swordsman was still utterly motionless. Tellius was more aware than most how quickly Hondo could close the distance. Even experienced men tended to misjudge how much ground a sudden rush could cover. At just six paces away, Deeds felt safer than he actually was, while his life hung in a balance he could not see.

'Guns that were stolen the night before last, when I was ambushed on the way out of the house in Vine Street.'

Deeds had no idea how long he had lain in the alleyway alongside that house, piled up with kitchen scraps and a dead dog. His head was splitting. He felt slightly detached, as if the world swam behind glass while he peered and tried to make sense of it. He was aware that he was making an appalling spectacle of himself, as if a cleaner, sharper version sat on his shoulder and buried its face in its hands.

Hondo suddenly cracked his neck and rolled the shoulder of his sword arm. Deeds sensed some tension fade in the scene and breathed out. He'd felt like an insect about to be pinned to a board, reprieved in the last instant. Instead, Hondo's attention seemed to be on . . . oh. Deeds sighed. The big man, the one he had called Hondo's bear, was staring at him with the same perfect stillness Deeds remembered from the house on Vine Street. Hondo was watching Bosin and, for a moment, no one moved at all and a breeze blew leaves across the yard.

'He's almost out on his feet,' Lady Sallet said. 'Perhaps we should have some soup brought.'

'He's not a stray dog, Win,' Tellius replied, seriously. 'You can't keep him.'

In truth, though, that was exactly how Deeds looked. Yet Tellius was more concerned with what might happen if Bosin or Hondo decided to avenge their fallen companions, right there in the courtyard with the ambassador of Shiang looking on. Tellius wondered how much of an insult it would be if the ambassador was injured in a brawl. He thought they might avoid a war over it, but his road would never be built. Slowly, Tellius raised both hands. He could see indecision in Hondo, which was strange in itself.

'Now then, Deeds. If you stand back from the gate, Masters Hondo and Bosin were just leaving, do you see? They are going home to Shiang. Master Hondo? I would prefer you to leave the business of Darien to Darien – and the business of Shiang to Shiang.' He sensed rather than saw a tiny nod from Hondo, though it gave Tellius hope as he went on. 'Ambassador? It has been an honour for you, I know. However, I will not keep you further. I look forward to receiving news of your safe return.'

Ambassador Xi-Hue looked confused, as if he had

encountered a mugging and only wished to see how it turned out. Yet Tellius was clearly dismissing him – a man who had been the symbolic ruler of Shiang just the night before. Xi-Hue bowed deeply, as servant-to-lord, then allowed himself to be helped to mount.

'I need a manservant,' Hondo said suddenly. 'And a guard. I am hiring. If you need work.' He spoke directly to Deeds, and Tellius had to struggle not to groan as the battered gunfighter blinked, turning his head one way and then the other to help him focus.

'Master Hondo,' Tellius began. To his surprise, Hondo held up his hand to interrupt whatever he had been going to say. As nothing else, it showed the shift in their relationship. Hondo was no longer his to command.

'As my employee, you would be under my protection, Deeds.'

'Until when exactly?' Deeds said with a snort. 'Until we're out of sight of Darien? No, I don't think I'll be taking you up on your offer, sir. I didn't come here for you. I believe Master Tellius owes me at least a new set of guns. I'm here for those.'

The bravado was visibly fragile, as if Deeds might break down and start bawling at any moment. As he spoke, he leaned more and more on one leg to spare the other. Hondo could see blood beginning to pool around one foot while he swayed. Yet Deeds still stood with his chin up, glaring at them all.

'I'll have a new set of guns brought, Mr Deeds,' Lady Sallet said suddenly. 'And clothes. You're the same size as a few of my guards – we should be able to find something to suit you. I'll have Doctor Burroughs look you over as well, if you don't mind. Those wounds will bring a fever otherwise, if they haven't already.'

Deeds raised his eyebrows at her. He had never met the lady of Sallet house before, but in that moment he just wanted to melt into her concern and collapse. Even the thought of unclenching his will and pride made the court-yard swim.

'Damn. I'm sorry, my lady. I think I'm . . .'

His legs folded at the knee and he fell in a heap. The ambassador for Shiang made a sound like a sigh and clapped his hands together twice.

'What an interesting fellow, Lord Tellius. I wish . . .' He looked around him, at Hondo and Bosin, at the crowds peering in from the road outside. 'I wish I could stay longer.'

Tellius might have answered, but Hondo turned on them both.

'Ambassador, I'll need another day to get him back on his feet and whole enough to ride. One of your men can take my seat and drive the cart. I'll purchase another mount and catch you up on the road.'

Tellius looked at the sword saint in suspicion. He flick-ered a glance at Bosin as well, who stood like a tree in his thick travelling coat, ready to mount a horse that had been retrained from pulling a plough.

'I won't let you take Vic Deeds, Master Hondo,' Tellius said. 'You can't expect me to stand by while he is removed from Darien to be killed – whatever he might deserve.'

Hondo looked squarely at the man he had called king just the day before. Tellius had won a Shiang title for him-self in the negotiation, so he'd been told. He spoke formally, choosing his words.

'I came to Darien originally to take you back, Lord Tellius. Events . . . overtook that intention. Yet I told you then that you could not stop me – and I say it to you now. If I choose to take Vic Deeds with me as I go, he will come with me.'

Lady Sallet made no obvious signal Hondo could see. Yet the scene changed as he finished speaking. Two of her Sallet Greens came around the side of the main house, accelerating as they went. Hondo had helped train the men within and they moved well in the armour, hidden from view so that the suits appeared like green insects. They were the primary offensive power of House Sallet, larger, faster and far stronger than any man. They skidded to a stop by the lady of the house and her consort.

The ambassador shrank back from the massive armoured figures, his mouth opening and closing. The suits looked like statues come to life and yet had moved with such speed, their destructive capability was obvious. Long green swords protruded from behind each of the pair, ready to be drawn. On the street, the crowd stood in frozen awe, their mouths open.

The Sallet Greens took up a watching position, turning back and forth to assess what threat had called them out. Lady Sallet patted the leg of the one closest as she might have a hound. She smiled at Hondo.

'I believe you are unique, Master Hondo. You fought one of my Greens before – yet you stand alive. Please don't threaten us in my home. Honestly, Hondo. I thought we were friends.'

Hondo winced. The last was perfectly judged to interrupt his rising anger. He had spent dozens of evenings with Lady Sallet and her consort. Some women are like a balm for men, he had come to understand. They nudge them to reflect on errors they would have missed alone, yet without bitterness. His mother had been such a woman. Hondo sighed to himself. Lady Sallet had drawn the sting from the moment. He knew she was capable of the most delicate manipulation, but that did not mean he could resist the injured gaze she turned on him.

'If you'll give me the chance to explain . . .' he began.

'Give instead your parole, Master Hondo. Your personal oath that you will not harm me or mine while you remain on my property.'

Hondo bowed to her. He had threatened Tellius. She had every right to force him to public obedience. More, she knew him well enough to understand his word was iron. Hondo dropped to one knee on the stones and bowed his head.

'I give you my parole, Lady Sallet. And my apology.'

'Very well. Come inside,' Lady Sallet said immediately.

She held up an arm as if to usher him into the house, though Hondo stood a dozen paces away with two massive green warriors between them. Nonetheless, he turned and followed her. He shot an apologetic glance at Ambassador Xi-Hue as he went. The ambassador could only stare from one to the other, still unnerved by all he had seen, not least the great bounding monsters that had come at him like something from the legends of Shiang. He wanted to know more of those!

'After you, ambassador,' Tellius said in resignation. He indicated Xi-Hue should follow them in. 'Perhaps it would be better to wait until tomorrow morning and get an early start on the road.'

As they entered the main house, Tellius turned his head and gestured towards the slumped form of Vic Deeds, still blocking the arc of the gate. Captain Galen himself strode over. He draped the younger man over his shoulder while the gates were shut, muting the sounds of the city.

The courtyard drawing room of the Sallet estate was fairly small compared with some Xi-Hue had seen. He thought there were probably too many chairs and paintings on the walls, though he could sense a sort of consistent taste in the room's clutter. A single log burned in the fireplace at one end and the room was at least warm. Lady Sallet's servants appeared to communicate with their mistress without the need for spoken commands. She chose a spot near the fire and it seemed to Xi-Hue that they were all seated moments later, with tea steaming on a tray and being poured into cups. The Sallet Greens had remained outside. They loomed behind the windows, clearly aware of all that went on around them. Xi-Hue found them fascinating and wondered how he might gain permission to examine one in more detail.

'Perhaps you should explain yourself, Hondo,' Lady Sallet said.

There was still a touch of frost in her tone, Xi-Hue noted. The woman had some iron in her and Hondo dipped his head, accepting tea from the servant who passed it to his hand.

'My lady, I feel I should apologise . . .'

'That is a wise instinct. How many times have you been my guest in this very room? And yet you speak to Tellius like some angry young fool? For what cause? Why this sudden interest in Deeds?'

'You did hear him admit he was the one in the loggers' camp, my lady. He is the man who shot Bosin and killed Master Hi.'

'Was he not defending himself and those around him? I ask only because that is what he claimed, Master Hondo. Be honest now. I would like to hear the truth of it.'

Hondo thought back to the moments in the logging camp. With Bosin and the twins, he had come out of the deep forest, after crossing tundra and mountain to reach that spot, all the way from Shiang. After two years living in Darien, it was hard even to remember the innocence, no, the ignorance of his younger self. Hondo breathed out, forcing himself to relax.

'He may have believed he was under attack,' he said. Lady Sallet kept her gaze on him, unblinking until he went on. 'He may have *been* under attack, yes. However, my lady, you should know that I have every right to claim his head even so. My honour does not rest on whether the man had some idea of self-defence or not.'

'Really? How strange that it does not. Perhaps you should re-examine your honour.'

Ambassador Xi-Hue made a startled sound and Lady Sallet turned to him. In all his life, he had never heard a noblewoman speak so to a swordsman, never mind a sword saint. Xi-Hue was appalled to have witnessed an actual rebuke. From that moment, Hondo would surely recall Xi-Hue had been present for it. It could very easily poison their own relationship beyond repair. The ambassador felt Lady Sallet's glare fall on him and looked determinedly into his tea.

'I will examine my role in this, my lady,' Hondo went

on. 'You may be certain. That is a private concern. I have said I could claim the right to take his life. He killed a companion of mine and wounded Bosin almost to death. This Deeds is responsible for Bosin's . . . condition now, more than any other. There is no court in Shiang that would deny me . . .'

'We are not in Shiang, Master Hondo,' Lady Sallet said. He subsided once more.

'No, of course we are not. I cannot seem to remind you that I did not demand his life. I offered him employment, as a servant of mine for the journey.'

'You expect us to believe you would not kill him, after all you have said?' Tellius broke in, speaking for the first time.

'Have you known me to lie, Lord Tellius? In any form? I am the sword saint of Shiang. I carry the honour of my home in me. And I do not lie. If I say I will protect Vic Deeds, though I think he is a scoundrel, I will do so. Indeed, I will give my life to save his. If I make that vow, I do not expect to hear anyone else doubt my word.'

Hondo heard his own voice rise and somehow he was not surprised to have Lady Sallet speak again. He was off-balance in conversations with women, he realised. Men were easier to understand, certainly to intimidate.

'Of course we accept your word, Master Hondo, if you choose to give it. I have known three men of Shiang well – Tellius first, then you and Master Bosin. If you are all examples of your culture, Shiang must be an extraordinary place.'

Lady Sallet waited while Hondo and Tellius shared a sheepish glance, as she'd known they would. Bosin sat with his head slightly bowed, as if in prayer. He showed no interest at all in the conversation.

Lady Sallet reached out then and touched Hondo on the knee.

'I know you are not a man for games. If your honour was less a part of you, I might fear some trick of words – that you would call him your servant only until you reached Shiang and then kill him at the gate, or that you would abandon him to starve there, thousands of miles from home. Yet I do know your honour, Hondo, I do. So why do you want him? What is he to you?'

Hondo hesitated.

'It is not what he is to me, my lady. It is what he is to Bosin.'

As one they turned to the enormous man who sat in perfect balance as always, his hands lightly clasped. Bosin's cup of tea remained untasted and he did not look up at their sudden scrutiny, as any other might have done.

'Master Bosin?' Tellius asked. There was no response, so he looked in frustration to Hondo once again.

'Bosin recognised him in the house on Vine Street,' Hondo said. 'I saw it at the time, but I was . . . distracted by my duties, then by my bout with the champion of Féal. After that, I was unconscious – a scratch from a sword coated in sedative.' He added the last in response to the look of astonishment from the ambassador. Xi-Hue recollected himself and sipped his tea as Hondo continued.

'It hadn't come back to me before I heard the name Vic Deeds at the gate. But I remembered him then. I know that name. I learned it on the night we came through that logging camp.'

Hondo glanced aside at Bosin, before his gaze drifted across the ambassador. Hondo wondered if he would be breaking some privacy to speak of the stones of Darien. He reminded himself he was leaving, that he had never been more than a visitor to the city. The thought was surprisingly painful.

'Bosin was healed by the Canis Stone. He became less as a result.' Hondo nodded as Tellius winced. 'Yes, my lord. "Less" is a hard word, but Bosin doesn't care if I use it. He lost interest in the world through that healing. Certainly he lost any sense of vengeance or justice. If I'd had to guess, I would have said he wouldn't know Vic Deeds, or more likely that he wouldn't care. The two events – being shot, being alive today – are separate in Master Bosin. He is fit and immensely strong. His reflexes are, I think, a little better than they were – and he is still a master of the Mazer patterns and knowledge. He is one of the greatest swordsmen alive today . . . and the man he was is dead. I am filled with grief to leave Darien, for reasons I do not completely understand. I will miss this city and when I return home, I fear Shiang will feel different to me. Bosin knows nothing of that. He is leaving because the ambassador brought orders to summon him home. He has no regrets and I thought he would shake the dust of Darien from his boots and never look back.'

Hondo reached out and tapped Bosin on the arm, to be certain he had his attention.

'Master Bosin, did you recognise Vic Deeds at the party on Vine Street?'

The big man's head rose smoothly and once again Tellius felt a subtle tension in the air. He knew the Greens were not the only defences in that room. Bosin sat very still as he considered.

'Yes. I knew him,' he said.

'And how did you feel when you knew him? Do you remember?'

Bosin frowned, his brow lowering as he thought back.

'Bad. Like illness,' he said. 'I cannot explain it.'

'Thank you,' Hondo said in satisfaction. He looked around at Tellius and Lady Sallet. 'How hard did the Canis family try to undo what they had done to their son? They must have been relieved to have him alive after terrible injuries – and they all knew the power of the stone. Did they even search for the boy he had been?'

Hondo drank his tea, by then barely warm.

'You want Vic Deeds to be . . . what, a key?' Tellius said after a moment. 'I think that is a fantasy, Master Hondo. I think that is your guilt speaking, for failing to protect your men.'

Hondo stiffened as he drank, though he knew Tellius preferred to speak bluntly rather than be misunderstood.

'Nonetheless, that is why I would take Deeds with me to Shiang. Even if I am a fool, I would like to know I tried everything.'

'That makes sense,' Tellius said. 'Though I will not send him with you –' he paused as Hondo began to bristle – 'as a slave. When he has been tended and fed, you may offer him paid work guarding the caravan. It is the sort of employment he knows and he will be useful. However, Master Hondo,' Tellius held up a hand, 'I will require your oath to keep him safe, as you said before. Even if you have to escort him all the way home again. And, of course, if he refuses, I will not force him to accompany you.'

'How would you feel about keeping that last part to yourself? You don't need to lead with it, not if I give an oath to keep him safe.'

Tellius raised his eyebrows, sorry once more that the sword saint was leaving Darien.

'Is there nothing I can offer to persuade you to stay, Master Hondo? That would solve your problem just as well.'

'I am expected to return, my lord,' Hondo said.

Tellius sighed.

'Then you accept my terms?'

Hondo glanced at the ambassador and waited until Xi-Hue gave the tiniest of nods.

'Very well, Lord Tellius. I accept.'

10

Gamble

For Prince Louis, the most surprising thing about Darien was how alive it came at night. He had spent part of his youth in a village to the far north where entire days could pass without a single cart or carriage coming through. He knew now that his mother had been kept in isolation until she was clearly pregnant, then returned to her home village to raise the child for the first seven years – as far from the distractions of the cities as it was possible to be. It was a compassionate system, in its way, she had told him. She had wept when the king's men came marching into their village on his seventh birthday, just as she'd always promised they would. They'd worn red, Louis remembered, a grand, bright colour in that drab place. He'd never doubted her word, though some of the other boys had said she'd lain with a minstrel and just pretended it had been the king. Children could be cruel, but she'd told the truth.

Louis could still remember her breath on his skin as she'd kissed him goodbye. As he walked, he raised his hand to the same place on his cheek. He'd told her not to worry, he remembered, with a pang of embarrassment. He'd thought then that he was his father's only son. The revelation that there were a dozen other women like his mother around the country had helped to harden him, to increase his resolve. His father raised children like wheat, to be the administrators and officers of his new nation.

Just about every year after Louis' arrival at court, some new brat from the country would be brought to the king's side. King Jean Brieland would inspect them with the same thoroughness he brought to his warhorses, then either pronounce himself satisfied or not. Those who were accepted were trained and educated. Louis had no idea what happened to the others. He had seen one bright little lad who seemed full of laughter and excitement. The king had taken one look at the boy's twisted foot and shaken his head, turning back to the supper he had interrupted.

Louis told himself they were sent home, back to the loving embrace of their mothers to live out village lives. There had even been times when he'd envied them, though he had seen their fear. He hoped they had known some kindness. He had been set on a harder, darker path.

His carriage trailed him around the ring road, a dozen paces behind and itself surrounded by a phalanx of Féal guards. The night was cold, though Louis wore a thick cloak, held clear of the pavement by a fold gathered in his right arm. Yet the sky was clear and he had not lost the sense of pleasure that descended upon him as he'd passed through the gates of Darien once again. He was walking in the city, not as an outsider, peering from behind glass, but as one of them.

His father had sent him back almost immediately, this time as munificent partner and ally to Darien – with a trade deal already agreed. Louis had brought the wealth of Féal, fortunes in gold and men. Two hundred had made up that second group, from his father's dark-coated clerks to men like Lord Harkness, who could start a gambling establishment with just a pair of dice and a cup.

Half of them would report directly to his father; Louis understood that very well. The rest were like spiders descending onto a sweet little plum, fat and full of juice. Did spiders drink juice? He thought not, though he had some vague sense of them draining insects . . . Louis waved the idea away. Entire armies had apparently failed to breach the walls of Darien. Yet the kingdom of Féal entered as friends, made welcome in noble houses and fine establishments across the city. In just a few weeks, they had begun some forty businesses, with the house on Vine Street as the hub. Another patch of new enterprise had sprung up on the river docks. Slow barges of Féal now made their way down the great river that fed the city.

The joy of it was that Louis and his clerks had not gone seeking the life's blood that ran in Darien. No, from the moment he had returned, merchants had come to *him*, pitching deals and trades and new ventures. Three restaurants had opened, serving dishes he had known as a child. They were packed out. It was a giddy time and Prince Louis wondered if his father might give him Darien when they had taken it over. It was a place more suited to pleasure than some of the dour northern cities of Féal. He thought Darien suited his appetites rather well.

He crossed the street at a spot where dozens of men and women stepped between raised stones, with gaps for carriage wheels between them. For a moment, Prince Louis felt like one of them, lost in the flow of people. It made him want to laugh aloud and he caught the quizzical expressions of a couple as they passed, pulling their little daughter back before she walked right into him. The night was cold and clear, and he had arrived at Lord Harkness' latest gambling house, 'The Darien Lion'. The man had a knack for a name, it had to be said. Straight and honest, Harkness wagering houses brought a torrent of gold to his father. Prince Louis had been astonished not to find some similar enterprises in Darien, not at the level that might attract true wealth. Let the poor people of Darien keep their coin games and grubby tavern cards! He and Harkness ran a clean house. If history was any judge, they would repay the initial investment in less than a year. After that, it was all jam.

His cloak was taken from him as he entered. Lord Harkness had been informed, of course, so that he stood ready to welcome the prince of Féal, bowing deeply. Half a dozen Darien men stepped forward to be seen and to greet him. Lord Aeris was first among them, dressed more finely than Louis had seen before. The man wore coat and trousers of his house white, with a glitter at the cuffs that could only be diamond studs. He looked . . . gaudy. Yet Louis smiled and clicked his heels as Aeris swept a low bow to him. His father had doubled the repayment, for the service of lending it at the right moment. More, they had allowed Aeris to buy a fifth share of the Lion, a stake that bound his fate to theirs as well as any chain. The new house Lord Aeris was building further along Vine Street was said to be a wonder of excess.

Beautiful women watched from the gaming tables, looking up from those they were with to see who had arrived. Prince Louis wondered how many sweet little flowers would brush by him over the course of the evening. Women seemed attracted to power, which at the age of twenty-two both delighted and occasionally exhausted him. They liked him to notice them, to pat his arm and to laugh, showing him their throats and wrists. It was not such a great trick to pluck some of the finer blooms. For that alone, he would have considered the Darien Lion a delightful enterprise.

Louis accepted a drink of something ice-cold and biting, with a twist of lemon peel in it, then wandered over to view the tables and choose his vice for the evening. As co-owner, he preferred to be seen in the public room, spilling light and warmth and laughter into the road. Everyone passing by the establishment would know they were excluded from something wondrous. The following night, they would take their savings and risk it, telling themselves they'd stay for one drink and go.

The games on the second floor were just as lucrative, though for those who preferred to see a little blood on a white cuff. There were no laws against betting whether a man could watch his finger being bitten to the bone by a beautiful hostess without making a sound. Or wagering for and against two boxers, each with one foot bound to the floor. Harkness was the master of hazards of all kinds. He could spin odds on anything. Such events sometimes aroused other passions in those who watched. That had been its own revelation, Louis recalled. There were bedrooms on the highest floor of the Darien Lion. Louis kept a silver key to one on a chain at his waist.

It was good to be alive that night, as always. To be in Darien, though, was a special joy. As Louis stood there and sipped, aware of the gaze of a blonde whose dress seemed to have been made for a smaller woman, he realised one reason he felt so content in Darien was that his father was so far away. The thought took some of the shine off the evening. Each day he spread his father's gold and influence was a day closer to Darien being a territory of the kingdom, a vassal. On that day, he would have brought the kingdom of Féal into Darien and made them both the same.

The prince raised his glass to the blonde, casting doubts aside. She left the side of the man she was with and began to make her way over. Louis showed his teeth as he smiled, rather hoping her companion might challenge him. He was in his prime, he reminded himself. Whatever the future held, he knew he would ride it and be young and strong and handsome for ever. If Darien had to fall to his father in the end, well, it made each day more precious until it did. He drained his glass and watched as a waiter prepared another on a tiny table, setting up the whole thing on the spot. Lemon peel spiralled into the air and appeared in a glass of clear liquor. Louis bowed his head to the waiter, giving him honour for a skill worth knowing. As he sipped and sighed, the blonde arrived as a pleasant distraction, pressing a delicious weight against his arm. The one she had left glared after her. Louis was aware of the man peering at the sword he wore, weighing his chances. He felt a tingle of anticipation. Instead, the fellow pushed through the crowd and vanished, taking his failing courage with him.

'You are too beautiful for the table games and gawkers in this room,' Louis said to his new companion. 'May I show you the ones upstairs?'

*

Deeds considered the problem of running. He had been a caravan guard before, though never with a destination so far beyond his usual haunts. It was one thing to escort a dozen carts of silver ore a few hundred miles to a foundry – quite another to cross forests and mountain ranges where no one even knew the name of Darien. Still, that sort of work often attracted men such as himself, without much in the way of ties. If they had families, they had probably abandoned them, or been thrown out. They liked to gamble and there were always one or two who liked to fight as well. In times past, Deeds had been those men. He still smiled at the stories he'd racked up over the years. Some of them were so dark, it was sometimes hard to remember what had made him laugh on the first retellings. He and one particular group of hardbitten roadmen had left one town in ruins. It had started when they'd set a feed store on fire, then the farmer had broken his neck clambering over a stile to chase them. The local men had turned out in force that night, to catch and string them up. Perhaps a dozen more had lain dead before the sun rose again. Deeds had come out of that with a few extra weapons and a fine gold chain he'd lost at cards the following week.

For over a year after, there had been vague descriptions on posters and Deeds had been forced to take work picking hops for beer. About half of his group of ne'er-do-wells had been caught by bailiffs and king's men, so he'd heard. He'd taken care to avoid the hangings. It was well known that experienced thief-catchers stood and watched the crowds. He'd stayed clear – and remained free. He frowned to himself, wondering if a man's luck could just run out, the way it seemed to happen at cards sometimes. Deeds recalled the old royal palace in Darien and watching it burn down. He'd made it out, but he'd left more than a few sins in the flames, and perhaps a good part of his luck as well. Certainly his life had taken a turn for the worse since that night. Damn Aeris. Damn Elias. Damn Tellius and all of them who thought he could be sent here and there like a damned puppet. Deeds was his own man – and no man's servant.

He wrestled another iron peg from the ground, letting canvas sag and the tent rope fall loose. The Darien road was long behind, as were the forests he'd known a little too well a few years back. He'd never gone further east than those before, but the plains before the mountains were beautiful in their way. Not that he cared for beauty. On a proper road, a man had choices. He could walk home, for a start.

It was typical of the heathens he rode with that none of them had seemed to appreciate the craftsmanship and labour of that thread of road cut through the wilderness. He'd asked when they were going to start building something like it and received only contempt.

'Stuck-up Shiang bastards,' he muttered.

In all his life, Deeds had been a man others watched, usually a little warily. He had a look about him that suggested he might laugh at your troubles – the sort who might throw a wild dog into a crowded tavern, just for the fun of it. He'd always been treated with caution, or fear, which were almost the same things. To be discounted as a threat by the swordsmen and their ambassador was galling. Deeds gritted his teeth and yanked another peg with a heave, seeing that part of the tent lean to one side, while a Shiang servant named Chen glared at him. They had a right way to do everything, but the tent went up and the tent came down. That was all that mattered. Deeds glared back.

Ambassador Xi-Hue insisted on his peach-coloured pavilion being raised every evening and dismantled the following morning. The rest of them slept on horse blankets or wrapped in a cloak under one of the carts. It was hard work and not the sort that Deeds enjoyed, to say the least of it. He might even have refused if Hondo hadn't taken his guns while he'd washed in a river. There was treachery! The guns Lady Sallet had given him may not have been of the quality he'd known before, but Deeds had been shooting them in each morning, which helped to wake the camp nice and early. Hondo had said it was too noisy and hidden them somewhere Deeds couldn't find. They'd had no right. He had enough cartridges and the weapons were his property. No right at all to take what had been his.

'And if I ever get them back, you'll be the first to know about it, Meneer Hondo, I tell you straight . . .' he said to himself, grunting as he pulled out a peg.

Sweat trickled down his forehead and when he wiped it, he could feel a smear of mud on his cheek. Four other men were folding and rolling sections of canvas ready for the carts that would carry them, brushing every speck of dirt away as they went. If they heard him speak, they'd learned not to begin an argument. Deeds tended to shove the Shiang servants out of his way, or help them past with his boot. He was sick to the back teeth with all of them. There was nothing in the world like dismantling a pavilion for turning men against one another, except for maybe civil war. Deeds wondered what would happen if he gave Chen a proper little tap to shut him up – and what the punishment might be.

Something of that calculation must have shown in his face. The Shiang servant decided to move on, complaining about lazy men as he went past. Deeds weighed a handful of spikes in one palm, seriously considering just tossing them down and going home.

He'd been promised astonishing pay, three times the usual rate. In the past, Deeds had enjoyed guard work – well, who wouldn't? Fed and kept warm for a few weeks, with a nice fat pouch of unspent coin at the far end. Not that he'd actually seen any coins. The ambassador refused even to notice a servant, looking through him like he was a pane of glass. Hondo had discussed payment easily enough when he needed an extra guard back in Darien. On the road, he seemed to think talk of money was beneath him. The sword saint just walked away if Deeds brought it up – and of course the one called Bosin was a little too much of a worry to press harder. The big man seemed simple anyway.

If Deeds just left them to their tea and breakfast and walked home, he had neither money nor guns. He'd starve to death after around two weeks of hard trudging, he reckoned, or perhaps be hanged for theft in some village where everyone married their sisters. Of course, he could just bide his time and continue to Shiang. The ambassador's servants said it was at least a month away, though he thought they might be mocking him. Chen in particular had a sly humour in some of his glances.

Deeds sighed and stretched his back where it ached from bending down, over and over. He'd fantasised at first about being young and free in a foreign capital, with guns on his hip and good money in his pouch. Old Tellius had described it as a chance for a fresh start – and for his enemies to forget about him.

Talking to the Shiang servants had disabused Deeds of any notions of available women, however. It seemed the society that produced Tellius had very strict ideas about allowing women into the company of strangers. He'd be lucky even to see an unmarried one, so Chen said. No wonder Tellius had left.

A sudden push from behind made him stagger into a rope, almost falling across it. Deeds caught himself and whirled on whoever had shoved him, only to find Hondo standing there.

'You neglect your work, Master Deeds, while you stare at nothing. I will not tell Ambassador Xi-Hue that *my* servant is the one responsible for holding us up this morning! Move!'

Deeds took a long breath. He'd had it up to here with being ordered around. He'd agreed to be a caravan guard, not some Shiang peasant. Darien didn't even have slaves! Yet he'd been treated like one, just about. Food, sleep and back-breaking work. He should have known not to expect anything better from Tellius. The man wasn't Darien-born. No doubt they looked after their own first. Deeds closed his eyes for a moment. Sod it. He dropped the bundle of pegs straight down, so that they clattered on the ground by his feet.

'I think I'm about *done*, Master Hondo. So I'll ask you for my pay and my guns. I'll consider buying one of the horses with that pay, if you'll give me a good price. Or I'll walk. Either way, I'm finished. I didn't sign on to be shouted at and treated like a f . . . like a skivvy. Still – I'm told you have honour, or what you choose to call honour, so I'll be having my pay now, thanks. And my guns.'

He snapped his mouth shut then, determined not to wilt under the man's dark gaze. Hondo did not reply for what seemed an age and the other servants bustled on with storing the pavilion on its cart. Chen came over to collect the fallen pegs, his gaze and head averted in the presence of the sword saint.

'Come with me, Master Deeds,' Hondo said at last.

Without another word, he strode away across the camp. Deeds hoped he was going to get the guns that were his by right, though he had a suspicion his luck wouldn't change that quickly.

To his surprise, Hondo stopped where Bosin was chopping logs. Wherever they found a fallen tree, Bosin would go out with his axe and break the thing up into smaller pieces over the course of an evening. It seemed to be his only hobby. One of the carts was already piled high with pieces of wood, covered in waxcloth to keep them as dry as possible.

Up close, Deeds was reminded of the sheer size of the man he had shot and almost killed a couple of years before. Bosin was working with his shirt off and was a fine specimen. Deeds found himself holding in the slight belly he'd been developing back in Darien. The truth was he had lost that softness somewhere on the road, though he had not realised it.

'Master Bosin,' Hondo called. It did not do to stroll right up to a man busy with an axe.

Bosin halted the upswing, his blade gleaming in the air.

He sank the axe into the stump block and brushed dust and wood chips from his hands. Deeds saw one of them was wrapped in a blood-stained cloth, where the skin had split. It didn't seem to trouble the man particularly. Perhaps it was his imagination, but Deeds thought Bosin's gaze lingered on him, even as he replied.

'Master Hondo,' Bosin said. He clearly considered the conversation at an end and began to reach for the axe handle once again.

'Vic Deeds wishes to leave, to walk back to Darien,' Hondo said. There was something like urgency in his voice and Deeds looked askance at him.

'Or to ride,' he reminded the sword saint. 'I don't mind buying one of the horses. The piebald isn't worth much, but she'll carry me.'

Hondo went on as if he hadn't spoken, his gaze steady.

'The man who shot you three times in the chest, Master Bosin.'

'Hey!' Deeds said sharply. 'Old times – and forgotten. Self-defence, which you agreed.' A whisper of fear came to him then. 'Tellius said your word was iron, Hondo! Was he wrong?'

Hondo turned his gaze on Deeds and the younger man almost took a step back.

'No, he was not wrong. I guaranteed your safety. Though you shot Master Bosin in the chest three times.'

'Well, you're wrong then, aren't you? Because he'd be dead if I had. No one survives three in the chest. Believe me, I would know. If I shoot a man, he damn well dies. So maybe it wasn't even me who did it.'

'It was you,' Hondo said, 'and he would have died, if not

143

for the Canis Stone. I brought him to Darien and Doctor Burroughs looked at him. Bosin ran a fever that got worse and worse – and then the city came under attack. I knew what the Canis Stone would do, or I thought I did. I made the choice anyway, for Master Bosin, because I needed him. Because *your* city needed him.'

'And I'm sure we are very grateful,' Deeds said. 'But bringing it up now seems like needling a man who can't defend himself, Master Hondo. In Darien, we call it water under the bridge. Understand? Like a river. You can't go back to before. All of that – all of this, it's just water under the bridge. So stop wasting my time, pay me what I'm owed, give me my guns and send me on my way!'

Deeds was cold, damp and miserable. He'd been treated like a labourer for weeks, without respect, without a proper drink of alcohol even, though he noticed there was always wine for the ambassador. His voice had risen to a shout by the end of it as his frustration overrode common sense and caution. He knew very well that Hondo could have carved him to pieces, but he also knew the man's convoluted sense of honour made that impossible. The thought emboldened Deeds. He raised his hand and prodded the air with two outstretched fingers. The sword saint looked at him in astonishment.

'You gave your word, Hondo,' Deeds said. 'To take me as far as I wanted to go – and not one step further. To protect me like I was your firstborn. Instead, I've been treated like the help, like a kitchen boy you don't much trust.'

With each point, he jabbed his finger forward. Deeds thought he saw the man's eyes actually darken and he began to reconsider.

'Either way, I am finished. Give me what I'm *owed* and get out of my way.'

Deeds sensed movement. He caught sight of the flash of silver as Bosin swung his axe with enough force to cut him in two. Then he was sprawling across the grass, thrown aside by Hondo as the man caught Bosin in a great embrace and went down with him, smothering the attack as they rolled on muddy ground.

'I'll *kill* you!' Bosin said, reaching for him.

Deeds shuddered at the rage in the big man's eyes. He could see how hard it was for Hondo to hang on to him and edged away.

'Is this what you wanted?' Deeds said to Hondo.

'Yes,' Hondo said through clenched teeth, grunting with effort. He was having trouble holding Bosin, though he had the man's wrist joint locked and his own legs braced against Bosin's so that the big man could not rise. Even so, Hondo was losing.

'Deeds?' Hondo grated.

'Yes, Master Hondo?'

'Please run. I cannot hold . . .'

With a roar, Bosin broke free. Deeds was off at a sprint, going as if all his demons were after him.

Fall

Prince Louis was drunk. He had not quite realised the potency of the liquid that lapped like clear oil against glass, cold and deadly with its little twist of lemon. The first one had made him feel like a hero, but the second had taken some of his balance – and the third, well, he wondered if he might see the third again at any moment.

It had been a wondrous evening, recalled in splendid flashes. The door hung open behind them as he and the blonde tumbled onto an enormous bed. He could hear cheering as some new match or bout began on the floor below. It made him grin, as if the merchants and lords of Darien were judging his technique. What an extraordinary aphrodisiac violence could be! Harkness had warned him about it, in his sour, old-man way. There were women and men who came to the gambling houses, not for the tables or the wagering, but the arousal they felt on seeing one man beat another half to death, or some private contest between enemies, where they touched burning brands to their flesh. The rooms up on the third floor were always filled at the end of the evening, so Harkness said.

The thought was matched by a laughing pair rushing by on the landing. Louis was struggling to undo a catch on her dress from underneath and caught a glimpse of a key held upright in a pale hand and a flash of eyes before they were gone. The door was too far from the end of the bed for him to kick it shut, he realised. He would have to ask her to stop for him to get up. That turned out to be a rare challenge all by itself.

Her eyes were dark with kohl and devilment as he began to raise himself on an elbow. A shadow blocked the doorway and Louis looked up sharply, instantly embarrassed.

'The room is taken, sir,' he snapped. It was his own fault, of course, leaving the door open and inviting gawkers by doing so.

To his astonishment, the man continued into the room, with others behind him. Louis was half-undressed, on his back and held down by the weight of the woman he had entered with. Even then, he might have thrown her off and gained his feet if not for the drinks that still swam in his system, refusing to drown.

With no warning, the first man lunged, punching him in the face. The blonde went flying in a heap and Louis saw one of the others raise some sort of black cosh over her, bringing it down hard. Her shriek was cut short and then Louis was fending off a wild attack, though more and more weakly as the dark figure batted away his hands and punched his head into the pillow, over and over. Blood spattered across the coverlet and Prince Louis had his own cry cut off as he tried to yell for help. Where were Harkness and his guards? He'd have the old bastard strung up for letting thieves into one of the rooms!

Louis was young, fit and strong, but all the fight was battered out of him in a distressingly short time. There was no sound from the blonde sprawled on the floor. A second man took hold of his left arm and held it steady, despite all his wrenching. The one who had beaten him with such precision then twisted his right arm, rotating the elbow so that it locked. He sat on the bed in horrible intimacy as he leaned on it, looking down at him. Louis felt both helpless and terrified. His lips were broken and he could feel his face beginning to swell. He had a sense of sick dread as a third man shut the door to the room. The noises and light were suddenly gone. Louis was alone, with three men and a woman, dead or unconscious. His heart beat hard enough for him to notice it and see lights flashing across his vision. He thought again that he might vomit.

'Get out,' Prince Louis croaked at them. He tried to pull himself free with the last of his strength and when that failed, just lay and panted.

'In a moment, son,' the one with his right arm said, adding to the pressure on his elbow so that it began to ache.

Louis could smell sweat and onions on his breath, as well as something else out of place, something he could not quite recognise. The man had hammered his head with a fist like a club and it was hard not to flinch whenever he shifted position. Louis glared back, but it was a poor show of defiance and they both knew it.

'My purse is in my jacket pocket,' the prince said. 'Take that and go.'

'All right then,' the man replied. He rootled around and fished out the pouch, putting it into a pocket of his own without breaking eye contact.

'Jones,' the one at the door grumbled in warning. 'You were told.'

The man on the bed just shrugged.

'Perks,' he said. 'No harm in it.'

Louis didn't want to ask them to leave again. He didn't want to hear himself plead, so he lay still, but then no one else moved either. He thought the pair holding him down seemed to be enjoying his helplessness. The one gripping his left arm was wiry and incredibly strong. He was grinning too, though there was only cruelty in it.

It was clear that they would not go on until Louis spoke once more. They had sensed somehow that he didn't want to, so they would make him. He thought of the blade hidden in his sleeve, a nasty little razor with one edge coated in his favourite paralytic. If he could bring that into play, it wouldn't take more than a stripe or two for him to be master once more of that room. The prospect was delicious. He would invent new types of savagery then for all three of them.

'You weren't meant to make a trade deal, my lord,' the man at the door said suddenly.

Louis blinked up at him.

'What?' he said weakly, though his mind was racing. Where was Harkness, or his guards? Was the old fool blind and deaf? Gambling establishments always had armed men to keep the peace. Did they not come up to the third floor?

'Your father was furious,' the man went on.

He was, Louis noted, rather better dressed than the pair holding his arms. They were all in long jackets, trousers and boots. The smell of shop-fresh cloth and polish was strong in the room. That was what it was, the scent that had seemed odd to him. He realised it was the sort of thing men might do if they wished to enter the Darien Lion without being hauled straight back out again as vagabonds. Now that he had a chance to think, he saw shaving cuts on both of the men sitting on his bed. They were more used to bristles. As he had the thought, one of them eased an itchy new collar, running a finger around it. The two on the bed wore pomade on their hair, Louis saw, as if they had taken a thick handful of the stuff from the same pot. Everything they wore was cheap but new-bought, a disguise for who they were.

In comparison, the man at the door wore a well-fitting coat that had seen better days. The elbows were a little shiny with wear, but the man's boots gleamed blackly and two gold bands glinted on his right hand, on the fourth and smallest fingers. Louis tried to see if one of them was marked with a crest, but when his nose had been struck, his eyes had filled with tears. They spilled down his cheek then and humiliated him – and he could see nothing with perfect clarity. The smile on the grinning one grew wider at the sight of the prince crying and yet Louis could not move his arms to dash the tears away.

'What do you want?' he said, choked.

'Why, nothing at all,' the man at the door said, leaning back against it as if he was utterly relaxed. 'Your father, though, he wanted you to blunder in and throw his weight and name and money around as you've always done before. He wanted you to be rebuffed by these people, in their pride and their arrogance. He wanted you *insulted*. Do you understand now? A little better?'

'You have no idea what my father wants,' Louis said. 'And if you are men of Féal, you know very well who I am – and who he is. He told me I'd done enough in borrowing money from Lord Aeris. Did you know that? He did. So if you want to live, you'll let me go now and disappear. I don't know your names.'

They all heard the desperation in his voice at the last, the way bluster turned to fear. His tormentors chuckled or glanced at one another in amusement, making his heart sink. They had seen all this before, perhaps many times. He would not get away with threats and he knew then that he could not bribe them. They were professionals, so it would turn out however it turned out, regardless of anything he might say. He felt himself relax in the face of an inevitable fate, though the little knife in his sleeve remained as a prickling awareness.

'I like you, Louis,' the man at the door said. 'Your father does as well. I told His Majesty that the best thing would be to kill you and outrage the body. To leave signs of Darien all around and maybe some local lad with a knife in his neck as one of the escaped murderers.'

Louis began to speak and the man leaned in closer, his voice rising.

'I *said*, we should leave you with your guts around your neck and a peacock feather up your arse – and the whole world crying out that it was them *nasty* Darien men what did it. And that would be that, Louis. Your father would have the war he wanted, at hardly any cost to himself. That was my advice.'

Louis stared at the man in shock. There was a deep malevolence there, he could feel it. The other two might be hired help, but this one . . . He shuddered. This one was enjoying his own description.

'Let me go,' he said, suddenly calm. 'Whatever my father

offered, you will need a friend someday, when you or someone you love is facing the rope. If I give you my word now, I will honour it then. Think! Everything you've heard of me. Has anyone ever said my word is not good? No, not once. So take what I offer you. More than gold, it will save your life, or the life of a daughter, or a son. When I am king.'

The one called Jones craned his neck to look back, one eyebrow raised.

'Mr Morris . . . ?' he said. 'I wonder . . . ?'

The one he addressed shook his head.

'Look at the blood! You've battered him, Jones. Do you think he'll just forgive that? Stay the course, now. Hold fast to your duty and *don't* give me cause to doubt you.'

It was enough of a threat to firm the man's resolve. Louis could see it in his face. He tried to work out whether it mattered that he now knew the names of two of the three, or if it meant they would kill him and so didn't care.

'I like you, Louis,' the one called Morris said. 'You're sharp enough to be your father's son. We're *his* men, though, Louis. Balls to bones, right through. You'll understand that, I'm sure. He calls us in for jobs he'd rather weren't seen by all his pretty lords and ladies.'

'You are making a mistake,' Louis said.

The man came away from the door and opened his coat, pulling out a wrap that clinked as he tossed it onto the coverlet.

'No. I'm not. Your father wanted you alive. He has a soft heart, son. Your death is the proper outcome. It gives your old man a reason to go to war – a good one. But I am his man, so if he says you live, you live.'

Louis breathed out and out, hardly daring to believe. Yet the man kept speaking.

'Though if you are to live and still bring us a war, it has to be with wounds that cry out to the heavens for justice. Nothing that will heal and leave you whole. Hold him.'

He said the last as Louis began to yell. The pair gripping his arms leaned in even tighter. The man called Mr Morris wrapped a greasy scarf around Louis' face, stifling his cries.

'I'm going to take an eye and a hand, Louis – and, yes, I think a stab wound in the side, along the ribs. No one would look at those wounds and think it was your own people, do you understand? It's all agreed, son. Nod if you understand. Stop weeping and nod. There.'

'I'll make it your left hand and I'll leave you the thumb. I tell you, if you have the thumb, you'll have almost full use. The things that matter anyway, like picking up a cup, or holding reins. I'll throw the fingers around the room and it will all look worse than it is.'

To Louis' horror, the man pulled out a small kindling hatchet, almost a child's toy in size, though it gleamed with wicked sharpness. They would have to let go of him for an instant, to bring it down on his hand, he thought. He imagined the action of drawing the knife from his sleeve, picturing the move so that when the chance came, it would be quick.

'We won't hit you much more, Louis. We want to make it look like you were left for dead, not tortured, do you see? If you make it easy for me, Jones will knock you out before I even do the eye, all right? We'll kick over a few chairs on our way out, kill a couple of the table hosts and the guards we bribed before. No witnesses, Louis, except for those who saw Darien men leave a Féal prince for dead. That's the story that will get out.' He paused. 'There's just one problem with all of it. Your father didn't have a proper answer when I pointed it out to him.'

Louis could not speak with the scarf around his face. He could feel it getting damp with tears and saliva, but he could only make a groaning sound. At least he could breathe through it. His nose was blocked with blood and snot, still dripping. The man they called Mr Morris saw his awareness and laughed.

'Yes, you see it. You are a quick one. If I leave you alive, the whole plan can come crashing down, can't it? Just like it did when you were meant to go into Darien and fail. One word from you about your father's men making a plan to cause a war – and, well, we'll still get our war, but they'll have time to get ready. You'll be killing hundreds, maybe thousands of your own people. And you won't be king then, Louis. No, mate. Your father won't forgive you a second time, the way he did before.'

Louis blinked slowly and Mr Morris shook his head as if in sadness.

'Maybe this don't feel much like mercy, son, though it is. The proper thing – well, that would be to kill you right now, on this bed. Only your father's forgiveness keeps you alive and blinking at me, moment by moment. So don't you *ever* doubt him. Or me. If you talk, I'll do worse than this, I promise. I'll take my time. Understand?'

Louis nodded, squeezing his eyes tight so that new tears trickled down. The man patted him on his cheek, then looked to the other two.

'Drag him off the bed. I'll need a hard surface to do his hand.'

Louis kicked and struggled at that, but he could not prevent his slide onto the floor.

Still, he took the chance for freedom when it came. As they struggled with his weight and position, he yanked his left arm from their grip, scrabbling for the knife in his sleeve. Some moments of panting madness followed. Before he could draw it out, his arm had been grappled once more, bent and twisted as one of them knelt on it. Louis gave a muted shriek as a bone in his wrist broke and the pieces ground together. He fell limp and then could only stare in shock as the hatchet rose and came down, cutting away two of his fingers and part of his palm. He could not scream, because he could not breathe.

'That's no good. I'll need to make another cut now,' Morris said irritably, eyeing the wound. The hatchet rose and fell again. When Louis finally pulled in enough air to make a sound, they took him up and smacked him with a cosh behind his ear. He fell limp, blood pooling on the floor in a room that was suddenly silent.

'What about the girl?' the one called Jones asked.

Mr Morris shrugged.

'I don't kill women. You'd better do it. Can't have a witness who might have heard. Remember now, both of you. You're Darien men, proud of killing some foreign prince who thought he could come here and take our women. Find someone to beat up on the way out, someone in fine clothes. Tell him it's what all Féal men will get if they come here. We need word to spread.'

He looked down at the young prince lying senseless.

'I'll do the eye. Gives me the shivers every time, but it will look good. Has to look like we thought he was dead.'

'Don't press too deep, or he will be,' the third man said.

'Yes, thank you, I *have* done this before,' Morris replied, kneeling alongside the fallen prince of Féal.

Deeds ran, with briars whipping past his face and leaving raised lines that stung. There was no road, so he was racing through wilderness and overgrown scrubland. He'd headed into the deep brush from a sort of primal instinct, taking him away from clear spaces and the two men after him. He'd hoped to leave them behind in the first wild rush. Hondo had to be twice his age, yet the sword saint seemed to be loping along at the same distance, just waiting for him to tire or burst his heart. Deeds had lost sight of Bosin, which was pretty much fine with him. There had been something animal and savage in the big man when he'd been red-faced and clawing the air, trying to reach Deeds. It had been unrestrained, like the time Deeds had fought with a bigger boy from the village and only stopped him with an almighty kick to the testicles. To his horror, the boy had been so eaten up with rage he'd begun to rise, staggering to his feet while the young Deeds looked on with eyes like saucers. He had thanked his stars when a teacher had come between them. Bosin's eyes had looked the same and Deeds ran like the wind.

He knew the first rule of running away is that you don't look back. Looking back doesn't achieve anything. He did it anyway – and felt his footing go from under him in a split second. The wet leaf mulch slipped and one step became a massive lunge before he was skidding down a wet stone. He felt Hondo grab him and though it was hopeless, Deeds fought anyway, kicking and flailing madly. His life was on the line and he hammered punches at the sword saint as the man tried to keep hold. Deeds caught a glimpse of the sword on Hondo's sash belt and knew that if he let the older man draw, it was the end. He felt his clicking jaw crack as he bit Hondo's knuckles where they held his collar, wrenching at the same time so that the cloth tore. Deeds had the satisfaction of hearing Hondo swear under his breath, but then both men sensed the shadow that loomed over them. It was instinct or hopelessness, but Deeds sagged as he looked up. Bosin was certainly tall, but it was his width that gave him the appearance of a barn door, or a bullock. The big man didn't seem out of breath, Deeds saw. A look of murderous rage faded like a fist opening, so that the blankness returned.

'You gave your word, Hondo,' Deeds panted.

Slowly, Hondo released him and Deeds saw there was blood on the man's hand where he had been bitten. It would have to be cleaned that evening or the wound would swell and grow hot. Deeds had known a man to die once when he was bitten in a fight . . . He shook his head, weary and fed up. He could not run any further, even if they gave him a good start. He was done. Deeds glanced at Hondo and wondered why he had ever believed his word.

Hondo was watching Bosin as a man might watch a viper in his bedroom. The sword saint rose to his feet in balance and seemed almost to have forgotten Deeds.

'Master Bosin?' Hondo said softly. When there was no reply, his voice hardened. 'Bosin!'

The big man looked up slowly, dragging his gaze from Deeds.

'I know him,' Bosin said.

Hondo nodded. 'He shot you.'

'All in the past now,' Deeds added quickly. 'And self-defence – and my duty as a guard for the camp anyway. I was well within my rights and you know it. You could have been thieves or . . .' He broke off when Bosin turned his gaze on him once more.

'He is . . . annoying. He is an annoying man,' Bosin said slowly.

He spoke as if from a great distance. Hondo blinked at him, at emotions he had not heard since Bosin had been healed by the Canis Stone. From instinct, Hondo nudged Deeds with his boot.

'Hey! Enough of that. Your honour guarantees my safety, Meneer Hondo. That's what you told Tellius, back in Darien. Your word and his. So if your ape has calmed down, I will thank you to treat me with a little more respect – and give me my guns and my back pay.'

Deeds rose to his feet, unable to understand the strange tension between the two Shiang swordsmen, or the way Hondo hung on every word Bosin said.

'Understand?' Deeds said, looking in exasperation from one to the other. 'Do you know what? Go your own way. I'm done. Just give me my things and the money you owe, with a horse. You can carry on kissing the ambassador's ring then. Give them all a bow for me in Shiang, would you? I'm for home.'

'What do you think, Bosin? Should I just let him go?' Hondo said.

The big man winced, shaking his head. It reminded Hondo of a bear he had once seen. The animal had disturbed a bees' nest and been stung, over and over, only his thick fur protecting him. As Hondo watched, Bosin twitched.

Deeds backed away from both of them. His guns had to be in the locked chest that was in Hondo's part of the caravan. Before that day, Deeds wouldn't have dared break the lock for fear of whatever punishment it would have earned him, guns or no guns. That sort of concern seemed a bit distant in that moment. Without another word, he turned and ran. To his horror, he heard Hondo giving a great ululating howl behind him, as if the hunt was on. Another sound joined it, a great coughing roar that lent wings to Deeds' feet as he raced back to camp. Behind him, the Shiang masters set off in pursuit.

12

Old Wounds

Deeds panted, the sound loud in his ears. At times, it felt like he was flying, barely in touch with the earth. The camp was actually closer than he had thought and he increased his pace now that he didn't have to hold anything in reserve. Whatever game those Shiang maniacs were playing, Deeds was going to get his pistols, if he had to break through some ornate lacquer and a brass dragon to do it. To be chased through ferns and bracken like a damned deer was just about the end. Deeds clenched his fists as he ran. Once he had his guns, he'd blast his way out if he had to. They'd no right to keep him a prisoner! He'd agreed to guard the caravan for triple pay, not be a slave to foreign devils.

Whether he took a better route or whether he'd lost them, he did not know. There was no sign of Hondo or Bosin as Deeds barrelled past the rearmost carts, swerving around a fire-ring of stones and a kettle hissing steam on a stand. Someone called out, but it was still early and the ambassador would be exercising on a nearby hill, going through his patterns of Mazer steps while the sun rose.

Deeds saw one of the ambassador's servants reach for a sword as he pelted past.

'Is it thieves?' the man called. 'Are we under attack?'

Deeds ignored him. He reached the third cart in the row, the reins neatly tied and waiting to be reattached to the draught horses cropping turf alongside. Hondo's personal chest was on that cart.

Sweat poured from him as he clambered up and ducked his head under a tarpaulin. It made a noise like cloth ripping as he pressed deeper in. Hondo's trunk was black and polished to a high sheen, though it showed dents and scratches too. It had been made in Darien, though perhaps to Hondo's specification, as it looked strange enough. Deeds cast around for something he could use to break the lock. He felt one of the tent pegs in his belt as he bent over it and grinned to himself.

He jammed the peg under the lip of the lid, wincing as the wood splintered. Well, they'd brought it on themselves, chasing him over the hillsides. Deeds flung back the lid and reached for the pair of guns he saw immediately inside. They were not his, but by the Goddess, they were better, with the mark of the Hart gun foundry on black-patterned hilts. They fitted his hand as well as his old ones and he rested the cool metal of one on his forehead and sighed, feeling whole again for the first time in an age.

As he stood taller, his head pressed into the canvas over the cart. He felt the lurch as someone leaped onto the driver's seat. Deeds spun to face the threat, but the bulge he made in the canvas proved a fine target. Something struck him with a clang and Deeds folded unconscious across the shirts and guns.

Hondo arrived at the cart in time to see Chen bring a ferocious blow down on the lump that moved jerkily under the canvas. The sword saint skidded to a stop and held up his hand to halt Bosin in turn. For once, it worked.

'He was stealing,' Chen said. The ambassador's servant could hardly disguise his glee at having been able to land a blow on the big ugly foreigner who scorned their ways and said foul things about Shiang food. It took a moment for Chen to realise he was not being congratulated.

'Step down from there,' Hondo said.

His voice was very calm and Chen sensed something was off. He clambered down quickly, standing with his head lowered and the mallet half-hidden behind his back. To his consternation, the ambassador himself approached them, drawn by the shouts.

'What is going on?' Xi-Hue demanded.

His servant chose the authority he knew best and answered.

'This man Vic Deeds was stealing from the sword saint, ambassador. I saw him come running through the camp, then climb onto the cart. I heard the noise of damage and I acted quickly.'

'I see. Where is this Vic Deeds now?' Xi-Hue said, looking around.

Chen indicated the canvas-covered cart with the handle of his mallet.

'I knocked him out, ambassador, before he could steal and escape, or do any more damage.'

'And you, Masters Hondo and Bosin? What have you to say for yourselves?'

Hondo was experienced enough to know the ambassador was asking questions as he came up to speed. There was no real malice in the schoolmasterly tone. It rankled even so.

'It is a private concern, ambassador, if you don't mind,' he replied. 'You'll notice Master Deeds was apprehended on my own cart. Injured, though my honour guaranteed his safety.'

Hondo said the last with a slight emphasis of disapproval and Chen dropped to one knee from instinct, though it was in part as his legs grew weak at the thought of offending a sword saint.

'Master H-Hondo, I a-am . . . sorry. I thought h-he was . . .'

'Enough, Chen,' the ambassador said irritably. 'Stand up.'

Xi-Hue had endured about enough foolishness. His morning patterns had been interrupted, which was unforgivable enough. His digestion would be disturbed for the rest of the day. Now he had to listen to some petty dispute? A 'private concern'? He was a long way from a court, or anywhere else. In that place, addressing men of Shiang, Xi-Hue was perhaps more himself than his usual mask.

'You should all be ashamed of yourselves,' Xi-Hue said. 'Private concern? *Private?* I am of the fourth noble rank, plenipotentiary and ambassador of Shiang! Where is your respect?'

Xi-Hue was oblivious to the way Hondo watched him steadily, showing no sign of submissiveness to authority, as the ambassador might have expected. Bosin too stood like a wall. The servant, Chen, sensed catastrophe. He chose to lie flat, prostrating himself in trembling silence. At the same time, they all heard Vic Deeds groan as he came round on the cart.

'I have said this is a private matter, Ambassador Xi-Hue,' Hondo said. 'Forgive me for any discomfort I may have caused. However, this is not your concern. Please. Do not let us take another moment of your time.'

His voice was deliberately calm, though there was tension in him. Ambassador Xi-Hue blinked in amazement at being so addressed. None of his usual tact and subtlety was in play. He was faced with disrespectful Shiang servants and his fury only mounted with each moment.

'It is not your *place* to tell me what is my concern and what is not my concern, Master Hondo! You forget your rank – and mine! Or did you earn some noble title while you were away? It could not have been by succeeding in the task you were set!'

Hondo watched the ambassador grow red-faced, but he could not bring himself to show the obeisance clearly expected of him, flinging himself to the earth like Chen. Xi-Hue was a stranger and perhaps Hondo had seen enough of rank to know it was all a fiction to those who had it. He sighed, weary of games.

'Ambassador, I have no wish to cause you distress. I ask you to withdraw and be ready to take to the road. I tell you for the third time – with respect to your rank – this is no concern of yours.'

'I am the representative of the court in Shiang!' the ambassador barked, refusing to back down. 'On this road, I *am* that court. The authority of the jade throne stands in me, in this place – a throne you are pledged to serve. Or is your word and your honour worth nothing, sword saint?'

Hondo stared without blinking for what seemed an age.

'You are . . . correct, ambassador,' he said at last.

Xi-Hue raised his chin and clenched his jaw.

'Then do not speak to me of "private concern". This is

my diplomatic retinue, Master Hondo – and I am of noble rank. Consider that, as you consider your response.'

Hondo decided to kneel, if it would allow the man to withdraw from the stand-off. Impatient as he was to examine the extraordinary awakening in Bosin, he understood the ambassador's pride had to be salved before they could go on. The traditions of centuries and the first decades of his own life told him to kneel. In the same moment, he saw how little it meant, a revelation that surprised him in its force. He began to drop to one knee, but froze as Bosin put his hand on Hondo's shoulder.

'You are the sword saint, Master Hondo,' Bosin said. 'Who is this ink-stained tea-drinker?'

The enormous swordsman turned his gaze on the ambassador, who stood in horror at what he was hearing.

'Leave us alone,' Bosin said to him. 'Go and compose a poem, or write a letter, but leave us.'

'You are throwing away your *life*,' the ambassador spluttered. His shock was great enough to abandon all caution and he went on. 'Do you think this insolence will be forgotten? The moment Lord Hong is confirmed as king, he will sign your death warrants. Kneel and ask for forgiveness, or I will have you flogged – and executed on our return to Shiang.'

Bosin laughed, the first time Hondo had heard the sound in two years. The sword saint looked up at the big man in delight, seeing the spark he thought had gone for ever. In that moment, the ambassador was an irrelevance. The sword saint began to laugh as well, overcome in his relief.

The sheet over Hondo's cart flew up in a crackle of canvas. Vic Deeds rose from amidst the cases and bags with a pistol in each hand. Hondo and Bosin reacted in the same instant, fading to the side before Deeds could sight and aim. The ambassador stood frozen as Deeds lowered his right gunsight to cover him, the other pointing straight up as he waited for a second target.

'I will be taking my *pay*, and these *guns* – and a *horse*,' Deeds snarled. 'Or I swear to the Goddess, I will walk over your dead bodies and take it all anyway. I have had about enough of this. If I have to rob you, I'll do that too. You can complain when you send someone back to Darien. For all the good that will do.'

Ambassador Xi-Hue had not been threatened in such a way since his days at the Mazer school. He could hardly believe the extraordinary events of the morning, but an attack on him merited the simplest response. He eyed the dark end of the iron pistol, with some awareness of what those diabolical weapons could do. His life hung in the balance, but that was nowhere near as important as another injury to his dignity, on top of all else he had suffered.

'Master Hondo? Kill this man.'

Hondo sighed. He had moved around to the side, out of sight. He knew he could probably throw something at Deeds, perhaps a blade to kill him, or just to spoil his aim long enough to close. That was not the point. He was more than a little weary of the ambassador's constant assumption of his service.

'If you move, he dies,' Deeds snapped.

The gun he held on the ambassador didn't waver, but the other swung back and forth, looking for a target. Hondo wondered if Deeds was as good as he seemed to believe, especially with guns he had never shot before.

'I have guaranteed this man's safety, ambassador,' Hondo said. Bosin was still grinning and he found himself smiling in response. Neither of them came closer to the furious man waving pistols around, however.

'Nonetheless, I order it,' Xi-Hue grated, without looking away from the madman threatening him.

'Then I refuse,' Hondo said, softly.

The words were significant enough for the ambassador to look around, despite the threat on his life. Hondo shrugged and went on.

'Deeds, you have very little time before this man's servants see that he is under threat and attack you.'

'I can take them,' Deeds growled back.

Hondo shook his head.

'You could if I had left bullets in that chest, perhaps. As it is, you cannot.'

'His guns cannot fire? He cannot shoot?' Xi-Hue demanded. 'Then what are you waiting for? Take them from him. Bind him for execution. You gave your first oath to the court of Shiang, Master Hondo. I am that court – and my honour has been undermined this morning. Weigh the conflict and respond to me. Now!'

Hondo closed his eyes for a moment. The ambassador was perfectly correct in his demand. There had been a thousand occasions in the history of Shiang where one oath had come into opposition with another. The most common was an oath of loyalty to a house lord who was then declared traitor. Every warrior had been brought up with those tales, as well as the mechanism and weighting to resolve the conflicts.

Hondo's oath of service when he had been made sword

saint pre-dated any arrangement with Deeds. If Ambassador Xi-Hue represented the royal court, he was right when he said the outrage to his honour outweighed any duty of care to Deeds. Hondo's responsibility was clear. Instead, he turned to Bosin.

'How would you feel about going back to Darien? I thought I'd be relieved at going home. I miss so many things. But now? I want to go back. I won't leave you, though, Bosin. Whatever has happened to you, I will remain at your side. What do you think?'

'I am starving,' Bosin said slowly. 'I feel as if I haven't eaten for years. Do you remember the Friday hog roast at the Old Red Inn? All you can eat?'

'Of course,' Hondo said, chuckling.

'I would like to see that again. I am too thin. There is nothing like that in Shiang.'

Hondo clapped the big man on the shoulder, feeling tears prickle in his eyes. He didn't know how to react to Bosin. He was almost afraid he would say the wrong thing and watch the terrible coldness of the Canis Stone return.

Hondo turned to Deeds then, watching them all with suspicion. Hondo noted how the guns had drooped. He hadn't been certain, in fact. There had been bullets in the chest, though well wrapped and deeper in. He'd thought Deeds might not have found them, but he hadn't wanted to bet his life on it. He breathed out slowly.

'Master Deeds, you've expressed a desire to return to Darien. I believe Master Bosin and I will accompany you.'

'With my pay and a horse and these guns,' Deeds said immediately, 'and bullets for them so I don't have to bluff you maniacs again.'

Bosin snorted and Hondo shook his head.

'You are the most irritating man I have ever met, Master Deeds. Thank you for that.'

'You are welcome,' Deeds said, though he had no idea what the sword saint was talking about.

Hondo turned to see the ambassador's indignation and humiliation mingling in equal measures. The news had spread through the camp and the man's personal guards had arrived in support. They did not look happy to find themselves on what appeared to be the opposite side of a sword saint. Hondo met the eyes of each man as they took position. He made a personal assessment as to whether any of them would draw a blade. He hoped not. They were loyal men, doing simple work. They did not deserve to die.

'Ambassador,' Hondo began, making his voice ring out. 'I apologise for any dishonour. I have weighed my oaths – including those you have not heard, made to Tellius of Darien in the years that he was king. I choose to return home.'

He said the last word without especial emphasis, though it caused confusion in Xi-Hue.

'To Shiang?' the man said.

Hondo shook his head, hearing the rightness as he'd said it.

'No, ambassador. To Darien.'

Tellius looked at the young man lying helpless, wrapped in bandages. Prince Louis had suffered terrible wounds in the attack. Tellius could only blame himself for not anticipating it. He should have guessed there would be some in the city who regarded the deal with the kingdom of

Féal as an insult, or an invasion. By the Goddess, that was exactly how he had felt himself. Instead, he had done nothing as the prince and his Lord Harkness had set up restaurants, gambling houses and trading ventures across the city. They'd lavished astonishing sums on the new establishments – all legally. In response, Tellius had spent more days sulking on the Sallet estate than he had in two years, feeling old.

He'd mourned a royal title he'd never truly had, as well as a council of Twelve Families that had chosen gold over dignity and freedom. It had hurt – and as a result, he'd missed the danger that he was not the only one who resented the prince and his people. The result was what he saw. One of the prince's arms had been broken, his fingers hacked away. One of his eyes had been ruined, with a gash down his cheek. It was ugly work and Tellius recalled the prince's youth and arrogance with something like regret. He would never again stand unaware of pain or loss. That was the terrible thing about serious injury. It stole more than just an eye or a hand. It took innocence.

The prince stirred and Tellius rose from his seat to cross to the bed. The royal physician, Master Burroughs, was down the corridor of the little hospital. Tellius stepped outside to the guard on the door.

'Send someone to fetch Master Burroughs. I think the prince is waking up.'

That done, Tellius leaned over the young man. It did not make him proud to feel a twinge of spiteful vindication as he did so. Tellius had wanted vengeance for the death of Lord Canis. He'd even kept an eye on the Canis boy for weeks, in case he tried some wild scheme, or used his family money to hire men. Could that . . .? No, Tellius shook his head. The boy was not yet subtle enough to escape the watchers Tellius had placed around him. There had not been one Canis meeting in the weeks since his father's death without ears to report the details back to Tellius. Yet it had not saved Prince Louis.

Tellius saw the eyelids flickering and the young man hissed to himself, drawing in a breath as he became conscious enough to feel pain. There was a brass bracelet on his wrist. Tellius rotated it as he had been shown, hearing it click. Burroughs had said it wasn't magic, that it dripped some numbing milk or other into a vein. However it was done, it seemed to work. Tellius saw Prince Louis' face relax. He thought the prince might go back to sleep, but without warning, the good eye opened, red-rimmed and sore as it focused on Tellius.

'Relax, son. You've been badly hurt. You'll live. Master Burroughs says the wounds were clean enough. He had to open you up last night to stop some bleeding inside. Can you understand me?' Tellius remembered what Burroughs had told him to say. 'Do you know who I am?'

'Speaker Tellius,' Prince Louis whispered.

He sounded hoarse and Tellius passed him a glass of water. To sip it, Louis had to struggle up and Tellius could see the young man's confusion at the mass of bandages that had replaced his left hand.

'No . . .' Prince Louis said, shaking his head as memories flooded back.

Tellius decided to get it over with. He knew he might have been more patient with a friend or family member, but the truth was he had other concerns than coddling a young fool who seemed to walk with trouble wherever he went.

'You've lost your right eye and left hand. You were stabbed in the side. Master Burroughs says you are lucky to be alive. If you hadn't been found so quickly and brought here, you would be dead. The young woman with you was not as fortunate.'

Tellius paused to see how much the young man was taking in. Prince Louis seemed stunned, though it might have been the pain or the drugs in his system.

'You will live. Do you understand that? As long as you rest, you have every chance of returning to full health.'

It seemed like a cruel thing to say to a man who had lost an eye and four fingers, but Prince Louis nodded. They both looked up as Burroughs entered. He smiled to see his patient awake and alert. With Tellius looking on, the doctor made a show of inspecting the bandages, though what he could possibly discern beneath all that white cloth, Tellius had no idea. Still, Burroughs looked satisfied.

'Excellent,' he said. 'Young dogs do heal well. I have salved the wounds in honey, sir. You'll need to have your dressings changed every second day for the first month. I'm happy to do it, if you remain in the city. Now, I've cleaned you up as best I could, but much depends on the fevers that will surely enter. Still, you are young and obviously fit. You should survive. Good. Must get on.'

The doctor nodded to Tellius once more and left the room. Prince Louis sagged back against the pillows, looking utterly defeated.

'I . . .' Tellius began. He hesitated, but he needed to ask before Prince Louis drifted back to sleep. 'I am aware that pigeons flew from the roof of the Darien Lion shortly after you were found and taken here. I assume your father will have been told of your injuries?'

Tellius waited. An age seemed to pass before Prince Louis nodded.

'I'm told you were attacked by men of this city. I assure you there was nothing official about any of this. If it is confirmed that men of Darien waylaid and maimed you, I will have them taken and prosecuted. As speaker for the council, I offer our formal apology that such a thing could happen. I am only pleased you survived, unlike poor Lord Canis.'

The single eye turned to watch him. Tellius thought he could see a terrible anger there. He could hardly blame the young prince.

'Do you remember the attack?' Tellius asked.

He knew his chief witness lay on the bed before him, though he was not certain what answer he wanted. Slowly, Prince Louis dipped his head once more.

'I'll need descriptions. Anything you can recall. One of them seems to have run foul of the guards and been killed on his way out, but there were at least two more, that we know of.'

Tellius took a deep breath before going on. There was no help for it.

'And to the best of your knowledge, were they men of Darien?'

After an even longer wait, the prince nodded again. Tellius felt himself deflate, though he had known what he would hear. He'd spoken to a dozen patrons of the Darien Lion that evening. The violent thugs who'd attacked a foreign prince on Darien soil had been triumphant and jeering as they'd left. One of them had even boasted about it in a tavern down the road, vanishing before city guards arrived to arrest him. The whole story was infuriating and yet Tellius had to press the prince further, for all he dreaded the answers.

'Tell me. How will your father react? Will he accept such things happen in a city? That violence on the street is not unheard of? Will he give us time to respond?'

The young man on the bed tried to lurch up and catch him by the arm. Instead, the bulbous lump of bandages on his left hand just knocked against Tellius and fell away.

'My father will go to war,' Louis said. His remaining eye blurred with tears.

13

Hunter

The village of Wyburn was a one-street sort of place, with a tavern and a smithy and a few houses dotted around. A day of hard riding from the city, Tellius felt as out of place as he once had entering Darien. After forty years or so, he knew the city well, but the outlying villages, where farmers . . . farmed, were a different world again. He thought people were probably still people, wherever they lived. Yet he'd heard rumours about village folk and their dark superstitions. He saw a few boys had gathered at the base of an apple tree nearby to stand and stare. He and his guards were probably the most exciting thing to happen in Wyburn since they'd been born.

When they came to the right house, Tellius nodded to Captain Galen and stood back. The door opened as Galen raised his fist, before he could knock. Tellius swallowed.

The man who came out to stand on the step looked as if he'd been dried on a stove. Elias was stringy and hard, like old wood. He wore leather trousers and a ragged old black smock, ripped open at the neck as if he hadn't cared enough to sew a seam. His beard was half white and half black, just about, with deep lines on his cheeks and around his eyes that spoke of years outdoors. There was no front garden, as the house opened right onto the cobbled road.

Two small plum trees had been placed in pots on either side of the door – a touch that did not seem like something the man facing them would have done. Tellius could smell meat drying on the air that wafted out. It was a rich, sweet smell, not unpleasant. He cleared his throat, but the man spoke before he could begin.

'No to whatever you want. I don't have any business in Darien, not now.'

He paused and Tellius had the uncomfortable sensation that the man was listening to a conversation only he could hear. If everything Tellius had heard was true, that was exactly what he was doing.

'My name is . . .' Tellius began.

'Androvanus Yuan-Tellius, yes. Seems you know who I am as well. I don't know how you found me, but if you know anything, you'll know you won't be taking me from my home, not today.'

'Meneer,' Tellius tried again, as the people of those parts said. 'If you know my name . . .'

'I know your name because you just told me. Then I told it to you, so you didn't. How did I learn it, if I stopped you speaking? Yes, exactly.'

To Tellius' surprise, the man stepped out further onto the step, pulling his own door closed behind him.

'Hold on. Just listen for a moment,' Tellius struggled on. 'You are Elias Post. That's clear. It took me long enough to find you.'

'How did you . . . Oh, I see.'

Tellius blinked. It was hard carrying on a conversation with a man casting for answers Tellius had not given.

'Meneer, you'll have to slow down. I am too old for games.'

'That I understand,' Elias replied, with a shrug. 'All right. If I ask how you found me, you'll say something about witnesses, the last time I was in the city. I had other concerns that night, beyond hiding. So I suppose I was seen.'

Tellius considered his next words carefully. The last time Elias had entered Darien, he'd ended up so covered in the blood of others that he'd been described as a red horror. No good description of the man had been possible in those circumstances – except that he had carried two small girls away from the fighting. It had taken all the resources Tellius had in Darien, dozens of men masquerading as tax inspectors, over many months. Some of them had even collected taxes as they'd visited every home, farm and village within a hundred miles of the city.

A hundred and eight families had two small daughters in that number. They'd all merited a second visit, this time by the women in his employ. As a rule, those families had been trusting enough when a sweet young lady asked their daughters if they'd ever been to the city.

Tellius' people had been thorough and whittled the numbers down to a dozen possibles. He'd set watchers on each of those – and one of them had reported a widower in Wyburn, living on his own with two children. Shortly after that, the watcher had vanished, disappearing as if he'd never lived. Which brought Tellius to the door of the man he privately considered to be the most dangerous individual alive.

'So. You confirm you are the man who killed the last king?' Tellius said.

'*No,*' Elias said. 'I was there, yes. I did not fire the shots that killed him. Now listen to me: I regret that day, every day. I went into Darien because a man had taken my daughters. I didn't want to kill *anyone* – and I ended up red with innocent blood. Have you any idea what that is like?'

Tellius nodded, slightly unnerved by his intensity.

'I believe I have,' Tellius replied. 'I fought that same night, sir. I fought against the Aeris legion as they came in. I held the line, standing in the road with the people of the city. I heard your part in it much later. If you say you didn't kill the old king, who did?'

It was not what Tellius had come to ask, but he could not let the moment pass without seeing if Elias would confirm what he had heard. To his frustration, Elias Post just frowned and waved his hand.

'Some young fool. I imagine he's long dead by now.'

'Perhaps I should thank you for what you did,' Tellius went on. 'You stood against the Immortals of the Aeris legion. You helped defend the city.'

'For a while. Yet it was your Lord Hart who killed their general, not me. You know, I wish it had been me. He was the one who took my daughters. He was the one who gave the order to kill the king and throw the Twelve Families and the whole city into chaos. He told us to cut the head from the snake. He *needed* killing.'

A whisper of an old rage began to gleam in the man's eyes and Tellius had to struggle not to edge away. Elias looked fit and brown from a life outdoors, but there was no obvious sense of danger from him. Yet he had survived traps of gunfire and sword. He had withstood a cavalry charge. This was a man who had walked into a royal palace and then out again, leaving a host of dead behind.

Tellius chose each word carefully, sensing Elias was still hearing them before they had been spoken.

'Why have you come here?' Elias said.

He seemed to listen to a response and Tellius felt he had to reply quickly to get a word in with his future selves. It was the oddest sensation.

'The past is the past, meneer. I have not come for vengeance . . .'

'If you had, I would make you regret it,' Elias said, interrupting.

Tellius hurried on, rather than challenge something he believed to be the truth.

'This is no small thing, meneer. Darien could fall, be in no doubt about that – I would not have come otherwise. I do not yet know the full strength of the forces that will come against us. Only that it is the result of a personal event. A king's son was maimed in Darien. His father's armies are marching south.'

Tellius found he was gabbling to stay ahead of his alternate selves. He had no idea of the extent of the 'knack' Elias Post was said to have. The man could see just a little way into the future, which made him almost impossible to hit and fearsome in a way no other warrior could be. The Aeris general who had taken his daughters had done so as a way to control him. That had not ended well.

'Listen to me now,' Elias said. 'I have not invited you into my home because I did not want to consider you my guest. I have no interest in the politics of your city. If Wyburn is attacked, I will fight to defend my home. Nothing else . . .'

'We need you. And you owe us a debt,' Tellius interrupted.

'I am the Speaker for the Council of the Twelve Families, consort to Lady Sallet. Do you think I'd be here if it wasn't absolutely necessary? I . . .'

Elias broke his stubborn stare, turning to look left, along the street. Tellius had seen small gates between some of the houses, with alleys leading to the rear of the terrace. One of those opened and a girl stepped out. She wore a dark smock dress that reached her knees, slender as a willow wand and about as pale, twelve or fourteen at the most. Tellius knew he was no great judge of such things. The resemblance to her father was clear, however, as was the man's instant concern and irritation.

'Not now, Jenny. Whatever it is, I will deal with it when these . . . gentlemen have gone.'

'I was listening,' the girl said. 'I think you should help the city if you can.'

'And I have told you before not to listen to conversations that are no business of yours,' Elias retorted.

'You said the city saved my life, though – and Alice's life,' the girl said. 'You said they tried to save mum as well. That's a debt, isn't it?'

Her voice was clear and although she seemed aware of the soldiers and Tellius watching her, she didn't look at them. It was as if Elias and his daughter were having a private conversation on the open street.

'It *sounds* like a debt,' Tellius murmured to her.

She looked up at him, clear-eyed and fresh-faced as she raised one eyebrow. Elias snorted.

'There was a plague a few years back. The girls and I were given some foul muck by a legion doctor, outside the city. They offered it to secure my service, then held my daughters prisoner so I would do whatever they wanted. It has nothing to do . . .'

'The Aeris legion is funded by the Twelve Families,' Tellius interrupted. 'It was then, and it is today. It remains a cornerstone of the city defences, though we have militias and gun regiments now.' He raised a hand as Elias began to colour. 'They are commanded by a younger Aeris brother, nothing to do with the one you knew.'

As Elias digested that information, Tellius nodded to the girl.

'Jenny Post, is it? So, you and your sister were saved by Darien. I'm sorry to hear we could not save your mother as well. I remember that plague, though I lived a different life then. Darien allows change, miss. And forgiveness, sometimes. I have come to ask for your father's help in an emergency, that is all. Perhaps to wipe clean some of the blood on him as well.'

He waited then for Elias to respond. The man was trembling, though it did not look like fear, but rather one who was barely holding himself under control. Tellius dared not risk a glance at Captain Galen, nor at the closest thing to a Mazer master he had left, now Hondo and Bosin had gone. Micahel was the best or second-best swordsman in Darien at that moment, but if Elias attacked them, Tellius suddenly realised he would sacrifice himself to get Micahel away. It had been quite unconscious, but Tellius had edged between them while the girl spoke, when he saw Elias growing angry and cornered.

Micahel's job was to keep him alive, to move so fast, perhaps not even Elias could stop him. Yet instead, Tellius' instinct had placed himself in the way. The realisation made Tellius smile in wry disbelief. The girl stared quizzically at him.

Elias had not missed the significance of Tellius' last words. Whatever part Elias had played in the death of the old king had not been brought into the light. Yet they clearly knew where he lived – and he could not say for certain that there was nothing in Darien that could not make him a prisoner once more.

Tellius took a plum from the bush by the door as he watched Elias think, hoping he would make the right choice. The fruit was still unripe, hard and green in his hand. Perhaps there was nothing Elias feared, but that night four years before had been dark and savage. No one had ever come looking for the killers of the old king, though rumours still pointed in a dozen directions. Elias had to have dreaded the knock at the door, no matter how hard he was to bring down. Tellius suspected the man felt some guilt, no matter what he told himself . . .

'No,' Elias said firmly. The trembling stopped and he mastered himself. 'Whatever they want, I am well out of it. You'll understand when you're older, Jen.'

Tellius took the little unripe plum. He stepped away from the doorstep and threw it at the daughter standing in the road. Even then, he sensed Elias beginning to move and then halting, his mouth twisting into a grimace.

Jenny Post caught the plum without looking, without taking her eyes off her father. Slowly, she turned her head and fastened Tellius with a gaze that made him shiver.

'If we wanted to keep me hidden, you would have thrown your life away just then,' she said.

'Perhaps,' Tellius replied, though he felt his old heart

skipping beats as it raced. 'But I had to know. If there is a war coming, I will need everyone who can stand and fight. Is your sister the same?'

'I don't think so. Not yet anyway,' Jenny replied. 'Though I'd speak to my father if I were you. He's more than a little annoyed with you at the moment.'

Elias stepped off the doorstep and walked forward, prodding Tellius in the chest. Micahel and Galen began to react but Tellius held up his palm.

'I told you I wanted no part in your wild schemes,' Elias said. 'I owe nothing to Darien. Yes, that's true!' he snapped suddenly, responding to a point Tellius hadn't been quick enough to make. He tried to guess what it might have been.

'If you witnessed the death of an innocent man and did not stop it, no matter what General Justan Aeris had threatened, you are guilty of something, Elias Post. I know it and so do you. So pay your debt! And be pardoned for your old sins.'

Elias looked at his daughter and shook his head.

'I'll go with you,' Jenny Post said suddenly. 'Yes, I will.'

'No, love. For your mother's sake, I can't let you do that.'

'You'll need someone to keep you fed, won't you?'

'No. I won't take you to war, Jen. I don't want you to see . . . to have you become what I am. Please. If I go, I'll need you to stay here and look after your sister. It's not an adventure, love. It's murder they want me for. It's always murder.'

Tellius felt a twinge of embarrassment at witnessing the man's pain.

'I'm sorry,' he said to both of them.

Without another word, Elias turned to face his front door and twisted savagely at the knob, opening it onto the gloom within. He went inside and Tellius looked to the girl watching him.

'Shall we go in . . . ?' Tellius began.

She spoke over him, amused at his nervousness.

'Of course. He knows you will.'

The ground floor of the home where Elias lived with his two daughters was a single room. Coal burned in a small black stove set into one wall. Tellius let the warmth relax him as he entered a space that was both crammed and comfortable. Spiderwebs had formed in all the corners and every surface was taken up with books, tools or, oddly, coloured stones – the sort of thing a loving father might bring home to his children, perhaps. Tellius looked around in something like surprise. Elias Post was a hunter, a good one, so it was said. Perhaps the little house was not so surprising for a man who had lost his wife and come home to raise two young girls on his own. It didn't fit the image of the blood-covered maniac who had walked through gunfire in Darien, stepping aside untouched from bullets in the air. The conversation on the step had confirmed for Tellius that the red man had been able to look ahead. Some of the witnesses from that night had sworn it had to be some form of air magic, or moving solid things from a distance. The city had witnessed air magic only too recently, Tellius thought, remembering the four Returned souls who had come from Shiang two years before. Darien had survived true mages turned against her defences. Yet she remained: battered, scarred and magnificent. He had no wish to see another army test those walls, which was why he had chosen to play this particular card.

Tellius accepted a cup of sweet brown tea and sipped at it. Micahel and Galen had come in with him, making the small room feel uncomfortably crowded. Galen seemed content to watch in silence as Elias and his daughter moved easily around, picking up cups and kettle and tea-strainer and water and even some thick brown sugar, brought down for guests from a high shelf. There was no sign of the other daughter, though Tellius found himself looking around at intervals, convinced he was being observed. He waited until the sensation prickled the back of his neck and then looked straight up, seeing an eye vanish from a crack in the floorboards above. He thought he heard a squeak of shock at being caught and smiled as he sipped his tea.

'So, you are my guests,' Elias said at last. He had laid out a dozen biscuits on a plate. Tellius watched as Galen selected one and munched it, checking for poison.

'Thank you for making us welcome,' Tellius replied. He chose not to mention how unwelcoming the man had been before. The presence of Elias' daughters had a civilising effect, Tellius could see. The cold hardness when speaking to men alone had eased. It was probably true for many fathers, or at least less surprising than it seemed.

'I have not agreed to anything,' Elias reminded him sourly.

Tellius nodded slowly.

'For the past months, we've been negotiating a treaty with a kingdom to the north – Féal. They sent their prince and he was just about ruthless enough to get what he wanted, though it was against my will and advice. Unfortunately, he was then attacked in Darien. He was blinded, stabbed and had most of one hand cut away. When I spoke to him, he thought it would mean war – and I believe him. Even if I did not, I had men watching his father's legions. They began to move as soon as the news reached them.'

'Were you behind the attack on him?' Elias asked.

Tellius shook his head without indignation. It had been an obvious question.

'I would never have been so crude about it. No. One of three attackers was cut down on his way out. Another boasted about cutting up a prince of Féal as he drank in a bar that night. He was not found and the third just vanished.'

Tellius trailed off for a moment. When he listed the fates of the three men together, a suspicion grew in him. No one had claimed the man found dead on the way out of the gambling house. Nor had any of the gambling-house guards claimed to have put him down. Tellius put it aside for later thought.

'If the army is on the way to attack Darien, I can marshal our resources. We will be a hard nut to crack for any small king coming our way.'

'Then why do you need me? Ah, of course,' Elias said.

His daughter looked from one to the other and Tellius understood she had not been using whatever her knack was. It did not operate all the time, but only with an act of will. That, too, he tucked away to be examined at a quieter time. He did not enjoy the sense of helplessness he felt around Elias. It was like tossing a razor blade from one hand to the other, never knowing when it would cut him.

Tellius hid his dislike of the situation. It would surely be worth considering ways to control such a man.

'Why do they need you, Father?' Jenny Post asked softly. Elias inclined his head to Tellius.

'To kill that king, dear,' Tellius said. 'If everything I've heard is true, your father can get into an armed camp and reach the man in command. It is my hope that we can then sue for peace. Without a personal reason to assault Darien lands, perhaps they can be persuaded to return home.'

'And if they keep coming, you will have had me cut the head off the snake,' Elias grated.

'Yes. I'm sorry,' Tellius said. 'Though you are uniquely suited for this.'

'I'm a hunter, meneer. I sit on the village council. I live comfortably enough here. I don't need your grand schemes.'

'I understand that. Your village may not lie in the path of the Féal king, but others do, to the north of the city. We can evacuate some in time, but they don't want to see fire and . . . murder any more than you do.'

Tellius glanced at the girl as he spoke, choosing how much of the horror of war to repeat in front of her. Not that he needed to remind her father. He could see that much in the stove glow reflecting in his eyes.

'You don't know yet if they will even come, do you?' the girl asked.

Tellius shook his head.

'They broke camp and moved as soon as they heard. Believe me when I say I want to be mistaken, but I must gather what forces I can before they do. Your father is a spearpoint, whether he likes it or not. I would be a fool to leave him in the traps when one hard strike might end it all.'

'You'd have me go in alone?' Elias murmured.

'No! I will go with you,' his daughter said immediately.

'You will *not*,' Elias said, cutting the air with his hand. 'You have no idea what it is to take a man's life, to be spattered with warm blood and see their agony and *fear* when they can no longer defend themselves. No, Jenny. Don't ask me for this.'

She clenched her jaw as she looked away, Tellius noted. The girl was more like her father than either of them seemed to know.

'So, Speaker Tellius,' Elias said, turning back. 'You'd send me alone against a camp I have never seen, facing what magical defences I cannot possibly know. To save a city I do not love. Is that your offer to me?'

'No,' Elias said. 'You are not my only spear, Elias Post. You would not be alone.'

Elias thought for a moment. He looked at his daughter and the girl nodded to him, accepting. Tellius looked from one to the other, understanding that some decision had been made.

'All right. Tell me who you have,' Elias said.

14

Killer

Lady Win Sallet pushed the shop door and listened to the chiming bell it disturbed. She wore a dress of dark green over white, complete with wide-brimmed hat and long green gloves that reached to her elbows. A Sallet coach waited outside, resplendent in green and black, with footmen in her house livery, staring silently ahead. The road wound through one of those parts of the city less used to the comings and goings of the Twelve Families. A crowd of gawkers and tradesmen had already begun to gather. It was one reason Win Sallet did not bring her Greens with her when she moved around the city. It was not only that they were most feared when no one knew how they worked, when sightings had the quality of ancient legends. It would also have created a crowd of the curious so deep they would have blocked the road and interrupted the humming trade of that district for the rest of the day. She could hardly describe her presence as discreet, given the family crests on either side of her coach and the dominant colour. Yet it was as quiet as she could manage.

The shop she entered was empty of customers and full of just about everything else. Whatever the original window display had been, a thousand other pieces had been packed into every slot and tiny opening. Further back, the same impression was only emphasised. On each side, right to the tall ceilings, objects had been shoved in wherever there was space. It was oddly fascinating, Lady Sallet realised. Wherever her gaze landed was something completely different – brass toys on one spot, a writing desk on another, beautifully figured in green copper. A basket of walking sticks sat askew on a crate of old planes and chisels, all resting against what looked like ornate stained-glass windows, removed from some house that had been demolished. Win Sallet wondered if she should send one of her staff to look through the collection. There would surely be treasures there. She had noticed no sign of anything magical, however. There were other shops and indeed an entire street for that sort of thing. Lady Sallet imagined the owners of those establishments would not take too kindly to a competitor. It would have been safer for the owner to sell items of strictly non-magical interest and beauty.

The ringing bell had not gone unnoticed, of course. Lady Sallet only wondered that the owner had so few customers that she could leave the place untended. Yet footsteps sounded, wending their way down from above, with each step creaking. Lady Sallet adjusted the angle of her hat and stood before the glass counter-top, waiting for the young woman who owned 'Beautiful Things'.

When the owner appeared, she was looking into an accounts book, held open in her hands. She was in her twenties, with her hair tied back and bound. She wore a neat dress that ended below the level of the desk, over a white blouse. A pencil protruded from over one ear.

Lady Sallet could see red ink in large quantities before

the book closed with a snap and the younger woman looked up and smiled.

The smile froze and vanished as quickly as it had come. To Lady Sallet's horror, the young woman let the book fall. Her right hand began to rise.

'Nancy, please! I have not come here to hurt you.'

The woman stiffened and blushed at her own name. She could see no threat. Apart from Lady Sallet, the shop was empty. In confusion, Nancy came round the counter to retrieve her accounts book. Lady Sallet saw flashes of red on every page.

'Is the business not going well?' she asked.

Nancy did not respond. She put the book down on the glass, over a tray of old rings and gold-coloured chains, then looked past Lady Sallet to the street outside.

'How did you find me? How did you even know I was here?' Nancy demanded. 'I haven't used my name. I haven't borrowed money. This place isn't anywhere near my old haunts, even!'

'You're a city girl, Nancy,' Lady Sallet replied. 'You told me that yourself. Where else would you go? Anyway, I always hoped you'd come home. I admit I hoped as well that you'd come and see me when you did.'

It had been one of Tellius' people who had spotted the young woman who had caused so much havoc on the night the Aeris legion attacked the city. Nancy had been terrifying then, Win Sallet remembered only too clearly. For years, the girl had believed magic to be a fraud, no more than a cruel trick. The truth had revealed itself when she'd soaked in so much of it she'd almost burned the city down. Her knack was that she could draw it in, like a sponge. On its own, that would have been enough to make her immensely valuable to the Twelve Families. Yet Nancy's control of magic was similar to liquid. She could drink herself almost to bursting, ruining any artefact or great spell around her – then spit it back in lines of fire. In all the histories Lady Sallet had read, there had been very few with abilities as powerful as the young woman watching her with suspicion. Or none at all. If Tellius was right, they no longer had the luxury of remaining hands-off on Nancy, while she tried to run a small shop in a rough area.

'I didn't owe you anything,' Nancy said, though she looked away as she spoke. 'I'd lost my . . . friend that night. I'd been forced to do some horrible things.'

The young woman shuddered and Lady Sallet wondered if she was remembering the attempt to save one of the Sallet Greens. The sound and smell of a man scorching to death inside had been obscene, a memory that had hardly begun to fade.

'I trusted you enough to lend you my family stone, Nancy. Do you understand what it meant to me? Do you remember that?'

'Of course I remember it! But that was another life – and I've left it behind. I have my shop now, bought with gold I earned myself.'

Lady Sallet chose not to mention the debtors already clamouring to force that shop into bankruptcy. Whatever Nancy was, she had no flair for running a business. The location was wrong and the stock was wrong for the location. The young woman paid too much for things that wouldn't sell and there had been at least two assistants who'd robbed the place blind. Nancy would have been better off opening a butcher's shop, which that part of the city actually needed. Lady Sallet kept that last thought to herself, however. She'd done her research before making this approach. Looking at the way Nancy raised her chin, ready to reject anything she would say, Lady Sallet decided to push her a little. The fact that Nancy had more offensive capability than any other living being in Darien was a concern she had to ignore. Even her Sallet Greens were useless against one who could draw their magic from them in a touch. Lady Sallet wondered how much was left in the young woman watching her with dark and worried eyes, flecked with gold.

'This shop is . . . what, a month from going up for sale?' Lady Sallet said, looking around. 'No customers today? But there are still the taxes to the council. No rent, of course, not for one who owns it outright. But I imagine the purchase of a house and a business on this street took a great deal of your windfall, is that right? I wonder how much you have left before the bailiffs come banging on the door? The council will force a sale for unpaid taxes, as I'm sure you are well aware.'

'What do you want?' Nancy said.

She had paled to hear her financial position discussed with such cold calculation. Not least for the suspicion that Lady Sallet knew about the gold mask she had brought back to the city and melted into fine, albeit counterfeit, coins. Nancy also knew better than Win Sallet how accurate a picture of her finances it was. There was one single gold coin and three silvers in a sock upstairs – with all of her stock not worth five times that. Yet the taxes were due at the end of the month. The thought made her eyes narrow.

'Is this blackmail? You think you have me at a disadvantage?' she said.

The golden flecks in her eyes seemed to deepen as she spoke and Lady Sallet had to steel herself not to lean away.

'Your own incompetence is disadvantage enough, I should say. What do you know of double-entry bookkeeping, of allowable expenses? Of company law and dividends? What events have you planned in this street to introduce people to the shop? That is, if it is worth saving. I don't see how you could ever advertise a place so full of random objects.'

'So you came here to insult me? To tell me I can't run a business? Well, thank you, my lady. Now get out of my shop, while it is still my shop.'

The last was an admission and Lady Sallet saw tears sparkle in the younger woman's eyes. Yet she had seen tears before and produced them herself enough times to strangle her first impulse to embrace and reassure. Instead she shook her head, slowly.

'I came here because we need you, as I'm sure you have already surmised. And no, it was not for your business acumen. We believe the city will be attacked by an army coming south to take every stone from every other stone. I want to stop that army in its tracks, before it even sees Darien. Is that clear enough for you? If you agree to this . . .'

The tears seemed to have vanished as Nancy listened, Lady Sallet noted. The younger woman nodded and raised one hand. Win Sallet tensed, but she did not flinch back, making Nancy smile at her bravery. Slowly, Nancy raised finger after finger, counting off her points.

'One. I want a hundred-year exemption on my business, from *all* taxes. Two – I want an accountant to visit each month, his salary paid by you, or House Sallet. Thank you for that suggestion. Three, I will also need a sign-maker and glazier . . . as well as a monthly stipend for cleaning and repairs.'

'Done,' Lady Sallet said.

Nancy shook her head and smiled.

'Not yet, no. If you need me, you'll set me up without a word of complaint. I find I like being a shop-owner, Lady Sallet. Setting my own hours, pottering about, searching through the markets for interesting things. And I have sold a few, whatever you may think. But not enough to keep me in good style. I heard about that gambling place in the north of the city. The Darien Lion? I want a share in that.'

'I cannot . . .' Lady Sallet began, then paused. Her instinct was to negotiate, but the price was low, considering what they would get in exchange. She sighed as if defeated, lowering her head to hide any sign of satisfaction. 'Very well. Five per cent of all profits, taken from the council's share. I will win a vote on it, or pay it myself from Sallet funds.'

'Twenty per cent,' Nancy said, her eyes bright.

'My dear, I might manage ten – and that is a fortune. You would not believe what that place makes in a month. The Twelve Families own half the establishment in common, so I suppose you could say each of us has four per cent or a little over. I might be able to bargain my share up to ten, but twenty would be beyond me.'

Nancy put out her hand.

'Very well, ten per cent, without taxes.' She noticed the way Lady Sallet winced at that and smiled at scoring a hit. 'And my other terms?'

With a twinge of genuine regret, Lady Sallet took Nancy's hand in her own gloved one. Tellius would think she had gone mad, but who knew how long they had? They needed to get the team together and Nancy was key to that. She just hoped he was having as much luck with Elias Post.

'Your terms are acceptable. I have a clerk in my coach, with all he needs to write it up for us to sign. You haven't asked the details of the work, dear.'

Nancy's grip was firm before she let go, hinting at strength.

'You said you want me to stop an army. That's clear enough. Lady Sallet, look at me for a moment. Tell me what you see.'

'My dear, I see a young woman in a difficult position, who has worked hard to find a way . . .' Lady Sallet broke off in confusion as Nancy laughed and shook her head.

'You might have said you see the woman who destroyed Sallet Greens, who stood in a fighting line and poured fire into the night. You might have said you see a killer, Lady Sallet. You make my point for me. I'll say this to you, because you are the only woman on the council and perhaps the only one who can understand this. Men think we are marked by what we do. They truly believe it. They think you can look in a woman's eyes and see how many she has slept with, or if she was . . . harshly treated. Or whether she has killed, even. It is an error, but they don't know it. *You* know, though. A woman isn't truly marked, not by anything that doesn't show – and bruises fade and cuts scar to pink lines. So when you look at me, you see a dusty young woman, managing a shop. Even though you were there that night, four years ago, it's hard to remember that I killed men. They came to attack my city and I stood in their way. Or they tried to hurt me and I burned them where they stood. And the truth is that I haven't lost a night of sleep, or worried overmuch about it since that day. So if I can win a quiet life for myself, with funds enough and time enough for peace, yes, I'll do it again. I'll burn the world for that. If they are on their way to Darien, maybe I'd have done it anyway, though I suppose we'll never know.'

'You'll need the Sallet Stone,' Win Sallet said softly. She did not know what to make of Nancy's words, not then. It would take time to sift them, like flour. 'We have a better idea now of what the family stones can do, since . . . we crossed paths. They have a store of magic in them, as much as you'll need.'

Two years before, Lady Sallet had watched the Bracken Stone dissolve into dust as its reserves were drawn into the Shiang swordsman known as Taeshin. The power had dragged his soul back and healed his body, but at the cost of the stone. The thought of losing the symbol of the Sallet house was a wrench that almost brought tears to her eyes. Her parents had touched it, as had her grandparents and every generation, back to the beginning of recorded time. Nothing Nancy asked could possibly have been the equal of the Sallet Stone, but it would still be a price worth paying to save the city. If it came to it.

'Bring in your clerk, Lady Sallet. I'll make tea for us

all – and there is a very sweet ginger cake upstairs, in my parlour.'

Nancy seemed lit from within, her hair more lustrous, though it was tied back in a long tail. Lady Sallet turned to signal her people and closed her eyes in a moment of relief. They needed Nancy to have a chance of success, in the way a stonemason needs his hammer.

Taeshin sipped pale green tea and stared gloomily out of the tiny window in the garret room above a laundry that he shared with Marias and the man they called the Fool. He and Marias were no longer master and slave. Darien had no slaves, Marias had told him firmly, watching for some objection. He had still been coping with a transition from something like a grey afterlife at the time. The details had faded quickly as soon as he was back in the world, with a purple stone crumbling to dust on his chest. The exact nature of servitude in a strange city thousands of miles from home had not been his primary concern. Perhaps it should have been, he thought.

He had resigned himself to death back in Shiang, just about. He still remembered the way the burden had seemed to lift as he'd made the decision to settle himself on a quiet hillside and put his sword through the cancerous growth in his side. It had seemed like sense, though when he had confided the memory to one of the Darien swordsmen in training, Micahel, the man had seemed coldly furious. Micahel had been brought up in poverty, without parents to keep him safe. Yet he had told Taeshin that every damned day had been worth knowing, that no matter how terrible things seemed, a man could sleep and wake refreshed and continue chipping away at his problems and his failures. That all men could be reborn, and all men forgiven. It had been an extraordinary lecture and Taeshin had withdrawn from it. He'd needed more time – to fit into a new city, to understand a culture that was radically different from the one he had known. Not that he had travelled to Darien! That was part of the strangeness he saw on all sides. If he had chosen to leave Shiang and cross the mountains, plains and forests, he would have had months of anticipation to prepare himself. He would have said a formal goodbye to everything he knew and loved, all the while welcoming his new home as it grew closer, step by step. Instead, he had been no more than a blind passenger as another man used the power of the Aeris Stone to take over his body. He still woke in the night sometimes, wet with perspiration, with the smell of acids and the touch of leather straps holding him down.

As a prisoner, Taeshin had been given glimpses of what was happening, no more than fragments. In the end, when the thief soul had been torn back to . . . wherever . . . he shook his head at wisps of memory. In the end, Taeshin had found himself on the street, as if he had woken from unconsciousness. He'd drawn in his first breath in months and the pain had been appalling. His body had been battered and scraped and broken, then healed and broken again, over and over. He had been strong and fit, but ruined, with a great eye-shaped scar on his chest. There, in the rain, he'd felt a stone pulsing through him, pouring in power until there was nothing left but a smear of colour on his skin.

Marias had been there – and the Fool who had crouched

at her side, beaming. The two of them had kept him alive even, while those around still thought he was the enemy. In those moments, Taeshin knew he had been like a child, utterly helpless. It still rankled. He remembered a married cousin who had lost a leg in an accident. The man had murmured to Taeshin that it was not that he resented his wife learning all she could do for herself. It was that he'd hoped she would never have to find out. While Taeshin had been swallowed up and lost, Marias had been forced to learn.

He sipped his tea. A stranger looking in would have seen a young man, strong and taller than most of his people, with black hair cut short, black eyes and high cheekbones that gave him an aquiline look. Taeshin sipped again, breathing in the scent that was not quite as he remembered it. He had fallen back on work, building and maintaining the walls of Darien, leaning out on ropes high above the ground for danger pay, to repair cracks or loose stones. When that had dried up, he'd found a place as an instructor at the Mazer school. That had been good for him, after he'd got over the shock of seeing strangers not born in Shiang learning the Mazer dances that strengthened every joint and bone. He suspected the one called Tellius had been behind the offer. Taeshin was grateful for that, though he knew better than to believe the man was truly related to the royal family of Shiang.

For months, Taeshin had kept his head down, making sure he was the first to arrive and the last to leave as he and Marias made a refuge for themselves. Or a home, he was not sure yet if it qualified. They were not master and slave. Nor were they husband and wife, though they lived in the same two rooms, with the Fool curling up by the fire each night. He at least seemed happy, though Taeshin was never sure how much he understood. No one had called the Fool back, perhaps because his name had been lost.

Taeshin knew Marias hoped for something more. He would have had to be blind not to see it. Her glances and her touch had lingered as he healed over the first year. Yet he had lived as a puppet or a tool of another and he found his temper surging at odd moments, clattering around the place and kicking a door off its hinges. In some ways, he was like a child again and he had been wary of this woman who had so clearly grown to love him. He owed her a great debt – and he was not sure that was enough. Taeshin had died. He was not yet sure how to live, or if he had missed the chance to try again.

He drained the cup. He grieved, he knew that much. For the loss of his home or the life he had known as a personal guard to Lord Hong, it was not easy to say. When his parents had died, life had gone on, but under a weight. It had taken years before he noticed it had eased. Not gone, but lessened enough for him to live and laugh once more. How he felt around Marias felt much the same, and completely different. He had been smashed and repaired. He had known agonies he was grateful not to remember. He had been to a grey land and been made to fight, over and over. He knew the heroes of old would have laughed off their trials. Hercules had gone into the afterworld to steal a dog – and when he returned, it had been the same dark and driven young warrior, strolling through the markets of Greece.

Such thoughts shamed Taeshin. He knew he had

withdrawn from Marias, that her eyes filled with tears when he would not answer. His body had healed and he could not recall how many of the scars had even come to be. Yet she would not entertain the idea of going home, even when they saw the new road Tellius was building and Taeshin had walked a mile from the city with her, looking at the rising sun.

Rain lashed the windows as he stood there, so that he could no longer see the city around them and only the pattern of drops moving on the glass. The truth was that he wanted to go home, to where he belonged – and Marias did not. Yet he would not abandon the woman who had travelled half a world to save him. He owed her more than that and his sense of duty was one thing he had not lost. He nodded a fraction at the thought.

He jerked at the sound of knocking on the outer door. Marias was working with the Fool in the laundry down below. Neither of them would knock, surely? He frowned as he crossed the little room, stepping around the table they put out whenever the bed was leaned against the wall. He slept in the other room, on a mattress of two folded blankets.

'Who is it?' Taeshin said. He had left a training sword by the door. Though it was a crude thing compared with the ones he had known in Shiang, it was nonetheless sharp and well oiled. There was more crime in Darien than Shiang and he was annoyed with himself and the city for the urge to answer a door with a blade to hand. He flung open the door with more force than was necessary.

Tellius met his gaze and Taeshin could only gape at the older man. Micahel stood to one side and Captain Galen of the Sallet guard looked on. The three were crammed into the tiny hallway, their shoulders touching.

'Good evening, Master Taeshin,' Tellius said. 'I am here as Speaker for the city of Darien. The city that saved your life at huge cost to us. There is an enemy coming and I need your help.'

15

Shield

Lord Regis used his sword hilt as if it was a walking stick, bracing his right arm straight. In his fifties, he was still a massive physical presence, though his breathing suggested the climb to the top of the city wall had not been without cost. The younger man at his side eyed him with his usual mixture of awe and exasperation. They stood together on the crest walkway, looking down on the snake of refugees entering the north gate.

It had started a fortnight before, with farming families abandoning their homesteads and villages and heading south to the city. Those first few had come with stories of ranks of Féal soldiers trudging through the night, of banners gold and black.

The numbers had grown considerably since then. Both Regis and De Guise looked down on a stream of hundreds, possibly thousands, stretching into the shadowy distance. Exhausted, stumbling, like cattle driven before whips. It was a troubling thought for the younger lord. De Guise frowned as he stared into the gloom.

'And still they come,' Regis murmured to himself.

'Do you think all this could be part of the Féal king's plans?' De Guise said after a time. He went right to the edge and leaned over, looking down at miserable families begging for admittance.

'What do you mean?'

'All these people. Adding to the mouths we have to feed.'

Regis shrugged.

'They can't lay siege to Darien, not while we keep the river access open. Not while we have warships patrolling, either – and trading partners only too happy to pay war prices on grain. We can't be starved out, Geese. And some of these angry farmers will be willing to take up a sword to defend themselves, I should think.'

'And how do we know they are all our people?' De Guise said.

Regis peered down at the trail of misery below.

'You mean there could be traitors among them?'

'Or assassins.' The younger lord saw the beginnings of a smile appear on Regis' wide face. 'Why not? Is it so hard to believe? The last time an army attacked this city, the king was killed first – to cause chaos. The enemy saw value then in trying to undermine order, in breaking the chain of command! Is there truly no danger of that now? I look at these people, Regis, and I see hungry mouths. Who knows who hides among them? We offer safety, but they bring us only risk.'

Regis looked at the man who had inherited the De Guise family sword. The previous owner had been his greatest friend – his only friend, in all honesty. It had not been so strange for Regis to hope for something of the same comforting relationship with the younger relative.

The obstacle was that Robert De Guise had a sort of callous disregard that made him, in his own judgement, superior to everyone he met. The young lord was healthy and fit. He was agile and as slim as a reed. He seemed to believe those who had grown weak or aged past forty were somehow worthless.

Regis eyed the younger man's cold expression and wondered if it would survive the army of Féal. War hardened some and broke others. Regis knew decisions had to be made, obviously – a man could be too much a weeping ninny, useless to all and worse than a woman. Yet there was such a thing as too cold-blooded, as well. It made the older lord think of the Canis family and their stone. Young De Guise needed to wince at the sight of those who walked on bloodstained rags, starving and dull of eye. Until he did that, he would be a royal pain to endure.

Though it was growing dark, Regis could still see the stain of villagers and carts coming in, always retreating, looking over their shoulders for something beyond the horizon. Each group of villagers that piled belongings on carts and abandoned their homes took the fear on to the next, like a carpet being rolled up for hundreds of miles. It was its own wave – and behind them, an army marched in sullen rage towards Darien.

Regis realised he had not replied. No doubt De Guise would think he had dozed off or something. What had he been saying? Assassins? He shook his head.

'They are all searched as they come in – any weapons would be found.'

'Small comfort when guns are sold in city workshops! I pray to the Goddess a quick search is enough, but we should have cells ready to take anyone who raises suspicions. Has that been done? Is anyone watching to see if weapons are thrown aside before they can be searched?'

'You have the mind for the task, clearly,' Regis said. 'Perhaps you should go down, Geese, and direct the guards on the gate.' He noticed the young man made no move. De Guise was one of those who preferred to point out flaws, not the sort who mucked in and put them right.

'I tell you, my lord,' De Guise said after a time, 'sooner or later, we will have to close these gates – and anyone still outside in that hour will be run down and lost. I'd do it today rather than let more in to weaken us, or invite in some killer. Yes, that's what I would do. And, Lord Regis?'

'Yes?'

'I would prefer it if you called me Robert, or Lord De Guise. Not "Geese".'

Regis was tempted to pitch him over the battlement in that moment. He could see exactly how to do it – one quick grab of his thigh, a jerk upwards and no more irritation. He resisted the temptation. As far as he knew, no other twig on the De Guise branch was able to carry the family sword – and the city truly needed that weapon, just as they needed the Regis shield and the Sallet Greens. Whatever the Féal king intended, his forces would be met with magic, gunfire and iron. Regis smiled at the thought, until he recalled how little they knew of the army all these refugees were fleeing. Would the regiments of Féal throw themselves against Darien if they had no way to break walls? It was a sobering thought and Regis hoped Tellius was on his best game. Regis knew the speaker and Sallet consort for a cunning and competitive man. Not likeable.

Occasionally more like a street-seller bawling his wares than a man with a claim to royalty and high status. Yet there was something unbending in the old Shiang bastard. That at least was something Regis could appreciate.

'Gentlemen – and lady,' Tellius said to the group of three standing before him. With the permission of the king, he had borrowed a gymnasium in the royal palace to introduce them to one another. Leather-clad pommel horses, weights and wall bars lay on all sides, with a floor of polished oak pieces that reflected the beams of the ceiling in shimmering lines.

'The army of Féal is marching south. I have scouts and spies watching, though they have a net of their own people far out. They certainly know we are there.'

He did not say that he had lost a dozen men sent to report and observe the approach. None of them had been reckless. Whoever ran the Féal counter-measures was both ruthless and experienced.

'It seems to be a disciplined army, with good order and chains of command. They keep cavalry on the wings, as a screen. They fortify their location each night, digging huge trenches, complete with gates and embankments. As well as the fighting lines, they appear to have a substantial support group. These remain behind during the day and come to the fore when it is time to assemble the camp.' He saw the grim expressions of the little group and chose his words carefully. 'Though I would prefer a group of savages or berserkers, there are weaknesses in those rigid structures that we will be able to exploit. At this moment, we assume their intention is to sack Darien. They have made no attempt to engage the villagers and townspeople running before them and seem content to drive them in like beaters and hares. Our biggest problem is that we have little idea of their strength. So I would rather strike fast, when they do not expect you, than wait and perhaps be overwhelmed.'

He paused to look at the three before him. Elias was there because Tellius had offered a pardon – and subtly threatened him in the same conversation. The man's daughter Jenny had remained at home to look after her sister, though she'd argued bitterly about that until she and her father were the same shade of brick-red.

Nancy had come because she had as strong a love for Darien as anyone Tellius had met. She'd demanded a high price, but four years before, Tellius had watched her burn a street rather than run or hide. If the city was under attack, he knew Nancy would stand in the line with whatever weapons she had.

The last was the one Tellius knew and trusted least, though the man had been born in his home city and trained in the Mazer steps. Taeshin had come to Darien as the unwilling host of another, made to march thousands of miles like a puppet. The power of an entire stone had been lost to send that host back and heal Taeshin. Yet he was a master swordsman by the standards of Darien – or the kingdom of Féal.

The idea of sending so few against an army was the spear-thrust Tellius had described to Elias – right to the heart. Tellius knew more about each of them than he could admit. He knew Elias and Deeds had been sent into Darien to kill the old king. There had been few survivors, but those who had lived had been able to describe both men. Tellius had put together a sequence of events that was close to complete. He enjoyed puzzles and mysteries of exactly that sort, spending evenings at a desk with a single candle until he had fitted all the pieces in their right places.

He knew Nancy had grown up around Fiveway, one of the roughest parts of the city. He knew she'd worked in the Old Red Inn and that she'd bought her current home and shop with gold coins melted down from some artefact she had found in the black desert.

When Tellius looked at Taeshin, it was hard not to see the face of the madman who had set a good part of Darien on fire in his death struggle. Yet Tellius had watched him instruct the younger ones in the first Mazer school of Darien, supported by Sallet funds. Micahel had learned from him – and without Hondo and Bosin, Taeshin was the best blade in the city at that moment. There were other reasons for Tellius to want him there, though he did not share them.

His assessment did not help their chances of survival, of course. There were just too many unknowns. Tellius bit his lower lip as he decided how best to go about it.

'You'll understand this has come quickly. We are reacting, not planning. The prince of Féal was left for dead and now his father is racing south. I don't need to be a genius to know the two things are linked. So we are moving. You are the first spear thrown. If you fail, we'll stop his army at the walls, with the Aeris legion, the militias and the artefacts. If you succeed, you'll save the lives of thousands of your people. Those are the stakes.'

He waited for them to stop glancing at one another.

'We don't have *time* to let you train together – to send you into the hills and have you tell how you . . .' He waved a hand in exasperation. 'How you learned to deal with bullies, or that summer you were . . . I don't know, touched by an uncle. Understand? If we had a month, I'd give it to you, but we haven't. The army is making twenty to twenty-five miles a day and they are one hundred miles north of this city. We have three, four days at most, so just accept this: each of you is extraordinary in your own way. I can give you this evening to work in this room, so that you understand what you can do. After that, I have horses waiting with one of my scouts to take you as close to the army of Féal as he can. You'll get past the sentries . . .'

'Just like that?' Nancy said.

Tellius pointed to Elias.

'Ask him. You'll reach the king's personal tent or head-quarters. If you kill him, the personal vendetta ends.'

'Or . . . his officers decide to attack the city that mur-dered their king and his son!' Nancy said.

'We only maimed the son, but, yes, that could happen. Which is exactly what they're doing now. Your point?'

'Nothing. I understand.'

'Good. I want you to go in, kill the bastard in a crown and get back to the city. If they keep coming, we'll need all three of you on the walls. Understood?'

'You expect me to fight for you?' Taeshin said. 'I have sworn no oath of service. Darien is not my city.'

'The lady you live with . . . her name is Marias, yes?' Tellius said. 'She was your slave back in Shiang.'

The swordsman's eyes narrowed, instantly hostile.

'Yes, that is true.'

'She has a life here now – and so do you. Yet some things have to be earned, do you understand? I came here from Shiang and I *paid* my dues. Do the same.'

Tellius held the gaze of the Shiang swordsman for an age, until Taeshin dipped his head, accepting. Tellius nodded in turn.

'And you should marry her, by the way. I will make you a gift of a house of your own when you do.'

Taeshin gaped at him. He had always known exactly how to react in Shiang. The rules of conduct were there to prevent weakness or confusion. He looked back on that earlier existence with longing. Nothing made sense in the same way, not since the moment he had woken up in Darien.

'I will not fight for this city . . . just because you offer me a house!' he spluttered.

'I did not say you should,' Tellius snapped. 'I said I would make you a marriage gift. Marias is a good woman – and more patient than you deserve. No, you should fight for the city because it is your city. Because for the rest of your life, when people ask you what you did when the army of Féal was bearing down on us . . .'

'I will say I don't want to talk about it – because such things are not for the ears of those who were not there,' Taeshin replied.

Tellius smiled tightly at the response. There were times when he missed Shiang.

'You will know what you did. Some things have to be earned, Master Taeshin. I was there when the Bracken Stone wrenched you back. I imagine you were spared for a reason. I want you to win against these people who think

212

they can break our walls and enslave our people. I am no longer the king of Shiang, though I retain an estate and title. I want you to win – I want them also to lose.'

Tellius saw the younger man's eyes widen slightly as he registered the form of the words. Taeshin nodded as Tellius turned to Elias.

'You should know my scouts report vast forces. We have the Aeris legion of five thousand and forty-two thousand in the militias. We can make Darien a fortress, believe me. Yet more than eighty thousand are on the march towards us. They have some sort of legion structure, with at least twenty separate banners. More, they have wheeled constructions at the far rear: huge things pulled by oxen and horses. They are very well guarded. I haven't been able to get anyone close. Siege engines or towers – at this point, we have no idea. For all we know, their weapons are capable of smashing down our defences. Beyond that, I cannot say, but I will not lie to you. Your task is appalling – an assassination in the middle of that armed force. However, we are not without resources.'

Tellius took a slim wooden box from a long pocket on the inside of his jacket. Nancy had seen it before and her gaze followed it like a starving man seeing food.

'This is the Sallet Stone,' Tellius said, sliding the lid open. 'As well as the signature colour and symbol of one of the Twelve Families of Darien, it is a repository of magic. We do not know how it was created, nor how to replenish it if it is used up. The Bracken Stone turned to pale dust when the last of its magic was used. I do not want to see that again here, though we will not stint, nor hold back from whatever you need to do . . .'

'What is wrong with her?' Elias said. 'Oh, Goddess . . .'

Nancy had begun to draw from the stone the moment it was opened. For lesser artefacts, a touch was needed for her to pull the golden threads into herself. For an actual Darien stone, it felt like a window opening onto summer, a vast warmth and light that poured into the room. Her hair darkened and became tinged with red, seeming almost independent of her in that moment. She knew too that her eyes would be more deeply flecked with gold as she opened them once again. Taeshin had taken a step away involuntarily and Elias seemed differently focused, as if his attention was on something else entirely. Nancy smiled and Tellius shut the box with a snap, startling her. At the same time, servants entered the gymnasium to light lamps along the walls. One of them approached to hand a sword to Taeshin.

'There,' Tellius said. 'Elias is the leader. Obey his orders as if they were my own. Work together, please. The servants will show you to your rooms when you are tired. If you leave at breakfast tomorrow, you should arrive at the enemy lines in darkness. Now, I'm afraid I must go. I'll see you at dawn. As important as you are, you are not my only iron in the fire.'

Without another word, he turned and left.

Deeds eyed the rider cantering towards him along the road. There wasn't much question of an ambush, not with Hondo and Bosin alongside. The two swordsmen of Shiang seemed to have no concept of hiding. They stood like trees on the verge of the road that stretched all the way to Darien.

The first part of Deeds' plan to return home had been

to get back to that paved stone surface. In the camp, the Shiang ambassador had watched in fury as Hondo and Bosin had selected horses for themselves and Deeds. Their right to do so was less than clear, though none of the other guards had been inclined to challenge them. Deeds had the suspicion they'd all be outlaws if they ever returned to Shiang. That was not something he'd said aloud, however. Presumably Ambassador Xi-Hue had kept his own counsel rather than risk being a loose end or an irritation to a sword saint.

The horse they'd chosen for Deeds had gone lame almost immediately on a steep slope, slipping and sliding down, then whinnying in distress and standing with one leg cocked. Rather than leave it to be torn apart by wolves, Deeds had dropped it with a single shot to its head. After that miserable event, Deeds had been forced to ride behind Bosin for another hundred miles or so, through plains and woodland he was always on the verge of recognising, but never quite.

When they'd finally reached the new road, it had been with the awareness of hunger, thirst and the desperate need for Deeds to have his own horse before Bosin lost his temper again and killed him. The awakening of the huge swordsman was not like flipping a coin. At times, Bosin was as blank and dead of face as he had been for two years. Then without warning, the big man would smile at something Hondo said, or perhaps a memory that amused him. It was like watching a corpse come back to life. Deeds could not help prattling nervously in the company of one who might take it into his head at any moment to avenge old wounds. Nor did he particularly enjoy having to hold another man around the chest – especially a chest so big it made Deeds feel like he was a little boy travelling with his father. He strode the world with lightning on his hip! It was humiliating to snore on someone else's back and go wherever he was taken. A man liked to choose his path. For that, a man needed a new horse.

Deeds drew both pistols and levelled them at the rider approaching. The fellow seemed to understand the threat Deeds represented and reined in.

'I bear sealed messages, gentlemen. I have no coin, nor anything of value. Let me pass.'

'You can pass on foot,' Deeds said. 'I need your horse to get home.'

'This is your plan?' Hondo said. 'To rob a bonded messenger? Why, Deeds, when you have a place behind Master Bosin? Would you make us thieves?'

Deeds did not take his guns off the man staring nervously at them. He replied through clenched teeth.

'I am not "making" you anything. And I'd prefer it if you didn't use my name aloud. I thought I had made that clear.'

'That was before I understood you were contemplating a robbery.'

'"Deeds"?' the rider said suddenly, looking from one to the other. 'One of my messages is for you.'

Deeds blinked, then holstered his guns and held out his hand.

'No tricks, son. I'll drop you if you make a move.'

He watched as the young rider slowly reached to a satchel under his leg, undoing the buckle with wide-eyed tension. A sheaf of papers came out and the rider had to dismount and hand his reins to Master Hondo, then lick his thumb and sort through them one by one. Deeds drew his pistol alongside his thigh and slowly reversed it, so that he could use the hilt as a hammer. Hondo shook his head slowly in warning while the messenger searched on, oblivious.

'I thought so. Here it is, from Master Tellius,' the messenger said.

'Hand it over, son,' Deeds growled to him. He backed away from the others to read it, knowing they would not do anything until they knew what Tellius had to say.

Deeds smiled. There were only three lines on the page. It was the sort of message a man might scrawl in a tearing hurry, with a dozen other things on his mind.

'Some sort of trouble with the kingdom. What kingdom?'

'The kingdom of Féal, sir,' the young man replied.

'That prince? I *knew* he was all wrong, the first moment I saw him.' Deeds thrust the paper at Hondo. 'Tellius wants us to come back. Terms to be discussed later. If it's war, he'll give you anything you want, I should think. And me too. I think I'll ask him for a patent of nobility. "Lord Deeds". That sounds like a man's ambition, doesn't it? Or Lord Hondo?'

Deeds looked at Bosin and couldn't imagine the massive swordsman being made anything else than what he was.

'You found us, son. Well done.'

The rider was in the middle of replying when Deeds cracked the hilt of his pistol on the side of his head. He folded in a heap.

'You have made road-thieves of us,' Hondo said.

'Well, you're Darien men now,' Deeds said with a shrug. 'Grasp an opportunity when you see it, would you?' He sighed at the hostile expressions. 'All right. I'll leave his horse at the next tavern – and perhaps a coin or two for his trouble. I'll have to take another one, though. Will that suit you?'

'It will have to,' Hondo said.

'So you're coming back with me?'

'If we are needed, Deeds, yes.'

'*Lord* Deeds,' he said.

'I will not call you that.'

The three men mounted. The road was paved and flat all the way to the city for another eighty miles. If they changed horses three times at road taverns, they could do it in four hours.

'You will if I make it true. Now keep up with me. If you can,' Deeds said with a grin. He whipped the reins back and forth and his horse bunched its back legs and launched at a gallop.

16

Spear

Tellius paused in the doorway, looking thoughtfully at the man who had caused his most recent troubles. Prince Louis of Féal lay shrouded in bandages. His head was wrapped tight, covering all his hair and one eye. The dressings on his hand had been replaced and were a touch smaller than before, in a clean white lump like a mitten. More strips wound around the young man's chest, while a sheet covered his legs.

The prince sensed he was being watched and turned. His remaining eye glinted as he recognised Tellius, though the older man spoke before he could.

'You asked to see me?'

'Asked? I yelled, didn't I? Until I was hoarse!' the prince retorted. 'No one tells me anything. Why am I being ignored?' He winced then and shook his head, humiliated by the note of pleading he had heard in his own voice.

'My apologies. I have been . . . a little busy,' Tellius said. 'Your wounds were very serious. Would you have had us bundle you into a coach, still bleeding through your bandages?'

Tellius entered the room and closed the door behind him, then half-sat on the edge of the bed. The prince made an attempt to appear unruffled, but he was weak and battered and terribly vulnerable. It hurt his pride to acknowledge it.

'I am well enough to travel now,' Louis said firmly. 'If you will send Lord Harkness to me, I will arrange a carriage and everything else.'

'Ah. Lord Harkness was escorted out of the city a week ago,' Tellius replied. 'Along with a surprisingly large number of Féal men and women.' Tellius smiled tightly, watching the prince as if he were a specimen pinned to a board. 'Your father's army began to move around that time – just when the news of your injuries would have reached him. Your Lord Harkness became then the citizen of a hostile foreign power, so we sent him packing. I could have executed him.'

'But you thought it might antagonise my father further,' Prince Louis said.

There was both spite and weariness in his expression, but it was hard to read him. Tellius thought he was probably still running a fever. The young man was certainly flushed and sweating. He made a note to ask Master Burroughs about it as he left.

'You know, Louis . . .'

'"Your Majesty" is still the correct term,' Louis said.

Tellius shrugged.

'Your Majesty, it takes time to get an army ready to move, did you know that? An army has to eat, so food and cups and bowls need to be stacked ready, with cauldrons and tables for all the preparation. Chopping vegetables just once to feed a thousand men is a massive undertaking. For ten thousand, can you imagine? It's like a town on the move. Eighty thousand? More?' Tellius was watching the prince's reaction to his words, reading him.

'What do I care?' Louis said, though Tellius hardly paused.

'When a march is called, all those things need to be packed away and put onto carts. Now, if an army has been in camp for weeks or months, it only gets worse. Some of the officers will be living in the nearest town, for example.' Tellius waved a hand. 'No matter, they can be summoned quickly enough. But new supplies still have to be purchased – and checked, in case the victuallers and merchants are putting sawdust in the casks instead of salt meat or millet. At the back of every army, there'll be someone selling food or weapons or even iron nails stolen from the blacksmith. So everything has to be checked and rechecked. It takes time, do you understand?'

'I don't understand why you are wasting *my* time with it,' Louis grated. 'I say again – what do I care?'

Tellius nodded.

'Exactly! I imagine such things are beneath the concern of a royal prince. My nephew would have been the same, I should think. For men like yourself, and of course your father, orders are simply given and then they are carried out.' Tellius scratched his nose in thought. 'Yet I cannot help wonder how your father's army could have been ready to move without the slightest delay. I had men in the hills, son, watching. Half a dozen of them, all keeping an eye on your father while you bribed and blackmailed the votes on the council.' Tellius paused a moment, smoothing away an old anger before he went on. 'I wondered then if you were a distraction, keeping our eyes on you while he crept closer. Yet he didn't move a step. He remained in camp, until those birds reached him with news of your injuries. And then – his entire army lurched into movement. It's almost as if your father was ready to attack before he had reason to, do you see? Can you explain that to me?'

Prince Louis looked steadily back. His father was coming and he had not forgotten the man peering at him was his enemy. His eye and his hand would heal eventually. He'd be lesser, but he'd live. If he betrayed his father, however, there would be no hiding place. His experience had shown his father's reach. After a time, Louis spoke clearly and slowly, as if to a child.

'My father is fighting a war to his north – against a more terrible foe than you will ever know. I imagine he was ready to march against them when the news came in.'

'So you think he will ignore that threat from the north to attack Darien?'

The prince gazed back without replying and Tellius shook his head and sighed.

'I wonder. Or could it be that your father intended all along to attack us, even before you were hurt? Does that sound possible? Or is he truly risking his army for personal vengeance? No, something is not right here. What could it be?'

The young man remained silent, understanding this was an interrogation of sorts. He flinched when Tellius leaned in and plumped his pillows for him.

'There. Comfortable? I wonder if you can help me, Your Highness. Your father knows you are in Darien. If his intention is to take revenge for the wounds you have suffered, he must know you might not survive his attack.'

'Doctor Burroughs! Help!' Prince Louis roared suddenly.

Tellius sat back and waited until the young man was certain no one would come.

'There's no need for that, Your Highness. You're in no danger, as it happens. There is no benefit to us in killing you. If your father reaches our walls and demands your safe return in exchange for peace, I'd look a little foolish if all I have is a corpse, wouldn't I? No, you are as safe as anyone in the city, at least until we know your father's intentions – and his battle strength. Yet it just eats away at me. I can see there is something off, but I can't work out what it is.'

Tellius tapped his lips with a forefinger as he stared at the younger man and thought.

'And still I wonder – for all the wealth and boundless power you must have at home, could you be tempted? You showed me you were a sharp operator, ruthless and quick to react. You know my word is good, Louis. What if I offered you a patent of nobility? For Darien to have not twelve, but thirteen families on the council? Freedom. A title, land, licences to continue your gambling houses. There is a new road being built into the east. You could have first pick of trading opportunities there. Despite your wounds, you are very young. With such a start, you could build an empire.'

'In return for betraying my father?' Louis said. His hand throbbed and he knew that a single eye would mean he would never again be feared as a swordsman. His father had taken a great deal from him and the offer was more tempting than Tellius could possibly know. He squeezed his eye shut and a tear escaped his lashes.

'Are you so afraid?' Tellius said softly. 'Is his army so terrible?'

'You don't know,' the prince murmured. 'Darien cannot

stand against him. I have seen it before. I have seen cities burn.' He leaned back against the bed and sobbed, for all he had lost, for all that was still to come.

Taeshin looked sceptically at the older man. Elias had white bristles on either side of his chin, with more grey at his temples. He looked wiry and strong, but he had to be fifty. For an unarmed man to beckon a Mazer swordsman half his age was peculiar enough to give Taeshin pause. The thought made him wonder what Marias would say about him taking up a blade in earnest. She had not minded the training sessions he'd overseen at the school. Taeshin had a skill and they had to eat. They could not live on the proceeds from the work she and the Fool did in the laundry, not and have Taeshin keep his pride, anyway. Yet there was a difference between training children and drawing a blade to kill. In class, he could smile on occasion, or congratulate one of the better pupils. In battle, he was as cold and different from that gentle teacher as the soul that had made him its slave two years before. He expected Elias to sense the danger as Taeshin stood before him with a bare blade in his hand, swishing it through the air. Men facing a living weapon tended to tense up, or back away, or tremble. Elias merely stood there.

'Well?' Elias said. 'Show me why he picked you. I already know why he picked me. Don't hold back – you will not touch me. Let's see what you have.'

Taeshin put aside all other distractions, including thoughts of Marias. He came forward at the careless speed of a master athlete, sparing nothing. In his youth, he could turn and drop and twist with no fear that his knees or back might 'go'. Instead, he just moved and expected everything to work. Which of course it did. There was a reason the Mazer steps were known as 'dances' and kept secret from their enemies. The patterns of muscle and balance were breathtaking, like a cat leaping, or a dog snapping a bird from the air as it whirred overhead. Taeshin attacked and Nancy's eyes went wide as she watched. She had stood alongside swordsmen before, but the only Shiang master she had seen was Tellius himself, in the midst of fire and smoke and chaos. She had not quite appreciated how beautiful danger could be.

Elias slid aside from the first lunge as if Taeshin waded through treacle. He *reached* into moments ahead and had begun to strain for the limits as soon as Taeshin drew the blade. Elias had seen Mazer swordsmen before and he knew how fast they were. His knack gave him time to think, but he always feared a possibility where all paths led to injury or death. Taeshin's advance seemed like a spider of moving shadows, with all the moves he might make branching out. Elias had time to see each final choice and lean or step away from it, though the young man was extraordinarily quick. Chances were, the rattlesnake speed would lose its edge in just a few years and be almost gone by forty. Yet Tellius had made a good choice in Taeshin.

Elias moved around the open space as Taeshin began to heat up. The younger man had good discipline, Elias noted to himself. Though a dozen attacks had failed, there was no wild flailing, no over-thinking himself into a panicky blow. Of course, all Elias had done was avoid the blade to that point. He believed it was probably true that you never truly knew a man until you fought him.

Elias moved into the attack. Instead of just avoiding the blade, he blocked Taeshin's striking arm over and over, stepping in or to the side, knocking him off-balance. Even then, Elias struck only lightly. He had no wish to break the young swordsman's confidence.

'Enough,' Elias said at last.

He was sweating by then and was pleased to see Taeshin was as well. The young man had a look of awe on his face, but he stepped out of range and sheathed his sword, then dropped to one knee with his head bowed.

'No, please, stand up. We don't . . .'

Elias found himself blushing. There was a beautiful woman watching their little display. He blushed deeper when he realised he had been trying to impress her like a little boy. Goddess, he was too old to be a fool!

'How did you do . . . that, whatever it was?' Taeshin said as he stood. 'I have never seen anything like it. Believe me, I did not hold back.'

Elias hesitated. His best protection lay in never explaining his knack to anyone. The more who knew and understood it, the greater the chance someone would find a way to counter what he could do. Yet Taeshin and Nancy were to be his companions against unknown enemies, in darkness. He had to trust them.

'I call it my knack. I look ahead, just a little, into future choices. I cannot see them until you decide to act, but when you do, I can see it coming – and move aside.' He thought for a moment. 'Master Taeshin, you are a superb swordsman. I can see why Tellius asked for you.'

The young man bowed again in reply, the instinctive response to one of great status and honour. Elias sighed and turned to Nancy, standing there. She was smiling in a way that made him uncomfortable, as if she were a cat watching mice playing. Had her hair moved in quite that way before? Elias wasn't sure. It shifted in tiny amounts, as if a breeze played around her. Her skin too seemed brighter than when he had seen her first, with the blood close to the surface. Had she been so beautiful before? It wasn't the kind of thing a man failed to notice, not usually. Elias sensed Taeshin's focus intensify as he became aware of her in turn.

'And you?' Elias said. In the presence of beauty, he ended up being gruff, his tone almost angry, as if she trespassed on a more serious conversation. 'What good are you?'

Nancy smiled and raised her hand. Elias felt his eyes grow wide.

Vic Deeds was exhausted. In his youth, he'd ridden a hundred miles once, for a bet. With a bit of experience and a different horse every twenty miles or so, it was the sort of thing any eighteen-year-old could do in a night. Recovery was swift for the young. Messengers who had to do it twice a week became astonishingly proficient – and needed hardly any time to sleep and eat before they could go out again.

Deeds surreptitiously rubbed the base of his spine, where the skin had been scoured away. He was not that man, or no longer that man. He could hardly believe the age of thirty had sneaked up on him, lying in wait like a damned ambush. Nor how his lower back had betrayed him, where once it had just worked. It was true he'd fallen hard a few times over the years. He'd been robbed and beaten up once or twice, yes. Those things all took a toll on a man. But what sort of milksop would he have been if he'd never lived the wild life? A milksop with a lower back that didn't feel as if a red-hot poker lay on it, he supposed.

He could see Bosin was actually asleep in the saddle, which was some comfort. Deeds took it as a win that he had remained awake longer than at least one of his companions. He enjoyed small contests of that sort with other men, though it produced better results when he didn't tell them. The big swordsman lolled as his horse ambled along and yet somehow never fell off. Hondo had said something about Bosin being brought up in the saddle by some nomadic herdsmen, but Deeds suspected it was one of those Shiang attempts at humour, the sort of wild tale told to a stranger that he was meant to swallow whole.

Hondo remained alert, of course. That was one thing Deeds had come to expect from the sword saint. Even from sleep, Hondo could roll from his blanket and come up with his hand on a sword hilt. It was as if his mind never fully relaxed. Deeds wondered why Hondo hadn't gone insane over the years, and then spent some time wondering if he had.

The road had been fairly empty for the last dozen miles heading into Darien. Deeds could feel his own weariness furring up his thoughts, but he didn't think they'd passed a cart for a while. He couldn't understand how there could be a trail of them snaking back from the city walls. It made no sense. Deeds reined in and Hondo trotted over to Bosin, slapping him lightly on the arm to bring him alert. All three of them came to a halt with the moon rising above the city. Hondo was in the process of turning back to ask a question when Deeds understood.

A line of stragglers wound around Darien – a ragged-looking trail of people. Some of them wrestled overladen carts over rough ground, while others were on foot, their heads bowed as they trudged on.

'The other gates must be blocked for them to make their way to this one,' Deeds said. It was irritating, to say the least. He'd ridden across hills and rivers, plains and forest. Like a man finally reaching a place to pee, his need had become exquisite with the city in sight. He wanted to go home. He wanted to collapse in a room at the Old Red Inn, with his pay safe in a pouch. Then he wanted to find Tellius and squeeze him a little. If something was important enough to summon him home, it would be worth paying for.

'Come on, gentlemen,' Deeds called to the others, then raised his voice to be heard for a hundred yards. 'Make way there. We are on city business. For the war effort. Make *way*, damn you!'

The crowd parted in confusion, responding to the man who sounded more important than they were. Deeds harangued anyone moving too slowly and made his way to the eastern gate, where the guards were watching his arrival with a jaundiced eye. Even they were not certain enough to challenge him, which is what Deeds had understood from the moment he'd read the letter calling him back. War broke the rules. It threw normal courtesies into the air. It was, in many ways, the way Deeds preferred to live.

'Gentlemen!' he greeted the guards with a wide smile. 'You'll want to send a runner to Speaker Tellius. Tell him the gunfighter has returned. He will find me in my room at the Old Red Inn.' Hondo cleared his throat and Deeds looked back at him. 'Very well. Tell him the sword saint has returned also.' Deeds looked further to where Bosin was watching him in the gloom, his features shadowed. 'And his ox.'

'Right you are, sir,' the guard replied. The name of Tellius had eased the last trace of suspicion from his face. It was just moments before a runner was racing off through the dark streets.

'Come, Masters Hondo and Bosin. My fortune and patent of nobility will not earn themselves.'

Deeds dug in his heels as the guards stepped aside and raised the barrier across the narrow gate. Hondo saw how each of them bowed his head respectfully as Deeds rode past. The man was infuriating, but he had brought Bosin back. That was all that mattered.

As Hondo left the walls behind, riding alongside Bosin, he found a sense of peace settling on him that he had not expected. He had ridden hard, with little chance for conversation. Even thought had been beyond him for most of the journey, as he'd concentrated on the road and speed and not breaking his neck. Yet the moment he passed through the gate, Hondo felt chains fall away. He was back in Darien. To his surprise, he was delighted about it.

The messenger who entered the exercise hall came to a sudden stop. He had been inside the room before. He'd smelled floor polish then, and seen the orange-stained wood, iron and leather that made up the exercise apparatus. He looked around in astonishment, trying to make what he could see match his previous memory.

A vaulting horse was still on fire and lying on its side. Scorch lines ran right up the walls and across the ceiling, like curling webs of soot. The floor itself had been torn up in a dozen places, with bricks of hardwood flung through the air. Many of those smouldered and the messenger would have called for help if his throat hadn't dried and his testicles weren't trying to creep back up.

Three people stood in the centre of the room, as if at points of a triangle. The only woman seemed to be smoking as she faced the others. The messenger cleared his throat, trying to wet his lips enough to speak. The noise caught their attention at least.

'Ah . . . urm . . . mm-mm. Speaker Tellius sent me to ask you to hold. There will be three more coming.'

'Well, I'm not sure we need them,' Elias said, watching the woman with the red hair. Nancy smiled at him. He'd seen stripes of fire across walls before, he realised. On the night he'd come into Darien to kill their king. The memory sat like a dark clot on his brain – and in the deep heart of it, he remembered the unnatural lash marks burning along the walls. He was convinced he faced the source of them. Yet it had been Deeds who'd fired the shots that killed the king. Whoever this woman was, she had not done half as much harm as Elias had.

Taeshin looked from one to the other of his companions. A man he could not hit and a woman who wielded threads of flame. He had rarely felt so overmatched in his life, but at least neither was a swordsman. Whoever else was to come, it could hardly get any worse.

17

Leader

The eastern sky had grown the pale grey of rabbit fur. Elias stared out of the window of the gymnasium, waiting. He knew Tellius expected him to lead the group. He was not yet sure he wanted to, or if they would truly accept him as leader. Trust took time to build, that was the problem. It was all very well being put in charge while they remained in Darien, but in the field, when Nancy wanted to advance, or Taeshin wanted them to follow? He was not sure.

'Where are these others?' Elias said in irritation to Taeshin.

The swordsman shrugged, continuing to test and adjust his armour. At his request, a set had been brought over from the training school. It seemed almost to be made of crow feathers, in long thin strips of enamelled iron. Taeshin seemed pleased with it and still moved well enough. Elias wondered how much he would slow down after a mile or so on foot in the dark. Unless Tellius delayed too long, of course. Then he, Taeshin and Nancy would be approaching the army of Féal as the sun rose again the next morning.

A flicker of movement in the gardens caught his eye. Elias leaned closer to the glass, cupping his hand around it to kill the reflections of the room. He *reached* from instinct and his expression hardened. His mouth became a thin line as he worked the catch and opened the window.

Jenny Post saw the movement and came forward. Perhaps she was pleased he could only look out and not grab her by the arm and shake her. She looked up defiantly, though the trials of her night showed. Her skirt was dark with mud or wet, while her hair had been tangled and knotted in some fall. She looked exhausted and his anger melted away in an instant.

'Come inside, would you, Jenny? The door is just over there.'

She nodded without saying a word and darted off. Nancy and Taeshin thought it would be the three warriors Tellius had promised, so they were surprised to see a little girl of twelve or fourteen, coming into her father's arms in a rush.

'You are frozen!' Elias said. 'Taeshin, would you have one of the palace servants fetch a brazier? My daughter is cold and wet.'

One was brought in moments, taken from a nearby office and carried in on poles. Jenny looked almost hungrily at the little glowing door and seated herself as close as she could. Her lips were bluish, Elias saw.

'Who is looking after your sister?' he asked her.

She took a deep breath, ready for the interrogation.

'Meneer Finch and his wife. She's safe there.'

Elias nodded.

'You know you can't come with me, love. All right? I won't take you where you'll see men killed. No father would.'

'You cannot stop me. Not even you, Dad. I can *reach*, with you, so I can protect you.'

233

The little girl folded her arms, but she was on the verge of tears even so. Before Elias could speak again, Nancy knelt by the brazier.

'Jenny, is it? My name is Nancy. How did you even find us, love?'

His daughter looked with round eyes at her father. She had no idea who the glamorous stranger was, of course. Elias nodded to her, replying when she would not.

'We can use the knack to find a path, sometimes. It's not much more than a feeling, but I've used it to hunt, all my life.'

'I want to go with my dad,' Jenny said in a rush. 'I'll keep him safe.'

'Nancy is going to come with me, Jen. You see? I won't be alone. This man too, in the armour. He is a great swordsman from the city of Shiang. They'll keep me safe.'

'Not like I can,' his daughter replied. 'I can *reach*, Dad, as well as you.'

Nancy smiled at the way the little girl jutted her jaw. It made her look obstinate and adorable at the same time. Jenny Post was pale and wet and probably starving, but she hadn't given an inch since entering the room. Nancy found she rather liked her.

A clatter of boots and men's voices broke the silent moment into pieces. Nancy rose to her feet from instinct, the better to run or attack.

Tellius entered first, looking twice at the girl and the brazier. Behind him came Deeds, Hondo and Bosin. They looked about as weary as Jenny Post before them, though Elias saw Tellius walked with a new bounce in his step. He noticed too how Taeshin's mouth fell open at the sight of the Shiang swordsmen. Elias bit the inside of his cheek as he wondered how this would affect the attack they had been planning. Two or three slipping into a camp at night might have been possible. Twice that number surely meant more chance of being spotted and caught – though if it came to that, perhaps they'd have a better chance to fight their way out.

'Meneer Elias,' Tellius called. 'I would like to introduce you to Master Hondo, sword saint of Shiang. Master Bosin, a swordsman with few equals. Meneer Deeds you know.'

Tellius said the last with a slight emphasis and Elias stood very still, accepting the omission of detail even as it rocked him. So Tellius knew Deeds had been his companion on that night four years before! Elias wondered if the old man knew Deeds was the one who had fired the shots that actually killed the old king. He set his own jaw, just as his daughter had done before. It didn't matter. Tellius was a cunning old devil, there was no doubt about that. If he preferred not to condemn Elias, well . . . Elias dipped his head, accepting. Perhaps there was a price to pay there, whether it was spoken aloud or not. For Deeds as well, though Elias saw no sign of contrition or greater wisdom in the young man's face as it beamed around and alighted on Nancy.

Deeds showed his teeth like a grinning wolf as he looked Nancy up and down. She was very aware of his scrutiny, though she kept her gaze on Tellius.

Elias leaned around to see past the swordsmen. If they were as good as Taeshin, he supposed he was pleased enough. Yet Deeds was a problem that had to be addressed.

'Meneer Deeds is a gunman,' Elias said, 'where we need

stealth and silence. I know how he can shoot, so I don't say it lightly, but he's no good to us, not tonight.'

'You'll need me if it goes wrong, though,' Deeds said.

There was no bluster in it, so Elias assumed Tellius had already promised the gunfighter a place. He nodded, digesting the new information.

'I won't go if you expect us to fail, Tellius. Now, my daughter is here, so I'll speak gently to you. If we are a diversion, or some part of a greater plan, I will come back, alone if I have to – and I will speak to you again. Do you understand what I mean?'

'He means he'll kill you,' Jenny Post said, with satisfaction.

Tellius looked from one to the other, seeing the family resemblance in the jaw.

'I understand. And the plan is the same. You enter the camp with Taeshin – or Master Hondo might be a better choice. Nancy alongside you. She is there in case it goes wrong. She can break you out. Deeds, Bosin, perhaps Taeshin can wait in support. If you are pursued, they will be vital. It will not matter then if Deeds lights them up.'

'I should take Patchwork,' Bosin said.

Tellius looked sharply at him, sensing the difference in the man. He shook his head.

'The Sallet Greens are part of the defence of the city. If you . . . when you . . . come back, you are welcome to use the one called Patchwork. You're the best I've seen in that thing, anyway.'

'You shouldn't have tested anyone else,' Bosin grumbled. 'Patchwork is mine.'

'Lady Sallet lent the suit to you. It is not yours . . . Are you all right, Master Bosin? You seem less ... less ...' Tellius struggled to find a way to describe what he was seeing.

'Master Bosin is just weary,' Hondo broke in. 'We have ridden hundreds of miles and gone without sleep. We should get at least a few hours now.'

'We have to leave,' Elias said. He disliked being rushed and there were too many new things to take in. It was making him feel overwhelmed. 'If the army of Féal is moving twenty to twenty-five miles a day, they will arrive in range of Darien tomorrow morning. We have to get going so we can intercept them before the sun rises again – and we do not know how long it will take once we are in the camp. If you can doze in the saddle, you should. I cannot wait any longer.' He made a growling sound in his throat. 'I don't like this!' he said to Tellius. 'It is too rushed.'

'Believe me, I wish we had a week, or six months! But we close the gates tonight. Either you stop the army, or you fall back to Darien. We'll drop ropes for you from the walls and bring you up if the gates are closed. Stay alive and come home, all of you.'

Elias nodded. He turned back to his daughter.

'You see, Jen? I'm not alone. These people will keep me alive and I'll come back to you when it's over. Shall I get you something from the markets, then? Do you think your sister would like another doll?'

'I want to come with you!' she said, her eyes filling with tears. Nancy moved to pick her up and the girl stepped away from her embrace, leaving her holding air.

'Nancy,' Elias said. 'Would you show my daughter why you were asked to come here this evening?'

Nancy stood up straight and snapped her hand at the far wall. A long tendril of gold lashed out from her, like a whip uncoiling. It was followed by threads in the air, alive and so hot that a warm wind washed over them. Jenny Post gaped in awe at the beautiful woman who had such power. Bosin had a very similar expression, though Elias noted Deeds had gone a sickly shade of pale. Perhaps he too remembered the lash marks on the walls of the palace, years before. Deeds and Elias had very nearly crossed paths with Nancy. Elias wondered if she knew. He leaned down and gave his daughter a hug.

'There, love. Do you see?'

She nodded and Tellius came over.

'I have a lady friend who would be happy to look after you while your father is away,' he said.

Elias stiffened and Tellius felt his eyes widen, suddenly aware of his mistake. He let go of the little girl's arm and held up empty palms.

'As a guest, Meneer Elias. Not a hostage.'

The man had torn the city apart and walked through the Aeris legion to get his daughters back the first time. Even the suggestion that they might be held against their will was not something Tellius wanted to revisit. Elias nodded to him, accepting the words as he looked to his daughter.

'I'll come back here tomorrow, Jen, to take you home. All right? You'll be safe.'

Elias knew Tellius well enough to understand he didn't have to mention the alternative. If he didn't come back, Tellius would return her to Wyburn. Any man could die in defence of his people. He was not immune.

He took his daughter's hands in his. She began to sob softly, understanding that it was an ending. Perhaps it did have to be said, after all.

'If I don't come back, love, you'll live with the Finches, all right? They have a daughter of their own and they always wanted more. They'll look after both of you.'

'I don't want that! I don't want you to go,' she said.

He smiled and kissed her cheek before drawing her into an embrace so tight it was hard for either of them to breathe.

'Now don't I always come back for you?' he said tightly. She nodded. 'These are my people, Jen. I can't just sit it out and see them slaughtered, not if I have a chance to do something about it.'

Tellius cleared his throat softly.

'Time to go,' he said. 'Good luck, all of you.'

King Jean Bricland came awake with a surge of energy, rolling out of the low camp bed and onto his front to lever himself up and down twenty times. When he'd finished, he was slightly flushed and the camp was noticeably busier all around him. A servant stood close by with a steaming cup of tea, while another waited to assist him with bathing. In all, four men and two startlingly attractive young women waited to play a part in his rising. The sky was clear and it looked to be a good day ahead. He did not look at the corner of the tent where his shadow had curled up to sleep. On some mornings, she seemed to come awake an hour or so after him, so that, for a while, he was alone and free of her whispering. He grimaced as he caught a sense of movement, like a cat stretching.

See how they watch you? They are all afraid, even your whores.

'And right to be,' he said, smiling. The man ready to hand him his tea made no acknowledgement. He had served the king long enough to be wary of responding to any comment not clearly aimed at him.

Where is your son, though? What did you do to Louis to keep him from you?

'I did exactly what I had to do. I taught him a lesson he will not forget – as long as he looks in a mirror!' King Jean snapped. All the servants froze and he heard a faint tinkling as the one carrying his tea trembled the cup against a saucer. He looked in reproach to the corner where the shadow lay. 'There. See what you made me do. I am frightening the staff.'

'Your Majesty?' the one with the tea ventured.

The king could almost smell his fear, like a sourness in the air around him. He took the tea to end the rattle of china, waving the man out of his presence.

'Bring me a pot, Tom, would you? I need to move my bowels. I am a little congested, though the tea will help. Have the results inspected as well. I have been feeling less than my usual self. No doubt it is the discomforts of camp.'

He spoke in a rattle of words, clearly aimed at the servants scuttling to fulfil his every need. He did not want them to think he had gone mad. As he drank the tea and peered at the leaves clustered in the bottom of the cup, he glared sideways at the shadow. She knew he was watching, of course. She always had, ever since she had followed him out of the priest's cave.

By the time he strode out into the sun, another hour had passed and the camp was beginning to pack up, ready to march. Word had taken wing in the ranks that they would see the city of Darien the following morning. One hard march, a night's rest and then an attack. As King Jean looked around him, he saw only eagerness and energy. His legions were used to victory. He was content for a moment just to stand and breathe it in. First the violence, then mercy for the survivors. After that, he would rebuild Darien. If Louis had told its charms aright, he might make it a southern capital after it had been bled clean. That was what the healers always said. A wound filled with corruption could be cut deeper and bled clean. Yes, it was a fine image for Darien.

Lord Harkness had seen the king leave his tents. They were already being taken down behind him, part of the mass rise and fall of construction that took place every night. It might have been astonishing to see what five or ten thousand men given a simple task could do, both quickly and efficiently. Yet it had become unremarkable over time. As Harkness approached the king, servants unfolded a table and chairs. Still more unrolled maps and placed cones of lead to hold them against any errant breeze.

King Jean clapped his hands together, ready for whatever the day would bring. Rather than sit, he leaned over the table, staring down at a map of the land ahead that made him feel like a bird flying far above.

'This is excellent work, Harkness,' he said.

The older man fussed with his papers, delighted at even a little praise.

'Your son and I had the city paced out and recorded,' he said. 'I think it's about as accurate as anything they have themselves. You see the docks there? I gave those lads a gold piece each. They spent a whole night on the river, with wires and measuring sticks. I thought the city guards would arrest them, but they brought it all back. This is the result.'

'Very good. Though we have to get *inside* the walls before any of it is useful. Most of it, I will burn. You still think they'll pull back behind the gates? I would rather they came out to meet us in the field, like the Savoyards. My God, do you remember them?'

'Of course, my lord. That was a fine campaign.'

The Savoyards had fought with extraordinary fervour to defend their land. Just a decade later, they were part of the new nation and seemed to have accepted it. Of course, barely a fifth of them remained. King Jean had kept the women alive and sent in regiments of his army to breed new soldiers. There had been squalling babies everywhere in the new Savoy territory, so he'd heard. One or two had been killed by their mothers, but on the whole, women everywhere were a forgiving tribe.

'Who knows, you might become a father again when Darien falls, eh? Would you like that, Harkness? To go in with the winning regiments? Or are you too old for such fun and games these days?'

'I fear I am, Your Majesty, though my son is a young ram who would be delighted at such an opportunity. If you wish to honour my service, you could give him a pass?'

King Jean waved a hand in acceptance, aware of the shadow smirking as she crawled into view. His mood darkened in her presence and Harkness was experienced enough to sense the change. He spread another map on top of the first. This one was to a different scale and showed the land around the city walls of Darien. The hills were marked in concentric bands, tight together to show a steep slope. King Jean had peered at every part of it before, though it was still a thing of marvellous enterprise. In its own way, the map was as impressive as one of his siege engines and at least as valuable. At that scale, he could see the coils of the river as it made its way out of Darien to the sea. King Jean prodded the river entrance.

'How will they know when to attack?'

Lord Harkness smiled, unsure if it was a joke or not.

'I imagine they will hear, Your Majesty. As soon as the gunfire begins, we will hit them where they are weakest.'

The two men spoke for a few minutes, discussing the exact formations and deployment of forces. It was looking good.

'I think I'll walk amongst the men today, Harkness. It inspires them to have me alongside, enduring the blisters and the hardships.'

'They will be delighted, I am certain,' Lord Harkness replied, though his heart sank.

You fool. All you can do is make them afraid. You are not even man enough to tell me what you did to Louis.

'He served his purpose,' King Jean hissed at the shadow.

Harkness remained very still, his eyes slightly glassy. He had never been quite certain how to respond to the king's odd utterances, so he simply ignored them.

'On the other hand, perhaps I will ride, after all. I want to keep my horse fit for tomorrow.'

'Of course, Your Majesty, I will have Ox-head saddled and brought up to you.'

Rather than leave, the older man hesitated. King Jean

raised his eyes briefly, suspecting he knew what the lord would ask. He wasn't disappointed.

'May I enquire as to the . . . health of your son, Prince Louis, Your Majesty? He was a most agreeable colleague and I was upset to hear of his injuries.'

'He remains in the city, Lord Harkness. When we have strung up their council by their own entrails, when we have cut down their men and their children and the old women – and herded the young women ready for the breeding camps – I'll find him and see if he still has the will to rule. Do not lose too much sleep over Louis, Lord Harkness. He was always a difficult son.'

'Of course, Your Majesty.'

Look out. One comes to kill you.

The king reacted much faster than the lord bowing his way backwards. From slightly behind him, King Jean heard running steps. He turned and barely blocked the knife hammered down at him. His arm rose under the attacker's armpit and, for a second, they were close enough for him to feel the bristles on the other's cheek.

With a wrench, Jean Brieland took hold of the man's wrist and twisted until it broke. When he was a young fellow of twenty, he'd taken work as a strongman in a travelling show. He had not lost the crushing power that continued to bend the man's arm though he shrieked and tried to pull away, made pitiful and weak by pain. The king maintained his grip on the broken wrist, controlling him with it.

'I don't know you, do I?' he said to the man.

The man shook his head, weeping and enraged.

'You took my wife, my daughters . . .'

'Ah, well. I imagine we had more use for them than you did. Still, where were you, eh? When was this?'

When the man did not reply immediately, the king gave a jerk to his broken wrist and laid a second hand on the outer elbow, locking it straight. He began to apply pressure there, jamming his thumb into the joint.

'Dalston!' the man said through hissing pain. 'Your men came there and killed everyone!'

'No . . . I don't remember a Dalston. Can you point in the right direction? With your other arm?'

Lord Harkness looked away. He had witnessed the same cruelty any number of times and it still turned his stomach. He knew the king enjoyed it to a degree that was somehow obscene.

In desperation, the man with the broken arm tried to point to his home village, anything to stop the agony being visited upon him.

'And what is your name?' King Jean said with another twist.

The man sobbed.

'Walter,' he said through clenched teeth. He wanted to find courage enough to spit in the king's face, Harkness saw. Yet Jean Brieland never quite gave him enough time between bouts of agony that left him gasping.

'I don't understand, Walter, how you escaped. If my soldiers killed all the men, as you say. Where were you?'

As the man sobbed and sagged to his knees, Harkness saw they had been silently surrounded by grim soldiers of the king's personal guard. They were ashen, as well they might be. Harkness saw the rage that lay under the light tone as the king twisted the arm enough to make him scream.

'Please! Please stop!'

'Then tell me how my men missed you!' the king said, as if Walter was the one being difficult.

'I was in the woods when they came. I ran away.'

'You left your wife? You left your children?'

'Y-yes.'

'That is a shameful thing, Walter. Isn't it?'

The man nodded, with his eyes shut. He was already thin and worn. The pain made him pale as paper and so weary he seemed to be almost asleep or close to passing out. The king shook him until he was a little more alert.

'There. A man who would leave his wife and girls for soldiers. What? Did you think you'd find your manhood here? By attacking me? You are not the first, Walter, believe me. Now I want you to see something before I pronounce judgement on you. Step forward, Captain Nicholls, would you?'

The guard captain bowed his head, resignation already deep in him, like claws. As the king watched, the man removed his helmet and placed it under one arm.

'Captain Nicholls, you have failed in your duty.'

'Yes, Your Majesty.'

'Hand your sword and helmet to your second in command.'

'I . . . would like to ask for mercy, Your Majesty, in recognition of my long service to you.'

King Jean waited until the man had been disarmed before he replied.

'Your request is denied. Bind him and put him on his knees.'

It was the second in command who accepted the task,

246

kicking hard at the back of his captain's legs. Rope was produced and once again Captain Nicholls spoke up.

'I have served you for ten years, Your Majesty. I ask for mercy.'

'Do you see how he shows no fear, Walter?' King Jean said to the one whose arm he still twisted. 'Captain Nicholls here would not have run!' He thought for a moment, licking the tip of his tongue over his upper lip. 'So his courage redeems him. Stand up, Captain Nicholls. You are demoted to second in command of your troop. Acknowledge your new officer, sir!'

The ex-captain climbed to his feet and stood with relief clear on his face as he saluted and was saluted in turn.

'Courage, Walter, do you see?' King Jean said more gently. 'It does not mean a rash gesture, or waving a knife about! It is endurance – of hard work, of building a country, of working for something to last beyond you. Do you see? Your women will bear children – and those children will call me king. I hope that is a comfort to you.'

Let me have him.

'Oh, very well,' King Jean said.

He released the still-sobbing Walter and stood back. No one else saw the shadow creep across the ground like spreading oil, nor how she wound slowly round one of the man's legs. Walter seemed to feel the touch, though. King Jean watched in fascination as the man's expression became confused and fearful, looking this way and that as the shadow climbed him, higher and higher, until a dark arm or leg coiled right round his throat. She squeezed. He clawed madly at himself, of course, though one hand flapped uselessly. Yet there was nothing to grip, nothing thicker than the air he could not draw in. The man grew dark with it and then blue-grey as his heart failed. He fell inert, with dead eyes staring.

'Go back to your duties, all of you,' King Jean said. 'Do I need to say I will not be so merciful again, Nicholls?'

The man who had risen from bed that morning as a captain knelt on the turf, sickened and disturbed by the strange death he had witnessed, that had almost been his own.

'No, Your Majesty.'

'Then pack up the camp. I want to cover some distance today. I feel the blood coursing in me, sir! For all that lies ahead!'

18

Assault

'Not yet,' Elias said again, as Deeds turned to him in the gloom. It might have appalled him how easily he'd remembered the companionship of the young gunman. Neither of them had mentioned their previous association aloud, but there had still been an instant familiarity in the shared memories. They had history. It was a history filled with blood and death, but perhaps that wasn't a disadvantage on that particular night.

The scouts had taken them to within three miles or so of the Féal army, then left them in a valley between two rising fields, with only the setting sun for company. Horses had been hobbled there to wait for dawn, just another blot of sleeping animals in the darkness.

Elias and the others had settled down to wait for the night to deepen, until stars were visible and no hidden Féal watcher would see them moving. When they were nothing more than shadows, he took point on their slender column, leading them closer as quietly and quickly as they could go. A hard day's ride out of Darien, the land was farmed there, with fields and patches of woodland of the sort Elias knew well. He'd led them through green wheat and barley, dropping flat at the slightest sound.

They'd gone slowly enough, willing to let time spool

away as the night grew cold. Elias had halted at last in a stand of oak and birch, near the crest of a small rise. Some farmers left them for the Goddess, as tribute, or just because it was hard to plough a hill. In truth, the spot was barely higher than the walls of the Féal camp that lay ahead of them. The six of them lay on black and frozen leaves, staring at the enemy for the first time.

That close, they could hear the army of Féal. So many men in one place made a rustling susurration, an evening murmur. Like the sea almost, if the sea contained laughter and orders and iron. There were lights around the perimeter and dotted throughout the camp, casting pools of light. It was not as dark as anyone had imagined. Along the edges were massive embankments where pole-torches burned, lighting up guards on watch. As Elias stared into the distance, he saw the last baskets being filled with earth and stones dug from the ground, then raised to the crest of a wall. Fresh earth was packed in over that solid core and, in just a short time, something like a defensive fortress was complete. Guards took watch on actual gates, assembled from great beams brought forward and bolted together.

'Tellius was right,' Deeds said in awe. 'I can't imagine assaulting that with an army. How would you even get in?'

'Keep your voice down, Deeds,' Elias said, as he had a dozen times before. Some men didn't seem to understand caution. He recalled Deeds' love of risk and suspected it had survived all his trials since. The man was dangerous to know, but he shot like the devil. Elias only hoped he wouldn't get them all killed.

Elias turned back and the rest of them huddled close. Even so, he kept his voice low.

'I can't see a way to scout the camp. They've built their banks on flat ground, with nothing much overlooking them, so until we breach the gate, we don't know what we'll face. Our only advantage is that they don't know we are here. That means Deeds and Nancy are the last resort. If they are forced to attack, the noise and light will bring the whole army running. So . . . Hondo, Bosin, Taeshin? You are with me. Deeds and Nancy? Behind us. Once we're through the gate, find a good spot and hide yourselves. Under a cart, or . . . you'll know it when you see it.'

'That camp is huge,' Nancy said. Her voice was calm, almost languorous. It put Deeds in mind of long, sunny afternoons in bed with a lover. He smiled at her. She ignored him. 'Deeds and I should stay with you as long as we can, or we'll be out of range when you need us.'

Elias nodded. The truth was, there was no way to make proper preparations for something they'd never seen. Tellius had chosen three of them and accepted three more with great pleasure. Elias had to hope the old man's judgement was sound.

'Use your common sense,' he said to her. 'But Deeds, if you trip and fire a shot or rouse the camp before we have found the king, I will come back and kill you myself, if I have to wade through them all to do it. Understand?'

'Yes,' Deeds said.

'Yes, "boss",' Elias added.

'Yes, boss.'

'How are we going to get through the gate?' Nancy asked.

Deeds smiled again, but it was a darker expression, with memory in it.

'I imagine Elias will kill the guards,' he said.

'All right, but then what? If they have watchers on the embankments – and they will – the alarm will be raised the moment we attack.'

Hondo cleared his throat and the others turned to him in the darkness.

'I can't see how to do it. Even if we can kill the guards we see, there will be others, as the lady has said.'

'As "Nancy" has said,' Nancy interrupted.

Hondo inclined his head to her.

'Bosin and I might scale the embankment and take down anyone up there, but the problem lies in that lack of knowledge. Do they have guns? If they do, will they fire them in the camp? The darkness could help us there. Yet we don't even know where this king lays his head, or if he is with his main force!'

'I haven't come this far just to leave,' Elias said gruffly.

'Nor have any of us,' Hondo replied. 'I just can't see . . .'

'If we have to, we'll break the perimeter and rush them,' Elias added.

Hondo blinked unseen in the dark, shaking his head.

'Tellius appointed you leader, sir, but . . .' He struggled to find words that would not undermine Elias. 'Our advantage lies in stealth, as you have said. Six cannot rush an army.'

'I am not being paid enough for that, anyway!' Deeds broke in. 'And the horses are at least three miles to the south – if we can find them at all. So don't be expecting me to run that far with the army of Féal on my heels.' He kept some of his usual wry tone, but Deeds felt the beginning of a sick sense of worry building. This group could punch their way through a door easily enough. Yet this had all the marks of a plan thrown together in too little time, against an unknown enemy.

'For now, we stay here,' Elias said. 'See how often they change the watch, what patterns they walk. We'll wait as long as we can, let as many as possible fall asleep. I want them cold and groggy and slow in the small hours. It's true we don't know what defences they have. So I need you to be sharp. Rest. Sleep if you can. I will take first watch. When the camp is quiet, we'll go in.'

They settled back in the darkness, making themselves comfortable as best they could.

'Then we come running right back out again, with an army after us,' Deeds muttered.

'Be quiet,' Elias replied.

Silence fell again.

'Six of us,' Deeds said after a time. 'None like us.'

'Shut up, Deeds,' Bosin rumbled.

No one else spoke as the stars turned overhead.

Taeshin had listened to the others argue, hardly able to believe how they bickered and sniped at one another. Elias was the leader. It was inconceivable to have the other five discuss orders, all while the enemy sat in front of them! Warriors did as they were told! Taeshin shook his head in the darkness. Even Master Hondo had questioned the plans. Master Hondo, the actual sword saint! Taeshin felt only awe in his presence. They all seemed to know what to do, while he could only gaze on the camp walls with a sense of dread.

Things had been simpler in Shiang. Or they had seemed so. Taeshin missed the peace and calm of never having to think for himself. It was certainly more restful than the terrible anxiety he felt at that moment. He wondered what Marias was doing and found to his surprise that he missed her. The Fool, too, came into his thoughts, whistling away like a kettle as he worked with steaming cloths and the huge cauldrons of the laundry. Just a little distance made Taeshin long to hear Marias laugh once again. He realised it had been a while since the last time.

Hondo came awake as Taeshin touched his arm. He, Bosin and Deeds had been exhausted. How long had he been asleep? He felt refreshed even as he glanced at the stars and saw it had been a few hours, perhaps a quarter turn. Still, it could mean the difference between being fast enough and getting killed. Hondo was some way off being a young man. He knew having slept might save his life, but he still tried to conceal his yawn and slight confusion, waiting for his mind to focus.

Bosin was awake and crouching at his side, which was comforting. Hondo didn't know if the big man had slept at all, but it was hard to imagine an enemy getting past Bosin. Hondo shook his head. The man was no longer a faithful hound. He had grown used to knowing him in a particular way, to the point where Hondo had half-forgotten how much the old Bosin had annoyed him. He sent up a silent prayer that the one at his side would be a gentler mixture of parts.

'Are we going?' Hondo whispered.

His eyes had adjusted well to the starlight and he saw Bosin dip his head. Hondo took a deep breath and rose to his feet. He felt stiff and sore from sleeping on broken ground, but he gave no sign of that. A sword saint was a leader of men. The others would look to him to show confidence, no matter how poor an enterprise this was. Hondo had some idea of what his companions could do. Yet an army faced them, an army with unknown numbers and hidden strengths. He and the other five were just a single thrust of a blade. If that blow were turned, the night would go bad very quickly. He clenched his jaw, knowing the others could not see.

Elias waited until they were all on their feet. He reached out and took hold of coats and jackets, pulling them in so his voice didn't have to carry further.

'Stay away from light as best you can. I will take the guards on the gate. Hondo and Bosin will clear any watchers on the crest. If they are there. When we get inside, two groups. Taeshin, Bosin, Hondo with me. Nancy and Deeds a dozen paces behind, moving with us.' He exchanged a glance with Nancy as she nodded. 'Be prepared to change plan, depending on what we face. I want quick thinking, understood? Good. Limited communication when we're inside, unless it's a low whistle – and then only in an emergency. Kill silently, or not at all.' Elias recalled the command tent of the old Aeris legion and frowned in memory. 'We're looking for any large structure, one that is well guarded. If it goes wrong, if the alarm goes up, be ready to get out – over the embankment, or cut your way past a gate. Then scatter. You all know where the horses are waiting. Keep the North Star behind you and head south. Don't try and fight when you can cut and run. Understood?'

'I have a question,' Deeds said.

'He did not ask for questions,' Taeshin snapped.

Deeds looked at the swordsman in surprise.

'Oh, really? Well, you know what you . . .'

Elias clapped Deeds on the shoulder, interrupting whatever he had been about to say. The group broke up as if that was the signal, spreading out as they stalked down the slight slope, the sleeping camp before them.

Elias *reached* as he went, catching shadows of movement in the darkness. He remembered how he'd found it calming to close his eyes in Darien, to move without distractions. There were parts of him that flinched from the violence of that day, but to his surprise, he felt a great peace settle. There was no ambiguity in him that night, no sense of doing evil because a madman had his daughters. The king of Féal was marching a huge army south towards Darien. Peace was not his aim. Elias felt a building surge of excitement, then anger at himself. By the Goddess, he should have been able to resist the young man's call to war! He was no guiltless maniac, not like Deeds. Yet as he ran, he thought perhaps, just perhaps, he had been made for bloody work. It was said no one knew his fate, but if the Goddess had ever worked through Elias, it would be as an instrument of vengeance. Elias dipped his chin as he ran, like a boxer avoiding the knockout punch. He could be a destroyer, for one more night.

It was strange to use the tricks of hunting as he approached the gate, hunched low to make himself small. The torches cast a pool of light perhaps two dozen paces from one side to the other. Beyond that wind-blown light lay darkness and those coming in fast. To reach the pair standing on guard, shifting lightly from foot to foot, Elias had to sprint.

Nancy timed it well, he saw. Tellius had said to rely on her and there she was. She and Deeds had looped around, making noise that subtly drew the attention of the guards. Elias saw one nudge the other alert, then both soldiers stiffened at the sight of a woman dragging what seemed to be an unconscious man.

Nancy waved them over, looking desperate. It was a weak ploy, but it didn't have to work. All that mattered was that both men were watching Nancy as Elias came out of the darkness and crossed the pool of light. They sensed him and began to turn, but it was far too late by then. Nancy saw Elias held only a small skinning knife, but the guards seemed to deflate as he passed, sagging forward.

Elias lowered them to the ground, *reaching* hard as he looked for the first alarm, or some shout of warning. At the same time, Hondo leaped at the slope. The angle was designed to be too steep for anyone to climb, but the sword saint was like a mountain goat and gained the top in a skittering sideways movement. There was the muffled sound of a struggle and the body of a stranger came sliding down the outer slope, wedging against one of the basket outlines.

Elias gestured to Bosin and Taeshin. Neither of them had tried to get up the outer slope, not when they were close enough to see it. Bosin had diverted to stand beside Elias instead and Taeshin had gone with him. The gate was still shut, but Elias heard the soft clunk of levers and Hondo appeared. For all its appearance of massive strength, a marching camp was not secure. They stepped through a narrow gap, while behind them, Deeds leaped up. He and Nancy followed them in, all nervous as cats. Deeds had his guns out, Elias saw. He could not curse him when silence was the difference between success and failure.

The camp lay in neat lines ahead, like city streets. Hundreds of pale tent shapes could be seen before night and distance swallowed them. Carts and tethered draught animals had been made to form roads, ready for their owners to pack them up in the morning. The whole place was well ordered, but there was no sign of any general's pavilion.

Elias and the others moved silently, trying to stay close to the tents and aware of every snore and grumbling sleeper. Elias *reached* as he went, seeing a sleeping man come out to empty his bladder before they stumbled across him. The six of them waited in a line of shadow while he peed onto the ground. There were toilet pits along the edges of the camp and so the man was breaking a rule. Elias waited for him to go back inside and then a minute longer, until he had gone back to sleep. Silence and cold ached in the delay.

The further they went from the gate and the outer perimeter, the more danger seemed to shriek in Elias' ears. The camp was huge and he saw how easy it would be to get lost in the middle of thousands of tents. He began to count rows just to keep a sense of how far they had come. He had just passed forty when the landscape changed ahead. Elias dropped to a crouch once again and looked over his shoulder to see Nancy and Deeds were still back there. Plans changed and he hadn't appreciated the sheer size of the camp on first approach. They were already a long way from the edges. Troubled, he reached out and collected a handful of dust, letting it trickle through his fingers and sending a prayer they would come through.

His throat was dry and he wondered if any of them had brought a flask. Hondo or Taeshin, probably. Someone had to get out, obviously, to carry word back to Tellius. Elias waited for his heart and whirling thoughts to settle and grow calm. He was a hunter first – and he had learned to wait and listen on lonely hillsides. He'd been hunted himself once, when a female bear had caught his scent and tracked him for miles of deep forest. Elias remembered the feeling very well. Something was wrong and all his instincts kept him perfectly still.

Elias could hear the sigh of leather and cloth as the other five shifted uncomfortably, waiting for him to move or give new orders. He could not make sense of what he was seeing, nor the sudden sense of dread that gripped him still. White tents were visible on both sides, seeming to run around the perimeter of a darker heart. It looked almost like open ground and he wondered if the army kept a space for meals, or weapons drill. If it was that last, he had to have reached the centre. Yet there was something odd about the ground ahead. Only the dull gleam of starlight lit the field as Elias slowly turned his head back and forth, using his peripheral vision to pick up details in the darkness. He could not smother the sense of panic that had flared in him. He imagined suddenly running in, straining his knack to see what would happen. The results made him pull in a sharp breath. Shaken, he turned to Hondo at his back.

'We need to go around this dark patch. Tell the others. No one is to go near it. I will take a route left. Stay close.'

'What if the king has his tent in the centre?' Hondo whispered, his lips so close to Elias' ear that they touched the cold skin.

'Then we cannot reach him. Do you know the Sallet Greens?' Elias had seen them defend the city, the armoured artefacts that were the most powerful defenders of the city.

To his surprise, Hondo nodded.

'There are more . . .' Elias halted. 'Oh, no . . .'

Ahead of him, shapes had begun to move, unfolding in the darkness. Line by line, hundreds of black shells roused from stillness. They rose in creaking ranks, darker than night and gleaming under the stars. Elias swallowed. A dog barked nearby and a low horn wail began to sound over the camp. Someone had found the dead guards.

'Fall back,' Elias said aloud. His words stuttered as he *reached*, looking for threat all around. 'These are Sallet Greens . . . blacks.'

He saw Nancy coming forward and began to move to stop her.

'Let me through,' she said.

He heard the snap of the slim box shutting and she was brimful of something that made the air crackle as she came past. Elias gaped at what would happen, in time to turn away before she lit the night with a huge ball of flame that cracked the air and vanished. Those who had been staring into the dark heart of the Féal camp were left reeling and blind.

Men began shouting panicky questions all around them, while officers sprang up from their blankets and added swearing and orders to the sudden tumult. More alarm horns sounded. Elias watched in awe as Nancy poured out threads of light in a ball around her. They lit the lines of black-armoured figures moving like oil, spearing through them. She had spent whatever she'd taken from the Sallet Stone carefully before. He realised she was letting it roar out then, as if there was an infinite supply.

On either side of her, more of the creatures lurched into life, revealed by flashes and strikes. They sighted on Nancy as the threat and clustered around her, bounding with extraordinary speed. The dark core of the camp stretched away into the night and Elias could not see any end to them. Yet as they reached Nancy, as she passed through them, they fell back like insect husks, drained and twitching. For all their fearsome strength and power, they were her perfect prey. She was a wasp to them and they strengthened her as she killed. Again and again the ball of light cracked into existence, incinerating anything caught within. Elias could smell burned meat and hair and he realised he had hesitated for too long. If he went in support of Nancy, he and the others would be lost in that maelstrom, with weapons that would have little effect against armoured warriors. Instead, he whistled for the others to follow and raced down a lane between tents.

'Are we getting out? What about Nancy?' Deeds said from just behind him. The three Shiang swordsmen were in his wake with swords drawn like an armoured charge.

Elias felt completely out of his depth. The camp was waking up. Men were grabbing weapons and armour and he still had not seen . . . He caught a glimpse of a tent higher than those around it.

'Over there!' He pointed. 'One chance and then we run. Nancy can catch up.'

Even as he spoke, a wave of hot air passed over the five men. Nancy was still going forward, only slightly behind and to one side of them as she drove a molten line through the very centre of the camp. The enemy could not contain her if she kept moving, Elias told himself.

Coming up alongside as they ran, Deeds began to shoot anyone in their path. Elias made no move to stop him, not when it was easier to send men leaping back from gunfire than to kill them one by one. His way was too slow and the truth was, men didn't fear a lone hunter with a knife, not the way they should have.

'Where is the closest gate?' Deeds yelled over the sound of his own guns. They were still using the explosions of light to navigate through the camp, though a deeper darkness returned whenever Deeds reloaded or Nancy paused to draw from the armoured Féal blacks. With Deeds shooting two pistols, Elias felt blind and deafened.

'We are not heading to the gate,' he called over his shoulder. 'That tent, there. It has to be the king. We've come too far and we're too close not to try for it. Stay on my shoulder.'

'You said we should get out if the alarm was raised,' Deeds said. In the same moment, he picked off two soldiers coming at Hondo with raised swords.

Elias heard only part of the words. He scowled.

'One chance, Deeds, to end it all. Stay with me, or I will kill you myself.'

Whatever Deeds said in reply was lost as Nancy lit the night in a crack of heat that shook the ground. Bosin and Taeshin had a slight edge over Hondo in speed as they raced forward, all of them heading for the single point of white canvas that had been revealed, looming above the rest. If it turned out to be a weapon store, Elias would curse himself for bad judgement, but he hadn't come so far just to run. With his eyes closed, he looked into moments ahead, stepping through or over dying men. One thing about Hondo and Bosin, they were born killers. They made Taeshin look like a farmer with a family heirloom.

Elias flinched.

'Guns!' he shouted, then cursed under his breath. He could step aside from shots he could see coming. The others could not. If the army of Féal included gun regiments, massed fire lay ahead – perhaps more than even he could avoid. Elias watched safe spaces appear and wink out as he moved. Hondo grunted as he was struck, spun round and slowed as his armour took the brunt. Taeshin gaped at him and swallowed.

Darkness and the distraction Nancy had created saved them. Anyone aiming weapons was looking in the direction of the balls of white threads rolling through their armoured section, not at five men running in silence through the lines of tents, sprinting past before it was even clear who they were. More bullets flew, but without light to see, the Féal soldiers were too wary of shooting blind and hitting their own.

Ahead, Elias saw a white tent three or four times the size of any of the others they had passed. He wondered if he and the others could still get out by then, even if they just raced for one of the edges. It was more than possible his orders had thrown their lives away.

No, the camp was still in chaos, he told himself. He had not come so far to wonder for the rest of his life if he had missed the king of Féal by moments! He had to see, before they ran. If the six of them split up, if they scattered, they still had every chance of clambering over one of the earth banks and just vanishing. Or it was too late and they were already dead.

Elias came to a halt, panting as if to burst his heart. Yet there he was, standing before a tent fit for a king, while white fire bloomed behind him and the night lit up in shades of gold and blood.

19

Armour

King Jean Brieland slept lightly at the best of times. For all the relative luxury of his tent, his mattress was thin and the air was always damp, despite the braziers. He came awake from restless sleep at the first crack of sound.

For a moment or two, he lay blinking up at the canvas, seeing it light in flashes. Then he rolled out of bed and shouted for his servants to move.

They were slower than he had been to come fully awake. In the dull glow of a brazier, he buckled his own breastplate and yanked on leggings. He had slept with the belt against his skin, the pieces of gold stone as warm as a lover to the touch. His hand drifted to it as his servants finally appeared, hair tousled and faces creased from sleep. The king felt his heart settle. The camp was under attack, but he would not be seen panicking. Such things mattered to the men. He buckled on a sword by the entrance and walked out into the darkness.

The night was frozen, so that mud and turf crunched underfoot. Shadows rushed everywhere and one of his officers was bellowing 'Light!' at intervals, desperate for some idea of what was going on. Jean tutted under his breath. No one had ever dared attack the camp before. It was a move of desperation, but because it was so unlikely, they had not prepared for it.

He heard no enemy soldiers tramping, no thunder of hooves. Yet men ran everywhere and shouted. He would certainly have words with his officers about that in the morning. It was a shambles and unbecoming of the dignity of his legions. Were they children to be spooked on a dark night? Ridiculous. Whatever it was, there was no excuse to go running around like chickens squawking about a fox.

King Jean narrowed his eyes as he tried to understand what he was seeing in front of him. He felt the blood drain from his face when he understood the sudden flashes of light in the centre were in the middle of his Black Guards, that something was actually attacking the heart of his army. And survived still! He would not have thought any force could face his Guards and live for more than moments.

He began to step forward, peering into the distance. The king barely had time to register someone running straight at him. He actually turned to shout an angry warning to whatever servant was about to bowl him over in their panic, when he saw the raised knife. There was no time to counter. As he scrabbled to draw his sword, he felt the chill of steel whipping across his neck. His belt was warm as he gripped it in his free hand, his fingers suddenly cold.

His attacker froze as the king drew his sword and lunged with it. Somehow the man swayed aside from the blow, though King Jean thought he had cut him. He had no time to follow up as another came out of the darkness, over the bodies of a line of his men as they formed up.

King Jean raised his blade once again, but the swordsman's speed and certainty were shocking. He felt hit after hit: against his neck, thumping into his chest and then, horribly, testing every part of him. As the king roared for help and flailed, the enemy warrior cut his armour to ribbons, looking for weakness. The king's head was rocked back by a cut across his nose that would have ruined him. That was followed by a kick to one of his ankles, so that he fell back onto the frozen ground. He saw stars blotted out above and then someone was leaning on the tip of a sword, pressing their full weight down. He gasped and yelled.

At last his guards had worked out he was under attack. They swarmed in to help the king, without thought for their own safety. Perhaps they knew their lives were forfeit if they did not. King Jean was not thinking clearly. He thought he saw those trying to kill him sweep his best soldiers aside, cutting through them like a reaper at the harvest. Unless he fought gods from the old centuries, they would be brought down. He tried to lever himself up and one of them kicked him in the face, deliberately, still testing to see what could hurt him. He felt the belt grow hot on his waist.

These are assassins, Jean, come to kill you. You have stirred them up and then gone to sleep like a good boy. Did you think your Black Guards would save you? I can feel them burning.

'Then fight for me!' King Jean roared to the shadow. He could not see her in the darkness, but he could always hear the hissing voice, wherever she placed herself. Ever since the day when he had killed the priest and found his Black Guards, set against the tomb of some ancient king.

He felt the difference when the swordsman keeping

him down twitched suddenly, as if he had been stung. King Jean grinned in the darkness, though he tasted blood in his teeth. The man was extraordinary. Only the belt had kept him alive. Slowly, King Jean rose to his feet to watch him die.

Hondo felt something bite him, low down on his ankle. It stung, and whatever it was, it seemed to spread rapidly upwards, for all the world as if something climbed his leg. He tried to continue his attack, battering at whatever magical defence had saved the king. He thought he might break through, or find some spot where the man could be cut. Armour fell away in pieces and he brought the edge of his blade against every joint and major vein, looking for blood. It was like thumping a corpse that would not bleed, or a piece of wood. Yet Elias, Bosin and Taeshin had taken up station around them, giving him time to find a way to kill this man. There was no sign of Vic Deeds. For one of his character, perhaps it was not too surprising that he had left them to die.

The spreading pain from his leg made Hondo gasp. With the king flat on his back, Hondo took a step clear and tried to brush off whatever it was. Instead, it seemed to transfer to his arm. The pain was worse and he felt fear uncoil in him. He could not see whatever it was, but on the edge of his hearing he thought he could hear whispering.

The king's guards were still charging in, responding to the clash of arms. That was their mistake against Elias, Bosin and Taeshin. Blood spattered from all three men as they killed anyone who came in range. Soldiers of Féal were already stumbling in the dark over the bodies of those who'd gone before. Elias waited only for Hondo to signal it was done, but every passing second was a blur and he could feel he was slowing down. He had already been cut twice and he felt light-headed as he risked a glance over his shoulder.

Elias knew time played tricks, especially in darkness, when blades sang and clashed. It had probably been just moments since the king had come out of his tent. The chaos and darkness were still as good as a hundred men, more. None of those who had ridden out of Darien shouted orders or identified themselves. While others in the camp ran with torches and drew steel on their own people, the ones who had actually entered the camp to kill Jean Brieland were silent and almost invisible. Anyone who came close enough to make out their faces was killed.

It could not last, but it did not have to. Elias had seen enough of Hondo's skill – and the respect shown to him by Bosin and Taeshin – to expect the job to be done quickly. His mind was flashing back to another assassination and yet he felt only anger still. This King Jean Brieland was no innocent, but a man who would happily see Darien burn, with all the villages around it. It surprised him with its force, but Elias discovered he could still hate and he could still desire to defend his own people from an invader. Perhaps he was not just a simple village hunter, no matter what he told himself to get out of bed on a winter morning. Perhaps he was a stone-cold killer and a man of Darien.

In the quiet calm of *reaching*, he worked, feeling the spatter of blood whip across him as he murdered with his little knife. At his back, Hondo had stopped his own attack and was jerking and writhing in silence, as if something burned him.

'I'm out. Hold fast,' Elias said to Taeshin and Bosin.

They had not trained together, but their shared knowledge allowed them to work in near-perfect unison. They accepted his authority and edged closer to one another as Elias darted in.

The king was on his feet and Elias didn't hesitate. Jean Brieland was no swordsman, not like any of the Shiang men who faced him. He was enraged and strong, however. The king attacked the one who appeared between him and Hondo as if he chopped wood. As he struck only air and recovered, the man faded aside and sliced a wicked little knife across his throat.

The touch made the king gasp. Before that day, it had been an age since anyone had actually brought sharp metal against his skin. Yet as Elias dragged it clear, no blood came. Elias blinked. In a moment of surprise and indecision, King Jean pushed him aside, as he might have shoved away a child blocking his path. Elias did not try to avoid it and staggered back into Bosin. He had to duck then as the big swordsman answered with an instinctive blow that nearly took his head off. Elias cursed.

'Save Hondo!' he called to the other two.

They turned to see what assailed the sword saint as Hondo began to make a hissing sound, in pain and frustration. He clawed at his throat and yet when Bosin reached past his clutching fingers, there was nothing to pull away.

Without Elias to go through them like a threshing machine, Féal soldiers began to flood their position. The initial sense of confusion in the camp was fading heartbeat by heartbeat, along with any chance of success. Torches had been sparked alight in every direction, with hundreds more lit and carried in the hands of searchers. Order was being restored through the discipline of forces used to a chain of command – and with every new order and answering shout, their deaths came closer.

King Jean seemed determined not to retreat. Whether it was because his men surrounded him by tens of thousands in that camp, or because they could not seem to mark him, Elias did not know. He recognised magic when he saw it and he made a decision, though it made him want to spit in the face of the king who stood laughing while Hondo strangled.

The sword saint made no more sound. His face had gone pale and he tugged weakly at his neck, his fingers tearing the skin.

'Bosin, lift him up,' Elias snapped. 'Time to get out.'

'Here! Defend your king!' Jean Brieland roared into the night. He stood with his arms apart as if he welcomed the forces arrayed against him.

They all looked up as the night lit, bright as the sun. Nancy had burned her way through the dark heart of the camp and she was still coming, bathed in light. Elias heard Hondo gasp, the first breath he had taken in too long. The sound seemed to reach the ears of the Féal king and he flinched away.

'Leave him then!' Jean Brieland yelled.

Elias saw a patch of darkness unwind from Hondo's arm and throat, dripping like paint to the ground.

'Come on then, witch!' King Jean roared into the night. 'See what we have for you!'

He walked forward in the moment that Hondo attacked once again, with a speed and ferocity that made experienced men cringe. It was like being in the presence of a storm and yet the king remained, uncut. He leaned forward and tried to stab Hondo with his sword, though his blade was knocked aside again and again.

'Move back, Hondo,' Elias ordered.

The sword saint disengaged, though he was shaking with suppressed rage and horror. The man's discipline held, even while Féal guards fell against them like a tide. For a time, Elias and the three swordsmen were hard-pressed and he thought they would all end there, with failure like dust grating between his teeth. He thought of his daughters, though he knew he would wade in blood before he ever gave up. He would come home, if he was the last of them.

The king was laughing again, though it was a mad sound, as if he had lost his mind completely. Elias heard it choke off and looked round. He almost got himself killed trying to see if someone had marked the king at last.

He caught a glimpse of the king's stricken expression as Nancy came close. There was a moment when she made it through the beetle-like creatures that were the heart of the Féal army. She came to within twenty paces of the king and she brought the light.

As she did so, with all eyes on her, Deeds walked up and shot the king in the centre of his forehead. He'd stayed away from the attack, though the Shiang swordsmen seemed to be making a meal of a simple task. In the end, Deeds lost patience. He hadn't come to that place to throw his life away and he'd been eyeing the closest ramp to get out and make a run for the horses when he saw Hondo jerking and stamping, while the king laughed at all of them. It was too perfect a chance to turn down and Deeds had felt like an avenging angel as he'd stalked forward and shot the man in the face. He'd killed a king before. The first one was always the hardest, so they said.

King Jean's laughter stopped as his head was rocked back. Elias saw the man reach up in astonishment and peer at a smear of red. Jean Brieland did not fall, but he did not laugh again either. His mouth opened in astonishment and he shook his head back and forth as if to deny the blood.

As Elias looked back to Nancy, she crashed through a line of the black-armoured guards, like smaller Sallet Greens in their darting movements. Whoever commanded them had seen she could ruin the ones she touched. As Elias looked in vain for her to move up, he saw half a dozen of the things launch themselves at her in great bounds from the side. She had no defence against the weight of them. They were leaping high, to crash down where she stood.

'Go dark!' Elias roared to her.

He thanked the Goddess for her trust as Nancy's fire-light winked out, plunging that part of the camp into blackness. There were no torches lit where she had stood. There had been no need for them, where night had been day. Suddenly, there were just shining after-images and a sucking black hole where Nancy had been.

Elias went to fetch her out. He saw the Féal king had retreated, pulling back with a wall of men forming around him, weapons bristling as they clashed shields and swords together. The message was clear.

Elias shook his head as he walked in the dark. The king still lived. He and the others had kicked a hornets' nest and now the nasty little bastards were defending the hive – and he had to go in and get Nancy.

'Hondo – get out now,' he shouted. 'The others on you. Deeds! Wake up. Go with them. Now!'

Elias had seen Deeds stunned at the failure to kill a man he'd shot in the head. Bosin gathered him up as the big man changed direction. They melted away into the dark, and as Elias strode in the other direction, he heard yells and a crackle of gunfire erupting as they went. He wished them luck and closed his eyes. Ahead of him, Nancy walked alone, like beauty in the night.

Nancy fought against panic as she crept away from where the black-armoured monsters still hunted for her, flipping carcasses right over as they searched. Elias had seen the best defence was in going dark, but they weren't fools. More and more lights were being lit and everywhere she looked, men ran with torches, peering into tents and piercing sacks of supplies as they searched. She prayed to be invisible, while magic still ran in her like a torrent, drawn from all the Sallet Greens she had touched. No, not Greens, clearly. She'd seen enough in the flashes to have some sense of what they were. Smaller than the massive Sallet Greens, they seemed to be armoured men, in a black and shiny carapace. There were so many! Nancy knew better than anyone how precious Lady Sallet considered her Greens to be. She'd had six and lost three in defence of the city. Even then, she only had two sound ones and the last the men called Patchwork, cobbled together from parts that flashed grey amidst the green.

Nancy was still unsure if the ones she thought of as black beetles contained men or were somehow, horribly independent. She'd heard no orders called between them, yet they seemed to move in unison and with purpose. She'd certainly seen them learn to attack her, relying on weight and height and speed instead of simply plunging in. There was intelligence there. More than one had leaped high, forcing her to respond with a blast of flame to incinerate them. She'd been spattered with droplets of molten metal. A spot on her cheek had been burned. When she touched it, she felt a splash of something hard and cold that she did not dare try to remove. One of her arms was curled into a crook at her waist and, though she could feel nothing at that moment, she thought it was a bad injury.

She'd been through hell for what had seemed like hours. She could still not believe there was no sign of the sun — on a spring night where the light would return early as well. Battle was chaotic and terrifying, Nancy knew that. She shuddered at all she had learned that night.

She made her way in the direction of Elias, heading down a long line of tents rather than crossing an open space. Nancy could hear running men nearby and she crouched as light bloomed along the line, like an eye opening and looking for her. Then she was up again and running. She didn't want to fight again. Exhaustion lay thick in her blood, like salt in a cask. She just wanted to get out, to get away from thunder and flame and shining black death.

She didn't see the three soldiers standing together where one branch of tents met another. They had their heads bent close in muttered conversation and there was no light in that part, which was why she had gone through it, staying away from the lit roads. She almost stumbled into them and one of them reached out and grabbed her by the arm, leaning closer to peer.

'Who are you?' he said.

The voice was high and clear and Nancy saw he was a young man, barely out of his childhood. She felt magic uncoiling in her, like acid rising in her throat.

'Please, let me go,' she said.

Something moved in the dark then and the men dropped, one by one, their throats cut. Elias was there and she almost wept. She had reached a point where she just wanted someone else to show her the way out, to take charge.

'Stay close to me,' Elias whispered. 'I can lead you out.'

Nancy nodded, not daring to reply. He set off on a path that would have looked like a child's game or madness if she hadn't known what he could do. Nancy rested her hand on his shoulder and lost count of the times they avoided a patrol or searchers by instants. Little by little, they left the charred centre behind them and drew closer to one of the gates. Men swarmed angrily there and Elias was reluctant to bring the whole camp running once more. He guided her away, along the edge of the earthen ramps that had made the men of Féal feel safe as they slept. Nancy doubted they ever would again.

She waited in silence while Elias slipped up the inner slope. Someone died on the crest and then she went up and over, skidding and leaping down the outer side of the wall. There were riders galloping around the camp by then, throwing torches down and giving a strange howl. Elias hardly hesitated as he made his way through the pools of light. He led her on and on, into the night, until the camp was far behind and all the sounds of murder and rage had faded.

20

Dawn

First light banished fears and alarms, the sense of anarchy and pandemonium. Just the faint grey gleam over the camp brought new purpose and calm. So Jean Brieland told himself.

The king of Féal sat very still while one of the legion surgeons dabbed at his wound. His wound! Since the age of fourteen, he had never been cut, not once. On a chair of leather and wood, he sat with his hands tucked into his waistband, in part so the surgeon wouldn't see how they trembled. The leather belt had been cracked and old when he'd found it, all the more so after another thirty years. He'd wound reinforcing thread around it in bands of black, white and red, like decoration. Resin had hardened it all still further. Only the pale stone nubs were still exactly as he had found them.

'There is no point in wrapping such an injury, Your Majesty,' the surgeon said. The man was in his fifties and as fit as the soldiers he tended. He breathed through his nose as he leaned in close. 'It will scab on its own by the end of today and be gone in a few weeks. Without a scar, I believe. It must have been the most glancing of blows, Your Majesty. Your luck is still legendary. Still, I tremble to think how close we all came to losing you.'

King Jean waved off the attempt at flattery. It had not been done well anyway.

There are dying men in the camp, Jean Brieland. I can feel them slipping. Yet you sit here . . . while the doctor inspects a scratch? I hurt, Jean. I am burned. What balm does he have for me in that bag?

'You need no balm,' Jean said angrily.

The doctor hesitated until the king lost his tight expression and settled back.

Jean tried not to hear, but the shadow rested between his legs as he sat, like a beaten dog come to its master for succour. In truth, she seemed lesser. The words came weaker than before, with long pauses. He knew he was staring into space trying to hear the whispering. The doctor looked worried as he tried to peer once more into the king's eyes, reaching to raise his eyebrow with a thumb.

King Jean knocked the hand away, startling the man.

'Go tend the wounded, sir. I am clearly well enough.'

'Are you sure, Your Majesty? A blow to the head can be dangerous. You should not be left alone today.'

'I am always alone,' Jean lied. 'Go.'

'Very well.' The doctor bowed deeply over his bag. 'Though I will be in reach. Please send a runner if there is dizziness or a headache that grows worse.'

'What will it mean if there is?' the king said suddenly.

The doctor was caught between wanting to reassure and telling the truth.

'Even a glancing blow could lead to bleeding inside, Your Majesty. I see no signs of it, but as valuable as you are . . .'

'Yes. All right. Now aid my men,' the king replied, losing patience.

The doctor scurried away, unsure how he had given offence. King Jean rose to his feet, searching for signs of poor balance. His legs felt strong, he thought. If it wasn't for the swollen patch between his eyes, he would not have felt so shaken and furious – and humiliated. Assassins of Darien had dared to assault the very heart of his camp. The arrogance of it was breathtaking. Yet instead of being impaled on the blades and spikes of his legions, they had shown up a host of weaknesses and got away clean. Perhaps they thought they had failed. He hoped so. From where he stood, it did not look like victory.

He'd have to kill some of the men, he realised. All those who had been on guard the night before would have to be hanged, while the rest looked on as witnesses. He and his legions had been complacent. That was clear enough. They'd grown used to lesser enemies, those who ran like sheep before them. He remembered the lone husband who'd come to kill him before. From Dalton? Dalston? It didn't matter. A king made enemies, he knew that. He might even have admired their courage if it hadn't been aimed at him.

Will you weep, King of Féal? Do you care at all that I was burned in the foul witch-light, that I might have died? What would you have done then, without me?

'Oh, I would have managed somehow,' he muttered. A thought struck him and he frowned. 'I did not know you could be hurt.'

There was no reply for a time and he wondered how he actually would feel if the shadow perished. Bereft, or relieved? He could barely remember the first day he had heard her voice, whispering in his ear. He shuddered, caught by the memory of a time when he had still been frightened by her. He'd been little more than a child, he recalled, telling a friend that the shadow was *there*, pointing over and over. He'd learned she could kill then, no matter how he had pleaded.

'More importantly, how was I hurt?' he said aloud. 'I thought the belt protected me? Is that not its purpose? You said the morning stones would seal my skin. How is it that I bleed, then? Did you lie to me? Answer!'

Be silent, you fool! See how the servants look at you, standing on your own and ranting to nothingness – addressing an empty chair! Would you have them think you mad? How long do you think you will remain king if your army turns against you? There is your work, little Jean Brieland, if you have the wit to see it. Are you a child or a king? Go and speak to your men. Show them you are interested in their hurts and their lives.

'You are angry with me, I understand,' he said, more quietly. 'I am sorry you were injured. I am sorry we both were. I *would* miss you, you know that. Does that satisfy you?'

There was silence for a time, but it seemed less strained. He tried to see the shadow as she moved across the ground. There was definitely a hitch in her movement, as if she ached, or had been broken. He winced in sympathy.

'Did the belt fail?' he whispered.

You were shot in the head and yet you stand here. The belt did not fail . . .

He waited. In the first years, he had felt the little creature was his tormentor, that he could never be private or have a moment to himself. He thought she had even driven him to madness for a time, making him more savage and more vengeful than he might have been. Yet those qualities had served him well enough as he had formed a kingdom from hill villages and seen how to make them a true nation. He had learned many things from those days – not least that the shadow seemed to need him too. If he refused to speak, she would become frantic over time, as bonded to him as he was to her.

He wondered when he had started to think of the shadow as female, but perhaps that was just what he preferred to imagine. Yet there was a wounded tone to her hurt that reminded him of his mother or his first wife, both in the grave many years past. He'd had little time for the gentle companionship of women after those failed attempts. Not when the shadow would bicker and berate all those he tried to love. She had not minded him breeding sons, however. He thought the way she doted on Louis was even close to a mother's love. Perhaps that was why he thought of her as female, in her blackness and whispering. That, and the fact that she was a terrifying killer of men, at least when he asked nicely, or allowed her to be.

Silence now? You will not drag my secrets from me, Jean Brieland.

Still he said nothing, just waiting while the sun showed a line of gold wire and then a blade. It was a good omen, he thought.

Oh, very well! Though I am weak and injured and you are cruel. One of the attackers drew magic. The belt is an artefact of old times, little Jean. Yet I overcame the bitch as she tried to hurt you, as she tried to steal you away from me. That is why you live. Because I saved you and kept you whole.

'And you were burned . . .' he said. 'I am sorry. You said "she", though? The one in the fire? I saw her coming.'

Monster. Whore. Thief.

Nothing more came, no matter how he pleaded. With the sun rising, King Jean throttled down his reluctance and went to see the destruction of the night before. Some of his twenty legions had not lost a single man. Those further north than his own tent had played little or no part and were untouched. They were working hard that morning in the camp, aware of their luck, and how it was judged by those who had faced fire and iron.

The king walked past rows of bodies as they were sewn into shrouds for burial, or more likely a funeral pyre. It would have to be the latter with so many of them, as it was after a battle. He chafed at the thought of such a delay. Should he give Darien another day as a reward for their attack? Or rush upon them, on the heels of those they had sent to kill him?

He had been frightened the night before, in the dark, feeling pain for the first time since childhood. That fear had gone. His army was in range of Darien. He wanted to have the men form up and just march, to expunge the shame of the night with action. He longed for it and it was an effort to walk slowly down the lines of the dead as they were arrayed, as if on a final inspection.

Most of them had been killed defending him, he knew that. They'd run to save their king and died on the blades of no more than a few men. The attackers had been astonishingly skilful, that was clear enough. They would not have survived otherwise, nor vanished in the night like ghosts. King Jean remembered a report from his son that had described a 'sword saint' and a duel with Emil Cartagne. He wondered if the same man had stalked through his camp the night before.

It was an act of war, of course. No ruler of men had ever been given a better reason to blow the horns than this. Jean Brieland no longer needed the excuse of his son's injuries. Darien had attacked his camp and slaughtered hundreds of his men. In response, he would burn their city down around their ears and perhaps he would not spare even the women and children. The thought both darkened his mood and pleased him. There would be other battles to follow, other territories that might refuse his treaties, or the presence of his army on their borders. There was a satrap kingdom that began leagues to the west. Perhaps that man would benefit from a tale of the mighty Darien burned to ash and bone. Fire made all corruptions clean – and it would be seen for miles and miles. The hub of the region would fall – and all the small kings would know. He would make his nation then, carved in stone for eternity.

He stopped when he reached the end of the row. He wasn't sure if it was right that their faces were hidden beneath cloth. Dead eyes cried out for vengeance and they seemed almost peaceful lying there, far removed from the horror of death in the dark.

A group of senior officers had taken up position around him as he walked, so that the king led them in quiet reverie, all the way to the end of the dead. Jean knew it was a moment of performance, but he owed them something. A nation needed stories, to inspire the generations to come. When they told the tale of Darien, it would include his anger at seeing his men killed by filthy traitors.

Jean stood with his head bowed and his generals did the same, standing as if in prayer.

'These men have gone on, though they watch us still. They cry out, though they lie silent. So I give you my word as king, to those alive and those who sleep: you were loyal and you gave your lives for us. We will not fail. We will not let you down.'

One of his clerks scribbled the words with pencil and a scrap of paper as he spoke. King Jean nodded his approval. He'd look over the exact wording later. He thought the ending could be improved before it went into the formal record.

With that done, Jean walked on into the centre of the camp, where his Black Guards had settled into their unnatural stillness the night before. They too had terrified him once, until he understood them. He'd learned to love them since. Deep in that mountain tomb, with the body of Father Cormac gone to withered skin and bone, he'd climbed down ropes to see what strange things lay there in the darkness of millennia.

The memories were strong in Jean Brieland as he looked upon devastation. For every battle he'd known, his Black Guards had been with him. He'd marched them into villages and recruited with them standing at his back, unmoving and silent. To see grey pieces lying, or worse, perfectly preserved Guards curled up like dead insects, gloss and colour gone, was disturbing, like nightmares come to life. They looked like statues of themselves, the dead ones, with life and magic torn out of them. He'd thought them immortal, his changeless warriors.

In all the years since he'd climbed down into that tomb as a young man, determined to learn what the old priest had been guarding, Jean Brieland had seen only two of them fail. They'd stood still for who knew how many thousands of years, yet when he'd called them, when he'd said 'Follow', they had climbed out of the shaft through the heart of a mountain and they had made him a king. Everything he was had come from that tomb and the courage it had taken to enter. It struck him to the marrow to see them broken and tossed aside, burned like traitors and unwanted things.

'How many have we lost?' Jean asked his most senior general. He was not sure then if General Petraeus would be one of those he was forced to hang before moving on. That was in the lap of the gods, if the general had been in charge of the sentries the night before. Until that decision was made, the man could still serve a purpose and answer his damned question.

'Of the six hundred, we have twenty shy of four hundred remaining. Two hundred and twenty lost, Your Majesty. I'm sorry.'

King Jean closed his eyes for a moment. His beloved Guards, torn apart. His six hundred with a third of their number ripped away. It felt like a knife in his chest and his eyes snapped open at the thought it might be his heart breaking. While General Petraeus waited for orders and a dozen other men stood with their heads bowed, or looking out over the field of the dead, he took deep breaths and calmed his racing pulse.

He could see the path the witch had taken. It was a furrow in the ground, burned in the turf and marked by bodies. His guards. Already, there were teams putting ropes on them. As the king watched, one of the grey husks was dragged away by two straining soldiers, leaning low against the weight.

'Are they to be buried, Your Majesty?' General Petraeus asked.

Jean recalled the man had been some sort of mercenary before swearing his oaths in blood to Féal. Petraeus had never let him down before. He knew it wasn't fair to fix the blame on one of his loyal officers and he struggled to keep his voice steady and not let anger spill out. There had to be blood. The men had to see the blame lay not with their king, but with those who had failed him. They had to know there was always a price.

He had no idea what to do with the broken ones. For the two he had seen fail over thirty years, he had gathered a group of engineers and watched while they levered the dead suits apart. None of them had understood the workings within, not even with them broken into levers of shining metal and rippled blocks like cubes of black clay. There was no space for men in that black armour, for which he was thankful. If there had been, Jean knew he would have been tempted to wear one himself, though the thought of being trapped inside had chilled him. Even more so, now that he saw them curled like moths touched by flame.

General Petraeus waited for a reply with infinite patience,

Jean saw. It would be a shame to kill such a fine officer, no matter the lesson. He made his decision.

'Yes, they are to be buried. Give the task to the camp followers. Have them dig a mass grave – well marked, so we can find it again, when this is done. I will not stay to see the burial. They are not men, Petraeus.'

The general chose his reply carefully. He had fought alongside the king's black soldiers and he had formed an impression of awareness in them. If they were not men, they were not mere toys or statues either, he was certain. Many of them stood close by the fallen ones, waiting for orders. They seemed alert and jerky in their movements, as if they felt the loss of their own.

'As you say, Your Majesty. They are not men – they are the Black Guards. I will ask for a stone to be carved for them, a formal tomb. We have craftsmen enough in the camp.'

King Jean looked at the general, sensing the stubbornness in him. He did not always understand his senior officers. They had values and attitudes that were sometimes utterly confusing.

'Who was responsible for the guard rotation last night, Petraeus?'

This time the response was prompt.

'There were ten senior captains responsible for manning the wall, Your Majesty. Under Generals Brown and Chivers. All twelve have been arrested and held pending your decision.'

'I see. I am glad it was not you, Petraeus.'

The general bowed his head slowly in reply. It hardly needed to be said that he was pleased as well.

'They will have to be hanged, though twelve does not seem many. Select an additional centurion from each captain's section, someone senior. They will share the responsibility and the punishment.'

Looking over the field of broken guards, he was tempted to keep going. A couple of dozen men hardly seemed enough. Yet Petraeus seemed satisfied and Jean took his cue from the older man.

'I will have the order given immediatcly, Your Majesty.'

'Outside the camp, I think. Get the men into marching ordcr, the cavalry ready. I will see Darien today and make camp before their walls. And they will see me. I don't want any more delays, general. We'll hang the men responsible and march.'

He thought for a moment.

'They sent their best to kill me, general. They broke into our camp as thieves and murderers. It is an act of war, of course. Let the men know they carry the honour of the kingdom of Féal with them. I will take down the walls of Darien. I will mix mortar and blood to rebuild them. Let us make a mark on the world, General Petraeus.'

The man's chest swelled as he drew in breath and pride at the same time. Petraeus nodded and dipped to one knee before the king dismissed him and his companions. The camp walls were already coming down now that the army was up and about. As the sun cleared the horizon, cooking vats bubbled with stew and the men ate quickly and messily, tossing down the cups and bowls. They knew there was every chance they would fight before they ate again.

In normal times, there might have been excitement and

laughter in those ranks, almost the sense of a fair. Not that morning, however. The men had walked along lines of dead friends and companions, waiting to be buried. They had seen the invincible Black Guards broken. They seethed with the dishonour done to them, but they were not down-cast. They had broken cities before.

21

Chains

With the boy-king of Darien, Tellius stood on the walls, just waiting. Both of them had to shield their eyes as the light turned to evening brass. The land around the city was a grassy plain for the most part, marked by roads and a few small taverns for the weary traveller. Tellius had horsemen too out there, waiting on mile markers beyond the limits of his vision, racing in as soon as each one sighted the army of Féal.

The name did not amuse him any longer, not with scouts galloping back to Darien as if hell was on their heels. He acknowledged them with a raised hand and sinking heart, before turning to Arthur and exchanging a glance. Each rider returning meant another two miles covered. The king of Féal was moving quickly, his anger to be read in the relentless pace.

Tellius looked left and right along the massive wall. The crest was a single-track road, wide and solid. Drainage had always been a problem and recent rains had made the trackway a little soft. He'd had a mixture of sawdust and dark sand sprinkled all the way round the city, collecting it from carpenters' workshops and the black desert over previous days. He knew some of the rougher bars used just such a mixture on their floors to soak up blood.

Regiments rested in the streets below, ready to march up and take their posts. Fully manned, it was hard to imagine anything able to breach those defences. Yet Prince Louis' men had scouted the city. Tellius had done nothing while they'd wandered all over as visitors and partners – as guests of some of the noble families. No doubt the men of Féal had written entire books of gate mechanisms and maps.

Tellius gripped the wall hard as he thought of the mistakes he'd made, then tried to put them behind him. No one had perfect foresight of what would come! Mistakes were always made – by both sides. Tellius almost smiled at the thought of the destruction Elias and Nancy had wrought in the Féal camp. Although they'd failed to kill this Jean Brieland and seemed only to have aggravated him, they'd brought back information that had been like water to a dry soul.

Each of his little kill team had noticed different things. Exhausted as they'd been when they'd arrived back at the gates and been let in, Tellius had questioned them, learning everything he could. Only then had he left them to sleep like the dead. Basker at the Old Red Inn had offered up his best rooms for the war effort, though he seemed to think he would be repaid, at least at first. Tellius had listed instead some of the costs the city had incurred to keep that inn safe from invading armies. After quite a while, the old soldier had given up and gone back to polishing glasses.

Tellius felt the breeze pick up. He breathed it in.

'There is only so much you can do,' Arthur said suddenly. 'You are one man, Tellius.'

'One Speaker for the Council,' he replied, looking down. He knew Arthur's origins better than anyone else in the city. As a rule, Tellius treated him like a young ruler, rather than a construct made for a grieving mother, goodness knew how many centuries ago. Arthur would not age and Tellius thought he would not change. In another thousand years, there was a chance Arthur would remain on those walls, or perhaps the ruins of them.

'Has this city ever fallen?' Tellius asked softly. There were other ears around them on that wall, with men waiting on the steps. Tellius thought he could smell metal and oil on the breeze as it blew from the north.

'The old Empire of Salt fell,' Arthur said at last. 'The last Salt king died without heirs and his cities split apart in suspicion. Darien, too, though it was not a capital then, but a city far from the centres of power. Now we stand on walls as great as any I have ever known.'

The boy-king shrugged expressively, looking back with a perspective that made Tellius shiver. When they had met, Arthur had been living like an animal on the streets, pretending to be a mute. Battered and made wary by experience, he had expected only cruelty. Yet he had been made for an empress.

'Empires come and go, Tellius,' the boy-king said, with sadness underlying. 'Those who rule them forget to protect old freedoms, or spend the army payroll silver on palaces. Or become afraid of the rough soldiers on their walls and send them away. Kings are just men – and men make mistakes they sometimes live to regret.'

Tellius smiled tightly at the echo to his own thoughts. He did not point out the obvious, that at least one king was a golem. Presumably, for all his strange origins, Arthur was no more infallible than anyone else.

'I don't want to see Darien fall,' Tellius said under his breath as he looked out. 'It has meant too much to me. She has meant too much to me. Whatever she was, she is my capital now.'

In that moment, it was not clear if he meant the city or Lady Sallet. He did not need to say how it was to find love, long after he had ceased to search for it. He was not sure Arthur would truly have understood. The boy-king knew loss and grief, though perhaps the length of his life blurred such things and smoothed them down, made ripples instead of jagged edges.

'It hurts to find a pleasant spot – and then see it lost,' Arthur said. 'I remember gardens, Tellius, that are untended briars now, or even forests, with huge oaks where I once played. Or city walls built over paths I walked.' He shrugged. 'Only mountains stay the same. Men and women change the world around them.' The boy paused again, weighing his words. 'For good or bad, but I think mostly for good. There are ruins of an older world wherever they dig a deep foundation, did you know that? Old coins and walls and pieces of painted tile. I have seen statues taken from the earth when we rebuilt the walls. Half-faces, or a single arm in white stone. The past lies beneath our feet, Tellius. We stand like gods over them.'

'And one day someone will stand like gods over us.'

'They will. The strange thing is that you would like to kill them.'

Tellius grinned.

'I would. I really would.'

'You are not a philosopher, Master Speaker,' the king said.

'No. I am a war leader. I am a loyal man of Darien.'

'Not of Shiang?'

'I have said what I am,' Tellius replied.

The wind strengthened. In the evenings, it sometimes rose up as it struck the walls, rushing like a wave over rock. Tellius shook his head at the thought, imagining the army coming. The king of Féal was arrogant and enraged. Part of the reason he marched was because the people of Darien had not thrown themselves to their stomachs, shrieking at the mention of his name. King Jean Brieland was apparently a man who thought the whole world should kneel. Tellius hoped they could bleed his ambition weak against those walls. He might learn a little humility in Darien. Most men did.

Tellius considered the information Elias had won, staggering with weariness as he came in. Hondo had confirmed it. Yet a king who could not be cut did not trouble Elias particularly. Such a man could be sealed in a box and buried, or crushed under stone he could not lift, and simply left. Or set on fire, perhaps. There were a hundred ways and Tellius knew he was ingenious. He was more worried about the armoured black warriors Nancy had described. If they were anything like the Sallet Greens, the thought of hundreds of them was terrifying.

In the distance, Tellius saw blurred movement, the entire horizon shift and lurch. He felt the skin of his face grow tight, but he smiled and bowed to the boy-king standing at his side.

'Your eyes are better than mine, Your Majesty. If it please you, can you tell me what you see?'

'I see a great host, Master Speaker,' the king replied. 'With banners and formations and horses, mile upon mile of them. More men than I have ever seen before.'

Tellius blinked at that, considering the source.

'They will regret coming here,' he said.

The king of Darien nodded. Tellius looked over the wall and clenched his jaw at the sight of stragglers still coming in. They would be crushed against the walls, but he was out of time.

'Blow the war horns. Let the city know they are here. And close the gates!' he called to the officer watching him. The order was repeated three times, giving warning. Tellius heard cries of fear and desperation outside and he saw exhausted families lurch on, desperate to get in before the wave broke over them.

The river was eerily quiet, with all the boatmen snug in taverns along the docks and merchant traders busy with war supplies in the warehouses. The twin water gates of Darien that cut the city across its southern half were an obvious weakness. A decade before, they had been closed off at night by moored pontoons and a single sleepy guard paid to spend the night on them, while all manner of smuggling had gone on. More than once, the pontoons had been set adrift for a lark, so the guard woke to find himself lodged on a mudbank miles downriver.

Those sleepy years were long behind. Since then, the Twelve Families had taxed and spent fortunes to improve the water defences. The river was the lifeline of trade and its merchant captains brought fortunes to the treasury. Yet it broke the heart of engineers to see a shining breach in the walls on two sides, where the river ran through. It could not be enclosed, not with hundreds of boats passing through to the docks each day. Instead, huge double chains had been installed across the river, to be drawn up, encrusted and dripping from the riverbed as the war horns sounded. It took the labour of dozens of men to turn enormous capstans in the walls, with each step locked so they could not whirr back like a weapon. The weight of the chains was frightening, the very limit of what they could bear as the men strained to get them out of the thick mud. It was a little easier after that, until they came almost taut and barred entry to anything afloat. Each link was the size of a man and bore the mark of a guild master blacksmith.

The walls that held the chains had been remade as a sheer drop into the water. No army could mass for an attack there, not while fire poured down from above and the quays inside. An entire gun regiment had been stationed to guard each water gate, both where the river entered and left the city. The old Foss river was drinking water to many of the poorest, and bathing for their children. It was a brackish, oily road for the merchants who brought salt and iron and coal from mines far away. With hearth and family, the river was not to be touched, not without an axe falling on the hand that dared.

In the cold of evening, war horns sounded across Darien. The long brass tubes made a single, low note, like the drone of a bee. They rose in strength and volume, then fell away as each signaller ran out of air, took a breath and began again.

The effect on the river gates was immediate, with red flags raised on the high point of the wall to signal shipping and capstan teams racing to their positions. In just moments, the men took the strain and began to force the machines round, step by step, wrenching the great chains from where they lay on the riverbed. The first part was an agony of straining, and the more experienced river captains knew it took time. It was not uncommon for the most daring to ignore the flags and keep going, risking their ships and cargoes to get in over the rising chain.

On that night, there was more urgency in the air than the monthly drills over the previous few years. The warning horns meant a real attack and two ships made no attempt to drop sail and anchor for the night, as they would usually have done. Though the river gate was only wide enough for one, both captains kept their course and speed, yelling furiously to one another to give way as they came.

The wall men sweated on the capstans, driven in a rolling chant by a gun captain so that they all heaved on the same beat. It was a song that had been created for this new labour and it kept them all in time, many with their heads bowed and eyes closed as they focused on raising the damned chains that were gripped by river mud and about as heavy as sin.

The men cheered when the chains came free at last. The weight was still huge, but they could move forward, the capstan clicking as each step was locked with pegs hammered into holes in the wooden floor.

Out on the river, the wind had been stolen from one of the ships by the other, so that it slid ahead and through the gate. They all winced at the sound of the rising chains scraping barnacles and slime off the hull, but the ship didn't snag and the captain kept his rigging and masts, wiping sweat from his face as a thousand soldiers glared at his lucky escape.

Outside the chains, the other man nearly rammed his ship into the bank. He'd left himself almost no room for manoeuvre and yet his speed had not been too great. He threw out both anchors and the soft hold of the mud slowed him until the bow rested against the huge chains. One or two of his crew even reached out to touch a link, knowing they'd never get another chance. The captain had enough style to remove his hat and bow to the men on the walls, then his crew set about raising the anchors and setting down a boat to tow them round and back to a wider part of the river for the night. The sun was setting and as they went, the captain leaned on the side and called to another ship still racing in.

'The chain is up!' he shouted across the strip of water between them.

No one answered and he gave up, having tried to do a favour for a stranger. The other ship steered in silently on the current, though he could see no one up on the yards and only one figure on the tiller and another at the prow, guiding her. As they passed, one of the merchantman's crew shouted out another warning, but the man at the tiller didn't turn. The captain shrugged then. They'd see the fellows again when they were forced to come round and anchor. He sniffed the air, frowning at the smell of smoke that came to him on the breeze.

It had been a mordant sort of wit to rename the little ship *Vengeance*, Denn Hallman thought sourly. The king's captains had declared it a fine idea and painted the word on the bow before they'd disembarked out on the coast. 'Are you not coming, then?' he'd asked innocently. They'd scowled and told him to mind his damned business and to watch himself, and all manner of pointless, stupid threats that meant nothing at all. Denn's wife and daughters would be freed if he did this. The king of Féal had given his word on it. That was all that mattered. Their threats and bluster were just wind.

He had been a sailor in his youth, so it all came back to him soon enough, with a sort of yearning. He'd never have been able to handle even a small two-master on his own, of course, not on the open sea. Yet it wasn't too hard to steer the old barge down the river, not with one other fellow calling out from the prow. He was a dark and surly lad, with a knife always in his hand, as if he expected to be attacked at any moment. He hadn't given a name and only sneered when Denn had volunteered his own and offered his hand. If there had been a chance of some fellow feeling, it had been clear it would not come from him. Denn had asked him a few questions, enough to discover he knew nothing about starboard and larboard, or points of the compass. Of course not, that would have been too much like common sense. With a sigh, Denn had told the lad to just point left or right, standing up tall on the prow so he could be seen on the stern. Beyond that, they'd not said a word. Denn thought the young man had the look of city slums about him, rather than a country boy, who tended to be healthier and better fed. He thought of him as 'Snipe', after a breed of urchins who'd terrorised him in his half-forgotten youth.

As the walls of the city came into sight, there were just two ships ahead on the river. Denn felt his heart beat faster in fear. He couldn't slow down. It was true there was an anchor lying on the deck, with coils of rope in neat loops alongside. He supposed he could leave the tiller and just throw the lot overboard, but his job was to steer the ship right up to the gate. In the distance, he heard low horns calling, closer and closer as the sound was taken up, growing in force and volume until he swore he could feel the vibration in the wooden tiller under his hand.

Snipe had left his post, Denn saw. His heart sank and he felt suddenly dry-mouthed when he understood what that meant. He thought he could already smell smoke, though it might have been his imagination. No, there was a flicker down in the hold. He could see the light through the hatch that led below. Snipe was down there, lighting the damned ship on fire.

Denn swallowed his horror, focusing on keeping a straight line. One of the ships had gone through ahead, while the other had launched a boat to be towed round. He craned to see if they would make it before he smashed into them. He fretted as the tiller shivered under his hand. Without eyes up on the prow, he was practically blind! Where was the little bastard?

'I need directions!' Denn roared. 'Get up here! I'll run us into the bank otherwise!'

He could see a faint haze in the air now, smoke rising from the hold. He'd asked what was down there and the soldiers had just laughed and told him to mind his own business and do as he was told or they'd cut him. Fools. He knew very well.

He saw Snipe coming up the rungs of the ladder from below almost at a run, so he seemed to rise from the deck like a vengeful spirit.

'*There* you are!' Denn bellowed. 'Get to the prow and tell me if I'm heading straight, quickly!'

The skinny little rat gaped at him, mouth opening and closing on an angry retort. Before Denn could speak again, the kid had clambered to the edge, taken one look at the dark waters below and dropped away. The splash was lost behind and Denn could only look after him in dull resignation. He knew what it meant.

On the larboard or port side, the ship that had turned round passed by him. The captain yelled something, gesturing, but Denn Hallman was thinking of his wife and children. It had been a good marriage, pretty much. He'd certainly loved her and he'd saved a little for their old age. If someone had asked him, in his youth, if he'd give his life to save the young bride on his arm, he knew he would have said yes, without hesitation. This was just that. Of course, she'd be furious if she ever heard what he'd done. The thought made him laugh and weep at the same time.

He staggered as his ship reached the chains. In the current, the ship hadn't been moving at more than a man's walking pace, but the prow still crumpled and timbers groaned and cracked, deep in the hold. He could hear rushing water and his heart leaped at the thought of the river extinguishing the fires beneath his feet. Smoke rose from every crack in the deck. He was wreathed in it as the barrels blew up beneath him. The explosion tore the boat and broke the chains in a crack of sound and light like the end of the world.

22

River Gate

On the other side of the city, Tellius heard it. He and the king turned to see a ball of fire rising where the river met the city. He clenched his jaw. He had done all he could, he reminded himself. He was just one man, as Arthur had said.

No. He was the war leader of Darien, appointed by the king and ratified by the Twelve Families. He would not let the people down. At his back, voices shrieked for the gates to open once more. Tellius felt overwhelmed, unable to think. He looked over the wall and saw a woman kneeling on the ground to face the city, holding her child up as if in offering. Behind her, a line of cavalry had ridden out ahead of the army of Féal. No doubt they could see the last of those stragglers and understood they were trapped.

There was a certain kind of man who enjoyed helpless prey. No doubt some of them had found their way into the cavalry of the kingdom of Féal. Tellius could see them readying spears. Laughing young men, wanting to hunt. They would risk their own lives just to terrify the people watching.

'Guns and archers to the wall,' Tellius ordered. 'Stay low. Let them come close.'

The tramp of soldiers was loud as they took their

positions. Every gun foundry in the city had been churning out bullets night and day and he knew they still were. They were already short of brass and the black powder they used that had become, for him, the smell of war. Yet the archers had better range than pistols – and a better rate of fire, though the regiments still bickered over that. Barrels of fletched arrows were brought up all along the walls, thousands upon thousands, waiting to be sent down the throat of the king of Féal. On a high wall, they had range to beat anyone marching with a bow or a gun down there. That was an edge and Tellius knew he would need anything he could get.

The explosion to the south nagged at him. He had regiments at the river gates, commanded by men he trusted. He could not be there to oversee that defence, not while the main army approached the northern wall. He shook his head in frustration. He *had* resources. There was no point holding the north if the army of Féal broke through somewhere else.

With a low whistle, Tellius summoned one of the boys waiting to take his orders.

'Donny? Go to the Red Inn and wake Master Hondo. Ask him if he would be so good as to report on whatever is happening at the entry river gate for me. He is to act as he sees fit, with the authority of the council –' he glanced at Arthur and received a sharp nod – 'and the king. Go.'

The boy raced away. Tellius had chosen all the messengers from lads he had known years before, when he'd fed and protected a couple of dozen street children, with a little thieving on the side for funds. It had been a simpler life.

'I think it is time for you to leave the walls, Your Majesty,' Tellius said.

Arthur had been staring out at the army of Féal. He turned to the older man.

'Why would I do that, Master Tellius?'

'If you fall . . .' Tellius did not want to finish, but he made himself. 'It would hurt us all. It would hurt me.'

Arthur stood very still, his expression unreadable.

'Even so, Tellius. This is my city. I'm either king or I'm not. If I am, my place is on the wall, with the defenders.' He smiled suddenly. 'And you know, I am not that easy to kill.'

Tellius nodded. He felt pride in the boy that was like a pain. For a moment, his vision swam. He blinked hard and looked up, holding the bridge of his nose between finger and thumb.

'Very well, Your Majesty. It has been my honour to serve with you.'

Arthur inclined his head in reply, turning back to watch the enemy approach. His face was quite blank once more, as if the discussion had already been forgotten. Tellius gazed at the calm profile for a moment. He knew he could speak for a long time and it would still not be enough. He also knew he did not have to, that Arthur understood.

With a low whistle, Tellius called another of the street lads, one who had been a quick-handed little urchin just six or seven years before.

'Andrew. Please run to the shop "Beautiful Things" on Dial. Ask the lady there if she would be kind enough to join me on the wall. Give her my apologies and tell her I need her to burn some bastards. She'll understand.'

The young man flashed a grin at one who had kept him alive and fed him when no one else would. He almost flew down the steps at a pace to make the older man wince in anticipation of a fall.

Tellius didn't want to look at the woman still holding up her child. It had begun to scream in her grip. He could see its red mouth opening and closing, though they were too far to hear. Tellius felt the boy-king looking to him and he cursed. He turned to the closest archers and gunmen where they crouched with their backs to the wall.

'You, you and you. This troop. Throw down ropes to fetch the people out there. Loop the ends and draw them up. Be ready to cut the ropes if they are taken.'

No one had expected such an order and boys went running for ropes in desperation. Tellius watched as the cavalry swarmed like armoured hornets along the front of the army of Féal, spreading and spreading in a wider line. There were so many of them! His eyes could make out a dark heart of black armour, as Nancy had described, but sheer numbers worried him more.

Without an obvious signal, the Féal cavalry whooped and dug in their heels. Thousands of horsemen galloped in, showing their disdain, knowing they were immortal. At the gate, perhaps forty men, women and children clustered. They turned to face the horsemen charging them, as if it was better to see death coming. The woman remained, with her child writhing in her outstretched arms, in silent prayer.

Tellius saw two lads struggling up the steps with huge loops of rope. He grabbed part of one himself and heaved it over the wall, winding a bight of it around an outcropping of stone. Those below had prayed for a miracle and they were not slow to understand. The weight came on and the men began to haul in, hand over hand. Then the rate slowed, as more and more of the people below tried to climb.

'Haul! Get more men in line,' Tellius roared at those around him. They swore and strained, but all they could do was hold the ropes steady while those below kept climbing.

Tellius leaned over the parapet to see and his heart sank. The cavalry were almost upon them. A dozen people were climbing, though as he watched, one of them fell, taking another from the line as he went. They were already exhausted. Climbing a rope over a hundred feet up a wall was beyond them. Yet even as he watched, more tried to grab on and heave themselves up. One rope had people like beads, all slipping and crying out. It would surely snap before any of them made it to the top.

Some of his soldiers showed themselves on the wall, shouting down for the people to get off, that they could not raise so many. They could all hear the thunder of a line of horsemen shaking the earth.

No one below was saved. Tellius watched the woman swallowed up like a stone in a flood as the Féal cavalry pulled up against the city walls. They were in a wild mood, drunk on the chance to draw first blood.

'Archers, mass volley on my order,' Tellius said calmly. 'Gunmen. Aim at their precious horses. We'll kill more when they are on foot. Ready?'

All along the lines, those who heard him nodded. Those who could not had their shoulders tapped by officers, drawing their attention to the commands above and away from the carnage below.

'Slow and steady,' Tellius called to them. 'Horses first!'

They stood and leaned over the walls to pick their shots. Smoke hissed white and thunder sounded in crackling, rolling fire along the wall. Arrows poured as hail, whining through the air. The Féal cavalry were milling around in the death zone below. More experienced riders just turned and went out at a gallop as soon as the first guns opened up. Tellius watched horses hit and sent tumbling, their riders landing inert and broken on the ground. Hundreds more rose to their feet and tried to walk out of range.

Archers picked their targets, showing skill. They still had shafts as the first pistols clicked empty all down the line and had to be reloaded. Tellius cursed under his breath. The Hart guns had a slightly longer barrel than the Regis foundry weapons. There were some who claimed a better killing range for them, but it was still too short and accuracy was poor. He wished he'd had more time and ammunition for gun practice at that height. Too many puckers of dust and earth showed missed shots. Given another month, he'd have put wine casks out there and had competitions while the men practised. He winced at the patterns of bodies on the ground. There was never another month. The enemy always came too soon.

The Féal cavalry pulled back in half-decent order, showing discipline under fire. Tellius saw some of them carried shields, while others wore armour that resembled the feather-plate he knew from Shiang. Too many survived their ride right up to the walls – and he could hear them cheering. There seemed to be enormous variation in the styles of their regiments. Yet one man had joined them all into a fledgling nation. Well, it would be Tellius' task to tear them apart again.

Hondo came awake and rolled off the tavern bed before he was fully aware of his surroundings. Everything ached. He had ridden and fought and ridden once more like a madman to get back to Darien. After that, Tellius had put him in a room with a little lamp and questioned him over and over about everything he had seen. He was not a young man! Tellius should have understood that much, though Hondo saw ruthlessness in him. It was not that Tellius didn't care, but that he would spend those around him like coins at a fair. It was a position Hondo under-stood, though a sword saint was usually considered less . . . expendable.

What had wakened him? He heard a creak on the floor-boards outside his door. His sword was on a chair with his coat, where he had placed it before falling onto bedsheets that were clean and soft from a thousand washes. As the door opened, Hondo took a step to stand behind it, his sword in reach. His dreaming mind had heard the steps creaking and he was thankful for it. A sword saint could not be found snoring.

The tavern-keeper with a steaming cup of tea in his hand was named Basker. They were not exactly friends, but Hondo had stayed at the Old Red Inn on his first arrival in Darien. It was, if not home, at least a place where he was known and welcomed. Basker had been a soldier and there was that air about him still, of quiet discipline and self-control. Hondo appreciated it. They all ended up in the grave, but some men never said a word in complaint. They never mentioned their bad backs, or the pain from a club foot. His father had been such a man and Hondo recognised a similar sort in Basker.

'Thought you might appreciate a cup of tea,' Basker said, setting it down on the dresser. 'There's more hot water coming, if Elise doesn't trip on the stairs!'

Basker said the last with his head turned to the young woman coming in with a bowl of steaming water, cloths draped over her arm. She raised her eyebrows to him, blowing back a curl of hair where it had fallen across her face. For a few coins, a man could ask for the tavern bath to be brought to his room and filled there, while he waited. For most, it was a bowl on the dresser in the mornings – and a little extra for hot. There was a rumour that a man could ask for Elise as well, though Hondo had not tried to find out.

Hondo bowed in thanks as Elise entered. He bowed to her too and she smiled at him, essaying a bow of her own that was actually quite good, had she been a minor lord's son. He did not say so, though it was another sign that Darien had changed him. As she went back down the stairs, he glanced out of the windows, suddenly unsure whether it was dawn or evening.

'How long have I been asleep?' Hondo said. He felt rested, which pleased him.

'Six or seven hours,' Basker said. 'I've had the whole place tiptoeing past your door all day. Your mates are in the next room along, barely out of their armour.'

'All of them?' Hondo asked.

Basker shook his head.

'I put Vic Deeds down in the taproom. He's up and about already, annoying Elise. No, I gave the big fella the bed. That other Shiang, Taeshin? He spent the night on the floor, with a bit of firewood under his neck. He's a strange one, Master Hondo. He doesn't have your way with people.'

Hondo blinked, absurdly pleased to hear himself described in such a way, especially by Basker.

'Taeshin fought well yesterday,' he replied. 'In the camp.'

'Oh, I don't doubt it,' Basker said cheerily. 'He looks a right handful. Proper minty little bastard, I'd imagine. Here, drink your tea. I'll leave you to wash.'

'Why did . . . why was I woken?' Hondo said, though he knew the answer from the change in Basker's expression.

'The army of Féal has come, Master Hondo. Weary as you are, you ain't the sort to sit it out, if I know you at all.'

There was some commotion in the taproom below, with the voice of Elise telling someone not to go up. Both men turned to the door at a clatter of heels on wooden steps. Once again Hondo took a step closer to his sword. Basker too turned from old instinct, though he presented about as much target in profile as he did face on. Either way, both of them were ready to defend or attack as Donny came into the room. He was breathing hard from running across the city, but he grinned at the sight of them.

'All right? Tellius told me to wake up the Shiang lads. You're on, mate. You're up.'

'Master Tellius wants me on the wall?' Hondo replied. He glanced at the bowl of water and took the moment to splash his face and slick back his hair, running his fingers through to the tips.

'Not the wall. He wants you to take a look at the river gate. There was an explosion there.'

Hondo swore, knocking over the water bowl as he turned and grabbed for his coat and sword.

'Lead with that next time, boy!' he said, pulling in air to bellow an order. 'Bosin! Taeshin! Deeds! With me!'

Silence fell below, in the tavern, though Hondo could hear stirrings and swearing from the room next door. Hondo felt his bladder groan. Some things could not wait.

'Give me privacy, would you? Go and bang on their door.'

The street lad grinned again, delighted by his work.

Hondo reached for a pot under the bed and balanced it on the covers. Basker looked away as the swordsman sighed and began to fill it.

'The er . . . river gate is where I grew up, Master Hondo, though it wasn't so grand then and the houses were packed a bit tighter. Near Fiveway and Red Corners. I took the name of the tavern from that, where they make the dyes and boot polish. I still have family there. If you're heading that way, might I take a stroll with you?'

It was barely half a question, but Hondo chose to answer. 'We won't be strolling, but take up your sword if you wish, Master Basker.'

'Right. Though if I'm carrying a weapon, son, it's "Colour Sergeant" Basker, if you don't mind.'

There was pride in his voice and the tavern-keeper stood taller than Hondo had seen before. He grinned and clapped the man on the shoulder.

'You don't look fit, colour sergeant,' he said.

'Some of it is muscle, son. I'm not much for sprinting

these days – but I can trot a fair way and I can walk the rest. I'll get there.'

Five men left the Old Red Inn as the last light of the sun faded. Basker knew the way better than anyone and led them to the river, though Hondo would have gone at twice the speed and fretted at the pace. Deeds complained he had not eaten properly, though he was the only one of them to have grabbed a piece of steak from another man's plate. The gunman folded it over in his hand as he trotted with the others, biting off pieces as he went.

After half a mile, they had all loosened up. Basker took them to the river and over the Regis bridge. There was a ripple of gunfire in the distance that went on and on. It dampened the mood as nothing else could, stealing the excitement of running through black streets under moonlight.

Hondo loped along with Bosin at his shoulder. He felt calm and purposeful, though his right knee was beginning to ache. He had not visited the southern third of the city before. He supposed he would have followed the route of the river if Basker hadn't been there. Yet more than once, the way through was blocked by some great mill or warehouse, the river disappearing underneath with barely enough room for a barge. Basker never hesitated and the others followed him, winding in and out along tiny alleys, trusting he knew the way.

The streets were darker there than the ones in wealthy districts. The houses were tightly crammed and there were more people actually on the street, though whether that was normal or not was unclear. Hondo sensed them as he passed, shadowy figures in doorways, or out to hear the news. Some of them called questions or even a challenge, then faded away as the size of the group became clear. The crackle of massed gunfire grew with each step.

Basker had set a pace he could maintain, but when they could see the flickering light of shots, Hondo and Bosin split apart and went past him. Bosin said nothing, but Hondo patted the tavern-keeper on the back in thanks. The man's intimate knowledge of the city had saved them time.

Taeshin too patted Basker on the shoulder as he ran on, though it was an awkward thing, almost as if Basker was a good-luck talisman. Deeds just chuckled. He was panting about as hard as Basker by then, which pleased neither of them.

'You can't shoot . . . if you can't breathe . . .' Basker said to him.

Deeds glared.

'All right, grandpa, you've done your bit . . . Now take a rest before you have a heart attack.'

Basker seemed to swell as he considered a reply. Whatever he might have said was lost as the light commanded their attention ahead.

The wall of the city loomed black on black, a deeper bar that cut across the night sky. Stars could still be seen through the breach of the river gate. That was lit in the constant flicker of thousands of gunshots, delicate sparks in the darkness. It might have been beautiful if it hadn't meant they were under attack.

Hondo, Taeshin and Bosin were just ahead, stopping on the closest bridge to the wall. A soldier there was trying to wave Hondo back, but the noise was so great it was almost impossible to hear normal speech.

'. . . bridge . . . coming down . . .' the man roared into Hondo's ear. 'Move . . . !'

The small group walked away from him, across what would have been an ordinary narrow street just that morning. Hondo turned to the barrage going on, uncertain what to do. As he stood there, the men at the bridge knocked out supports with hammers and the entire assembly of stone and wood roared into the waters with a huge splash.

'To block the river!' Basker shouted. 'They must have ships.'

'What?' Deeds yelled back, cupping his ear.

Basker didn't try again as he thought it was just a dig at his age. The gunman never missed a chance to challenge man or woman, as far as the tavern-keeper could tell. He let his anger drain away. Perhaps they needed that sort of cocky devil, at least for the moment. Deeds was no longer breathing heavily, but neither were they moving forward. Basker spread his arms and shrugged in silent question at Hondo, but the sword saint stood still on the quayside.

In the gap between the walls, there was no sign of the massive river chains Basker knew were meant to be there. He thought he could see iron links hanging limp, vanishing into the river current. Even as he had the thought, a small two-master came into view, easing across the shining surface though gunfire battered her on all sides. The light was almost constant, but pistol shots could do nothing against the weight of a barge coming in. Every inch of the vessel was pockmarked and Basker could see flames flickering in her hold – but on she came, spinning slowly in the current.

Hondo watched the ship come. There was nothing he could do to stop it. A dead man was revealed in flashes by the tiller, two more on the prow. They had been riddled with bullets, but the current still drew them into the city. The vessel was burning, making the night around them even darker. He thought he saw movement on the banks behind, but as long as the walls held, the army of Féal would still have to swim or climb to enter Darien.

As he formed the thought, the second fireship exploded. The current's drift had taken her close to the southern part of the wall and the crack of white light and fury silenced the gunfire on that side completely. The sound was a physical thing to those on the wall – and those watching with Hondo. They all felt it as a thump in their chest and they dropped flat, the instinct of fragile life in the presence of all gods. A blast howled overhead and pieces of ship and stone whirred like daggers through the air.

Hondo could see nothing but flashing green lights. He blinked and held his nose, trying to listen for anyone taking advantage of the lull. He could hear nothing. The air had been robbed of sound and he wondered if he had been made deaf.

It had to have been worse on the wall, he realised. Hondo came to his feet with Bosin and Taeshin, faster than either Deeds or Basker, who was rubbing an arm. Deeds said something to him and Hondo saw the tavern-keeper clip the gunman across the back of the head, sending him staggering forward. Deeds reached for his pistols and Hondo touched him lightly on the arm.

'They will come now,' he said, relieved to hear his own voice. 'Be ready, Master Deeds. Perhaps tonight you will wipe the past clean.'

'It's already clean,' Deeds said in wide-eyed innocence. 'Though I will add the murder of a tavern-keeper if Basker touches me again.'

The right wall was silent, while only a few guns still fired on the left. Compared with the mass volleys of moments before, it was pitiful and all too clearly desperate. It meant Hondo's eyes had a chance to adjust to the night again, however. He squinted back and forth, turning his head. Another ship was sliding down the river. He wondered if the walls would take a third explosion. Perhaps that was the plan – to just batter them down, to rain stones on the defenders and then walk in over rubble.

'Another one coming. Any ideas?' Hondo called to the others.

He felt helpless. Outside the walls, the banks shifted. Hondo grew still as he tried to be certain, though some part of him had been looking for them, dreading the sight. He did not fear soldiers gathered there for the assault. Soldiers were men. Yet he'd seen that particular patch of darkness in the Féal camp. It shifted like foam on a seashore under moonlight, like spilled oil. As someone organised the defenders, as gunfire began to light the night once more, Hondo counted them in flashes, in groups of three or four. The armoured black warriors Nancy had driven a sword through were there. He counted at least a dozen of them, waiting, milling like ants.

'The dark ones from the camp,' Hondo said. 'We can't let them into the city.'

The thought of such pitiless creatures let loose in the tenements and alleys they had run through was terrifying.

'We don't have Nancy, though,' Deeds pointed out. 'And without her, we can't stop them.'

They turned to watch the other fireship coming closer. For all they knew, there were a dozen behind her.

'Maybe we can stop that,' Hondo said.

He turned to Bosin, but the big man suddenly spun on his heel and vanished into the darkness. The other four watched him disappear back the way he had come with varying degrees of incredulity.

Deeds waited for someone else to speak and took a step away from Basker.

'Well, I didn't . . .'

'Deeds?' Hondo interrupted. 'I swear I will kill you myself. Be silent.'

He looked out at the ship on the river, already with a gleam of red showing in its heart. The forces on the right side of the river gate were still silent and dark.

'Come, gentlemen,' Hondo said. He drew his sword and they were all struck by the ringing note, almost like a bell. 'We can stop that ship.'

23

Armour

Tellius bit his lip, wincing as he saw enormous wheeled constructions slowly brought to the fore. Oxen lowed in distress as they were driven on, whipped and struck in their exhaustion. Tellius swore under his breath, angry with himself. He had sent three men in to report on the massive things being hauled behind the army of Féal. Two had gone out filthy, reeking of sweat and horses. The third had relied on a simple cooking pot, saying men rarely challenged servants struggling with a heavy burden. All three had worked for Tellius for years and he'd trusted their skills. While the army marched on Darien, his people had lit out in the dark, circling right around and joining the teams there, trying to get a glimpse of whatever threats lay waiting on the huge carts. Wrapped in tarred or oiled canvas, they had been better guarded than the king himself – and that had made Tellius fear them. Not one of his people had returned. The three men had vanished in the night, as if the army had simply swallowed them.

Whatever the things were, they seemed to need dozens of oxen to pull them into position. Tellius leaned forward, resting his hands on the wall as the thick canvas coverings were peeled away, all down the Féal line. He frowned at the sight of massive black tubes, surrounded by men standing to attention as the animals were unharnessed and driven to the rear to eat or be eaten. He saw braziers being lit and curved wooden shields assembled. A few of his officers tested the range for pistol fire, but out on the plain, the teams didn't even flinch from the shots. The black tubes looked a lot like barrels themselves – and Tellius felt his heart sink as if he had dropped down a well.

Cities had time and leisure and the *markets* to make weapons – Darien was the proof of that with its pistols and crossbows, even the artefacts of the Twelve Families like the De Guise sword. Perhaps nations like the kingdom of Féal had similar resources to bring to the field of war.

The enemy seemed to need light more than privacy to set up their positions. They sparked huge torches and lamps to life and Tellius watched as they scurried around in preparations. He hated the feeling of standing still while others made all the running. It was the reality of remaining behind a defensive wall, of course. Yet before the sun had set, he'd seen an army that stretched to the horizon. Eighty thousand? More? There was no question of sallying out against so many. All his plans were to hold and bleed them against the walls, with contingencies for what would need to be done if they broke through.

The boy-king of Darien was further off along the wall, speaking to the men and awing them that he remained in their midst at such a time. Tellius hoped Arthur would not be killed. There was no heir ready to take over if he fell. They hadn't thought they would ever need one.

Tellius turned as Nancy reached the crest. She saluted him and smiled, though it looked adorable rather than particularly military, like a woman wearing a man's shirt. Tellius nodded to her, putting thoughts like that out of his mind.

'You called, Tellius?' she said. Her expression darkened as she saw the line of torches and the army of Féal revealed. 'There are a lot of them.'

'We've taken a piece out of their cavalry,' he said.

Tellius didn't mention the woman he had seen with her child, or the other families that hadn't made it to safety. Nancy knew the realities as well as he did.

'Here,' he said, holding out the slim box. She had returned it to him when they'd come back to the city, but it was made for her, in defence of Darien. 'Keep it on you. There'll be no holding back against these. You'll need it if they reach the top of the walls.'

She took the box with the Sallet Stone reverently, as if he passed her a relic of the Goddess. Tellius watched as Nancy made it vanish into a pocket of her dress. She nodded once, accepting the seriousness of his words and the charge he laid upon her.

'I'm not so good over long range,' she said.

He shrugged.

'Long range doesn't worry me. They can stay at long range until they starve, as far as I'm concerned. It's short range I'm concerned about. It's those things swarming over there.'

He pointed to the black-armoured creatures she had seen in the camp. Nancy recalled a nightmare while she'd slept, there and gone in memory, though it made her shudder. There still seemed to be hundreds of them and they were never still, as if they had to move or fall. They were not men, she recalled, though they'd seemed aware. She felt her fingers clench.

'They burn well enough,' she said. 'But I see no towers. How can they reach us?'

'Pray they can't,' Tellius said.

Along the vast front of the Féal line, huge banners rose, signalling something. Tellius opened his mouth to speak again and then jumped as a rippling line of shot sounded in a roll, from one end of the line to the other. The cannon teams worked in unison, almost as a display, so that each weapon fired a moment after the one alongside.

The results shook the wall. Tellius could feel a shuddering beneath his feet, that built and built. Smoke hid the Féal army completely and Tellius heard them cheering. He hated them then.

'What are those things?' Nancy whispered.

'Just guns,' he said and shook his head. 'The Aeris legion has some small ones. We've been working on casting iron barrels of that size, but I turned the master smiths onto making chains for the river gate instead. It seems the army of Féal has solved the problems of scaling them up.'

As the smoke cleared, Tellius saw one of the big guns had burst, killing those around it. Yet the rest were being reloaded. He watched in sick fascination.

'Will the walls hold?' Nancy asked. 'Against those things?'

Tellius looked at her.

'That was a show of power, to frighten. They will turn them now on the gates. After that . . . no. I don't think the walls will hold.' She thought how exhausted he looked as he went on. 'You should go back to the streets below, Nancy. You're too valuable to lose if all this comes down.'

The south side of the river gate was a grim place. The previous fireship had come right up against it, actually touching the stone piers before exploding. Hondo found the first bodies at the base, where men had been standing in groups, perhaps to reinforce those on the crest, or change the watch. They lay still, as if asleep, yet they were cold and dead. Some had been sent tumbling and lay sprawled, while others had been caught by some piece of wood or chip of stone as deadly as any bullet. They lay in lines and curves, like script, putting Hondo in mind of the aftermath of a great battle, where the officers walk amongst the dead, looking to learn from the action for next time. Further back, he could hear voices weakly calling for help, but he ignored them. He had different duties, different skills.

The street entrance to the wall itself had been barred with iron gates. They hung twisted and awry and Hondo wrenched them open to step through. He thought the stone walls would surely have protected those within, but the opposite seemed to be true. As he climbed the steps to the crest, he saw blood splashed across the walls and more bodies, though whether they had been flung or crushed or flattened, he had no idea. They did not look like men so much as piles of cloth and metal. Hundreds lay dead where they had clustered on one side to shoot down at the invaders.

Every one of them had been a young man desperate to defend his people and his city. They would have known what the ship represented, from experience of the first one. Yet they had leaned over even so, cramming themselves in to pour fire against that enemy.

Hondo bowed his head, giving them honour. They had not run, because they stood on the walls of their home. Because their women and children waited within. It was not a small thing – and he was pleased Taeshin bowed his head as well as he reached the crest. Even Deeds was silent, though it might have been the bulk of Basker at his back that kept his tongue still in his head. Where was Bosin? Hondo cursed his friend, feeling a spike of worry that the big man's mind had broken, after so many shocks.

The only way past the river gate was one not available to those outside. No one could get through the water entrance without swimming – and that was impossible for men in armour. Had any of the enemy been so foolish as to strip off to get in, they would have been easy meat for soldiers on the city side of the river.

That left the wall itself. In the darkness, some enterprising officer had rigged a rope walkway on the inner edge, no doubt to stop his men falling to their deaths. It was held by iron rods driven into sand and stone. The rods had survived the blast, though they leaned outward and the whole scene was blackened and charred. Hondo sent Deeds after the other end of the rope. When he hauled it free, the sword saint pulled it towards him in great loops. Hondo went to Basker then and spoke quietly.

'I'll need someone up here to pull the rope back up. I can hardly leave it for the men of Féal to climb.'

Basker tried to hide his relief that he would not be asked to shimmy down a high wall. He was strong enough when standing still, but against his own weight, he did not think that would be enough. He nodded and Hondo clapped him on the shoulder once again.

Hondo, Taeshin and Deeds tied the rope on. Deeds checked it carefully, showing he did not trust the other two to have made a decent job, though their lives would rely on it as well.

There was no time for speeches and the three of them just vanished over the side. Basker waited until the rope went slack and then pulled it up, hand over hand. After that, he was alone for the first time since leaving his tavern. He leaned against the wall and panted, trying to keep his heart in his chest. When that had ceased to be a concern, he went and took a pistol and bullets from the hand of a dead man. After a while staring out at the next fireship slipping along the current towards him, he fetched two more and stuck them into his belt.

Hondo had seen the night before how poorly an army fares against a small group of hostiles. The entire structure of regiments and officers and massed lines of infantry or horsemen was a bureaucracy not dissimilar to a city. As soon as numbers were too great for men to know one another by sight, they needed signifiers of armour or shields or flags – and boundaries. Those outside were the enemy, while those who walked purposefully through the ranks would surely already have been challenged if they were not one of us. It meant he only had to get past the outer ring of guards and sentries to be able to move swiftly.

There was no mercy in him. He and Taeshin worked together in pair patterns, changing position back and forth as they approached a guard, appearing out of the darkness and leaving him dead. One of them distracted while the other killed – and Deeds had to scramble to keep up, so quickly did they move. It was not even as well ordered as the formal Féal camp had been. These were regiments of men waiting on a dark field to assault a city, or for fireships to blow enough of it to pieces that they could walk in. Torches of the sort they had used in camp would just have made them better targets, so the darkness was absolute there, with all men as shadows.

Those closest to the walls had mounted ranks of shields on wooden frames against pistol shot. Some of the soldiers actually slept, while others sat by cooking fires or played dice and cards. Their kit lay all around and Hondo only worried Deeds would trip on one of the shields or spears left in piles by their owners. The sword saint and Taeshin went through the army like ghosts, staying as close as they could to the river bank.

Hondo could see the fireship coming closer. One of the masts had been unstepped, so that only a single cross showed. It made it harder for any breeze to get purchase and spoke of careful planning. He needed to get on board and at that moment the barebones ship was too far from the bank to consider leaping for it.

He sweated as he ran, more from the sense of helplessness than exertion. He had to get aboard! He could not watch another ship drift by to blow the walls of Darien apart. He'd seen the cracks on the right side of the river gate as he'd set the ropes, great yawning openings where the mortar had broken. He was not sure it would hold even until the morning, but another explosion would surely bring that entire section down.

Looking into the night, Hondo did not see the line that snagged him until it tangled his steps and brought him down with a crash.

'Watch what you're doing, you fool!' came a voice.

Hondo didn't reply as he was still held. His priority was getting free. Taeshin crouched at his side and found the fishing line, cutting it in two places.

'Are you . . . ? Hey, don't cut it!' the voice went on.

In his consternation, the man did not notice they were not his people. Hondo killed him quickly and silently, letting the body slip into the waters. The voice had been very young. It was odd to think of some enterprising soldier setting a line and hook to fish in the river while he waited. Hondo felt no pang of regret, however. He had walked through hundreds of the dead up on the walls.

As he crouched there with Taeshin and Deeds, flames began to lick out of the fireship's side, illuminating a rickety pier and a fishing boat with a single mast, forty yards or so ahead. Taeshin saw it as well and they set off together, ignoring Deeds as he hissed questions.

Hondo searched for oars, but they had been taken by the owner, no doubt to prevent exactly this sort of opportunistic theft. He cursed. An army rested alongside that bank and they were not all fools. Guards and sentries were up and alert, looking for anything out of place. Yet he sat in a boat, with a fireship about to pass him, looming large over the water and casting its own shimmering light on the surface reflection. In a moment, Hondo knew the light would reveal the three of them, sitting like helpless mice to be captured or killed.

'Use your hands as oars,' Deeds hissed in the darkness.

The gunman tried to reach down, but even lying flat, he was too far from the surface of the river.

'Your swords, then!'

'I will *not* do that!' Hondo replied, appalled. The Ling sword was a year's work from a master and incredibly valuable. He had won it in a tournament of all Shiang and its provinces. It was not a tool!

'Then that ship will go past,' Deeds said. He did not sound disappointed, not now he had seen the gleam of flames in the hold.

Hondo cursed. He drew his sword and cut the rope with it that bound them to the little pier. With a huge shove, Taeshin pushed them out into the current as the fireship came alongside. For just a moment, Hondo thought they might reach it, but the current took hold and they began to drift, moving further from the larger hull.

Hondo swallowed as he lay on the bow. He could hear the cheering of thousands as he had accepted the Ling sword.

'Please, sword saint,' Taeshin said. He handed over his own blade, still in its scabbard. 'Use mine. Not the Ling.'

Hondo nodded in relief and Deeds muttered about foreign idiots as Hondo swished the scabbarded blade through the water, poling them into the main channel. Shouts sounded on the bank, not a dozen yards away. Deeds ducked down in the boat when he realised they would be silhouetted against the fireship for precious moments. As he had the thought, he heard a crackle of gunfire and swore.

'Paddle with it, would you!' Deeds growled at Hondo.

There were wooden steps set into the side of the little ship and Hondo leaped for them, scuttling up and in like a cat. Taeshin followed him and Deeds returned fire to keep the heads down of those pricking shots at him in the dark. He jumped then, and missed, plunging into the river.

Hondo heard the splash, but there was no time to turn back, not with the walls of the city coming at them. Barely forty yards remained before the fireship would drift between the stone pillars. The last one had been well timed, Hondo thought, as he ran the length of the ship. His life hung in a balance he could not see.

The tiller had been tied in place. He slashed the ropes cleanly with Taeshin's sword, then threw his weight against the wooden bar, pushing it over. Both the current and the forward motion of three or four hundred tons of ship fought the rudder. Hondo struggled with the weight until Taeshin joined him and heaved. Together, they shoved the bar right to its stop and the two-master began to turn, groaning, presenting its side to the city. Hondo had a moment of sick apprehension when he thought it would continue on and wedge right in the river gate. Yet the turn continued, though flames showed through the planking under his feet.

Hondo shouted in pleasure as the boat ran aground in the soft bank, the prow crumpling as it dug into mud and rose up. Without needing to say another word, both he and Taeshin ran for the prow and jumped off it into the deeper darkness of the river bank. They did not stop when they hit and rolled but tore into the night, images of dead men on the wall flashing into their imaginations. They made it into a wheat field before an explosion made them stagger for the second time in the evening.

Hondo turned on his back and shielded his face with his sleeve as a blast of air and splinters whined past. He found he was panting and began to laugh in giddy relief as he sat up.

Ahead and to the left of him, a section of the wall groaned as if in pain. As Hondo watched, a huge part suddenly slumped, like a man giving up on life, then slid with a roar into the river. There would be no more fireships passing into the city, but the wall itself was open and Darien lay unprotected.

Hondo came to his feet and dusted himself off. He became aware of the night moving around him and drew the Ling sword before he understood the nature of the threat.

In the darkness, the black figures were almost invisible, silent as they'd crept up on his position. Hondo bowed to Taeshin and took up first position, readying himself. He knew the ferocity of the enemy well enough to know this was his last day, but no fear or weariness showed in his face, though every joint and muscle ached.

'Master Taeshin, you are dismissed from service,' Hondo said. 'By my authority. Make your way back to the wall. That is an order.'

Taeshin blinked as he raised his sword with both hands on the hilt. He thought of Marias and the Fool and he cursed. He had come a long way to die in a foreign city. Though it would be a rare honour to fall at the side of a sword saint, to be mentioned in the great tales, he could not shake the desire to live. He remembered facing death once before and the sense of calm that had descended upon him. Yet he had been spared and it had taught him to value the hours of life.

He closed his eyes for a second, bidding Marias

goodbye. The Fool would protect her. He wanted to live, yes, but he would not leave the sword saint of Shiang to be brought down by creatures of darkness. He would not. They creaked as they moved, he realised. It sounded almost like speech.

'I believe I will stay, Master Hondo,' Taeshin said.

The black figures seemed to writhe in the darkness and he swallowed a knot of fear as he prepared to take some of them into death, whatever they were.

'You are disobedient,' Hondo said.

Taeshin shrugged, dropping into a ready stance, in perfect balance.

'There are no slaves in Darien,' he said.

Something crunched over the rubble of the wall, sending another pile of stones crashing down. It was a distraction and Hondo glanced quickly back to the broken river gate and froze. He knew the Sallet Green armour known as Patchwork. He knew the man within, as well.

Bosin came bounding in with a steel sword in one hand and a green blade in the other. He crossed the distance between the wall and the Black Guards almost as a blur, crashing into them as they drew their own weapons and attacked.

24

Tellius

Tellius stood before the northern city gate, listening to the thump and crack of iron balls hitting. The sounds were different, depending on whether they struck metal or stone. Metal rang out, while stone had no give in it. The walls were like a fat man getting hit in the gut, with each blow causing pain deep inside. The surprise was how well they were holding up under the barrage. His first fear had proved false and the slow thump, thump, crack, thump had settled into a rhythm, though the end would come all the same.

He had not been idle. When he'd confirmed they would concentrate fire on the gates and thanked the Goddess for the sheer weight of the iron beams and the mechanism that kept them shut, Tellius had put out a call for builders and masons in the militias, ordering them to fetch their tools and materials, to build an internal wall.

As he watched, the thing went up, layer on layer inside the gate. Mortar and stone was slathered together and the road for a mile around would be back to mud, just about. Every paving slab or doorstep they could find had been brought to that place, over the protestations of shop- and house-owners alike. The men had told him the mortar would never set in time, but Tellius had Nancy there to warm the stones. Perhaps even then it would not be as solid as it would have been after a few nights of drying. He thought it would do well enough.

If the gates were broken down, the soldiers who rushed in would find themselves in a narrow passage between massive curving bulwarks of stone, the height of a man and at least as deep, as they blocked the road for twenty paces. Tellius had wanted to close off the end, but one of his captains had pointed out the Féal gunners would just settle back then, hammering the same spot until the inner wall fell. It would be better to leave a funnel for them to get through – and have gun regiments ready for them.

Tellius smiled at that thought, though he jerked at another booming blow, exactly where he was staring at the gates. The sound was a bell tolling. He'd already seen the iron spheres littering the ground before the city, half-sunk into the turf under their own weight. Yet each hour of the night that passed was a thumb in the eye of the king of Féal, Tellius could feel it. To arrive at sunset and then attack was a mark of colossal arrogance. If that sun rose again and the city still stood defiant, the king would have lost face in front of his entire army. Such things mattered.

Each move the man made showed more of who he was. Tellius had begun to see defence, not as a passive, waiting thing, but as a chance to humiliate a king who thought he could just arrive and command the walls to fall. King Jean Brieland thought they could not stand against him. Every hour they did proved him wrong.

As Tellius watched, a string of carts appeared along the ring road, their owners whipping tired old nags who would have preferred to spend the night in a warm stable. They brought oak beams and piled stone slabs that looked suspiciously like gravestones. Tellius thought he should probably leave them to it before he found out where they had come from.

He walked back to the steps and groaned at the sight of the messenger coming down. Donny was a good lad on the whole, but he had a sort of twisted delight in bad news. Tellius saw it in his face as he reached the yard below.

'There's those black armour things coming, boss. In a rush.'

Tellius stood still for a moment. He was tempted to shrug. The walls and the gate still stood. What did it matter . . . His stomach swooped away from him. He'd heard the reports. The things could leap. The things could climb.

'Nancy! To me now!' he called to her. 'I need you on the wall!'

She stood with awed builders around her, like the Goddess herself brought to life, as she placed her palms on mortar and stone and warmed them. He saw her nod and he was off, climbing the stairs to the crest of the wall once more.

'What about these walls?' one of the workmen called.

Tellius looked down on them as he reached the top. They carried trowels and iron spikes with string wound about them. At the side were the swords and guns and pikes they had laid down. He was proud of them all and he chuckled.

'Build higher! You are clever men,' he roared down to them. 'We are a clever city. Build!'

Vic Deeds was afraid. He understood fear well enough to know it, to welcome it even, in the right place. In more normal times, it sharpened a man. It kept him focused when his life was on the line, so it wasn't always a bad thing, at least not for him. Being dropped into a river in complete darkness, with a gleaming fireship passing overhead, had introduced him to a different sort of terror, where he could hardly move for a sense of doom rushing down on him. Ruining his cartridges, so that his guns were barely better than clubs, was also part of it.

He was unarmed, in the middle of an enemy army rushing towards a breach in the walls of Darien. Only their focus on that breach and the darkness kept him alive as he went reluctantly with them, squelching with every step. Deeds had lived most of his life in expectation of the hand on his shoulder, the voice calling him out. Yet he didn't want them to spot him. He didn't want to die there, not that night.

Ahead, he saw the black-armoured creatures, clambering over one another to get to . . . yes, Hondo was there. The sword saint had survived the blast. Deeds found he was running towards Hondo in a line of hostile soldiers, all unaware of his presence in their midst. He tried to slow his pace. He had seen Hondo move in the deep forest and in the enemy camp. Deeds had no desire to be mistaken for one of them.

He was looking for somewhere, anywhere, to throw himself down when Bosin came bounding out of the city wearing the Sallet Green suit they called Patchwork. It gleamed deep jade as the big man crashed into the Féal beetles. Deeds felt his line slow further and he flung himself flat as if he'd been shot, lying still as those behind rushed on past. More than one trampled him deeper into the mud, making him wish for dry ammunition as he tried not to yell out. It was still better than running into range of the maniac in Patchwork, Deeds told himself. For an age, he was battered and kicked and sworn at as an obstacle, unseen in the dark.

The Sallet Green suit was huge in comparison to the beetles. They hung on Bosin's arms and he spun them round like a father with his children at the harvest festival. Then he flung them down with huge force, plunging swords green and steel into black joints, hacking limbs and pieces away. More leaped at him, making him stagger. If the creatures had just run past, Bosin could not have stopped them all. Yet they seemed to see only him, as if his presence was an ancestral challenge they could not ignore.

Hondo and Taeshin stood on either side, letting Bosin have the centre. The big man's face was hidden by the armour, though Hondo thought he could hear Bosin laughing as he tore the creatures apart and crushed them underfoot. He did not know if that was a good sign.

The charging line of Féal soldiers reached them, howling. They saw only two men and edged away from the whirling monster in the centre, draped all around by black-armoured things.

Yet they could not pass the swordsmen. The first casual shield strikes were knocked aside, their owners killed. Both Shiang men then picked up fallen shields when pistol fire crackled in angry disorder. The night lit in flashes and they were never there when men of Féal adjusted their aim. Bosin's armour flashed and sparked as they fired at him, but he did not fall.

Step by step, the three defenders were forced back rather

than allow the enemy to get round and into the city. The gap in the wall was barely six paces across, though another column of stone looked as if it might fall at any moment, widening it.

'Back, Master Bosin,' Hondo called to the green-armoured figure.

Bosin had torn through the black creatures. He was a master swordsman of Shiang, in a suit that magnified his strength and speed. Hondo knew he would be in agony the following day, if he lived. Yet he and Taeshin could not have stood alone against the beetles of Féal. Bosin had saved them. At least for a time.

Up on the walls, Hondo heard orders called. He had no idea how long he'd been out in the dark, but someone had clearly reinforced the gate position.

'Be ready to retreat to the wall!' Hondo called. He tried not to flinch when the order to fire sounded. Surely they would see him, or if not him, Bosin?

The range was short as gun companies opened fire. They had assembled in the breach itself, as well as high along the walls. Bullets whined past and Hondo ducked, knowing how easy it was to be hit when frightened men poured fire into the night.

He found himself edging towards Bosin and the big man widened his arms to shelter Hondo and Taeshin as he walked backwards, still with two swords outstretched. The last of the black creatures vanished back into the night at last, leaving a dozen or so in pieces on the ground. Hondo did not think he imagined the baleful quality in the stares they turned on Bosin. He could feel their hate, he was certain of it.

The ranks of Féal broke under those massed volleys, fired from higher ground. The darkness was just too comforting and they turned and ran, knowing they could not be seen. Hondo was left panting, facing a field of the dead. One of them rose suddenly and ran towards him, so black with mud it looked like one of the creatures. Hondo reached over and tapped Bosin on the chest-plate as he raised a blade. The panel flickered grey in response.

'That is Deeds, Bosin. He lives.'

'Hold your fire!' Deeds yelled as he ran. 'Darien man coming back in. Don't shoot your heroes, you bastards!'

The men on the rubble actually cheered, patting Deeds like a lucky charm as he and the others clambered inside the boundary of the city. Hondo saw the river was well and truly blocked. There were men running everywhere to make a barricade across the breach, with still more examining the broken walls to see if they should pull down part of it or work to make it safe. The walls were a hive of activity and Hondo smiled as Bosin turned and looked down on him. The cold expression of the green armour reminded him of the man Bosin had been, a little. Yet Hondo could hear him chuckling inside.

'I was pleased to see you,' Hondo said.

Bosin clapped him on the back and sent him staggering.

The river was dark beyond the city. No more fireships drifted in to the walls. Hondo saw massive wooden beams coming to cover the breach, and as he looked up, the streets beyond were filled with militia regiments, gun and sword. The entire city had turned out to face the threat and he did not think the enemy would get through them, not there.

Deeds had found Basker and been given new pistols

and cartridge belts. He was reloading, with relief clear on his face. He had begun to shiver in his wet clothes, so that the bullets rattled against metal in his hands.

'This was more than a diversion,' Hondo said. 'There were, what . . . two, three thousand? Twenty or so of those beetles? And the fireships. They wanted to force a breach here.'

He watched as beams were hammered into place. New stone blocks had been procured from some store and were already being lifted by rope teams and straining men. The officers had cleared the bodies of the dead without ceremony, leaving decencies such as funerals until they'd survived the night.

'I'm happy to stay here,' Deeds said. 'We've done enough.' He was bone-weary and he could see the Shiang madmen were just itching to get back to the fight.

'No, son,' Basker said. 'Not yet.'

They stood in a rough ring. Taeshin, Hondo and Bosin faced Basker and Deeds. It was a moment of silent communication that none of them could quite have put into words. Yet Deeds dipped his head, accepting.

'Fine. But no more water. No damned rivers. I like the way they cheered me then. But if I am to be a hero, I want to get onto the wall. And after that, the next person to cross my path gets a bullet in the face.'

Tellius arrived at the top of the steps, panting. He was in time to see the first of the black beetles clamber over the wall and leap amongst the defenders. They were fast and vicious, like crickets with black blades. Some of the dozen regiments along that section tried to shoot them as they climbed, but in that, they resembled spiders, gripping and flinging themselves upward. They arrived then like scythes in the midst of packed soldiers. It was carnage. He heard shock in the cries and shouts of dying men, while all along the wall, others pressed forward to attack. Their courage was a kind of madness, but they could not just stand aside. They could not let such things down into the city.

'Nancy, you're up,' Tellius said.

She slid open the box and slipped the green Sallet Stone into her hand. He watched open-mouthed as her hair darkened and writhed with life. Her eyes seemed to gleam and then she went past him. Men dived for cover as she spilled white threads into the night, drawing power from the stone.

The creatures she reached began to die, crumpling back in grey husks and falling inert, or tumbling back to the ground far below. Yet there were so many of them! Tellius felt the stones shudder again as the heavy fire intensified. He could hear the tramp of marching, armoured men coming closer. This was the great push then, the surge that King Jean Brieland expected would bring the walls tumbling. He cursed the man. If they could just hang on till dawn, they would have won something. They could wear his damned pride like a pendant then. Or his balls.

Nancy had become the focus for the beetle creatures as they clambered over. He saw her cry out in warning as two of them leaped high. Her life hung in the balance and yet she was brimful of the stone's power and she could not halt her own reaction. The ball of light and heat cracked out around her, incinerating the two beetles as well as a dozen men who could not get far enough away.

Tellius winced and swore, but there was nothing they could do. Neither swords nor guns seemed any use against the things climbing and whirling against them. He needed artefacts.

The thought galvanised him. It had been moments since Nancy had gone in and he'd stood watching her like a fool. He could feel exhaustion making him slow and stupid, but he had to keep moving.

'Regis!' Tellius called along the line. 'Regis and De Guise here!'

He heard it taken up and an answering shout in reply. Regis was coming. Tellius knew the man would not be far off.

As he had the thought, one of the black-armoured things climbed over the wall where he stood, facing him. Nancy was too far away to call. Tellius could only stare in sick fascination as the creature looked for other threats or targets. He was just one old man and it darted its head back and forth, discounting him. There was awareness there, judgement, some sort of mind. When it caught sight of Nancy, the thing froze and began to go after her.

Tellius hacked his sword with both hands against the creature's neck. As he did, he felt a pain across his chest and down his left arm. Something clicked under his blade, as if the metal had cracked. He felt it run right through him.

The beetle tried to turn back, but he had damaged something. Its head grated and dipped to one side. It lived, even so. He understood it would rush him, the eyes gleaming like black glass.

Regis arrived at a run, the shield of his family held before him. He cracked it into the black figure and knocked it over the wall to the plain below. He turned in delight to Tellius, but his grin faded when he saw the man's grey expression. Lord De Guise had come with Regis, carrying the family sword. The younger man was quick enough to catch Tellius as he fell and laid him down on the steps.

Below their feet, a great crash sounded. The wall around the gate had given way and one of the massive iron plates had been smashed back, yawning open. The city was falling and on the plain the army of Féal roared victory, their voices like the sea. Tellius could not take a breath for the pain that tore into him. He was going to die without her!

'Find Win, would you?' he tried to say.

He did not know if De Guise had heard. The young man was saying something to Regis, already looking away. They could not stay, of course, not with those creatures leaping and scuttling along the wall, killing as they went. Tellius understood. Yet the thought of dying without having the chance to see Win Sallet again was almost worse than everything else.

'You, boy. Sit with Master Tellius, would you?' Lord De Guise said.

Tellius felt himself raised to sit and dragged against the inner lip of wall. He was grateful for it. His strength had gone and his chest seemed to have a piece of broken glass in it that tore at him with every breath. He looked over, expecting Donny. He was surprised to see the face of Henry Canis instead. The boy was weeping again. Why was he weeping?

'You should not be up here,' Tellius told him, his voice a whisper.

The boy patted him on the shoulder, in clumsy mimicry of something he had seen.

'They are fetching Lady Sallet,' Henry Canis said.

Tellius shook his head. He tried to push himself up, but the pain surged immediately and made him gasp. Breathing was getting harder, he realised, trying to control panic. He did not want to die choking. He'd ask Regis to kill him first, to make it quick.

'I liked your father,' Tellius whispered. 'He was a good man.'

He watched the boy's eyes fill with new tears. Goddess, he was always weeping!

As Tellius looked away, Henry Canis reached into his pocket and pulled out a flat, black stone, flecked in gold. He reached out with it and felt his arm gripped in Tellius' right hand.

'No,' Tellius said.

'I can *save* you,' Henry Canis said.

'It would not be me,' Tellius replied, though he spoke through agony. His eyes were wide, with longing and desperation, but he still held the boy tight enough to hurt. Henry Canis scrambled back with a cry then, breaking his grip and running off along the wall.

'Tellius?'

He heard a voice he knew. A voice he loved. Tellius tried to turn his head as a green gleam lit that part of the wall. She had come. She had brought her two remaining Sallet Greens and she had come. He felt himself lifted away from the wall and then settled back into her arms as she knelt on the sand and dust and looked into his eyes.

'Didn't want to go . . . without seeing you,' he said.

She kissed him on the cheek then, a touch that was surprisingly warm. At her side, a little girl settled down, her eyes wide. Elias' daughter, Tellius recalled. There were so many things he had to do, still.

He glanced up as Arthur knelt on the muddy ground at his side then. The news was spreading and though the battle raged further along the wall, others were coming in to that spot. Tellius looked at Micahel from the Mazer school as he too knelt, and then at Donny as the lad skidded and dropped alongside them, his mouth twisting. Tellius felt his breath growing shallow and the pain in his chest only increased, never giving him rest. He saw they needed him to speak to them and so he did.

'I never *had* . . . children. I was never a father, but . . .'

'Yes you were,' Arthur said. The others nodded. The king's eyes shone and tears spilled down his cheek.

'Please don't go,' Win said. 'Please. I love you.'

He did not want to, but he had no choice. His head sagged and life went out of him, leaving him less. Tellius felt the pressure of her final embrace and then he was gone.

25

Broken

Nancy fought to control the power that boiled in her. She seemed to draw the beetle figures like iron filings, as if they remembered her from the camp, or sensed she was the greatest threat. As soon as they saw her coming, they broke off their attacks on the wall regiments and scuttled in her direction.

She walked on dead things and bloodstained sand as she moved along the wall, trying to check over her shoulder as she went until Lords Regis and De Guise came at a run and took station there. She'd faced a swarm of the things at that moment and barely had time to shout for them to keep their distance before she'd triggered a ball of light that left stones a fading gold. Sand crunched underfoot, cracking like ice on a pond. Yet there were still hundreds of them and they were determined to bring her down. The light she brought cracked out again and again, though good men died in it. She could not save them, though she cried out for them to get off the wall. Their duty and their beautiful stubbornness held them there – and she brought death as she went.

Every step was a struggle for control as power flowed from the Sallet Stone and out through her. She could feel it like a river of acid and, after a time, it seemed to burn her as well, so that she hurt, worse and worse. Still they came – and she made ash of dark shells.

She held up the stone like a shield and felt her fingers digging into it, so that she gripped it like a bar of soap, leaving deep marks. Another blast of white heat tore through three of them as they flung themselves towards her. One had a grip on her neck and was bringing a sword down when she charred it. Regis was battering another pair further back, while De Guise aimed his sword at the things, spearing them in dark light.

Nancy felt the stone fail as her grip collapsed. She was left with stiff fingers and a handful of pale dust. As she gaped, it began to blow away. No more magic roared through her in a torrent. She had used it all and her first horrified thought, before even her own safety, was how she would tell Lady Sallet.

The remaining black creatures clustered before her, expecting death from her hand. She could only gape at them, helplessly. Slowly, they began to unbend, to stand tall. They were still suspicious, she could see it, but they would attack.

'Regis?' Nancy called without turning away. She heard running steps behind her, but she dared not take her eyes off the beetle things that could move so frighteningly quickly. It was with fear and confusion that she felt her sleeve tugged and looked down to the upturned face of a little boy.

'No! Get away from here!' Nancy said. 'You'll be killed.' They would all be killed, she realised. There were still too many of the things alive.

'Here,' the boy said. He pressed a stone into her hand,

the same shape and size as the one that had turned to dust, but black and flecked with gold in its depths. 'Use this. For my father.'

He was pale, but determined and he did not look afraid. Henry Canis patted her on the arm then and walked back the way he had come, past the astonished figures of Regis and De Guise.

Nancy turned to the beetles. She felt the power in the stone and let it fill her, like water into a dry well. The creatures froze for a moment, understanding that something had changed. White threads cracked out from her once again and her hair writhed a deeper red.

'How *dare* you threaten my people,' she said to them. She blinked at that, as she had not meant to say the words aloud. Whether they understood or not, they rushed her and she burned the air itself as her response.

Elias stood on a street that had previously been cobbled, but had then lost those stones in great swathes, torn up all around the gate. Within a short time, the sandy base beneath had been churned into the thick muck he'd known on his first visit to the city, when Darien had been a strange and frightening place. In some ways, it still was.

Tellius had told him to stay close, to wait until he was called. 'There is always more than one plan,' the man had said. Elias had seen only glimpses of him after that, running up and down the steps, marshalling the resources of the city and sending them where they were needed most. Whatever those plans had involved, he had not yet called Elias on deck.

Elias looked up when light flashed on the crest of the

wall, recognising instantly that Nancy was up there. He clenched his fists, feeling useless for the first time in years. He was no good to anyone on a defensive wall, not really. For all the extraordinary power of his knack, he could not stop the massive guns arrayed out on the plain, nor scratch the beetle creatures he'd seen in the Féal camp. It hurt to admit, but his knack was good for murder and his own protection, more than war. As Elias watched Tellius race back up the steps, he thought it seemed a selfish thing.

The speaker for the council did not come down again and Elias waited while the gates were hammered. He saw the wall the men were building, though without Nancy there to warm the mortar, the new sections would be weak. Elias winced with the others as strikes hit the gates at the same time, in twos and threes. The men there cringed away from the impacts and some of them were flung aside with killing force when one of the gates slammed open, smashing through part of the wall they had built.

Elias looked up as he heard the roar of the army outside. They knew what it meant. He heard, too, the tramping feet of the regiments stationed around that gate. They were coming up to defend the breach, readying weapons to repel the assault.

He heard a low whistle behind him and turned sharply to see Bosin and Hondo, Taeshin and Deeds. Elias knew Basker as well and was somehow unsurprised to see the big tavern-keeper with a sword in one fist and a pistol in the other.

'Evening, meneer,' Basker said, cheerfully.

Elias nodded to him.

'Tellius told me to be ready for orders, but he's been up on the wall for an age.'

'Then we should go up,' Deeds said. 'Let the men see me, that sort of thing.'

'He is right,' Hondo said. 'We can be useful.'

Elias smiled in relief, pleased to have someone break through his indecision. He trotted to the stairs and the group followed him up.

They found chaos and blood on the sand. In the east, the grey light known as the wolf dawn was showing, a smear across the horizon that seemed to make the world colder. Lady Sallet knelt near the top of the steps, with Tellius across her lap. Elias could see the man had died and his heart went out to her.

Standing at her side was a figure Elias recognised. A pair of royal guards stood ready to defend the king of Darien, wary of armed men appearing. Elias felt his knees buckle for a step and he froze, glancing over his shoulder. Deeds had also met Arthur, when the boy had stood like a statue in the old king's palace, with flames licking up the walls. Elias felt his eyes widen further as he recognised his daughter kneeling straight-backed alongside Lady Sallet, in skirts like a lady-in-waiting. Jenny looked up at her father in a mixture of nervousness and defiance he knew very well.

'Your Majesty, Lady Sallet,' Elias said, recovering from his surprise.

Sounds of fighting still dragged at his attention along the wall. In the presence of the king, Elias dropped to one knee before rising. At his back, Hondo did the same. Arthur looked up at them and Elias saw bright tears in the boy's eyes. Four years before, Arthur had spent a month of summer with him in his village, part of their family as he healed and recovered, before returning to Darien to be king. Elias put out his arms and both his daughter and Arthur came to embrace him in the same moment. He put one arm around each and held them tight.

'I'm sorry,' Elias said over their heads. 'Tellius was a good man.'

'Yes,' Lady Sallet replied. 'And he pushed himself to this. I don't know if I can forgive him for that.'

Elias hesitated, unsure how to go on. Hondo saw one of her servants was standing nervously nearby, without the authority or nerve to break through to his mistress. Hondo nodded to him. He understood.

'Son, this is a dangerous place,' Hondo said firmly. 'You should take your mistress to safety.'

'And my daughter,' Elias said. 'And the king.'

As he spoke, Win Sallet glanced up, understanding his fear. Smoke drifted along the wall like morning mist. The battle still crashed on below, so that stones trembled and dust danced. She laid Tellius gently down and placed his hands over his chest. Without a word, she reached down and kissed him, then rose to her feet. She looked worn, her eyes red and swollen.

'He is right,' she said to her servant. 'Take Master Tellius down. Go with him, would you, Jenny? To look after him. Fetch a couple more of the lads to help you.'

A young man neither Hondo nor Elias knew stepped closer then.

'I'd like to help carry him, my lady, if you don't mind. My name's Donny. He was kind to me, when I was a kid. To be honest, he saved me.'

'Why thank you, Donny,' she said, though her vision swam with tears and she could hardly see. She watched as Donny and Micahel and then Arthur took position around the man she loved still. One of the king's guards stepped in to help, but Arthur waved him back.

She could not bear it. Lady Sallet turned with an effort of will and looked over the army of Féal outside the walls. They were pressing closer than they had before, pushing in through the breach. Below their feet, pistol fire erupted in massed crackling, with grey smoke rising through the air. It was the smell of war and the city would bleed out those trying to bring it down.

'Do you see there, Master Hondo?' Lady Sallet said suddenly, pointing. 'On the plain. Do you see those swirling banners, those horsemen?'

'Yes, my lady. I can make them out.'

'*That* is where he will be,' she said. 'The king of Féal. He waits for his men to establish a safe boundary inside the walls. Like a cancer growing inside us, Master Hondo.'

She looked past Hondo to the others clustering in that spot. Deeds was there, with a pistol in each hand. Taeshin stood with Hondo, a dark and troubled young man who had never been at home in Darien. Win Sallet knew Patchwork as well as anyone alive. She had been the one to allow Bosin the use of it earlier that night, when he'd arrived panting at her estate house. Elias was known to her only from planning sessions with Tellius.

'Tellius sent you all against the Féal camp,' she said. 'He sent you out to try and stop this from happening. And it failed.'

'We reached the king,' Elias said. 'But I could not cut him down.'

'He has some sort of protection,' Hondo murmured. 'Though Deeds shot him in the head.'

'And drew blood with it,' Deeds said. 'If Nancy hadn't been ruining my aim with her fire-starting, I'd have taken him down.'

'Nancy was close to you?' Lady Sallet asked. 'When you shot the king?'

Her eyes widened as she understood. She looked over to Tellius as Donny and Micael and Arthur lifted him up, gripping folds of his clothes. He was no great weight. Elias' daughter went with them, though she let her father draw her into another embrace before she descended the stairs. Win Sallet wanted to call out and stop them, to go with him. And she would, she told herself, just as soon as she had pulled the bow back and sent these people against her enemy. There was a season for grief. There was a season also for vengeance.

'Nancy draws magic in,' she said. 'It is her "knack". If the king was injured while she was close, it is because she was draining his protection. Ruining it.'

'Permanently?' Deeds said. He looked over the walls to where the king of Féal sat surrounded by horsemen, his banners like fluttering shadows. The gunman's expression was wolfish as he smiled.

'If you had fired a second shot, he would be dead,' she said, wiping the grin from his face. 'But take her with you.'

'Sorry, what? Take her with me where?' Deeds asked.

Hondo pointed over the wall.

'Lady Sallet is sending us out, one more time,' he said.

'One *last* time,' Win Sallet added.

Deeds looked from face to face, frowning. Basker spoke before he could.

'You did say you wanted to be a hero, son.'

'I wanted to be a live hero, with women and free beer. Not to charge an army in the dark again. The old Goddess doesn't like me testing my luck like this.'

'The sun will be up any moment,' Hondo said. 'Would you rather charge an army in daylight?'

As one, they all looked to the east. Already the light was changing.

'If we're going, it has to be right now,' Hondo said. He could see Nancy coming closer, summoned by one of Lady Sallet's men.

'How, though?' Deeds said, peering over the inner wall. 'There is an army down there, all pushing to get in our gate.'

Hondo jerked his head to the ropes that had been brought up for the last refugees. Deeds sighed. Every time he made an objection, it was countered.

'Pull them back up as soon as we are down,' Elias said. He was already uncoiling one and as Deeds watched, he dropped a mass of loops over the edge and began climbing down.

'Nancy?' Lady Sallet said. 'They are going to try and kill the king. I know I can't . . .'

'I'm going with them,' Nancy said.

She followed Elias on his rope, with Taeshin behind her. Deeds looked over as Bosin threw down another and clambered after it, with the rope wrapped around the armoured arm of the Patchwork suit.

'I liked Tellius,' Deeds said. 'The city will be poorer without him.'

He saw her eyes harden.

'Yes. Yes it will. Now go, Master Deeds. Pay your debts.'

He blinked at that and wondered how much she knew. As he climbed down, he suspected it was probably all of it.

Only Basker still stood there. He looked apologetically at Lady Sallet.

'I can't climb down that rope, my lady. Maybe twenty years ago. Not now.'

'Then remain on the wall, sir! As long as you can, until you have done all you can. Given all you can. *That* is all that matters. Do you understand?'

Her voice trembled at the end. With the others gone, he saw she had let her grief return. Or perhaps she was just no longer able to hold it in. Basker turned away to give her what privacy he could. He heard her weeping and gave up on that. He had daughters and he knew what to do. When he turned back and opened his arms, she fell against him and sobbed her heart out, just a girl again.

The army clustering like blackflies against the walls of Darien had not expected to come under attack. Elias grinned as he landed on turf. As a hunter, he knew well that the best time to take prey was actually not in the dark, nor in daylight, but in the hour between, when the eye of man is confused in greys and shadows. He killed his first soldier within moments of reaching the ground, clearing a space for the others.

They came down one by one and the ropes vanished like snakes writhing back up the wall.

'Slow and silent,' Elias told them. He *reached* as he spoke and he was already turning to a shadowy soldier running at them when Deeds shot the man in the head. The sound seemed especially loud against the walls and the entire army of Féal seemed to become aware of them in the same moment.

'*Damn* it, Deeds,' Elias said.

There was no time for anything else. He felt the wash of heat and the grey light became full day as Nancy threw out threads. Elias *reached* hard and strode forward with his little knife held to cut throats. At his side, Hondo and Taeshin took station, guarding his flanks. Within a few steps, Bosin went ahead of them, with one green sword and another steel blade of Shiang.

They moved away from the walls like a thresher, through a close-pressed enemy, leaving a trail of dead. There was still surprise enough, in that no one in the army of Féal knew what was going on, or believed they could possibly be under attack in the moment of their victory. The city gates had been blown in! Most of them were still howling their delight, clashing shields and swords.

Yet something was wrong. Somewhere close by, men were yelling, screams were cut off – and a green figure trampled them down. The six of them came out in a spearpoint and Elias killed and killed as they went. It was not long before he and Bosin were mired in blood and filth. Of course, Hondo remained somehow clean, as if even death could not touch the sword saint of Darien.

Hondo blinked at the thought. That was what he was. He had joked with Tellius that the city school would one day produce a sword saint, but Darien already had one. Him.

It felt like a revelation, rising like the sun that peeked over the horizon in the east and cast gold across the army of Féal. Hondo just hoped he would live long enough to tell Bosin.

The light brought a more concerted response. The Féal horsemen were armoured and ruthless enough to ride down their own ranks to face whatever enemy was cutting a trail from the walls towards King Jean Brieland. As dawn grew clearer, enough soldiers pulled out of their way to allow a rank of heavy cavalry to reach a decent canter, heading into the centre.

Elias knew he could not stand against a mass of iron and horseflesh. He was grateful when Bosin peeled off to face them, spreading his arms wide and rushing suddenly terrified horses.

Elias pressed on between Taeshin and Hondo. He could still hardly believe the level of their skill. He was not certain he could survive a bout with either of them, but the one they called the sword saint seemed to move like a ghost, though he had to be older than Elias by a dozen years or more.

To the sides, Deeds kept up a withering barrage of gunfire against anyone who raised gun or weapon. He was extraordinarily accurate, as Elias knew very well, though the army had woken up to them and the protection of Bosin's armour was some way behind. Elias knew there was only so long they could keep going, before surprise was choked off and they were surrounded and cut down.

Bosin caught up with them, looking battered. He had lost his green sword against the cavalry line and one of his legs kept flashing grey, so that he had to drag it for a few steps. Yet Elias was grateful for his presence.

Without warning, they broke through a line of heavily

armoured men to open ground. Elias jammed his little knife into an armpit and pushed another warrior into Hondo's path, where he was instantly cut down.

The sun was still rising and Elias found himself facing the dumbfounded figures of the king's mounted personal guard. In their midst was King Jean Brieland of Féal. The man made a flicking gesture with his fingers and two of his beetle creatures leaped forward, but not at Elias. They went for Bosin and he grunted as he caught them and began to twist.

Elias did not hesitate. As the king's guards spurred their mounts to ride at him, he slipped through the spaces between. The king drew an ornate sword and swung it, but Elias leaned aside and pulled the man off his horse in a crash of armour. He punched him then, over and over, then knelt on his chest, a king who threatened his daughters . . . and his city. Elias felt the beat of it, deep in him. Darien had been a distant place once, but he had fought and bled for it. He had earned the right to call her his own.

He felt something touch his hand, like the whisper of wings, or the silken creep of a wasp. Elias was too used to sitting still in bracken and fern to react sharply, but he could not help glancing over. He saw nothing, but he felt the skin tighten and constrict, the stinging touch moving higher. He blinked as he felt the sensation reach his shoulder and chest. It felt sickeningly intimate. Even as the king looked up at him, he wanted to jump up and take off his shirt.

A cold hand gripped his throat, exactly the sensation of strong, chill fingers on his skin. He swallowed, understanding that it was some magical thing. Elias shifted his knee to the king's arm and brought his little knife up as something squeezed him and he found he could no longer breathe.

I have him, my love.

King Jean Brieland was staring up at Elias. He tried to say something, but even as Elias choked and began to go purple, he still brought down his blade. He jammed his knife into the king's throat and made sure he would not rise again.

There was no air to be had. Elias felt his vision darkening and he tried not to panic, though he knew everyone did in the end. He did not see Nancy coming closer, though the world spun gold around her and, in the light of the Canis Stone, all shadows were made rags. Elias heard something shriek in despair and pain – and then he was gasping and coughing, more grateful for air and life than he had ever been.

Exhaustion came like a wave then. Elias stood, swaying. The army was still roaring in and even in that place of flickering light, though Bosin stamped and Hondo moved like a wraith, he knew they would not get out. Even Nancy would be overwhelmed in the end, though he thought she might make floating cinders of half that army before they brought her down.

He heard Deeds curse as his guns clicked empty. Elias dipped his head and looked down on the man who had brought so much misery. It was easy to see the face of the prince in his father.

Elias looked up. Tellius had chosen him as leader of their little group. Perhaps for this.

'In the name of the king, I command you to lay down

your arms!' he bellowed. The volume and certainty of it shocked some of those around him out of their battle rage. One of the king's generals had been unhorsed in the chaos. He took a step away from the strangers who had walked right into the camp. The man's face was coldly furious.

'He isn't saying a word, you murdering . . .'

'Not this dead man. His son,' Elias said. 'The new king.'

He felt Hondo and Taeshin turn to him and shrugged.

'There is always more than one plan,' Elias said. He turned back to the officer.

'If you kill us now, it will be against the orders of the heir, Louis. At least hear what he has to say before you continue. King Jean Brieland is dead. Long live his son. And blow retreat, lad. I do not want to have to kill you, or anyone else today. Pull the army back from the walls of the city.'

He rose up from the dead body of Jean Brieland to address the king's officer.

'What is your name?' Elias asked.

The man could not seem to look away from the blood that spattered his chest and throat. Elias reached out and broke his trance with a tap on the chest.

'General Petraeus, sir,' he said, automatically.

'The king is dead, General Petraeus. His son commands you to stand down.'

'I can't . . . take your word for that,' the man replied through clenched teeth.

'Then give me till noon. Pull your army back and wait. We'll keep the gate open. Before noon, you'll have word from King Louis.'

'He lives, then?' the general asked.

Elias nodded.

'I'm glad. I heard . . .' The man made a decision. 'Very well. If I don't hear by noon, we will attack. Give me your word you will not reinforce the walls and gates in the meantime.'

'You have my word,' Elias said immediately. 'Anyway, it would hardly be fair.'

He felt giddy and chuckled, surprising the man. Elias turned his back on him then, looking to the city. Up on the walls and around the broken gate, Elias could still hear the clash and cries of fighting. He and the others had come barely two hundred paces, though it had seemed longer.

'Blow retreat, general,' Elias said. 'Or go against the command of your own king.'

As Elias walked back, Nancy and Deeds fell in beside him. Bosin joined them, though his leg dragged and he was exhausted and slow. Taeshin and Hondo brought up the rear – and ahead of them, the ranks of Féal parted like the sea. The soldiers did so in confusion and visible anger, but the horns began to sound and the army blew retreat.

'Six of us,' Deeds said. 'None like us.'

26

Patient

Prince Louis looked up at the sound of footsteps. He felt his heart pound faster at the thought that they had finally come for him. One of the nurses had told him his father was attacking the city the night before. She had glared at him like it was his fault, while the truth was his stomach had tied itself into knots of fear at the news. He did not know what he hoped for in those moments of indecision. He watched the door handle turn and imagined his father entering the room and sitting on the bed. Fear uncoiled in his stomach.

Lady Sallet entered. He knew her from the council meetings and his mind raced with implications. She rustled as she moved, filling the room with whispering. Without a word, she closed the door and settled herself on a chair by his bed. He tried to frown at her with one good eye, but he was too desperate for news.

'Your father is dead,' she said. 'He fell on the field of battle, attacking this city. His army waits for word that you are alive. You are his heir?'

He nodded, mute. It was too much to take in.

'Then in this moment, though you are yet uncrowned, you are the king of Féal, Your Majesty.'

He narrowed his eye in suspicion.

'Where is Tellius? I would like to hear from the Master Speaker.'

Her expression tightened as he spoke and her eyes grew cold.

'He died in defence of the city. No one could have done more.'

'I'm sorry,' he said. 'He . . . I'm sorry.'

'Yes,' she said, taking a moment to arrange the green skirts. He could see pockets sewn into them as she smoothed the material with her palms. 'There will be a funeral. Perhaps you will attend, as representative of your nation. Yet you present a problem to me, Your Majesty. A problem I can resolve in a number of ways.'

'Most of which involve my death, Lady Sallet. I understand. Does my father's army wait under a flag of truce? Is that why you have come to me?'

'It does. And it is your army now, Your Majesty, not your father's.'

He sighed. She did not know him, nor how his view of the world had changed. His father had taken an eye. At that moment, his main feeling on hearing the man was dead was just relief he would never see him again.

'So you are considering whether I should be allowed to leave, or whether it would be better to kill me.'

'You are perceptive,' she said softly.

He inclined his head, accepting the compliment.

'I don't know how I can convince you. If you let me return to my army, I will take them home, to rebuild, to trade. I will not return here.'

'Perhaps. Or perhaps we will see your son or grandson marching south once more.'

'Well, I cannot speak for them!' he snapped.

She raised an eyebrow and he coloured.

'My point, Your Majesty, was that if you leave as a beaten enemy, peace will always be fragile. My wish is to continue our trading agreement, exactly as you had it before.'

'The new Lord Canis will vote against it,' he said. He had the grace to blush deeper as she looked at him.

'But . . .' She hesitated and thought of Tellius. Yes. She would take a risk. 'But I will not. I will vote for trade and peace. It has come to my attention that the world is wider than these walls. Either way, I have had enough of war, Your Majesty. Though I would remind you that we won. Darien was breached, but your father was far from victory.'

He nodded slowly, accepting her terms.

'I will need to have something signed and sealed in your name, of course, as king,' she said. 'And you must be seen by your generals. I will have something suitable found for you to wear.'

'Will you let me take the body of my father?' he said.

She saw how tears blurred his vision. Love was a strange and twisted thing, Louis realised. He had been afraid of his father all his life. He had hated him more times than he could remember, with a dull forge-heat. Yet the thought of King Jean Brieland being humiliated in death was still unbearable. Louis realised he wanted to see the body, needed to see it. To say goodbye.

'Of course,' she said. 'He is yours, Your Majesty.'

'Please. Call me Louis, Lady Sallet.'

'Then he is yours, Louis. As Tellius is mine.'

She left him then and a dozen servants bustled in her wake to shave and wash and dress him, making him fit to be seen. He wondered which of them would have killed him if he had refused her offer.

When Louis went out beyond the walls at last, it was with fresh bandages and a black silk patch sewn for his missing eye. His army cheered him, waving weapons and banners. He acknowledged them from the back of a grey gelding, weak and pale, sweating from the exertion. Yet he lived.

He wept when he saw his father, cold and still upon a bier. Jean Brieland lay before the walls of Darien and they still stood. The spring sun was at noon and it looked as if it would not move again.

DARIEN

Turn the page to see
how it all began

I

Risk

He was a hunter, Elias Post, a good one. The village elders
spoke of his skills with enormous pride, as if they owned
some part of his talents. The people of Wyburn looked to
him to bring them meat, even in the darkest months of winter when other places lost their old and young.

The land around them was exhausted, though they still
worked it hard, forcing some small crop from each scrub
field, guarding slow-growing things from crows and raven-
ous pigeons. Sheep still roamed the bare hills. Doves pecked
and glared in their boxes. Bees drowsed in lines of hives.
It might have been enough to feed them all if some of
the woods had not been burned and sown to grow oilseed
for the city, earning silver over food. Elias did not know
the rights and wrongs of those choices. When the grain
store was down to a crust of years past, when the warrens
were trapped out and empty, thin-fingered hunger crept into
the village, peering in at old men as they rocked by the fire.

He'd gone out first when he'd been a boy, coming back
to his mother in triumph with ducks clutched together
or hares all tucked up under his belt like a skirt of grey
fur. There was an abundance in the summers, but it was in
the deep winter where Elias earned the praise of the village
council. When the frost came down and the world was
white and silent, he had been a sure source of venison and

partridge, hares – even wolf or bear if the snows were deep. He drew his line at fox, though he trapped them to let the hares thrive. The meat was foul-tasting and he could not bear the smell.

As he reached forty, he'd been offered a place on the village council himself. He took pride in attending the meetings on the first day of each month. Along with his skills, there was an authority in him that grew each year, like a cloak he was made to wear whether he wanted to or not. He did not speak often – and then only when he knew the subject well enough to be sure of his judgement.

The one source of disagreement was his refusal to take an apprentice, but even then they knew his son would follow him when the boy was grown. What did it matter if Elias preferred to teach his craft to his own kin? There were always some who grumbled when every other hunter went into the forests and returned thin and empty-handed, with frost on their beards. Elias would come in then, hunched and bowed by the weight of a carcass draped over his shoulders, all black with frozen blood. He did not laugh or boast to the other hunters, though some still hated him even so. They were proud men themselves and they did not like to be shamed in front of their families, no matter how he shared the meat, in exchange for other goods or coin. They held their peace, for they were not fools and the village needed Elias Post more than the other hunters. No one wanted to be cast out, to have to go to the city for work. There were no good endings there, everyone knew that. When young girls ran off to Darien, their parents even held a simple funeral, knowing it was much the same. Perhaps to warn the other girls, too.

The plague had arrived that summer on the cart of a

potion-seller from the city, or so they said. It had first become a scourge there, where people lived too close and rubbed cheek and jowl with fleas and lice. No doubt it was a punishment for sinful couplings. You did not have to live long to know that healthy lives had hardly any pleasure in them. This plague began with rashes, and for most of them it was no worse than that. A few days of fever and itching before good health returned. They all began with that hope, only for some to lie cold and staring after a week of misery and pain. It was a cruel thing that year, and it knew no favourites.

When the proctors of the village met that autumn, they were not surprised to see Elias' seat standing empty. They murmured the name of Elias Post in sorrow and pity then. They had all heard. Wyburn was a small place.

His son Jack had gone in just a week, a little boy of black hair and laughter who'd been struck down and snatched from life, leaving a piece of river ice in his father's heart. The hunter had aged as many years as the boy had lived in that last night, sitting with him. Towards the end, Elias had walked a mile to pray at the temple outside Wyburn, that stood alone on the road leading to the city. He'd made his offering – a wisp of golden hay from the harvest. The Goddess of the reaping had turned her face from him, spinning on her iron chain. By the time he'd trudged back across the fields to his house near the village square, the boy was cold and still. Elias had sat with him for a time, just looking.

When the sun rose, his wife and daughters were weeping and trying not to scratch the welts that had risen on their skin, dumb with fear, pale as plucked flesh. Elias had kissed them all, tasting the salt of bright sweat. He'd hoped for the plague to take him, and when he slept for a while and woke again, it was almost a relief to discover his own welts swelling, his forehead damp. His wife had wailed to see him sick, but he'd gathered her in with their two daughters, a knot of arms and tears and grief.

'And what would I do on my own, my love? You and the girls are all I have left. Now that Jack is gone. I had one chance to be happy and it was *taken* from me. I will not be left alone, Beth! No. Wherever we are going, I will walk with you. What does it matter now, love? We'll go after Jack. We'll catch him up. We'll fall into step beside him, wherever he is. He'll be pleased to see us, you know he will. Why, I can see his face now.'

As darkness came, Elias found he could not bear to sit and listen to breaths crackling in the silence. He rose from his chair and stood for a time at the window, looking out on a moonlit road. It was an early dark then and he knew the tavern would be open. Yet it was not ale he wanted, nor clear spirits. He had no coin to waste on those and no taste for it. There were other things to be found in the light and the noise of a crowd.

He knew he would be thrown out or even killed by frightened men if they saw the raised patches on his arms and stomach. He grimaced, uncaring, driven wild by the itching. Perhaps it was murder he was considering, though he did not think it was. Some men were taken, others were spared. That was just the way of it then. They knew it was spread by touch; no one really understood the manner of it. There had been plagues before. They rose in summers and burned out in the cold months that followed. In some ways, it was as ordinary as the seasons, though that was no comfort to him.

Elias shrugged. An old shirt and a long coat would hide

the marks. There was a patch of swelling under his hair and another at the crook of his throat. In the mirror, it looked like a map of islands, white in a pink sea. He shook his head, then buttoned the shirt up high.

Hunting was clean, especially in the dark and the cold. He went out and he used his knack and he caught deer with his hands. It was a thing he had not shared with anyone, though he had hoped his son would learn the craft of it when he was older. That thought brought such a wave of grief that he could not bear to remain in the house. He pulled thick clothes from a reeking pile and yanked them on, adding a felt hat with a broken brim that would hide his face. He could not just lie down and die. That had always been a weakness in him.

There was medicine in the city, everyone knew that. There were doctors who could make the dead stand up and dance, so they said. Yet such miracles required more coins than a village hunter had ever seen. In the autumn, Elias butchered hogs on local homesteads and took away some chops and kidneys for his labour. Or he cut wood in exchange for a pot or two of honey. When he caught white or red foxes in his traps, he saved the skins and sold them all at once to a fellow a few miles downriver, for real silver bits. Elias had never been to the city himself, but he knew they had all sorts of learned men there, who could do just about anything. For money, anyway, not for kindness or for love. That was understood and he could accept it. The world owed nothing to anyone. He had made a living from it even so.

Elias kept his precious coins in a pot on the mantel, saved for the years ahead when he would not be able to hunt in the snow, when his fingers would not grip the knife too well. Perhaps too for when his knack would surely wither in him, like a man's sight or hearing. He touched the pouch in his pocket, its contents taken down and counted out on the kitchen table earlier that day. Perhaps he'd intended this thing all along, he did not know. The mind was a strangely complex beast, slow and deep, layer upon layer. His father had said he felt like a boy riding a great ox at times, without very much idea of what the ox was thinking.

The fruit of a dozen years of fur and meat trading could be held in one hand. Yet even his precious pieces of silver would never be enough, Elias knew that. Doctors were rich men. Rich men expected gold, with the heads of other rich men pressed into the soft metal. Elias had never seen a gold coin but he knew there were twenty silver to one noble – and they were somehow worth just the same. It was a little like the captains of the troops of soldiers who came through sometimes in the spring, looking for young men to recruit. Each captain lorded it over twenty men, telling them what to do and where to step. Elias wondered as he walked how many captains a general would command. A dozen? A score? Was there a metal they valued more than gold? If so, he had never known its name.

He considered this and other things as he made his way down the road towards the inn, his mind whirling in grief and anger and recklessness. He had worked hard and raised four. One had gone into the ground after just a few days in the world. Back then, he and his wife had been younger, more able to put it behind and try again. He'd told Beth they'd given one back, comforting his wife in that way. He said they'd paid the tithe of their lives in that grief.

It had not been part of the bargain for his son Jack to follow, nor for the itching plague to touch his daughters. Elias had known that most of those who grew sick survived it.

He'd been calm and utterly certain it would pass at first, denying what was happening right to the moment when he'd felt his son's hand had somehow grown cool. The flesh had kept its colour, but it always had been warm before. He'd known then.

He'd been teaching the boy how to read, letter by letter. It just wasn't possible that the lessons would stop, that he wouldn't hear one more halting word or feel the boy's laughing weight as he leaped on his father from a doorpost. Perhaps it was a kind of madness, but Elias felt no check or curb on him that evening, as if he'd seen his life through glass and understood at last that *nothing* mattered, but those he loved and those who loved him.

He knew that night was one of two in the year when farmers sold their wool. The great Harvest Eve was coming and that would be a day of celebration, where hams were cut thick and for one day the villagers drank one another's health and ate until they could hardly move. First came the wool sale, at the end of summer. There were men with real silver in the tavern that evening, pleased with themselves and drinking jug after jug of the rich brown ale.

Elias wet his lips with his tongue, feeling the cold air dry and tighten them once again. He had never used his knack amongst men before. That secret heart of him was for the deep silences, for the dark hills and the frosts. The thought of using it with eyes on him was akin to walking in with his buttocks hanging out of his breeches. He found he was sweating and began to scratch himself. No, not that night. He would just have to keep his hands still, no matter how much it was a torment. The whole countryside was alive with warnings of plague and they all knew his son had been failing.

He remembered then that the Goddess had turned her face away from him when he asked about his boy, Jack. Elias had to bite his lip for a time at that thought, until the pain made him shiver, anything rather than curse her. She might be deaf to those who needed her help, but she heard every word spoken ill. It was hard to pull his mind back from the furious words that simmered and seethed in him. He stumbled along to the light that spilled onto the street, drawn by the sound of laughter and the clink of brown pots.

He just wanted a decent book to read ...

Not too much to ask, is it? It was in 1935 when Allen Lane, Managing Director of Bodley Head Publishers, stood on a platform at Exeter railway station looking for something good to read on his journey back to London. His choice was limited to popular magazines and poor-quality paperbacks the same choice faced every day by the vast majority of readers, few of whom could afford hardbacks. Lane's disappointment and subsequent anger at the range of books generally available led him to found a company – and change the world.

'We believed in the existence in this country of a vast reading public for intelligent books at a low price, and staked everything on it'
Sir Allen Lane, 1902–1970, founder of Penguin Books

The quality paperback had arrived – and not just in bookshops. Lane was adamant that his Penguins should appear in chain stores and tobacconists, and should cost no more than a packet of cigarettes.

Reading habits (and cigarette prices) have changed since 1935, but Penguin still believes in publishing the best books for everybody to enjoy. We still believe that good design costs no more than bad design, and we still believe that quality books published passionately and responsibly make the world a better place.

So wherever you see the little bird – whether it's on a piece of prize-winning literary fiction or a celebrity autobiography, political tour de force or historical masterpiece, a serial-killer thriller, reference book, world classic or a piece of pure escapism – you can bet that it represents the very best that the genre has to offer.

Whatever you like to read – trust Penguin.